The. Hoosier. Girl.

A Memoir.
Radical Religion. White Trash.
And Coming of Age in the 1980's

by Harry Sneed

Published by
TypePunk Publishing
510 A South Main St.
St. Charles, MO 63301
Visit our website at www.TypePunk.com

This is a work of fiction. While some locations may be real places that have existed or currently exist, all characters of this novel and the story within is created by the imagination of its author and are purely fictional.   .

LIBRARY OF CONGRESS CATELOGING-IN-PUBLICATION DATA FORTHCOMING

Sneed, Harry
The Hoosier Girl:
By Harry Sneed / First Paperback Edition

ISBN
9781950919017

10 9 8 7 6 5 4 3 2 1
Printed in the United States of America

This book is dedicated to the "Lakers." Those of us who were lucky enough to have been raised and lived in Spanish Lake, Missouri during the good ol' days.

CHAPTER ONE

"Hello, Vagina Hunter." Those were the first words she ever said to me. She vehemently denies she said it. However, I'm almost positive she did. Almost.

As I look into the mirror of my memories, I mostly see a moving picture of my life. It rolls out before me like a ribbon whose satin is smooth and soft. Shiny. Those are my childhood years. Smooth with the innocence that all children possess. Carefree. Uninhibited. A discarded tablespoon. A Matchbox car. A patch of raw earth filled with worms and bugs. This was my amusement park. I could cradle myself within the soft arms of its happiness for hours upon hours. Building dirty cities that flooded with a twist of a downspout. Turning roly-poly bugs into invading monsters or worms into giant snakes that were trampled upon by a hero's scratched and dented, little metal Jeep.

Blissfully playing in a sea of ignorance. But this ignorance wasn't a bad ignorance. It was a good ignorance. A child's ignorance. And I would drink myself to a drunken stupor of its bubbly intoxication at this very moment, had I the opportunity. But I can't.

The silky ribbon of my life that once was glib and glorius became twisted and intertwined. And now I am a decade old. The little human larva is now a pupa entombed into a crusty cocoon of Education. Religion. Maturity. Especially Religion. But unlike a moth or butterfly whose pupa stage is dormant and peaceful. I was perpetually busy. My mouth could not keep up with the galaxy of questions that formed in the black hole of my brain and shot forth like the USS Enterprise at warped speed.

My skin too, was slow to grow at a syncopated pace with my bones. From my twelfth to my thirteenth birthday, I sprouted like a milkweed a full two inches in height. I jumped from wearing a boy's size small to men's small. Thus, bypassing the normal fashion metamorphosis of boy sizes. Medium. Large. Extra-large. This sudden skeletal expansion caused me to have stretch marks on my legs. Long, embarrassing, shiny and hideous. These, what appeared to be evil scratches, ran up my outer thighs on both my tall, skinny legs. But these cicatrices didn't stop there. They assaulted my self-esteem.

No other boys I knew had these scars. I never saw a single scout swimming in the lake at Camp Beaumont possess them. I know because I looked carefully. I looked in gym class too. Especially in high school when we were gestapo-ed into the showers after class. Between the acreage of bare bodies and among the forest of skinny, fat, long, short, hairy, and bald legs and the same defined dangling penises, not once did I ever discover another boy with stretchmarks on his legs. I was a freak.

And if God or Satan or both hadn't thought such physical scars weren't enough to mentally scar an adolescent boy, then puberty was nothing more than sadistic icing on the teenage cake.

Like the temperatures of each season, the tonal pitch of my voice changed daily. High. Low. Partly sunny sounding one day. Mostly cloudy during choir practice the next with a chance of cracking continually. Eventually the fine-tuning fork within my throat settled at a pitch that was somewhat masculine, but not yet manly.

Then came the peach fuzz and pimples. They were simple enough to control with a Bic razor and some Clearasil.

It was what was within my head that was nearly untamable. Hidden from my radically religious parents was a teenage boy's brain fueled by testosterone that perpetually pumped out thoughts, fantasies and desires of sex.

Now I am a senior at Hazelwood East High School. No longer does my memory seem to move with motion pictures. Now they are all of the Polaroid type. Quick. Flat. Still snapshots that eject from the front of my forehead. Some are as muted and colorless as the real Polaroid photographs that sit in several albums upon my bookshelves. Others are perfectly focused. Microscoped quality memories that are as real and tangible to me today, as they were back then. Before the clicks of time turned the present into memory. Now. Click. Memory.

One day when I get to heaven, I'm going to have God rewind the story of my life and stop at my eighteenth birthday. Saturday, December 13, 1980, at around 7:15 p.m. I want to see the exact moment we first met. Prove to myself that I was right. She indeed called me Vagina Hunter. That's what she called all the guys. But she'll deny it to her grave. Maybe then she can have her God; the omniscient, omnipotent, and omnipresent One that possesses a vagina rewind her life, too. She'll see that I was right.

Of course, she'll deny it even sitting face to face with God. But that's how she was. Stubborn to a fault. Beautifully strong-willed. Deliciously defiant.

CHAPTER TWO

"Hello Vagina Hunter. Would you like to see my pictures?" she said, sporting a smile that made Alice's Cheshire cat look innocent and timid. There were no introductions. It was just an out-of-the-blue offer to look at her school pictures.

"Lucy says they're the best ones I've ever taken." I had no idea who Lucy was, but I smiled anyway. One could only smile when she talked to you. It was like the queen was giving you an audience and you felt honored because you knew others were watching too, wishing that she was talking to them. Before I could answer, she opened, what I thought was a book, but it turned out to be a little purse made out of a hardcover copy of L.M. Montgomery's classic children's novel *Anne of Green Gables*. She took out several pictures and spread them on the counter in front of me as a jeweler might do presenting a selection of his finest, sparkling diamonds. I looked at them, trying hard not to show any particular interest. But they were stunning, as the jewel that she was and she knew it.

I raised my eyebrows and gave a polite smile of satisfaction. "Nice," I said.

"You're Ruth's brother, aren't you?" I nodded yes. Surprised at the question. I had never "officially" met Amanda Marrow. I had seen her occasionally at school. But we had never spoken. Our paths had never crossed. I knew her by rumors and reputation only. She was the beautiful new freshman who was already infamously popular. Gym class. Mike Simmons said she gave him a hand job in the backseat of the bus after football practice yesterday. Lunch table. Renee Rudolph swore she saw Amanda stealing a pack of cigarettes out of Shawn Eisenberg's locker.

"My sister Sara absolutely adores Ruth." Amanda pointed to a cute, petite, dark-haired girl dressed in a pink sweatsuit roller-skating next to my sister. "She says she's a perfect angel and the nicest girl she's ever met."

Amanda picked up one of her pictures and held it up to study it. She unconsciously bit her lip. I watched as she slanted her head and stared at it in the same proud way people often do when they've accomplished a grand feat. My best friend, Chuck, had the same look on his face when his car won the pinewood derby race in Boy Scouts. My mother wore that expression on a weekly basis in spring when her daffodils were at full bloom.

"That's saying a lot considering we've attended five different schools in the past eight years." Amanda set the picture back on the counter.

"Ruth, a perfect angel? Not. But she is a great little sister..." I said. "...as far as little sisters go."

"So is mine...as far as little sisters go." She gathered the little stack of pictures and shuffled them back into her *Anne of Green Gables* purse.

"I'll take a size six," she said and handed me her skate ticket. I turned and was ready to reach for a pair of the ugly brown leather skates that came with the price of admission. But instead, I picked up a pair of pretty pink leather skates with orange wheels that cost an additional dollar to rent that were sitting on the shelf above and handed them to her. Her eyes grew big. "Merci beaucoup!" she said with an accent that sounded partly French but mostly made up.

"Five schools in eight years? That's a total bummer." I moved the conversation from behind the counter towards the benches and motioned for Scott, the skate attendant, to take over. He saw the queen was giving me an audience and in return, I was presenting her with gifts. Scott smiled and gave me a thumbs up.

"Are you a military brat?" I asked, as we walked to the skate-changing benches.

"No, I'm just a brat," she said with a sinister smirk. "But I had an asshole for a father who couldn't keep a job for more than a couple of months. So we kept getting evicted and moved around a lot."

"Had a father?"

Amanda sat down on a bench, took off her shoes, and proceeded to put on her pretty pink skates.

December was in full swing. Most girls in Aloha that evening were snuggled in long pants, tight designer jeans, long-sleeved shirts or sweaters. The coat racks and lockers were packed full of Parka coats and acid-washed jean jackets. Beneath the carpeted benches where one sat to put on their skates were piles of boots and tennis shoes and an occasional knit cap.

Amanda had on a two-tier, denim rah-rah skirt and a tight pink cropped t-shirt that exposed her stomach. The sweater she had worn into the building was now draped over her shoulders with the sleeves tied across her chest. If one had never known her or heard of her reputation, she looked sexy yet studious. For the others, her attire appeared scanty and slutty. I was still forming my opinion when she put her left foot on her right knee to tie her skate. Slowly. Her skirt climbed up her thighs exposing what I thought was a pair of tight purple panties.

Badum. Badum. My heart immediately began to race, causing my palms to sweat like the armpits of a runner that had just won a marathon. It wasn't like I hadn't seen a million girls' panties before. As the manager of Aloha roller skating rink, not an evening went by when some silly female sporting a dress or skirt took a spill and totally exposed her underside. But this wasn't some silly girl. It was Amanda Marrow, the Freshman Fire.

She paid no attention to her fully exposed crotch. She made no effort to shut her legs or pull her skirt down as she tied her skate. No morals. No inhibition. The rumors were unfolding as true each second she sat with her legs spread wide open. I was in the front row of my own personal peep show. I looked sheepishly around to see if anyone was watching what I was watching. Several boys behind me were doing the same thing. My stare was subtle and cautious. Theirs were bold and belligerent. Almost vulture-ish. Amanda always had eyes upon her. Always.

She stood up and blatantly hiked up her skirt. It was then, I realized to my great disappointment, those weren't sexy purple panties she was wearing. They were just a pair of stupid spandex shorts. The kind figure skaters wear under their skirts.

"Yea, I sort of had a father. Unfortunately, he's not dead." Her purple spandex shorts were now camel-toed into her crotch. She began pulling them out by their bottom hems. I tried with the intensity of an umpire to look her in the eyes as she did it, envious of the boys behind me taking mental pictures. "He's just serving eight years in prison for drinking and driving."

"Eight years for a DWI? That seems kind of harsh?"

Amanda pushed her skirt down. The show was over. She rolled her eyes and took a deep breath. "Ok," she said and paused. "I'll make this long story really short." She paused again. Each verbal break acted as an invisible leash that physically pulled me unconsciously closer to her. Until finally, I was fully encroaching her personal space. Does a girl like her really have a personal space? I wondered.

Or was she psychologically pulling me next to her because she was about to tell me a secret and she knew that for every pair of eyes that were constantly glued upon her, there were the same number of ears. Listening. Ready to fuel the gossip mill. She began to tell her tragic father story in a dry and monotone voice.

"The stupid son of bitch attempted a U-turn on a highway because he forgot his pack of cigarettes at the bar. (She took a deep breath) In the process, he pulled in front of another car with two teenage chicks in it. They slammed into him sending both cars into the concrete median. (Another deep breath) Two other cars got caught in the middle of the whole fucking traffic turmoil and before it was over six people went to the hospital. (Big dramatic sigh) The two girls spent several weeks in the ICU. An off-duty fireman, a schoolteacher, and her two children went to the ER, but were released with minor injuries. (Final deep breath and then with a bit of bitterness) The son of a bitch walked away unhurt, but he walked right from his car to a police car and into jail. Which is right where the asshole belongs."

"Wow, sorry to hear that."

"Don't be sorry because I'm not. Lucy, Sara, and I could have been in the car and you may not be talking to me right now." I was immediately not sorry it happened. "Or those two girls he put in the ICU could be Ruth and Sara." She pointed to our sisters skating side by side. They happened to be looking our way and saw we were talking about them. They waved and skated towards us. "I'm sure you wouldn't be one fucking bit sorry if that was the case."

Both sisters greeted us with a Hi. Ruth put her arms around me and gave me a big squeeze. "Sara, this is my big, handsome brother, Christian. But only mom, dad and I call him that. Everyone else just calls him Chris."

I put my hand out and Sara shook it. Then she introduced Ruth to Amanda.

"And Ruth this is my short, ugly sister, Amanda. That's her real name, but everybody calls her all different kinds of other names."

We all laughed and took turns shaking one another's hands. I suddenly realized this wasn't just any Sara. It was THE Sara. The new girl Ruth had met in school and incessantly talked about. "Sara's not scared of stink bugs." "Sara's going to make a life-size gingerbread house when she grows up." "Sara draws cats better than our art teacher." How convenient. My kid sister was becoming best friends with Amanda Marrow's little sister. What a small world.

"Ruth talks about you all the time." Sara said as she bent down. "She says you're the best big brother in the world," Her petite slender fingers fidgeted with her skate laces. "I have an awesome big sister, too. Of course, she can be a you-know-what sometimes, but I guess it could be worse." Amanda gave Sara a playful push. She tumbled but grabbed Ruth's leg, steadied herself, and stood back up. "Although God knows, I wish she didn't dress so sleazy, so I could at least wear some of her hand-me-downs."

Amanda tossed Sara a scathing stare and started to drop the F-bomb but caught herself.

"Fu...Forget you! You only wish you could wear clothes like these." Amanda twirled around on her skates. "I just bought this skirt with my first paycheck," she said proudly.

"Well, isn't that a coincidence?" Ruth chimed in. "Christian is wearing new Jordache jeans he got for his birthday today."

I struck a pose like the models in *GQ Magazine* and did a quick turn and showed them the gold designer stitching on the back pockets.

"Nice ass," Amanda said and whistled. Sara giggled. Ruth covered her mouth with her hand and gave me a look that said, "I can't believe someone just said my brother had a nice ass right in front of me." The song *"Crazy Little Thing Called Love"* came blaring over the speakers. Both girls let out an excited scream and skated off leaving Amanda and me alone once again.

"Well Happy Birthday...Chris...tian." She smirked. "How old are you?"

"I'm eighteen and old enough to vote now." I don't know why I tossed in that stupid stuff about being old enough to vote now. I guess I was a little nervous and at the same time wanted to make it seem like I was an older man. I knew Amanda had a thing for older guys. Just that past October there had been a buzz all around school because the extremely popular senior football captain, Mike Bergmeister, had taken Amanda to homecoming. Mike Bergmeister was USDA prime choice male. The cut of meat that belonged to the taste of only the best and prettiest female palates. The seniors. The cheerleaders. At the very least the pom-pom squad. But Amanda didn't fit in any of those categories. And that is what made her public enemy number one to the dozens of snobbish girls, the moment she accepted Mike's offer. The shooshes, as they were often called, didn't like the fact that some new floozy freshman was whoring in on their jock territory. Senior Class Hall. Kristie Soundermeyer said that Mike Bergmeister said that after homecoming they went parking at the airport PVA and Amanda was such a sex fiend that after she rode him, she then proceeded to straddle the stick shift of his Camaro and rode that too while he watched.

"Congratulations," Amanda smiled and her face lit up. "But guess what?" she asked.

"What?"

"My birthday is Tuesday! I'll be sixteen and finally able to drive. Is that totally awesome or what?" She raised her hands in the air and did a little celebrational dance. "I swear, I almost have Lucy talked into letting me skip school and take my driver's test. I have no doubt that I can pass the written test. It's the driving part that makes me nervous." She toyed with the arms of the sweater wrapped around her until they were once again tight around her slender shoulders. "The thought of parallel parking totally paralyzes me." She chuckled at her wordplay.

"I surmise Lucy is your older sister?" I asked.

"Surmise! Oh my God, did you just say surmise?" Amanda's face flushed with excitement. She began to jump up and down forgetting she was on skates. Suddenly one set of wheels shot out from beneath her and she started stumbling forward. Right. Towards. Me. I quickly reached out, opened my arms, and she fell into them.

Focus. Click. Flash. It was at that exact moment. The moment her body pressed against mine. The moment I felt her warm breath against my neck and her sweet-smelling perfume filled my nostrils. The moment I carried her weight and held her steady until she was once again stable. That was the moment I fell as I saved her from falling.

The entire incident lasted maybe five seconds. I could have let her go. I could have

laughed and asked her if she was ok. I could
have joked about her clumsiness. But I didn't.
　　Some　　strange,　　unstoppable　　reflex—a
subconscious nerve—that reached deep beyond
the strains of my physical muscles, suddenly
twitched. I pulled her to my chest. I shut my
eyes. I hugged her. No, it was more than a hug.
I couldn't have explained it then because I
was young and not all of my childhood
ignorance had been sucked out of me. It
resembled a hug. But the fact was, it was more
than a hug. It was a I'm-never-going-to-get-
the-chance-to-hold-you-in-my-arms-ever-
again-and-therefore-I'm-going-to-cherish-
this-second, squeeze. Today I like to think of
it as a miracle from God.

When I opened my eyes, Amanda was staring at me. Or maybe I
should say, she was staring through me. Her eyes. Her beautiful and
radiant amber eyes whose hues could only be describe as the color of
coffee at the precise moment you pour cream into it. When it swirls and
twirls and becomes little golden storm clouds. The exact color where
the dark tones of coffee fights with the white tints of milk, each wanting
to dominate the battlefield of blackness before the spoon comes and
destroys them both into merely a tan-ish toffee. That was the color of
Amanda's eyes.

She slowly shook her head back and forth. Perhaps trying to shake
off the residue of the cheap thrill I had just pressed upon her. I blushed.
My heart sank. I was no better than the other guys who pinched her ass
on the crowded school bus or purposely brushed against her breasts
during dance classes in PE. But I swear on a stack of Bibles as high as
the heavens. I swear on the life of my little sister. I didn't consciously
and purposely mean to do it. As I said, it was a weird, unstoppable
reflex.

I waited for her condemnation. A disgusted rebuke. A verbal ass-
kicking. To my surprise, she acted as if nothing had happened.

"Thanks," she said. "You saved me from falling on my face." And
just as quickly as she stumbled and fell into my arms, her countenance

immediately changed. She smiled and I judged it to be a thousand watts brighter than the flashing lights that bounce around us. "I've been in this town for six goddamn months and you're the first guy that's actually said something sexy and sophisticated." She reached out with both her hands and grabbed my shoulders. "Please, say it again."

"Say what again?" I asked.

"What you just said, "I *surmise*, Lucy is your older sister."

I paused, not quite sure why I needed to repeat myself. But I did as she commanded. After all, she was the queen. Only this time I said it in a slower, lower, James Bond-ish manner with my right eyebrow cocked up.

"I...surmise...Lucy is your older sister?"

"OK, you just made my panties wet!" Amanda screamed as shook my shoulders.

How does one reply to a statement like that? The subject alone is enough to open an encyclopedia-sized conversation that centers around volume Fl-Fu. Flirt. Foreplay. Fuck. I'm sure the vulture-eyed boys that incessantly soared around her could have come up with some type of response. "Prove it." "Show me." But I just swallowed. A gulp so deep and so strong that I felt my Adams apple slide up and down in my throat. Once again, my face turned fire hydrant red. But this time I bowed my head in an attempt to hide my childish embarrassment. Amanda let out an enormous laugh which only stoked the embers burning in my cheeks.

"Looks like I made the birthday boy embarrassed," she said. "Sorry, but I love beautiful and unique words. Matter of fact, I collect them and it's just nice to stumble upon someone who randomly uses one." She tilted her face to the heavens to think. "It's like finding a beautiful, rare verbal seashell on the beach of life." We both smiled at her poetic analogy.

An anonymous guy's voice called from the skating floor. "Quite flirting Amanda and come skate." Several girls also begged for her to come join them.

"Looks like the queen's court is calling." I mustered a brave response and motioned toward the skate counter. "I have to get back to work anyway."

"More like the queen's jesters," she said and stuck her hand out as sort of a peace treaty for embarrassing me. "It was nice meeting you...Best big brother in the world."

"You, too." I shook her hand and immediately released it. I didn't want to touch her too long. Lest I do something stupid and unexplainable again. "By the way, you smell great." I complimented. "What perfume are you wearing?"

"Heaven's Scent," she said, then turned and skated through the crowd of kids and towards the lockers to put her shoes away.

Heaven. Sent.

I watched her incredible ass swing back and forth without trying to hide my stare and then went back to the skate counter.

For a moment I felt sorry for every plain or ugly girl in the world. The fat ones. The tall and gangly ones. The short mousey ones. The ones that had no physical defects whatsoever, other than they were cursed with a face that was simply unappealing. An over-sized nose. Eyes set too far apart. Teeth that were yellow and crooked. How unfair life was for them. Theirs was a world of social struggle and predestined prejudice against them. No stares turned towards them as they enter a room or walked down a hall. No one rushed to open doors before them or hurried to help them with their spilled bags. They walked anonymously in the world during the week and sat solitarily alone on the weekends with nothing more than a book, a TV or a pet to placate them.

While girls like Amanda, with their slender, perfect bodies, that would make a Grecian sculptor weep with desire, white teeth and facial features that our society has ordained as "attractive" are placed celestially high on pedestals. A mere flirtatious smile from their lips and a whirlwind of honeybees begin bumbling compliments about them and tossing complimentary gifts to them. "A large coffee for the price of a small one," says the man behind the counter to the beautiful blond. The beautiful ones always have a pre-approved credit of approval.

I didn't know anything about the real Amanda Marrow. She could have been the sister of Satan. The evilest bitch two humans have ever birthed. But because she was blessed with beauty, I tossed rationality to the wind and was whipped.

My eyes moved with magnetic gravity once more towards her direction. She suddenly turned and began to make her way back towards me. I continued handing out skates, pretending I didn't give a hoot's ass she was still in the building, let alone standing in front of me.

"I forgot something," she said as she approached the counter. She opened her *Anne of Green Gables* purse, took out one of her school pictures, and handed it to me. It wasn't a little picture that came in sheets of ten. Or the medium ones that fit perfectly in a boy's wallet. It was a big picture. The five by seven-inch kind that was typically given to grandparents or special aunts and uncles.

"Happy Birthday," she said. "Oh, and you surmised wrong. Lucy is my mom."

CHAPTER THREE

I immediately put the picture beneath several phone books we kept under the skate counter to keep it safe from other guys who would have killed to possess such a treasure. The rest of the evening remains out of focus. Blurry. Foggy. Part of me was skating on clouds because Amanda Marrow, the Freshman Fire, gave me her picture. But not just any picture, a big picture. That was the upper part of me that went from my shoulders to the top of my head. I was on an emotional high. The kind that only a newly infatuated teenage boy can feel.

The lower part of me, the testosterone part from the waist down, was thinking more sexual thoughts. Thoughts like, "Could I possibly have a chance to see what's really hidden beneath those purple spandex skater shorts?"

Then there was the middle part of me. The area deep in my chest that felt a slight tightening each time she skated with another boy during the couples skate. I hid behind the pinball machines and secretly watched as they skated hand in hand slowly around the rink with the lights dimmed and love songs playing over the speakers. I know it was ridiculous and stupid to feel that way. I had just "officially" met her. But my heart ached three times that night. Three times. Once for each couples skate where I was not the one holding her hand. The fact that she didn't repeat any of the couples skate with the same guy only buried the sword deeper into my fevered flesh.

But the biggest torture came when Steve Tolerson, a popular soccer jock with long hair and a dark complexion, left to go outside with Amanda by his side. They returned sixteen and a half minutes later. Not that I was paying attention or keeping track or anything. She was wearing her sweater when they left, but when they came back in she was all bundled up in his letter jacket. She looked disheveled and tousled. I wanted to believe with all my might they went out to the back of the building to smoke. However, because of her soiled reputation, the only mental movie that played in my head was of them outside screwing in the back seat of a car. Fogging up the windows as she took off those purple spandex shorts and gave him her sexual gifts that I wanted. I took her picture from beneath the phone books and looked at it.

"One day." I thought. "One day."

The night dragged on. My duties and responsibilities as rink manager forced my mind back to a semi-sense of sanity. Then came closing time. That's when every part of me, from my nose to my toes, began to splinter and shatter with disappointing pain as I watched Amanda leave without even giving me as much as a nod as she walked out the door. Thankfully Sara, with Ruth still at her side, came to say goodbye.

"It was nice meeting you, Chris," Sara said as she put her ugly brown skates on the counter and then her sister's pretty pink skates next to them. "So what does a girl have to do to get cool pretty pink skates like these?" She smiled.

"Be friends with the rink manager's little sister," I said. "It'll get you pretty pink skates and sometimes even a free soda and popcorn at the concession stand."

"Totally. Awesome!" Sara said and high-fived Ruth. Ruth beamed with pride of her big brother, the rink manager. She escorted Sara to the front door. They said their goodbyes and promised to call one another. I would be encouraging Ruth to do that regularly.

CHAPTER FOUR

As manager, it was my duty to make sure the rink was properly cleaned after closing and readied for the next day. It usually took about an hour. Ruth loved hanging around during this time. She had the entire rink to herself. She'd climb into the DJ booth that sat on a raised platform in the corner of the rink and make the strobe lights flicker and dance across the state-of-the-art, baby-blue painted, concrete skate floor while listening to her favorite songs. When she got bored playing DJ, she'd help vacuum the neon pink and green speckled carpeted walkways around the lockers and benches. Sometimes she helped organize the skate counter.

"Did you have fun tonight, munchkin?" I handed her a pair of skates and she put them back on the rack.

"Yes, it was fun." She smiled then got a frustrated look on her face. "Except when Tommy Klaus kept skating really fast past us. He'd almost run right into us. A couple of times he even knocked Sara down flat on her rear end." She picked up another pair of skates and started to put them on the rack but stopped. "Of course, he apologized and everything, but neither Sara nor I thought he meant it. Sara asked me why I thought he was being so mean to her. I told her I surmised it was because he liked her. Just like that time when Mike Pervell kept bumping his desk into the back of my chair in sixth grade driving me crazy and you said it was probably because he liked me."

"Well, you probably surmised right." I had to laugh and silently give mom and dad a big thank you for constantly using the word "surmise" around the house so their son could one day appear to be sexier and more seductive than he actually was.

When the rest of the staff was gone and all the skates had been put away, I went into the office and told Mr. Abernathy, the owner, we had finished for the evening. He thanked me and asked if I wouldn't mind turning off the lights on my way out. I did as he asked and while under the cover of darkness, and out of Ruth's view, I went behind the skate counter, took Amanda's picture from beneath the phone books and secretly slipped it into the inner pocket of my coat.

Most guys would have proudly boasted to the world that Amanda Marrow had given him her picture and displayed it like a flag on the Fourth of July. But it was more than just a picture to me. It was a sacred and mysterious gift. Rumor had it that she liked to give her body away. I'm sure there were plenty of guys that claimed that prize. I, however, possessed one of only two five by seven-inch school pictures of her. The questioned remained, why would she give such a prized possession to a guy she didn't even know?

The ride home started out quiet which was unusual for Ruth. Ever since she had spoken her first word "baba," it seemed as if God had put a switch on Ruth's mouth called her tongue. And by doing so, He created a chatterbox of biblical proportion. Whenever that switch was turned on, just about breakfast time, her mouth didn't stop moving until her tongue switch turned off, which was about the time she went to sleep.

"Sara seems like a really nice girl," I said, turning her tongue switch to the "on" position.

"She is, Christian. Especially for all the things she has been through. Did you know her daddy is an alcoholic and in prison for almost killing somebody? And her mother works so much that she was practically raised by Amanda? (Deep breath) And they live in a small house with only three rooms and she has to share her bedroom with Amanda and Lucy. And she hasn't ever been to church except for three times. Twice on Christmas and once on Easter. Three times in her whole life! (Deep breath with eyes rolled.) That's about how many times we go in one week."

I nodded my head and looked surprised. I acted like I was genuinely interested in everything she was saying. And I was, but my interests had more selfish and sexual motivations. Ruth continued to spill her guts about everything she knew about Sara Marrow. I wasn't about to stop her.

"Sara said Lucy works full-time as a seamstress at some clothing company and waits tables part-time at Steak 'n Shake. But that wasn't enough to pay the bills, so Amanda had to go to work too. She got a job as a cashier at Waldenbooks at Jamestown Mall. Now they have enough money, but nobody's ever home. Sara has to be all alone all the time. And she told me, Christian, that sometimes she gets really scared and hears noises and has to call Lucy at work. But Lucy just tells her, 'It ain't nothing...and that's exactly how she said it, 'It ain't nothing...' I told her she can call me if she ever gets scared and if Lucy or Amanda can't come home then I'd have you take me over to her house. You wouldn't mind doing that would you Christian?"

"Of course not. What are friends for?" I continued to shamelessly use my little sister as an information pipeline. I made a mental list of my discoveries about Amanda Marrow:

Her birthday was Dec. 16. (She'll be sixteen years old.)
Ruth had her phone number.
She lived in a small house.
She shared a bedroom with her sister and mom (whom she called Lucy.)
She collected beautiful and unique words.
She worked at Waldenbooks.
The mysterious puzzle named Amanda Marrow was slowly being pieced together by my secret little weapon called Ruth.

"And they call their mother by her first name, Lucy. How weird is that? I can't picture calling mom by her first name, Rosemary, like she was our friend. (Deep breath) Can you imagine that Christian?"

I looked at her in utter disbelief and shook my head. "Not." I smiled. "Rosemary, would you please pass the peas?"

Ruth gave out a big laugh and in the same breath nonchalantly asked, "What do you think about Amanda?"

"Oh, she seems nice enough, and she's not bad looking, I guess." I faked a look of noninterest.

"Not bad looking!" Ruth let out a crazy scream. "No duh! She's probably the prettiest girl at Hazelwood East. Maybe in the entire St. Louis area!" Ruth had somehow freakishly read my thoughts.

"Yeah, she's a pretty girl I guess, but I think she may be a," I hesitated to say the word, "hoosier."

The H-word hit Ruth hard. I could tell she was also toying with the thought that mom and dad might not approve of her befriending Sara.

Over the years, I had come to the conclusion that our radically religious parents could get past their children being sinful because, after all, the Bible says that we are all created as sinners. However, there was one thing that my parents had zero tolerance for and that was being a hoosier.

For the first eighteen years of my life, I didn't know the word "hoosier" had any other definition other than white trash. Someone who was low-class, uneducated, crude, dirty, vulgar, and sleazy. And if those weren't enough adjectives to describe a hoosier, mom could always find more.

Smoked. Cursed. Drank. Fornicated. Satan may be the reason for the fall of humanity but hoosiers were the ones that kept kicking them down the hill to hell.

"The world doesn't need more God." I once heard my mother say to my father after listening to the nine o'clock news in which a drunk driver had killed a family of three. "It needs fewer hoosiers." She then went on to explain that preachers and deacons were put on this earth to save the souls of the unbeliever. But all the other Christians, the regular Christians, like her and dad, were there to fight the war against ignorance, alcohol, tobacco, drugs and every other adjective that defined a hoosier. "If there was more of that," she preached to dad. "There would be less of that," she said pointing to the television. Needless to say, I was brainwashed to believe that hoosiers, were Bad with a capital B.

"Christian, I don't know about Amanda, but I don't think Sara is a hoosier. We've had some talks and she agrees with me that smoking is stupid. I told her that stuff you taught me about how if you put a drop of antifreeze in a cup of soda that nobody in their right mind would ever drink it because it's poison. But how, when people smoke, it's just the same thing and they do it all day long and they even pay to do it. That's about the stupidest thing in the whole wide world to pay someone your hard-earned money to slowly kill you. She said she was going to have to tell Amanda that story because she hated that Amanda smoked. She was too pretty to do something so ugly."

Ruth stopped to catch her breath and then continued. "She said that she saw her daddy do all kinds of evil and mean things when he was drunk. Unthinkable things that she can't even tell me. She swore she wasn't ever going to drink alcohol because he was an alcoholic and that's a sickness that's hereditary and can be passed down from a parent to a child. Sara said that she's never going to drink alcohol so she would never have to worry about getting his sickness."

"Sara seems like she's a pretty smart little cookie for being in seventh grade."

"She's even smarter than me when you think about it."

Ruth pointed to a house buried chimney-deep in Christmas decorations. The rainbow glow of lights was enough to land a 747, let alone Santa's sled. "Wow," Ruth whispered. I slowed down as we visually inhaled the heralding of the holidays. The stoic faces of the life-size nutcracker soldiers that stood guard before the blow-mold nativity scene. Where Mary, Joseph and the three wisemen, dressed in dazzlingly colored robes, stood solemnly staring down at the baby King who rested peacefully wrapped in cracked and faded swaddling clothes.

"I mean, she doesn't get better grades than me and everything." Ruth continued. "But, Christian, you and I aren't hoosiers because mom and dad taught us not to be hoosiers. But Sara's mom and dad are hoosiers and she's not a hoosier. Not because she was taught not to be, but because she watched her parents do all those bad things and was smart enough to say, "I don't want to be like them. I don't want to smoke or drink or do drugs and all those bad things.' She learned not to be a hoosier by living in the wild. While we learned not to be a hoosier by living in a zoo where our mom and dad trained us. I think it takes a smarter animal to learn things like that out in the wild, as opposed to the safe comfort of the zoo."

It took my simple brain a couple of seconds to digest the brilliance in her fourteen-year-old analytical mind.

Ruth wasn't finished. "I haven't ever been over Sara's house yet, so I don't know how clean or organized she is. Her locker isn't very organized. It's not like she's got dirty clothes in it or old food rotting away, it just isn't as clean and organized as mine."

"And we both know how you can be a little clean freak."

"Cleanliness is next to Godliness. That's what I've been trained to believe in our zoo, ever since I spilled my "baba" of milk on the dining room chair."

"Thank God, it was covered in plastic."

The last mile home was once again quiet as Ruth analyzed our conversation. In addition to having attitudes and mood swings, you could add "must analyze everything," to the terrible traits of a female teenager.

"Christian, even if Sara is a hoosier, can't people change?"

"Of course, they can," I assured her. I believed that people did change. It was that belief that would later become the driving force of my life.

I was mentally wrapping up the day as we turned into the driveway and pulled into mom and dad's clean and organized garage. I turned off the car and opened the door.

All in all, it was a pretty damn good eighteenth birthday. I got a new pair of Jordache jeans. I met Amanda Marrow and personally got to know her on an intimate basis. Sort. Of. And then, without laying a finger on her flesh, I orally pleased her and got her panties wet by presenting her with one beautiful, rare, verbal seashell. I wonder how many other boys could boast of such a feat. Very few. If any. And if that wasn't enough to doodle a big asterisk mark next to the day's entry in my imaginary diary of life, as a day never to be forgotten, she gave me her school picture. But not just any picture, a B-I-G picture. I reached into my coat to caress her perfect, paper face.

"SHHHHIIITTTT!!!" The word boiled out of my lips. I didn't even attempt to put a lid on it.

My scream startled Ruth. She turned with a horrid look on her face. "What's wrong?"

I felt around the inside of my coat. Nothing. I jumped out of the car and began frantically looking between the seats and around the floorboards. Nothing.

"What are you looking for, Christian?" Ruth asked.

"Nothing," I said as I moved the car seat up and picked up the back floor mats and looked beneath them.

Ruth started looking around the car, too. Not exactly sure what she was looking for.

The picture wasn't there. It must have fallen out of my coat at Aloha. DAMN. It was too late to go back and find it. Sobering sadness seeped into my veins. I let out a frustrated moan. I would drive back after church tomorrow. "Dear God, please let it be there." I prayed. I couldn't stomach the thought of some other boy finding my paper jewel and soiling it with his grimy fingers or fantasies. I'd rather it be lying soggy and smashed on the parking lot. Ruined by the raindrops and forever decimated to the rest of the world. I shook my head and slammed the car door in frustration.

"What were you looking for, Christian?" Ruth asked once more.

"It's not important!" I lied.

We sneaked into the house trying not to wake up mom and dad. But there was a lamp on in the living room. And next to the lamp, mom was sitting on the couch watching TV. She immediately stood up when we walked in.

You could always tell what kind of mood my mother was in by how tight her robe was tied around her waist. Loose. Happy. Tight. Not-so-happy. Tonight, the belt on her pink velvet robe was so tight she looked like a pork loin about ready to go into the oven. Her hair, which was usually pristinely in place, was unkempt and tussled from climbing out of bed at midnight.

"We just got a phone call—and you know how much I hate late night phone calls," Mom said as she shook her finger at us. "I immediately thought something was tragically wrong. But it was some girl named Amanda and she asked for you." Mom set an evil stare upon me.

Ruth and I looked at each other.

"I told her that you weren't home." Mom turned off the TV with an agitated click of the knob and picked up a piece of paper sitting next to the phone. "She sounded funny like she was exhausted or maybe even," she paused. "Intoxicated." She vomited the thought out with her lips and then touched her fingers to her forehead and began to rub them around. Soothing the skin where the treacherous thought had once sat. "I asked her if everything was all right. She assured me that it was and apologized for calling so late. She gave me her number and asked if I wouldn't mind telling Christian, not Chris, to call her tomorrow."

Mom handed me the piece of paper with Amanda's phone number on it. Ruth and I stood there with blank expressions. Oblivious. Curious.

Mom took her interrogation pose—arms folded across her chest, right shoulder shifted up, and her left hip shifted out.

"So young man, who's this Amanda girl?"

CHAPTER FIVE

I lay in the darkness of my bedroom. Wondering. Contemplating. Tempted. Why did Amanda Marrow call me? She didn't even bother to say goodbye when she left Aloha. And now she was waking up my parents with a late-night phone call. I didn't know whether I should be excited or pissed. You don't call someone at 1 a.m. unless it's very important. Hmm. Could she have forgotten her purse and wanted to ask me if anyone had turned it in? Maybe she had second thoughts about giving me her picture and now she wanted it back. I wasn't even sure I still had the picture to give back. I kept racking my brain for reasons. Then it came to me.

A dark thought in the recess of my mind.

Could it be that she was drunk? Mom said she sounded funny. My suspicions of her being a hoosier were being validated. She smoked. Cursed. Dressed sleazy. And then there was that boisterous and embarrassing comment about her panties getting wet right in the middle of a bunch of people. Decent and respectable girls didn't talk like that. At least not in public. She had no class. No sophistication. Yes, she was beautiful. But that appeared to be the one and only positive asset she had going for her.

I continued to stare at the ceiling. No, she couldn't be drunk. She had left with Sara just

over an hour ago. I watched them get into an
old beat up Impala that I presumed to be Lucy's.
But? Perhaps she had snuck out with that
long-haired, soccer jock and went to a party?
Or? Maybe she was one of those teenaged closet
alcoholics that Mike Wallace talked about on
Sixty Minutes. The ones who keep a bottle of
vodka hidden under their mattress. "Ok
Christian," I thought. "Even if she is drunk.
Why is she calling you?"

My mind raced in a million different
directions, but always sling-shot back to one
particular incident. The one that began with
her falling into my arms and ended with her
saying. "OK, you just made my panties wet." As
hoosier-ish, uncouth and embarrassing as it
was, the thought that I could make Amanda
Marrow's panties wet was simply too
overpowering for my brain.

And then my dark thoughts got even more
dismal.

"Oh Lord, please let her be drunk and
calling me for phone sex." I shut my eyes and
prayed. A tinge of guilt reverberated about
my consciousness for asking such a naughty
request.

To be totally honest, I was a virgin. I
possessed all the anti-hoosier traits that mom
instilled in me. I didn't drink, smoke, do drugs
or act like a hoosier in any capacity. Except
one. When it came to the subject of sex. Or
should I say, because of my lack of sex, my
mental senses were in a constant state of
delusional dry-humping via impure thoughts.
I was always thinking about sex. Fantasizing.
And there were lots of HMSs. Which was sexual
code between my group of male friends. It stood
for Healthy Masturbation Session. As sinful

as I was taught they were, HMSs were just that.
Heathy. Euphoric. Stress-releases. A physical
high without the use of drugs or alcohol. And
they could be done without the knowledge of
anyone ever knowing.

Realistically, Amanda's phone call wasn't
anything sexual at all. It was probably
something totally legit and lame like she
forgot her makeup compact in the restroom and
wanted to see if anyone had turned it in. I lay
there like a teenaged girl analyzing
everything. Piece by piece, I broke up the
entire evening into little thought segments
that stacked upon one another until I had
sifted and inspected every word that was said
and every action that took place. I looked over
at the clock. 2:08 a.m.

It had been nearly an hour since we had
gotten home and mom had given me her
interrogation stance. Everyone was surely
asleep by now. As much as I knew how wrong it
was, I had to do it. I had to call her. I knew I
was taking the risk of waking up mom and dad
and potentially getting grounded for life for
talking to a strange girl in the middle of the
night. And although she was a strange girl,
she was more than strange: she was Amanda
Marrow, the Freshman Fire. I crawled out of
bed and went to my door and listened. Nothing.
I quietly inched open the door, tip-toed
through the tulip-pink carpeted hall, picked
the phone up off the table and walked it back
into my room. By the time I shut the door, I
could hear the beating of my heart echo in my
eardrums. Thank God the phone had a long cord.

I picked up the paper with Amanda's phone
number and the emergency flashlight tucked
inside my slippers beneath my bed. Only

functional dysfunctional families had
emergency flashlights stuck in slippers
under their bed in case of fire, tornados or
the second coming of Christ.

I had to make that phone call, or I would
have gone stark mad and lay awake the entire
evening analyzing, analyzing, analyzing. I
buried my head and phone beneath my covers,
dialed the number and prayed to God that
Amanda would answer.

Just as it started to ring, I suddenly
remembered they all shared one bedroom. I was
bound to wake up the entire family. Oh my God,
I was acting like a hoosier just like her! I
went to push the receiver button down.

CHAPTER SIX

"Hello?" the sleepy voice on the other end answered.

"Amanda?" I whispered.

"Yes?"

"It's Chris..ah...Christian from Aloha. Sorry to call so late, but you called?"

There was a pause. A slow awaking of thought. "Thank God," she whispered, with a sigh of sleepy relief. "Hold on." I heard her move about as she jostled the phone. Then there was another silent pause. "Sorry, I had to go into another room," she said softly.

I wondered if she knew that I knew she lived in a three-room house. Was she now in the kitchen or living room? But more importantly what was she wearing? If anything at all.

"Are you and Ruth safely home?"

"Yes." I answered. "Why?" I was slightly disappointed that she didn't sound drunk.

"I know this is going to sound really weird because you don't even know me, but I was exhausted when I got home and crashed on the couch and had a dream about you."

"You had a dream about me?" I almost dropped the phone.

Thank you, Lord! My prayers have been answered. Amanda Marrow had a dream about me! Was it a good dream? A bad dream? Or perhaps...a wet dream? Do girls even have wet dreams? Please do tell and be specific.

"Well, it was more like a nightmare." She paused, let out a subtle yawn, then continued. "We were at Aloha and everyone was skating. I heard this knocking on the side door. I opened it and my dad was standing there. He had a big truck filled with watermelons backed up to the door. You came over to see what was going on and dad said that the police chief said he could keep the watermelons there to keep them cold. But I knew he was lying because if my dad's lips were moving, he was lying."

"Watermelons?"

"Yea. Watermelons. Weird eh? The next thing I know Aloha wasn't a roller-skating rink anymore it was an ice-skating rink. Dad and several other guys started taking the watermelons off the truck and rolling them onto the ice. Nobody thought it was weird. Matter of fact, everyone was enjoying it. The watermelons became like an obstacle course. They were skating around them and jumping over them. Until this one guy hit one with his skate blade and sliced it open. I started smelling vodka and I realized what was going on.

"Not just watermelons but vodka in watermelons?"

It was definitely a hoosier dream.

"Yes, vodka in watermelons. I'll tell you why I was dreaming about vodka in watermelons." The sleepiness in her voice faded as she began to narrate her story within a story. "One time when I was a kid, the glass company my sperm donor worked for..."

"Your what?" I interrupted her story.

"Sorry, sometimes I like to call my father, sperm donor. I once heard Lucy call him that in the middle of one of their arguments and it rang a nice chord. So, I call him that at times." Amanda regained her thoughts. "Now, where was I? Oh yea, my father worked for a glass company and they had a big annual picnic for all their employees and their families. Everyone had to bring a dish or dessert. It was sweltering hot so dad thought he would be fucking funny and he bought a big watermelon. He cut a hole in the middle of it and then poured half a bottle of vodka in and put it in the fridge to chill. When we got to the picnic, they cut it up and served it to the grownups. Everyone thought it was fantastic, like chilled cold watermelon shots on a scorching summer day. They patted dad on the back and congratulated him for saving the day. Everything was going great. Free food. Free Drinks.

All you could eat cotton candy, popcorn and hot dogs for the kids. There were clowns and games like the water balloon toss and the clothespin milk bottle drop. And then they did a wheelbarrow race. You know what wheelbarrow races are right?"

"Yea, one kid holds another kid's legs while they walk on his hands in front of him." We did it many times at Sunday school picnics and church camp.

"Right." Amanda's pace picked up. "So Chat...fucking...Riley, whose dad, Mr. Riley, owned the glass company—I'll never forget his pimpled, pug-nose ugly face—is holding this other kid's legs and when they take off, Chat...fucking...Riley thinks he's going to be funny and starts running fast. Well, the kid he's pushing tries really hard to keep up at first, but then he can't keep up and falls smack on his face really hard right on the parking lot. Chat...fucking...Riley can't stop and he tumbles right over the top of the kid. You should have heard everyone gasp when it happened; like they had just witnessed a bad car accident. The wheelbarrow kid, I forget his name, got these horrendous scrapes on his chin and forehead and Chat...fucking...Riley sprained his wrist.

Well, come to find out, Chat...fucking...Riley had been sneaking and dipping into the vodka-spiked watermelon and had gotten slightly inebriated. When old man Riley found out, instead of giving his spoiled asshole kid an ass whipping he deserved, he started yelling at dad for bringing the vodka watermelon. They almost went to fists." There was a reflective pause. "That was a hard one to watch because one part of me wanted to see my dad get his ass kicked and the other part of me wanted my dad to tell Chat...fuckin...Riley's dad to shove it up his ass."

"Wait a minute, you wanted to see your dad get his ass kicked?"

What kind of daughter wants to watch her dad get his ass kicked? Or what kind of dad is so bad that his daughter wants to see him get his ass kicked? Hoosiers.

"Yea, you have to know my dad. Real asshole. But anyway, everyone knew that watermelon was spiked. But Chat...fucking...Riley thought he was the first man on the moon and he could get away with anything. So it wasn't my dad's fault. It was the little prick's fault. But I didn't want dad to get into a fight either because I knew that would cause him to lose his job which meant we'd have to move again. And

I didn't want to move because the house we were living in had this charming little birdbath in the back yard. I loved sitting next to it watching the birds splash in the water while I read...," she paused. "...why in the hell was I telling this story?"

"Your nightmare, watermelons on the ice..."

They didn't have a name for it back then but today Amanda would be called ADD.

"Ok...ok...ok...soooo the skating rink was filled with watermelons but not just watermelons, vodka-spiked watermelons that dad was going to sell. All the sudden, one of the guys with dad shoved his cigarette in one of the holes in a watermelon and tosses it at a stack of watermelons on the ice rink and it explodes. Next thing I know, all the watermelons are exploding and everything's on fire and people are frantically screaming and running out of the building." Amanda's voice got louder and more excited. "I'm fucking freaking out running through the burning building looking for Sara. I find her outside by the front door standing with Ruth. They're both safe but Ruth is hysterical because you're nowhere to be seen. Suddenly you come running out of the side door carrying this crying kid in your arms like a goddamn superhero. You're all black with soot and choking and everyone's applauding you."

She paused. "You're not going to believe what happened next, Christian."

"I'm on pins and needles."

"I'm almost embarrassed to even say this and I don't get embarrassed."

Of course, you don't get embarrassed you're a hoosier.

"You don't have to be embarrassed, just tell me."

"I asked you if you had the picture I gave you. You got this horrid look in your eyes. Then Christian, without a word, you turned around and started running right back into the burning building. Sara, Ruth and I kept screaming and yelling for you to stop but you just kept going. You disappeared into a cloud of smoke that was billowing out of a door. Then there was a huge thundering explosion and the entire building collapsed. Oh my God, I was screaming and shaking and...it was just terrible, Christian...terrible." Her distressed words were sincere.

"So, let me get this straight. I died in your dream, trying to save your *picture*?" I grinned at the thought.

"Yes, isn't that terrible?'

"I don't know. I think it's kind of cool. It's one thing to die saving a person from a burning building, but to die saving the person's *picture* from a burning building, that's the kind of stuff that books and movies are made of."

"That's the kind of stuff that books and movies are made of," she repeated. "Oh my God, that's such a sensational phrase, I love it! Can I borrow it?"

"You can have it free of charge," I said.

"Thanks." She made a mental note. "So I woke up yelling and trembling. I told Lucy and Sara about the nightmare and Sara said I should call to make sure everything was all right. When your mom said you weren't home yet that freaked me out even more. So we got out the Yellow Pages and called Aloha. Some man answered the phone. I figured if he answered just like normal, then everything must be normal, so I hung up on him."

"Well, we're both home and safe," I assured her.

"I have to tell you, Christian, I dream every night and I remember my dreams. People say you don't dream in color, but I dream in color all the time. They also say that you never die in your dreams because if you did, you'd die in real life. But that's a fallacy, too, because I've died in my dreams several times. Do you remember your dreams?"

"Yes." I lied.

I seldom remembered any dreams. But I had Amanda Marrow on the phone and I didn't want to sound boring. So I lied to keep the momentum of the conversation going. It wasn't the drunk dial that I had prayed for which had us mutually masturbating. But still, while the rest of the world, including every guy at school, was asleep and dreaming about Amanda, I was talking to her in real life about how she had dreamed about me. How incredible.

It was just her and me. One on one. No one
else around. No distractions. No interruptions.
That was more than an answered prayer. It was
a miracle. God had given me a second chance.

I had blown it the first time hours earlier
at the roller rink. Acting like a bumbling
idiot. But now I was hidden in the darkness
beneath my blankets while she was miles away
on the other end of the phone. I was not going
to be the shy and easily embarrassed boy she
had met earlier. I didn't know who that red-
faced dork was, but it wasn't me. I was
outgoing, personable and confident, sometimes
to the point of arrogant. I needed to take
control, grow some balls and take advantage
of this God-given opportunity.

"Matter of fact, just last night I dreamt…"

"Oh, one more thing, Christian," Amanda interrupted. "Some of my
dreams actually come true. Last year I dreamt this pregnant girl named
Lizzie who works with my mom, went into labor and my mom helped
deliver the baby. It was no sooner than a week later that Lizzie did go
into labor at work. My mom had to take her to the hospital and she said
she almost had to pull over and deliver that baby right there on the side
of the highway, but they got to the hospital just in time. Is that crazy?"

"That's crazy," I said and assured her. "Well, if I see anyone
bringing watermelons into the skating rink, I'll make sure to
immediately tell them to leave."

We both laughed, which took the edge off the crazy nervousness I
was feeling.

"I'm sorry that I called so late," Amanda said.

She apparently did not hear my "last night
I dreamt" statement. Which was fine because it
meant that I would have had to lie again and
make up some kind of dream.

"I didn't mean to wake your mom up. I thought you'd be home and awake and get to the phone first. Your mom didn't sound so happy."

"She has one of those late night phone-call phobias that all moms have. If the phone rings after ten o'clock, she automatically thinks it's the police, hospital or the morgue."

"Phone-call phobias." She chuckled at the wordplay. "I wish my mom had that."

"I'm sure she does, she's just doesn't show it."

"Yea, maybe."

"I was…," I pause a moment and finished in my James Bond voice. "…surmising why you were calling so late."

Amanda laughed. "I'm sure your mom was doing the same thing."

"Yea, she'd kill me if she knew I was talking to anyone on the phone this late."

"Oh, I'm sorry," Amanda apologized. "I don't want to get you in trouble or anything?"

Are you freaking kidding me? TROUBLE? Trouble is exactly what I want to get into with you. Let's keeping talking. Tell me what you're wearing or not wearing right now. Describe to me in those fancy words you're so fond of, what your body looks like and what you'd let me do to you if I was there right now. Oh, if only I had the guts to say such things...if only.

"I'm cool," I assured her. "It normally takes me a little while to wind down and go to sleep when I get home from the rink." I tossed the ball in her court. "But if you need to get off," I paused, "I mean... hang up...I totally understand."

As God as my witness, I did not mean to pause right after I said, "get off," but when those two words came out of my mouth it was like my thoughts raced three seconds ahead of my lips and said, "Oh my God, did I just ask her if she

needed to "get off?" And that caused me to
pause momentarily.

She caught the faux pas and parried. "I don't need to get off." She
gave a sarcastic and almost naughty giggle. It was her turn for a
resonating pause. "Or hang up." Another giggle. "I'm wide awake now
and I don't have to get up early so we can chat a little if you want."

CHAPTER SEVEN

Praise Jesus! She wanted to keep talking. But did I continue to act like the wholesome best big brother in the world and talk about safe, boring and platonic things?

Or should I reveal my true sex-starved nature and try to make her panties wet again by tossing out beautiful and abstract words?

My mind was overflowing with erotic thoughts and entirely void of beautiful and obscure words.

"Hope you liked the picture I gave you for your birthday." She woke me out of my fantasy.

"Yeah, it's awesome. Thanks." I verbally bowed before her and then regained my composure. "But not so awesome that I would actually die for it or anything." I laughed. "You're really photogenic. You should be a model."

"I tried but I'm too short. They like girls over five ten and I'm a whopping five two. But thanks for the compliment." She pondered. "I'm curious to know what you did with my picture."

I didn't know if I should lie and tell her it was sitting next to me on my nightstand. Or maybe I could say someone stole it. The little devil and angel that perpetually sat on my shoulders began warring with one another again, each begging for my attention. The devil had won the first battle and gotten me to call her. But the angel on my shoulder won this time.

"Um, well to be totally honest, I forgot it at Aloha underneath the skate counter."

"Well thanks! I guess that shows how much I mean to you." She teased.

"Look who's talking, I didn't even get as much as a wave or nod when you left tonight," I said defensively, leaving the hurt out of my voice.

"I didn't say goodbye to you?"

"Nope."

"Sorry about that." Her tone softened. "Why do I always forget to say goodbye to the nice guys?"

The words came out of her mouth not so much as a real question but as a rhetorical question. One that I wish I had not heard.

So there it was, I was the ignored and invisible nice guy. You know what they say about nice guys and how they finished last? I pretended to ignore the comment and continued the conversation.

"So...um...how's working at Waldenbooks?"

"How'd you know I worked there?" she said, surprised.

"Oh, word gets around." I implied something more sinister. She took the implication and defended herself.

"Yeah, it's funny how words get around so fast at this school. Unfortunately, most of those words are lies. So don't believe everything you hear, Christian." She began to say more but held back, not sure how her words would come out. "I admit...," she said in a strictly platonic manner, "I enjoy sex. But contrary to the rumors," she cleared her throat, "I cannot suck the chrome off a car's bumper."

Silence. Did she just say what I thought she said? And was it possible to get embarrassed while hiding in the darkness under your blankets and talking to someone miles away on the phone? Yes. And. Yes.

"I bet your face just turned fifty shades of red didn't it?" She laughed. "I made the birthday boy embarrassed three times tonight." I could tell she was enjoying the moment. "Really, you don't ever have to be embarrassed around me. Nothing...," she began but caught herself mid-sentence. "...well, very few things offend me or make me uncomfortable. I've seen, heard and done it all."

What exactly have you seen, done and heard Miss Marrow? Please tell me so I can decide how to carry on this conversation.

"Well, maybe not everything but from the stories that go around school, you'd think I'd fucked every guy in it. That shit gets back to me, you know." I could almost feel her shake her head back and forth in angered frustration. "It doesn't matter. It's all lies, started by jealous douchbagettes."

I heard her flick her lighter and seconds later inhale her cigarette. I imagined the glow of the burning cigarette illuminating her sleepy face as she blew the smoke out into the darkness like a shady villainess in a black-and-white movie.

"Your mom lets you smoke in the house?"

"Yes, she's been smoking since she was Sara's age, so she can't bitch at me for doing it. As long as I pay for my own cigarettes and don't steal hers, she's cool and copacetic with it."

"You know that's stuff bad for you."

"Yeah, I know. It's like drinking soda with antifreeze in it. Isn't that right, best big brother in the world?" She took another long drag. "I know it's stupid and nasty and bad for me and I'll quit one of these days when the spirit moves me. Or it kills me."

Ah, the informational pipeline of our little sisters' friendship was already flowing.

"So what are your bad habits, Chhhrrristian?" She drew the word out as if to mean, "What bad habits does a Christian boy like you have?" Her voice suddenly echoed like she had walked into a different room. Then I heard what sounded like a stream of water...like she had turned on the kitchen sink or...wait...was she actually peeing while she was talking to me on the phone?

My manhood immediately came to attention.

"Um...are you peeing?" I asked nervously.

She giggled. "Yea, you weren't supposed to hear that. Sorry, I couldn't hold it."

My hand found its way to my manhood. Amanda Marrow was peeing while I was talking to her on the phone. This was almost better than phone sex. Almost.

"Wow, that's a first. I've never talked to a girl on the phone while she was peeing."

I acted like it was nothing exciting. However, the truth was, it was the most exciting thing to ever happen to me in the first eighteen years of my life.

"Oh, I'm sure you have, you just didn't know it. Unfortunately, it's kind of hard to cover up at two o'clock in the morning, while you're whispering on the phone and there's not another sound in the house."

I began masturbating.

"I am now about to wipe myself, just in case wondering minds want to know. But don't worry, I won't flush because it's loud and I don't want to wake up Sara and Lucy."

My breathing got heavy and all the moisture in my mouth vanished like the water in a flushed toilet. I repeatedly ran my tongue around searching for salvia or an abandoned puddle of spit lying forgotten in the back of my mouth that I could suck and produce some kind of moisture. Nothing.

"Christian, you there?"

"Ah-huh," I said, then turned the phone away from my mouth and held it upside down as I attempted to keep my heavy breathing away from the receiver while I played tug of war with both my mind and manhood.

"What are you doing?" she asked.

I believed she probably had a good idea of
what I was doing, but there was no way I was
going to tell her. I didn't care how much of a
hoosier or slut she was. You don't randomly
start masturbating on the phone while
talking to a girl.

Well, horny male teens do it all the time.
And, in most cases, the girls on the other end
of the line don't know. But it's kind of hard
to cover up at two o'clock in the morning,
while you're whispering on the phone and
there's not another sound in the house.

"Just...talking...to you," I whispered, in short, dry, gasps while
fantasizing about her nakedness and her naughtiness and the thought of
her wiping herself dry.

"Well, it sounds like your masturbating or something."

And about the time she said "masturbating",
I had finished. Eighty-three seconds from
start to finish. A new personal record. That's
the effect Amanda Marrow had on me.

CHAPTER EIGHT

I took a deep, refreshing breath. "Hold on a second. I think someone's up." I lied again. I put the phone under the pillow and quickly removed my messy pajamas bottoms and tossed them onto the floor. I took a couple more quick deep breathes in an attempt to settle my breathing. The moisture was slowly coming back to my mouth. I picked the phone back up. "I can't believe you actually thought I was masturbating. Oh my God, that's just crazy. I don't even know you." I took another deep breath away from the phone and continued with my lie. "I thought I heard someone walking around outside my room. I was freaking out a little and went to my door to listen. As I said, my parents would have a conniption fit if they knew I was talking on the phone this late."

One-way phone sex and blatant lying all in the same deep breaths. The devil on my left shoulder was doing a happy dance.

"Conniption fit...another exquisite phrase. You keep talking like that and I'm going to start masturbating!" She giggled and realized what she had just offered. "I'm just kidding! I didn't think you were either but nothing about Vagina Hunters surprise me anymore. It sounded like you were masturbating. I've heard that sound on other occasions while talking to guys on the phone."

"Vagina Hunters? Is that what you call guys?"

"Yes. I postulate, as oppose to surmise, that pretty much the entire male population possesses this pre-historic animalistic instinct of wanting to stalk, capture and conquer. But...since we've evolved to getting our food from the grocery store and no longer need men to hunt for the evening's dinner, man is now left with this empty feeling or longing to keep hunting, capturing and killing. So they've made women, or more specifically a woman's vagina, their new game per se.

You might say they've gone from hunting tigers to hunting pussies. Oops, did I just say the P-word out loud? I hope that didn't embarrass you." She lied and chuckled at her wordplay. "I've yet to find a guy who has proved this theory wrong. Well, I have met a couple of guys who I thought were the exceptions, but they turned out to be fags. I guess they're more Penis Predators as oppose to Vagina Hunters." She immediately changed the subject. "By the way, I don't think you answered me about your bad habit's Christian?"

"I don't have any bad habits." I chuckled. "I'm a perfect angel."

"I'm sure if I asked Ruth, she could come up with some. Everyone has some kind of bad habit."

"Well, to be honest, I don't drink, smoke, do drugs or rarely cuss." I proudly proclaimed. "I also don't cheat, steal, and I try my hardest not to lie."

"Wow, you are the perfect little Chrissstian boy aren't you? Does the name fit you or do you fit the name?"

"I don't know what you mean?"

"Are you a goody-goody Christian boy because it's your name and therefore you want to uphold that image?" I heard her take another long drag of her cigarette. "Or did someone place that label on you at birth and now you have to uphold that image?"

What an amazing, almost genius-like question. She summed up my entire life in one sentence. Was I Christian by name or by virtue? There was a time when I could answer that question without reserve, but as I grew older and spent less time at my domestic zoo and more time out in the wild, the distinction between the two became hazy and muddled. She wasn't helping making matters more definable at all.

"I'm not particularly a goody-goody boy," I said defensively. "I just try to make smart and healthy decisions that I don't regret. I was also raised in a decent and respectable home." I emphasized the words. "And have been taught there are things that make God happy and things that He doesn't like."

I really hated to bring God into the conversation. My mother always brought God into every conversation and God knows, I never wanted to sound like her. But I wanted Amanda to understand her way of life was radically different from my way of life. We each lived on the opposite side of the social spectrum.

She was a hoosier and therefore destined to a life of mediocracy at best or destitution at worst. Hoosiers girls didn't go to college and make something of their lives. They met Vagina Hunters at bars and clubs and went home with them and had sex. The hoosier girls got pregnant and became struggling single moms that had to work two jobs just to survive.

Or they married lying and lazy hoosier guys that abused them and treated them like shit. Once they popped out a couple of kids and got fat and ugly, the Vagina Hunters divorced them and went hunting for younger and more robust vaginas.

When it's all said and done, the hoosier girl became a hoosier old lady left with an empty, unfulfilling and unhealthy life and a couple of hoosier kids. Because hoosier begets hoosier. She remains single into her senior years until succumbs to a woman's worst fear. She dies alone.

That's the hoosier girl's life in a nutshell. Not my nutshell mind you, but my parent's nutshell or more specifically, my mom's nutshell.

However, should she like to change her hoosier ways and interject some class and sophistication into her wretched lifestyle, then she has the potential to move in different circles. If she cleans up her mouth and dresses more respectfully, then she'll reap what she sows. She'll meet other decent and respectable people who make better choices. And we all know that life is nothing but a perpetual stream of thoughts, choices, and actions. When you make right ones, you're bound to experience a greater amount of happiness, health, wealth, and wisdom. That's the non-hoosier destiny I was taught in my zoo.

But it doesn't stop there! Accept Jesus Christ as your personal savior and you have a first-class ticket to an eternal life of peace and prosperity. Do I hear an amen?

"What about sex?" Amanda examined. "Are you just another Vagina Hunter?"

She was calling me out like the lions were called out after the Christians were tossed into the arena. It was the old question, "How can you call yourself a Christian and have any sexual thoughts, desires or God-forbid, sexual actions before you're married?"

I've been confronted with that question on different intimate occasions with other girls. I've learned in my short, stupid, sex-starved, eighteen-year-old life that the best defense was to pick a Bible verse and use that as a shield against your shortcomings and then change the subject.

"Well, we all sin and fall short of the glory of God," I said knowing she had probably never heard that Bible verse once in her life. "Besides, one of the things I was taught was not to stereotype people. Like all men are Vagina Hunters."

"It's not stereotyping." She quickly defended. "I call it stereo-truthing." Another Amanda original. "There are blanket statements that you can say about groups of people and it's the truth when it comes to the majority. Women are more emotional than men. Italians like to eat. Irish like to drink. Black people have more rhythm than white people. Lucy says Church people are the worst tippers. Of course, you're always going to have exceptions to the rule, but the truth is, guys are Vagina Hunters. You put a hundred of them in a room and at any given moment and the majority of them will be thinking about vaginas, breasts or butts. Put an attractive woman in that room and watch the Vagina Hunters watch the vagina like a cheetah watches a slow gazelle."

Stereotruthing versus stereotyping? Very interesting. My entire zoo life I was trained by my mother to stereotype people and yet I was telling this hoosier girl it's not proper to stereotype.

CHAPTER NINE

"So...let's talk about something else," I offered. "I don't think you answered me about how you like working at the bookstore."

"I didn't?"

"Nope, we "got off" on another subject about not listening to the rumors that go around school."

"That's right." She drew her thoughts in a new direction. "Working at Waldenbooks is awesome. Well, besides the manager telling me I have to dress more conservatively."

"What? He doesn't like the short skirts and tight shirts?"

It was probably the short skirts, tight shirts and who knows what else that had gotten her the job in the first place.

"No, *she* doesn't," she said. "But I absolutely love working there! It's the perfect job for me." Her tone became light and animated. "I'm going to be a famous writer and own a used bookstore one of these days. I can conceptualize it all in my mind. It won't be dark and dingy with lots of wood and leather like most used bookstores." She spit the sentence out. "It'll be bright and breezy with lots of windows and sunshine. Maybe a big water fountain right in the middle of it. And there's going to be a little café in the back that sells eclectic imported coffees and a smorgasbord of teas. Next to the café will be a quaint small stage surrounded by tables and chairs for book signings and hip trios that play jazz." She took a deep breath and inhaled the scent of her imaginary bookstore. "Ah, I can almost smell the ambrosial aroma of used books and hot brews wafting around the bookshelves. That's why I'm going to call it.....," She suddenly stopped. "I don't know what I'm going to call it yet." She pondered and then asked. "Do you like to read, Christian?"

"I only read when I have to, like at school or church. I'm not much of a reader. It puts me to sleep."

"That's because you haven't had your reading cherry popped yet. I used to be the same way. I hated reading, especially when I was forced to in school. Until Mr. Nothstine, my fourth-grade teacher, assigned the class to read, *Anne of Green Gables*. That one book changed my life."

So that's why she had the *Anne of Green Gables* book purse. "And how did *Anne of Green Gables* take your reading virginity?"

"I believe that everyone has the potential to be a bibliophile...do you know what that is?" she asked.

I had no idea, but I took a guess. "Well, let's see, a pedophile is a person who likes to have sex with kids, so I'm thinking a bibliophile," I spelled the word. 'B-i-b-l-i-o', is someone who likes to have sex with...Bibles?"

"HAHAHA!" She laughed so loud I had to pull the phone away from my ear. "Oh my God, that's hilarious!" She roared one more time and ended with a snort. I didn't mean to be funny, but I'll take the laugh and hope that she doesn't think I'm a total idiot.

Her voice got suddenly soft. "Oops. I hope I didn't wake anyone up," she continued, 'Phile' doesn't mean 'loves to have sex with', but simply 'a lover of.' A bibliophile is someone who loves 'biblios' or books or reading." There was a residual giggle. "I had an epiphany about four years ago that went like this....," She cleared her throat.

"I believe when God creates us, She puts little hidden virgin bibliophiles inside us. Part of our purpose in life is to find that one soulmate book. Oh, we can play the field of fiction and non-fiction and not even enjoy reading, like we're forced to do in school, but then we finally meet...," There was a dramatic pause. "*It*," the one book that sweeps us off our minds and takes us to places we've never been. It makes us laugh and cry and seduces us into going to bed with it every night. It consumes our daily thoughts and when it's not in our hands we miss it. The more we read our soulmate book, the more we fall madly in love with it.

Until finally, we get to the last line. We're now heartbroken, yet ecstatic. We're tragically sad because our reading relationship with those characters is over, gone, like the death of a loved one. However, we're also elated, because our literary cherries have been popped!

Before our soulmate book, we were just readers. But now, we've become bibliophiles," she said in a tone that took her from being a mere mortal girl to a reading goddess.

"As a bibliophile, our minds constantly hunger for new fiction or facts that entertain and educate us." There was a final pause. "Yep, because of that one soulmate book, our lives are changed forever." Amanda took a deep breath. "Wow, sorry. I didn't mean to sound like I was giving an acceptance speech for the Nobel Prize in Literature; it's just....," She tried to find the right description. "…Well, until you become a bibliophile, it's hard to understand."

"So bibliophiles are sort of like Vagina Hunters but instead of hunting vaginas they're always on the lookout for new books and stories to read?" I interjected.

"Exactly," she laughed at the comparison. "Let's call them Story Stalkers and don't be disappointed when I say they're mostly female. I read an article once that said women out read men by twenty percent." She added one final epiphany. "The stereo-truth is women are more intelligent than men. That's why I always call God a She." I could almost see her smug smile through the phone line.

"What-ever!" I defended the entire male population. "Women may read more, but it's mostly those stupid romance novels. Men probably read more non-fiction stuff and that makes us more intelligent." I then used my mother as an argumentive shield. "My mother would also have a heyday with your epiphanies," I explained. "She'd tell you there's only one book that really changes people's lives and that's the Bible. She would also tell you that God is not a she with a capital S. But a He with a capital H."

And ironically, I think I'm starting to learn that Satan isn't an ugly, horned, male creature with a pointed tail but in reality, a beautiful, horny, female creature with an awesome tail.

"Well, everyone's entitled to their own wrong, biased, and stupid opinions, I guess." She laughed, smoldering the argumentative flame. "And while the Bible does change the lives of many people, it doesn't have to be a big religious book or literary classic to impact your life or take your reading virginity. It can be something as simple as *Peter Rabbit* or as complicated as Carl Sagan's new bestseller, *The Cosmos*.

"Or *Anne of Green Gables*."

"Yes. Exactly." Amanda began to explain. "I started reading it and immediately realized Anne Shirley--that's the girl in the book--and I were kindred spirits. I couldn't put the book down. I'd swear to myself that I was going to stop reading at the end of one chapter, but by the time I got there, I had to see what Anne was going to do next. I was like a plot nymphomaniac and I couldn't get enough of the story." More Vagina Hunter verbiage to keep me interested. "I consumed the entire book in about a week which was a miracle considering I despised reading. After I read *Anne of Green Gables*, I read the other seven books in the series. Then I found other authors who had written stories about head-strong and determined girls and read them. The next thing I knew I was reading all the time. I woke up one day and realized I was a bibliophile."

And soon I became a 'logosist'." She knew I had no idea what a logosist was, so she continued, "You don't know what a logosist is because I made it up. It means a collector of words."

"Logoist," I repeated.

"No, you forgot the "s" in the middle. It's lo-go-sist. 'Logos' is Greek for 'word' and 'ist' is someone who collects something, like botanist or linguist. Well, it doesn't really mean that, but you get the idea."

"Lo-go-sist." I tried one more time.

"Very good."

"Actually, I'm a numismatist, myself." I felt proud that I had a big word to toss out at that moment. "Do you know what those are?"

"Duh. It's someone who collects coins or money." She tossed the definition out like I had asked her to solve 2+2. Making me feel a little self-conscious of my own intelligence. "Well, speaking of money, or the lack of, that's exactly why I became a logosist. We were very impecunious...or poor...growing up, so I never had any money to collect anything tangible. However, being a bibliophile, I did the next best thing: I started collecting fascinating and beautiful words. They were all free for the taking from the books I read from the library and bookmobile. I got a notebook and started filling it with words that were captivating to my mind or pleasing to my ear. I also collect old words that you never hear any more. Sort of like someone who collects beer cans or baseball cards. Words like 'bequeath,' 'genteel' and 'hastened.' And I like making up my very own new and original words like 'stereo-truths' and 'logosist.' So far I have three notebooks filled with my word collection."

"That's really cool. And here I thought you were just trying to impress me with a great vocabulary. 'Conceptualize', 'eclectic', 'ambrosial', and 'epiphany', you never hear people say words like those, well, at least not ninth grade girls."

Especially those who are hoosiers. I mentally added.

"Hopefully, I do impress you with my vocabulary. As the world's only self-professed logosist, I'm very proud of my words, just like you'd be proud of a rare coin in your collection. That's also why I was so excited to hear a guy say a beautiful word like 'surmise' or a funny phrase like 'conniption fit.'"

"Ok, Miss Logosist, how do curse words fit into your collection?" I wanted to see if she could justify having such a filthy mouth. "My mom always taught Ruth and me that people curse because they're ignorant and can't think of anything intelligent to say."

"Well, you can tell your mom that's bullshit." She snickered. "Or you can tell her she's incorrect." She paused. "Now tell me, which one of those sentences has a greater impact or is more profound?" She let the question sit on a conversation table for a second and then continued, "I'm sure most people cuss and swear because of their ignorance but I do it because, as a logosist, I find curse words to be like...," She stopped, and I imagined her mentally searching her notebooks of words. "...the bagpipes of banter."

"I guess my mom was just stereo-truthing about people who curse and as you said, everyone's entitled to their own wrong, biased, and stupid opinions."

"Touché," she laughed.

She didn't have me totally convinced that her potty-mouth was part of a bigger logosist plan. I'd been brainwashed for eighteen years to believe differently. It wasn't going to be wiped away in one simple and eloquent example.

I would also have to remind her that it didn't
matter how much of a logosist she was, she had
to refrain from cursing around my mother if
she ever met her.

    To be perfectly honest, I did find her hobby
very fascinating. I had never met someone who
seemed so creative and original. Strangely, I
found I was being drawn into her personality
just as much as her beauty and sexuality
sucked me toward her.

CHAPTER TEN

There was an awkward silence. Once again, I heard the click of her lighter. Another long drag of her cigarette. It was a good sign. She wanted to keep talking. I obliged.

"What's your favorite word in your word collection?" I asked.

"Leafs," she said without hesitation. "Spelled l-e-a-f-s as in the plural of a leaf."

"But that's spelled l-e-a-v-e-s." I corrected.

"And that is why my word 'leafs' is better and much more beautiful. "L-e-a-v-e-s" is such an ugly and negative word. It's so good-bye, going away, and final," she almost snarled. "Leaves sounds like something that would be attached to the dark and dirty part of a tree like it's roots or bark. But l-e-a-f-s aren't dark and dirty. They're gorgeous and represent new life in the spring and provide shade in the summer and they burst into a kaleidoscope of colors in the fall." She sounded like a tree-hugging poet. "And that's why I spell them the way God intended them to be spelled l-e-a-f-s."

"But they turn dark and dirty and die in the winter," I noted.

"You may see them as dark and dirty and dead. But I see them as golden senior citizens of the season." She matched my alliteration and trumped it. "Leafs" is my most beautiful word because I actually own it. The rest of the goddamn world has a billion words to share amongst themselves but 'leafs' is all mine!" Her unbridled enthusiasm ended. "Sorry, I get a little carried away when it comes to my words."

She sounded like Ruth on caffeine and my mother on religion.

"No really, that's awesome." I didn't want her to think I was totally void of literary intellect so I added, "Ask me anything about the Bible and I can pretty much tell you whatever you want to know. Over the course of eighteen years of going to Sunday school and church two to three times a week, I figure I've probably read it about a half a dozen times."

"Really? I tried reading the Bible once but the chapter with all the "thou begat thou" gave me a fucking brainache."

Did she just say the Bible gave her a fucking brainache? I was shocked. In one quick, silent gasp, I inhaled all the oxygen from under the covers. I threw the blankets off my head, took a refreshing breath, and dived back under them.

How many times in my life had my brained ached because of the Bible? Almost as many as there are days in a year. I remained peacefully still as I listened to her glorious blasphemy and wondered when the bolt of righteous lightning was going to strike us.

"And the entire Noah's Ark story just bugged the hell out of me. How could you possibly fit two of every kind of animal on one boat?" She went back into teaching mode. "Let's say there are one hundred thousand species of animals on this planet. There's probably way more than that, but just for now, let's say one hundred thousand. Now we're going to double that for the two of each kind. So you have two hundred thousand animals on this one boat. But...that's not all." Her frustrated excitement continued. "How much food storage are you going to need to feed almost a quarter of a million animals? Probably about one more boat size. And how do eight goddamn people take care of feeding that massive herd?"

"But....," I tried to interject they weren't god damned people, they were God blessed people, but I was stopped.

"Yes, let's talk about butts--you've got two hundred thousand animals and they have to be fed and what goes in one end has to come out the other end. Now you need a place and people to clean up tons of shit on a daily basis. It used to take me an hour to clean up all the dog shit in my backyard and we only had one dog! And yet I'm expected to believe eight people took care of feeding and cleaning up the shit of two hundred thousand animals. I can't buy that." She took an irritated puff of her cigarette. "It's one thing to pass down folk tales from one generation to the next, but trying to make those folk tales pure truth, is a hard pill for me to swallow. Now, what were you going to say?"

"But God is all about miracles, so could it be possible that those animals were put into a dormant sleep so they didn't have to eat, drink or go to the bathroom?"

"Then why in the hell doesn't it say that in the Bible! Why would they tell all about the building of the ark and give us the exact fucking measurements and how many animals to bring on it but forget to mention the important "miracle"? How all two hundred thousand animals went to sleep and didn't eat, piss or shit so Noah and his family of eight didn't have to take care of them twenty-four seven for the entire one hundred plus days they were dilly-dallying in the deluge. Why'd they leave that part out?"

"There are things about the Bible we're just not to know about," I said in the exact tone my mother used when I asked her unanswerable questions about the Bible. Shivers went down my spine. "It's called 'living in faith.'"

"Well, that's bullshit, too. I'm supposed to have faith in a God that kills all His creations with one swoop of a flood. What the hell kind of loving God is that? Then let's talk about how the Earth got repopulated. With only four men and four women, there had to be some cousins fucking each other and some incest going on because to my unfaithful mind that's the only way you can go from eight people to five billion people. I guess that was just another "miracle" left out of the Bible so people like you would believe it and people like me find it to be a bunch of bull--and two hundred thousand other kinds of animal--shit."

I was being psychologically drawn and quartered. But not really quartered just halved. One half was high-fiving her for having the courage to speak freely on what she really thought of the Bible and God.

I had never heard words like "brainache," "bullshit" and "incest" used while discussing the Bible. It was more revealing than anything that I had ever read in Revelations.

However, the other half was chanting and encouraging me to wage a theological war with her. To stand up and fight for my beliefs and religion. But I couldn't muster enough

faith to face the fact that I was not battle worthy to fight her words. Or, to be totally honest, I didn't want too.

"I may not be a good Christian girl, Christian, but I believe in God and I believe in right and wrong and I really try to be nice and kind to everyone. Not because the Bible or God says I have to, but because it's in my human nature. Like the nature to stalk, capture and kill are born into Vagina Hunters. And even though I may not believe the Bible as the whole truth and nothing but the truth, so help me God, I believe in heaven and hell."

She moved the phone about and I could tell she was re-adjusting her thoughts as well as making herself more comfortable. "Funny, but last week I was walking through the aisles at work and making a mental note of all the books I wanted to read. I decided that when I die, I hope I spend eternity in heaven. That way I'd have endless time to just lounge around and read every book ever written." Her words made me smile. "So I could talk to God on Her own intellectual level."

"And if you go to hell?" I asked.

"A world with no books would be hell for me," her words echoed from the phone.

Once more, the conversation had taken unwanted twists and turns, this time into the theme of theology. As much as I wanted to keep talking and get to know her more and possibly even get into some phone sex, I was becoming tired and conversationally spent. I asked one last question.

"Did you talk your mom into letting you skip school on Tuesday to get your driver's license?"

I started to say Lucy, but I had a hard time calling parents and adults by their first names. It was a zoo training thing. Even Mr. Abernathy, whom I've known almost my entire life and work with on a weekly basis, wasn't called Kent. In my mind's eye, he's not a Kent. He's an adult, my boss, and Mr. Abernathy.

"Yeah, no. She said she didn't mind if I skipped school, but she needed the car. She works two jobs and she's working both on Tuesday.

I tried to talk her into calling in sick in the morning so she could take me, but she said it was almost Christmas and she needed the money. Now I'm just going to have to wait until our Christmas break. Hopefully, we can both find some time in our busy work schedules to do it." There was a disappointment in her voice.

"Your mom doesn't mind if you skip school?" I was subconsciously hinting; she made a bad parental choice. She picked up on the accusation.

"It's not like she lets me skip school all the time. But since it's my sweet sixteenth birthday, she said it was OK. I think she was feeling guilty because she has to work on my birthday. Poor thing. I love my mom to death. She's like my best friend. She'd been through some terrible shit married to my sperm-donor. We all did. But she's awesome." Amanda yawned loudly and continued, "She used to be one of those hippie activists. I have a great picture of her hanging on my wall. She has long hair and a flower headband. She's wearing big mirrored sunglasses and shorts cut off at her crotch and a white blousy, angelic shirt. With no bra. She's holding me in one arm. In her other hand, she's waving a sign that says, 'Bombing for peace, is like fucking for virginity.' Is that classic or what? She was protesting the Vietnam war."

"Do you want me to skip school and take you to get your license?"

Even as the words came out of my mouth, I wanted to lasso them and pull them back in. Was I crazy? What the hell was I thinking? It was totally out of character. But then again, she was slowly drawing out of me a character that was different from the one I had become. I had been confident and personable. Yet, in her presence, I became this blubbering idiot. I had told the truth and acted rationally. And now I was lying and one-way masturbating on the phone.

Worse yet, I was about to skip school for her. I had never skipped school in my entire life. The closest thing to it was in ninth grade when I faked being sick to get out of

Miss James's algebra class because I hadn't
studied for an important test. I was a
religious radical and she was neutralizing
my radicalness.

"Are you serious? That would be totally awesome!" She practically
yelled.

I was now obligated. In the deep recesses of
my genetic code, I also realized that it wasn't
just the effect Amanda Marrow, the Freshman
Fire, was having on me, it was more.
I couldn't hide the fact that she was right.
I was a Vagina Hunter. It was in my nature.
That was also why I had offered up my skipping
school virginity. My Vagina Hunting
instincts were kicking into action. By going
out of my way and doing her the incredible
favor of skipping school and taking her to
the DMV so she could take her driver's test, I
was opening a trap. She, in turn, would then
be obligated to me. We would spend more time
together. Talk more. I would get to know her
and learn her ways.
I remembered Marlin Perkins once saying on
my dad's favorite TV show, *Wild Kingdom*, that
if you really want to know how to stalk an
animal, you must first learn to know their
ways.

We spent the next fifteen minutes scheming and devising a plan
filled with lies and alibis. She was going to call school, pretend to be
my mother, and say I wasn't feeling well. How in the hell she was ever
going to pull off sounding like my mother was a complete mystery. It
didn't matter. I was like one of those bobblehead tigers that sit in the
back window of a hoosier's car. Whatever she said, my head just shook
up and down and my mouth readily agreed with it.

"Oh my God, it's 3:36 a.m. We've been talking for an hour and a half!" Amanda whispered.

"Yea. I know. And unlike you, who doesn't have to get up early, I have to be up at 7 a.m. so I can be a good Chrissstian boy and be at Sunday school by 8 a.m. So let's say goodnight and pray that we don't have any more nightmares, just sweet dreams and I'll see you in school on Monday."

"Sounds like a plan," she agreed and suddenly got serious. "Hey...," she paused, "Thanks."

"For what?"

"For having a very stimulating and non-sexual conversation with me. That's very rare. It's like every guy I talk to is in a constant state of horniness. And that's cool sometimes, but you can get sick of it constantly. That's another reason why I stereo-truth all you guys as Vagina Hunters."

I took the compliment at face value knowing that she had done most of the talking and I had been just another stereo-truthical Vagina Hunter filling in the empty spaces with my rhetorical fluff and hypocritical fantasies.

"You're welcome," I replied.

"Good night."

She hung up and I lay there with the phone next to my ear thinking a billion thoughts.

Then I heard it. In the darkness of the night when sound is pure and perfect, I heard it.

Click — the sound of another phone receiver hanging up.

CHAPTER ELEVEN

Sleep came quickly after my stimulating conversation with Amanda. But the morning came even quicker. Then time seemed to stop and move backward during Sunday morning church services. Neither mom nor dad showed any signs that they were aware of my dubious deed with Amanda last night. Had either one been last night's eavesdropper I would have already been verbally hogtied, whipped, and grounded permanently. I sat in the church pew listening to Reverend Monty doing his damnedest to save our damned souls, but I didn't hear any of it. I was as nervous as hell.

To be totally honest, the entire skipping school idea was scaring the hell out of me. It's one thing faking an illness to get out of a test. That's an academic misdemeanor. But a pre-planned full day of skipping school and deceiving your parents, teachers and the school administration? Well, that was an academic felony. A crime that had long-term consequences. Grounding. Suspension. Negative marks on your records that lasted through college and into your employment years. And why was I doing this?

Because I was getting some attention from the girl of my dreams. Didn't matter that she most probably didn't give a hoot's ass about me. She was probably using me like a doormat. But I had my Vagina Hunting motives and agendas, too. I was determined to get something out of this situation.

Once again, I was walking a tight rope. As many tightropes as I walk in my life, I might as well be a circus performer. Constantly balancing and balancing. Saint or sinner? Zoo or wild? Cool or clown?

I was currently teetering between Vagina Hunter and Mr. Nice Guy. But we all know where nice guys finish, don't we? They end up walking another stupid tight rope. Finishing first or last? Going to heaven or hell? Being a friend or foe?

I knew I was going to follow Amanda and her toxic ways. Even it if meant going against my parent's will. Just as I rode my bike into the toxic mist of the bug spray man as he drove down the street. Inhaling the pungent poison specifically because my parents told me not to do it. Perfume or poison? Or are they each the same? I wondered.

After church, I gulped down a hurried, healthy lunch with the rest of the family and quickly changed clothes. I had said a little prayer in church this morning. I asked God to let me find Amanda's picture. Now, I wanted to get back to Aloha to see if my prayer was answered.

"Where ya going?" Ruth caught me at the front door.

"I have to run up to Aloha."

"What for?" Ruth asked.

"I have some things to do," I said. I didn't think it was necessary to announce to the world that Amanda had given me her picture. Like the late-night phone call and the academic felony we were planning, the less anyone knew, the fewer chances there were of getting busted.

"I'm going to shut my eyes and read your mind," Ruth said, as she put her hand on my head and began talking like a gypsy fortune teller. "I'm picturing...a picture...of a beautiful girl."

"So you're the one who was listening to my phone conversation last night, you little shit!" I pushed her hand off my head and snapped, "Don't ever do that again or I'll..."

"I didn't listen to your phone conversation!" Ruth's eyes widened with hurt. "I promise. I just got off the phone with Sara and she told me why Amanda called last night. She also said that you and Amanda talked on the phone until three a.m..." She was about to chatter on, but my angered look stopped her cold. "But I promise I won't say anything to mom and dad."

That didn't make me happy. "Amanda told Sara that she gave me a picture and I forgot it at Aloha?"

"Yes, they talk about all kinds of things Christian. Amanda tells Sara stuff that mom would absolutely kill you if you told me. They're not like our family. They actually talk and discuss things." She reflected on her own words. "Oh, they argue a lot, too, which I think is a good thing. That way you don't store all that anger and frustration up inside and all the sudden explode like those watermelons in Amanda's dream." Ruth smiled. Hoping to earn a shared laugh. But it didn't work. "Can you believe she had a dream about watermelons with vodka in them and fire and you dying? Is that freaky or what?"

"Yeah, that's freaky." I was still profoundly perturbed. I opened the front door then stopped. "Is there anything else Sara told you about our conversation last night that I should know about?"

Like I'm going to commit a felonious academic crime and skip school with her sister because I'm trying to get down her pants? Did she say anything about how she thought I was masturbating on the phone while she was peeing? Spill your chattering guts, little sister, and give me the low-down on everything you know.

"No," Ruth answered. "But that question makes me wonder why you asked and what you talked about that you don't want me to know." I could see her genius-like analytical mind begin to turn.

"Don't worry about it," I said, and walked out the door, knowing that she would worry about it.

When I arrived at Aloha, the Sunday afternoon skate session had already begun. The parking lot was packed. The day was gray and cold. I was no better. I walked around to the front of the building and paced the parking lot intently in search of Amanda's photo. If it had dropped from my coat on the way to the car, it was sure to be ruined. Both the thought and wind made me shiver.

Nothing. I went in and greeted Mr. Abernathy at the front door and walked over to the rink where my best friend, Chuck, was patrolling the skaters. I walked around the building looking in trash cans and under counters and over shelves. I went through the lost and found, tossing the discarded coats and sweaters around. Nothing. I went into the men's bathroom and tore through the trash. I asked a woman coming out of the lady's room to stand guard for me as I went in and looked in their trash. The entire search netted me nothing other than crazy looks from the staff.

Chuck rolled off the skating rink, bobbed around several kids, and came to a stop in front of me. "What the hell are you doing?" he asked.

"I was just doing a rink inspection," I said. "I think as the manager, I should do those more often. This place is a mess."

"Oh brother, you're so full of shit, your eyes are brown." He leaned against the counter. "This place is never a mess and you've never done a rink inspection in your life. What's up?"

He was right. Mr. Abernathy was a Navy veteran who ran a tight ship when it came to Aloha. It was my job to make it clean and tight and I excelled at it. I was a poor liar at times and Chuck could see right through me. Best friends have that way about them. The Rolling Stone's song "Emotional Rescue" began playing. Maybe it was a sign from God. I had no other alternative but to confess. I needed an emotional rescue before I exploded like one of the watermelons in Amanda's dream.

I could count on Chuck to keep my secrets. We've covered each other's ass numerous times in ploys, plots and parental deceptions.

Like the time he told his mom and dad we were going to see Star Trek: The Motion Picture, but he was really taking Elizabeth Stanton to the sold-out Rush concert for Valentine's Day. His parents had forbidden him to go to a sacrilegious, pot-smoking concert, so he had no other alternative than to lie to them.

I had watched the movie by myself on his dollar and was right there the next day on the phone telling his mom how we had enjoyed the movie. Embellishing my lies with detailed accounts of the movie. How the wormhole scene, when Captain Kirk and his crew were talking in slow motion, had been really awesome. I denied her accusation when she said, "Chuck smelled like pot when he got home." Even though he did.

After the concert, we had met me at Burger Chef and I drove him home. He had taken his shirt off and held it out the window to try and get the pot smell to go away. I didn't enjoy lying, but sometimes you had to do what you had to do for a best friend.

Chuck, on the other hand, could lie with a straight face, so convincing that it would earn him an Academy award if they gave one away for parental deception.

One time during Vacation Bible School, or VBS as it's called in the Christian world, Trisha McDonnell and I had slipped out of the arts and crafts macrame-making portion of the day and sneaked into an unused classroom where we necked behind the locked door.

"Hey, Mrs. Hayes," Chuck said to my mom as she walked towards the VBS classes. "If you're looking for Chris, he's praying with some others down the hall." He motioned towards the nursery rooms. "We just had a lesson on repenting and Mrs. Maze asked if Chris would take them into the other room and talk to them and pray with them." He paused and added. "He's going to make a great preacher one of these days."

Those words were like gospel music to my mom. She smiled from ear to ear and told Chuck

that she was just stopping in. It wasn't
anything important. She'd be back at the end
of the day. When Trisha and I snuck back into
class, Chuck told me what happened.

Obviously, I was elated that he had covered
for me. But at the same time, I felt guilty as
all get out. I was lying, sneaking and necking
in the bowels of church and the depths of VBS
while Chuck was lying and making it look like
I was a missionary. All that moral tug-of-war
can toy with a teen's psyche.

While I knew it was safe to share my Amanda secret with Chuck, I
didn't want to share it with him or anyone else for that matter. It was
only a picture and phone call for Christ's sake. I didn't want to make it
into a bigger deal than it had the potential to be. I also didn't want to
open myself up to peer harassment should nothing come of it. But on
the brighter, more positive side, ...it was...I mean...it could be...a
Vagina Hunter's dream come true. You just can't put a cap on that and
call it a day.

"I'm going to tell you something, but it has to remain just between
us." I gave him our no-bullshit look.

"Ok, what's up?" He returned the look.

"Last night, Amanda Marrow gave me her school picture. I thought
I put it in my coat pocket when I left, but when I got home it wasn't
there. So it must have slipped out when I was walking to the car to
leave."

We both stared at one another in anticipation, each waiting for the
other to make some kind of astonishing response to the secret that had
just been revealed.

"And?" Chuck asked.

"And...I can't find the freaking picture!" I looked at him like he
was stupid.

"What part is supposed to stay just between us? Her giving you the
picture or you losing the picture?"

"Both!"

Chuck let out a big laugh and walked behind the skate counter.
"The last time I saw it, it was right here under the phone books." He

lifted up the books, but nothing was there. "Well, it was there." Chuck scratched his head.

"Last time you saw it???" I almost choked on the words.

"Yeah, everyone saw it. Mark and I were even talking about it. We wondered why she gave it to you. Is there something you're not telling your best friend, Chris?" Chuck returned the no-bullshit look once more.

I should have known. Eyes are always on Amanda. I bet she can't even piss in a private bathroom stall without someone watching her. Here I thought I was the only one in the world who knew she had given me a picture and the entire goddamn roller-skating rink staff knew about it.

"No. I swear. I don't know why she gave me her picture. Maybe because it was my birthday. Or maybe it was because I gave her those pretty pink skates," I said, pointing to the row of pretty pink skates. "I'm clueless."

"Yeah, right." Chuck rolled his eyes. "That wasn't a friendly little picture you give a stranger for their birthday. That was one of those big ones that come only two in a package." He looked around the floor behind the counter. "It was a damn good picture, too. She's so freaking hot. Did you see those purple skater's shorts she was sporting? I thought they were panties at first. Damn."

I ignored him. A numbness swept through my thoughts. Some other anonymous Vagina Hunter probably picked the picture up and took it home for his own personal HMS use. "Well, it's not around here. I looked everywhere." I moaned. Disappointment seeping out of my pores.

"That sucks for you." Chuck grinned sheepishly. Even though Chuck and I were best friends and we cared for each other like brothers, we still had our Vagina Hunting rivalries. "I think she's just using you to get to me anyway."

"Whatever." I rolled my eyes.

"I wouldn't worry about Amanda Marrow." Chuck patted me on the back. "She's out of your league. Besides, there's going to be so much snatch at my New Year's Eve party, you're bound to get a..." He made the universal sign for a blow job. "...or something."

"Your parents gave you the green light to have the party?"

"Yep. Showed them the B I got in Advanced Algebra and they Ok'ed it. Got a guest list as long as my arm. Shelley Gerst told me she's

inviting a bunch of girls from St. Elizabeth's all-girls slutatorium."
Chuck pushed away from the counter and started gyrating his hips in
an attempt to dance, and I say that graciously because Chuck had the
rhythm and dance moves of a one-legged, epileptic, cheerleader. But
Chuck never let his total lack of dancing hamper him from always
being the first and last one on the dance floor at our school dances.

When it came to Aloha and his dance skills on skates, it was only a
little more tolerable. He looked like a drunk cowboy riding through a
swarm of angry bees. His entire upper body flopped about while his
legs stood motionless. There he was in front of me, trying to wash away
my troubles by dancing to Prince's '*I Wanna Be Your Lover.*' that was
playing on the stereo.

He bit his lower lip and held it (we called it the white-boy bite) and
made his hands into fists like he was curling dumbbells and shoved
them forward and back as he thrust his hips in the opposite direction.
We've all seen the movements before: the universal sign for sexual
intercourse. Chuck loved doing universal sexual sign languages.

CHAPTER TWELVE

It was weird. Just three days ago when I shut my locker door and left school for the weekend, I was the normal, but functional dysfunctional Christian Hayes. My life was routine and status quo. School. Work. Chores. Church. Tick tock. Tick tock. Tick tock. That was my life's clock.

But that Monday morning everything was different. The ride to school. The trudge from the student parking lot, up three flights of steps to the senior lockers. Even opening the same locker that I shut last Friday. Everything was a little offbeat. Almost surreal. I smiled and said Hi to people just as I did every day. But today, I smiled, not because I had done it my entire life. But because I was, well, for the lack of a better term, a kaleidoscope of emotions.

I'm sure Amanda could have come up with a better phrase that described the montage of madness that was monopolizing my mind. Fear. Excitement. Curiosity. Just smile Christian. Smile. No one will ever know.

"Hey stranger!" She screamed from behind me. I jumped. She laughed. I turned red. She pretended not to notice. "How's it going?"

"Wonderful." I smiled as I mentally reached into the air and pulled a random phrase out of my thoughts that I thought she might like. "Everything's status quo!"

Be cool Christian. Don't be a dork.

"Status Quo?" She looked at me oddly as she reached over and pulled my folded shirt collar out from under my backpack strap, adjusted it, and patted me on my shoulder. Like we were married, and I was heading off to work slightly disheveled. "That's too bad," she said and added. "I do not know status quo." She chuckled at her wordplay.

"Status quo makes life easier." I defended.

"Not." She countered. "Status quo makes one lame and boring." She surveyed my meticulously clean and organized locker. "Like your locker."

Amanda smelled of Heaven's Scent mixed with the stench of cigarette smoke. She had probably just come from the student smoking area. I surveyed what she was wearing. Blue jeans that looked as if someone had painted them on her. Yellow pumps. A short sleeve t-shirt with a big yellow smiley face on the front. Above the smiley face was the word "Bibliophile" and below it was "Smile." Its teeth were the spine of books. She caught me looking at it. I wondered if it was a coincidence that her breasts were right where the smiley eyes were, giving them a three-dimensional look. She stuck out her chest to show me her shirt, her breasts or probably both.

"Bibliophile...Smile," she said as she pointed to the words on her shirt. "You get it? Lucy got it for me a couple of Christmases ago." She smiled like the smiley face on her shirt. "I wore it just for you."

And that's precisely what I mean when I said I was a kaleidoscope of emotions. Three days ago, we were at the polar ends of high school both academically and physically. She was Amanda Marrow, the Freshman Fire. First floor. I knew who she was, but only by her beautiful looks and sleazy reputation.

I was Chris Hayes. Anonymous Senior. Third Floor. But now, I'm Christian Hayes, Aloha Rink Manager and Ruth Hayes' older, best-brother-in-the-world.

And there she was standing in front of me fixing my collar, telling me she wore a shirt "just for me." She gave me a school picture. Dreamt about me and pretty much pulled her panties down and peed in front of me.

I, on the other hand, had anonymous one-way phone sex with her like the Vagina Hunter that I was and talked with her until the morning hours like the Mr. Nice Guy that I was. We plotted and schemed together. I was about to commit a felonious academic crime for her. And the one question that kept beating against the shore of my thoughts was;

Why?

Why was she giving me so much attention?

"Did you find my picture?" She asked.
"Yes." I lied as I buried my face in my locker to hide the guilt.
"What are going to do with it?"
"What should I do with it?" I replied. My face still in the locker.

Not that it mattered. The picture was gone. Lost. Never to be found again. I was making conversation. Warming up my brain. Steadying myself psychologically while enjoying the attention of her and those around us. Trying to be worthy of both.

"I think you should hang it right there." She pointed to the inside of my locker door. "That way every time you opened your door, you'd see me. Then your locker, ...and life…for that matter…, wouldn't be so status quo." There was condescending sarcasm in her tone.
"Why?"

There, I said it. Why? It was now out in open ready to be sliced, diced and made into Julienne Whys. Tell me why you gave me the picture? Please explain to me why I should

hang it on my locker door when I don't even
know you. Why is it that last Friday when I
stood here at this exact spot, I didn't know
you or give a hoot's ass about you and now I'm
an emotional freak who can't think of
anything but you?
Why?
The three-letter word, so simple and plain
yet had done more to change the course of
mankind's history than any other word, except
for two.

"Why not?" She countered with those two other words. And thus,
the sails of fate are repositioned and life's journey changes forever.

"Because." I paused to think, not of a good reason, but the best
reason. "Because...because..." My lips tried to express what I was
thinking but my mind wouldn't let me.

"Because, because, because, because, because..." Amanda began
singing. "Because of the wonderful things he does. We're off to see the
wizard, the wonderful Wizard of Oz." She danced around. Silly. Crazy.
Carefree. But she wasn't acting. She was being Amanda, the constant
attention magnet. I couldn't help but laugh. Neither could the queen's
audience that was standing around watching. When she finished her
little impromptu performance, she bowed to the watching crowd and
once again turned her attention to me.

"*The Wizard of Oz.* One of the few times where I loved the movie
better than the book," she said. Then her eyes got big. "Except when
the fuckin' flying monkeys came around. They scared the shit out of
me! Oh my God, I think they mentally scarred me as a kid."

I think it was more than fuckin' flying
monkeys that scarred you as a kid.

"So are we still good for tomorrow?" She asked. That was the
whole reason for her visit to my locker. To see if I was still going to
stay committed to the obligation that I offered up in the predawn
morning hours when my mind was weirded out. Had I not made the
offer or even called her back that evening, we'd still be worlds apart

separated by two floors and four school years. But I did make the promise and I'm a man of my word. Now it was time to face the fact and grow some balls and start working my Vagina Hunting plan.

"Sure." I didn't sound too convincing even to myself. "I'd be more than happy to skip school and take you to get your driver's license tomorrow for your sweet sixteenth birthday." I stopped and leaned towards her and quietly said. "What's in it for me?"

She got a hurt look in her eyes and momentarily gathered her thoughts. "I thought Chrissstain..." I realized she always drew the word out whenever she wanted it to mean 'Follower of Christ'. "...was being a good Samaritan."

Good Samaritan? Now that reply surprised me. What TV show did she learn that phrase from?

However, she was reading way more into the question than I had attended. Of course, as a Vagina Hunter, I was out to win her trophy. But as Mr. Nice Guy I would never go in for the capture that fast and sleazy. I intended to take my time, get to know her, and get into her good graces.

"I am being a Good Samaritan. But don't you think it's only fair since I'm taking this huge risk for someone that I hardly even know that I should get something in return?" I tried to rephrase it in a more platonic manner, but no matter how the words came out, they had the Vagina Hunting accent about them. It must be one of those osmosis things that happen. Like when you visit your cousin in Alabama for a week and you come back with a slight twang and say things like "ya'll" and "cain't." As an adolescent male teenager, your words and voice resonate with sexuality and a lot of the time you don't try or even notice. Words like "What's in it" and "I should get something" take on an entirely different meaning, especially to the opposite sex.

"You're sounding like another Vagina Hunter, Chrissstian." She rolled my name and her eyes at the same time. "And I was getting the impression that you may be the first truly nice, non-Vagina Hunter guy I knew." I could slice her disappointment with a mental sword. I stood there and watched her enthusiasm for me quickly fade. "You know I didn't ask you to take me to my driver's test, you offered." She shook her head one more time. "Never mind." She turned and started to walk away then looked back with a smug expression. "I can find someone else." Within seconds she was lost amongst a school of students.

CHAPTER THIRTEEN

"Damn." I slammed my locker door.

What the hell are you doing Christian Hayes? Somehow, I knew this would be my third strike and just as her picture disappeared out of my life, she too was on the verge of being gone forever. I took off after her and caught her at the top of the stairway to the freshman floor. She was already surrounded by a group of people, mostly guys, who were worshipping her every word. I walked right in the middle of the group and looked her in the eyes.

"Can I have a second with you?" The bold and brave Vodka Watermelon White Knight was growing some balls. There was a slight uncomfortable pause and then she turned to her court.

"I'll catch you guys later at the smoking area." She dismissed them with a smile. Some left willingly. Some looked perturbed that I was stealing their royalty away.

"OK, I didn't mean it had to be something sexual." I began defending myself. "You need to stop thinking that all my motives are sexual and stereo-truthing me as a Vagina Hunter." She defiantly stared back. Just then a group of Vagina Hunting jocks went walking by. Several said Hi to Amanda. She smiled, waved, and returned their hellos. One called out loud enough for everyone to hear.

"I love your smiley eyes!"

"Thanks!" She laughed and turned back at me and immediately removed the smile from her face.

I nodded towards the group of passing jocks. "Did you catch what he just said?" I asked.

"Yeah, he said he loved my smiling eyes." She got a cocky expression on her face and batted her eyes lids. "So?"

"No, he said he loved your smiley eyes." I pointed to her breasts darting out from beneath her Bibliophile Smile t-shirt. It took a couple of seconds for her to catch what I was trying to convey. A slight grin began to form from her frown as she realized the Master wordsmith had missed the sexual innuendo.

"Can you see how people can mistake what others say?" I asked. She got a guilty look upon her face and I don't know why, but I started to feel a little embarrassed for her. To ease her guilt and increase my own embarrassment I said, "Amanda, I'm going to be totally honest with you, I have never skipped a day of school in my entire life and I'm nervous as all get out."

"You've never, ever skipped school before?" The words were spoken in disbelief. As if I had just confessed that I still believed in Santa Claus or the Tooth Fairy. I was feeling a little dorkiness resurfacing and my cheeks were once again beginning to warm.

"No," I explained my hesitations. "You don't understand how strict and radical my parents are. If we get busted, I wouldn't just get a scolding and be done with it. I'd get grounded until I graduated. They'd take away my driving privileges. I know I wouldn't be able to go to any school activities or most definitely any graduation parties." I was looking at the floor as we went down, not only the stairs before us, but a long line of atrocities that would be inflicted upon me should our felonious academic crime be spoiled. "I'd probably have to write a letter of apology to every teacher and school administrator I deceived and go to a Christian counselor." I sighed and tossed my book bag over my shoulder and stopped at the bottom of the steps. "And I swear to God, if there were a dungeon in my basement, they'd toss me into it."

I could tell the improvised parental pity party was playing on her psyche. As God as my witness, I didn't mean to play that card. I was just stating the facts. But sometimes when the facts come out about the "status quo" of my zoo life, it takes on the appearance of "status fuck-upist" or whatever the Latin word is for the opposite of status quo.

"Are you kidding me?" She asked. We both shook our heads. Mine to say 'no' and her's to say, 'you have to be fucking kidding me'. She tilted her head to the side and squinted her eyes like she was about to have another one of her epiphanies. "So, it's my understanding that even though you risked all that crazy bullshit, you were still going to do it for me?"

I bowed my head. "Yes."

"Hmm. That's very noble ... or should I say, that's very Chrisssstian of you Christian." She got a renewed look about her. "Just like the hero in my vodka watermelon dream."

The halls were getting empty and we both looked at the clock. We were going to be tardy.

"I have to get to class," she said. "I'll meet you at your locker after third hour." She sprinted off.

Seconds later the class bell rang. I was still walking down the hall about to receive my third tardy in my four years of high school. The other two were justifiable. There was no excuse for this one. And the truth of it was, I didn't give a hoot's ass.

CHAPTER FOURTEEN

Why is it when one waits with baited anticipation, time moves in slow motion? Two hours can turn into two days. But when you're having fun or doing something sexual you merely blink your smiley eyes and its over? I was thinking those Freudian thoughts in my first-hour Psychology class. They somehow fit in and helped the hour go by.

During my second hour, Intro to Typing class, I practiced my pecking skills by typing the assigned phrase one hundred times:

Now is the time for all good men to come to the aid of their country.

But I kept leaving the T and I out of "their" and the O, R and Y out of "country". More residual Freudian slips or Vagina Hunting feelings?

Third hour English Comp went relatively smooth. Until Mr. Howell pointed to me and asked...

"Chris Hayes..." he said in his booming professor-ish voice, "Finish the following sentence with a metaphor, "Her hair was soft as....?""

I thought for a quick moment then tossed out, "Dryer lint." Mr. Howell and the entire class burst out laughing.

"Dryer lint?" Mr. Howell smiled. "How does one come to compare a woman's hair with dryer lint? And please pay close attention to his answer class." He had other motives for asking the question.

Everyone's eyes turned upon me. "Well, this morning I took a load of whites out of the dryer and when I went to clean the lint catching screen, I couldn't help but notice how soft and fluffy all the lint felt. It was even softer than cotton balls." I shrugged my shoulders. "And that was the first thing that popped into my mind."

Laughter once again echoed around the room and Mr. Howell stood up from his chair and walked to the front of his desk and leaned on it.

"There you have it class." He crossed his arms. "Some of the greatest metaphors in life and literature magically appear from the bleakness and blackness of our daily lives." Then he walked up and stood in front of my desk. "With that being said, Mr. Hayes, I wouldn't quit your day job." The class laughed once more. "Or...perhaps..." He stopped mid-sentence and stroked his chin with his fingers. Then stroked the entire class with his dramatic pause. "...if you keep that up you just might become a Pulitzer Prize-winning author."

The dismissal bell rang and I hurried from Mr. Howell's class to my locker. I didn't usually go to my locker after third hour because my fourth-hour chemistry class was on the other side of the school. So when I got there, I just pretended like I was doing something while waiting for Amanda. A group of people came walking by that had the appearance of paparazzi surrounding a celebrity.

"I'll talk to you guys later." Amanda once more dismissed herself from the center of its attention and made her way over to my locker. I noticed the "Why in the hell are you talking to Chris Hayes?" looks on some of her court as they walked away.

"OK," Amanda stared into my eyes with renewed interest. "I was thinking about this all morning and you're right. I was wrong to think you wanted sexual favors in return for skipping school and taking me to get my driver's license. I was stereo-truthing you as being just another Vagina Hunter." She paused and offered her hand to me. "My apologies." I took it and shook it in acceptance.

I was completely taken off guard and impressed how easy she admitted to guilt and her quickness to seek forgiveness. The truth was, I would have loved sexual favors and I was a Vagina Hunter. But she didn't know that and yet she still came to me asking for forgiveness.

Your normal person wouldn't notice such a seemingly trivial act, but it resonated within my entire being. This was a heathen and hoosier girl I was shaking hands with and yet, she was showing abnormal signs of decency and dignity that very few Christians, let alone non-hoosiers, show. If she kept that up,

I was going to have to start calling her, Amanda Marrow, the Anomaly.

"Thanks," I said. "That means a lot to me."

"And it means a lot to me that you were...or hopefully are...still willing to take me to get my driver's test even with all that crazy shit you'd be punished with if we got caught."

I nodded my head yes.

"Ok, then it's a deal. Skip school with me and take me to the DMV and I promise, cross my heart and hope to die, stick a needle in my eye, that I'll return the favor in some capacity."

"Deal," I said. And for the second time in a matter of minutes, we shook hands again.

We quickly went over the game plan once more. It sounded extremely plausible as she explained the best way to go about tricking school secretaries into believing a parent was calling in sick for their child. I would explain everything here but I'm afraid there would be a spike in school absenteeism, once the word got out. So I'll just say that to the degree of her beauty, sexuality, and logosist-ism, she was just as cunning and conniving to scam the high school administrative system.

"Call me in the morning," she said as we began to part ways. "Oh, and did you hear we might be getting a snowstorm tonight. If that's the case, we'll have to use Plan B?" And with those words, she walked away.

"Um...Plan....B???" I shouted down the hall. My words were absorbed by the roar of the students. She was gone. Plan B? What the hell was Plan B? I was ready for a Felonious academic crime and now there's a mystery Plan B? What the hell. What was I getting myself into?

Later that evening, after a dinner of pork chops and Cajun Rice-A-Roni, dad turned on the evening news. Sure enough, all three stations were predicting a mild blizzard to hit St. Louis just about the time school was supposed to start the following morning. Ruth and I watched the little scrolling marquee at the bottom of the TV screen that listed the school closings, hoping and praying Hazelwood School District would roll by. It never did. Just as the weatherman was wrapping up his final forecast, the phone rang. Mom picked it up.

"Hello?" Pause. "Who's calling?" Another pause, this one a little more annoyed. "Hold on." She tossed me a bothering stare as she handed me the phone. "Amanda would like to talk to Chrisssstian." She raised her eyebrows.

"Hello."

"Ok. Here's Plan B." We're the first words out of her mouth.

CHAPTER FIFTEEN

I liked Plan B. Plan B was a good plan. It didn't involve as many high-level lies and only a little parental deception. But most importantly, it allowed me to sleep in late in the event of a snow day. There is absolutely nothing better in a student's life than hearing those two words, snow and day spoken together. If Amanda can take the word leaves and turn it into her most beautiful and beloved word, leafs, then I'm going to take the words snow and day and make them a single word, snowday and make it my favorite word in the world. Not so much for the beauty of the word but for what it represents—one of life's best non-sexual ecstasies that rate right up there with getting the high score in Pac Man or finding any piece of paper money.

The feeling of being wrapped warmly within several layers of blankets as Mother Nature unleashes her own heavy blanket of white sleepiness. Your alarm goes off. You stir to start another cold school day. But. Wait. Mom opens the door. Snowday. What follows is a flood of coziness that settles upon your weary studious soul. You smile because you're in one of life's happy places and drift back to a snuggly slumber. Snowday.

That's exactly where I was when mom knocked on my bedroom door and announced. "No school today Christian; it's a snowday!" I reached over and turned off the alarm clock. I was at the beginning of Plan B—call Amanda when I wake up. I followed the plan by bringing the phone into my room and dialing her number. God, please don't let mom come upstairs and see the phone cord stretched into my room.

"Hello." Her sleepy voice answered.

"Happy Birthday! Birthday girl." I was half asleep and hidden beneath the blankets whispering but I greeted her with the best warm and wide-awake voice I could muster.

"Thanks." She almost slurred the word through her tiredness. "What time is it?"

"Time to get up and go get your driver's license!" I paused. "If they're open. I have no idea how much it snowed. I just woke up myself." My cheerful whispers once again trying to motivate her to get up and get going.

"Ohhh," she groaned sleepily. "I shouldn't have talked on the phone so late." She let out a big yawn and by doing so, verbally slapped me in the face.

It really shouldn't have been a verbal slap. But you have to understand, I was young and stupid and walking a tight robe between lust and infatuation.

I didn't associate with hoosier girls and when she said, 'talked on the phone so late', the first thing that flashed through my mind was—she's having another late-night phone call with someone else. But this one wasn't Mr. Nice Guy. He was a Vagina Hunter. Or maybe he was more than a Vagina Hunter. He was one of her Vagina Conquerors. One who had already stabbed her with his spear and now they were having phone sex into the early morning hours.

Meanwhile... Mr. Nice Guy is laying wide awake late into the night. I can't sleep because I don't know if I'm going to be committing a felonious academic crime in the morning. Or I'm going to be switching to Plan B.

Of course, there's no way I could ask her who she was talking to so late into the night because that would be out of place. Psychotic. Obsessive. I had to think positive. It could have been a female friend who just wanted to talk. Yeah right. I probably wasn't the first one to wish her a happy birthday either.

"JUST KIDDING!" Her voice suddenly brightened and became alive. "I've been up for an hour. I've already shit, showered and shaved." She paused just long enough for me to interject.

"I'm surprised you didn't wait until you were talking to me on the phone," I replied half joking and half not.

"Whatever, that's just an alliteration my grandpa used to say." I heard her take a drag of her cigarette.

Mental Note: Alliteration, a sentence or phrase that contains words that have the same beginning sound. Shit. Shower. Shave.

The excitement in her voice increased. "Guess what?"

"What?"

"This is the very first time I've ever seen real snow in the wild!"

"What do you mean this is the first time you've ever seen snow *in the wild*." I asked. Was my sister's information pipeline passing our conversations down the line to Amanda or was this one of her logosist terms?

"I mean, like, I've lived in Southern Florida my entire life. I've never seen real snow."

"Really? You've never experienced a snowday your entire life?" The thought made me suddenly feel sorry for her.

"Duh. When you don't have snow, you don't have snow days. Sara and I have already been outside and made snow angels in the front yard."

"How was it?"

"It was weird." She gave me one of her naughty snickers. "Normally when I spread my legs that wide, it's not outside and I'm not wet and cold. Well, I'm not cold at least." She waited for my response, but how in God's creation does one even reply to an answer like that? Silence. "Christian, you there?"

I didn't know what to say, so I started breathing heaving. "Can you keep (heavy breath) talking like that? (Big inhale) I want to masturbate again (Loud exhale) while I talk to you."

Did I just say "again"? Holy. Fuck.

"AGAIN!" She screamed. "You said you weren't masturbating! You lying Vagina Hunter!"

"Oh my God." I frantically tried to cover up the Freudian slip. "I didn't masturbate then and I'm not masturbating now. I was being facetious!" I said a little too loud for my own comfort.

There was a nerve-racking hush and after a long several seconds, she whispered. "Did you just say, facetious?"

"Yes, facetious. As in fake or teasing."

"Or flippant, frivolous, joking or jocular." She began to breath heavy.

"That is so (slow moan) seductive sounding. (Deep breath) Can you keep talking like that (another moan, this time a little louder) I want to masturbate now." She giggled.

"Facetious. Surmise. Conniption fit," I said erotically. "Tell me if you want more. Eclectic. Ambrosial..."

Suddenly, a loud KNOCK. KNOCK. KNOCK. echoed from my bedroom door.

"I got to go!" I didn't wait for a response. Mom was at my door and she was probably pissed. I freaked out and hung up the phone.

CHAPTER SIXTEEN

"Christian, hurry up off the phone!" Ruth's voice begged from the other side of the door. "I want to call Sara and see if she's made a snow angel. It's the first snow she's seen in the wild."

Heart. Attack. Avoided. Last night's snowstorm, the stress of lying to my parents, and Amanda's sexual teasing were getting the best of me. I imagined the knock on the door was my mother freaking out because she had picked up the other line and had been listening to what we were saying.

"You're going to have to wait," I yelled. "I'm talking to Chuck. I'll let you know when I'm done!" I said it loud, secretly hoping that mom heard me. There would be no problem with me talking to Chuck this early on a snowday. We were planning a morning of making money shoveling snow.

The lies just kept on coming.

I immediately dialed Amanda's number.
"Hello," she answered.
"Sorry about that. I thought my mom was calling me."
"You thought your mom was calling you, so you hung up on me?" She asked puzzled.
I let out a resigned sigh. "Well, to be totally honest, I thought my mom might have heard our conversation and that was her knocking on my door. But it was Ruth. She wanted to call Sara and hear about her first snowfall, in the wild." I didn't want Amanda to keep questioning my motives of why I was so freaked out that I hung up on her, so I

asked. "Why do you call it 'in the wild? Is that another one of your logosist words you made up?"

"No. Well, sort of." The ploy worked. She was now onto another subject. "One time when I was about five years old, Lucy and I were in a grocery store waiting at the checkout when a midget came walking by. Lucy said my jaw dropped open and my eyes got really big as he passed. She was afraid I was going to say something embarrassing. I didn't. But when we got outside, I looked at her in amazement and asked, "Was that a munchkin? Like in the Wizard of Oz?'

'Yes,' she said and then I proudly proclaimed, 'Wow, I've never seen a munchkin out in the wild before.' Lucy thought it was hilarious because I was calling everything that wasn't on TV, 'in the wild'. She tells the story all the time. Now every time something happens for the first time after seeing it on TV we say, 'in the wild'."

"So, I was about to skip school in the wild today. But now I don't have to because we're on Plan B," I said.

"Exactly. And there's almost six inches of snow in the wild of our front yard, so it's on to Plan B." She laughed.

I looked out my window and saw with my own Doppler eyes at least a half of foot of snow sitting on top of our patio table in the back yard. "That's not good." I thought out loud. "If the streets are too bad, my parents aren't going to let me take the car out." My dreaded words echoed into the phone. Damn, this could jeopardize everything. No car for either of us meant there was no Plan B.

There was silence on the other end.

Christian, you didn't come this far to let a little snow stop you from making Amanda Marrow, the Freshman Fire obligated to you in some cross my heart, hope to die, stick a needle in my eye, capacity.

"OK Plan C." I announced. I had to take charge of the situation like a skating rink manager has to when vodka watermelons are exploding and burning down the rink. "Has your mom left for work yet?" I asked.

"No, but she's getting ready to."

"Ok, here's the game plan, you ride to work with Lucy and I'll meet you there. If I can drive my car, then I'll pick you up from there and we'll go to the DMV. But if my parents don't let me use the car, I'll meet you there and we can take your mom's car. If you don't think she'll mind me driving her car?"

"Hold on, let me ask." She put down the phone and I could hear the sound of a blow-dryer buzzing in the background and some mumbling.

"No, she doesn't mind if we take her car." She got a concerned tone about her voice. "But how are you going to get there if your folks don't let you use the car?"

"Don't worry about that. I'll get there." I was clueless. "Give me an hour and I'll meet you at Steak 'n Shake. OK? And don't forget your birth certificate and social security card. You'll need those at the DMV."

"Are you sure?" She was now nervously hesitant. "This is becoming way too complicated and I'm starting to feel bad."

"Well then, you can seriously start thinking about giving me some sexual favors in return," I said demandingly.

More silence from her end.

"JUST KIDDING!" I laughed just loud enough for anyone in the house not to hear. "See, two can play that just kidding game."

"You are so going to get your ass kicked when I see you."

"Promises. Promises."

CHAPTER SEVENTEEN

Plan B was to lie to mom. I would tell her I needed the car to go shovel driveways in Francis Farms Estates, one of the wealthier subdivisions in Spanish Lake. The people who lived in Francis Farm Estates had bigger driveways and bigger wallets that paid a premium wage for child-labor snow removal. It was going to be an easy deception because I had shoveled driveways in Francis Farm Estates many times.

Instead, however, I was to really go to Steak 'n Shake, pick up Amanda, take her to get her driver's tests, and be home before lunch. Our plot was falling into place. If everything went as planned, I would get to spend several quality, one-on-one hours getting to know the hottest chick in the city.

I took a quick shower and put on a layer of thermal underwear, a flannel shirt, jeans and two pairs of socks and went down to the kitchen. I was more concerned about giving mom the impression that I was really, in fact, going to shovel driveways, than impressing Amanda with my sense of fashion on our first unofficial, official date.

Mom was making a batch of Cream of Wheat. I could smell the bread toasting in the toaster as I poured myself a glass of orange juice. She greeted me with a smile.

"I'm going to drive over to Francis Farms and make a little money shoveling driveways," I said matter of factly as I sat down to the bowl of Cream of Wheat.

"I don't think so, young man. Did you look at those streets out there? There must be a foot of snow on them and they haven't plowed them." She put the toast on a plate and set it down in front of me and sat down to her own bowl of Cream of Wheat. "I don't want you to drive in that stuff." She nodded to the kitchen window. "There are too many crazy drivers out there and you'll get yourself killed."

"But it's just down Bellefontaine road." I semi-pleaded.

"Well if it's just down the street, then you can walk there and get some exercise on the way." She began eating.

I didn't want to keep pushing the issue and raise any red flags, so I agreed. My mind was moving forward at a hundred paces per minute. Time was quickly ticking away before our one-hour deadline.

I now had two ways of getting to Steak 'n Shake. The first was calling Chuck to see if he could give me a ride. That wasn't an option. I knew for a fact he would still be sleeping and there's no way I would have asked him to take me to Steak 'n Shake to meet Amanda Marrow. As much of a Vagina Hunter that he was, it would have been like inviting an alcoholic to Oktoberfest.

The second option was to walk up to Bellefontaine and catch a bus over to Steak 'n Shake. As bleak as the option was, taking the bus was the only one I had.

I went back up to my room, put on my snow boots and gathered my hat, coat, and gloves. I also snuck into my secret stash of cash and took out three $20 bills. I was going to need proof to show mom I had been working all morning—sixty dollars made for a very profitable day.

I went to the garage and dug out the snow shovel from beneath a layer of garden tools where it had been hibernating since last winter. Then I headed up the street towards Bellefontaine. The frigid air fought with the snow flurries and I watched them wrestle through the pine trees and over the rooftops. A few houses down the street I encountered two entrepreneurial boys huffing and puffing as they filled their shovels with snow and hurled it to the side of the driveway. Each cautiously eyed me with my snow shovel in my hand. They glared at me like two polar bears eating a freshly hunted seal. "This is our street.

What are you doing here?" Their cold, red, faces read. I walked past them. I had no interest in their drive-way seal. My game was sitting at a Steak 'n Shake.

On the corner of Redman and Bellefontaine, stood my alma mater, Twillman Elementary School. Usually bustling with buses, teachers, and parents coming and going at this time in the morning, now the school sat peacefully still and dark. Snowday. A row of dumpsters hid the door to the cafeteria's kitchen. I shoved my snow shovel behind them. I would get it on the return trip.

I looked at my watch. Thirty-five minutes had already passed since I got off the phone with Amanda. It was going to take me at least ten minutes to get to the bus stop and God knows how long before the bus arrived then another ten minutes to get to Steak 'n Shake. I was not only going to be late but really late. Why didn't I give myself more time to get there?

If Amanda ever asks for one of my bad habits again, I would have to confess that I did actually have one. I don't necessarily know that this is a bad habit as much as an obsessive one.

I was, and still am, a punctual freak. I'm hyper-anal about being on time and radically pissed when others are late. It's all part of that non-hoosier upbringing in my zoo. However, this punctuality personality trait wasn't based on any religious dogma mom tried to force feed me. It was dad who taught me this lesson.

I was in Boy Scouts. We were getting ready to go camping. It was miserably hot and humid outside. The entire troop, along with our tents and supplies, were waiting in the church van sweating our asses off. One boy, Steve Baker and his father, who were habitually late still hadn't arrived. It had already been twenty-five minutes past departure time. We all knew the later you arrived at Camp Beaumont, the worst camping spot you got.

Mr. Howard, our Scout Master and the rest of us sat in the van getting more agitated by the minute. That's when my dad spoke up.

"Hey scouts," Dad said as he stood and turned to the eight excited boys squeezed into the seats between backpacks. "If I hired you to cut my grass for twenty dollars and when you finished, I didn't pay you, would that make you mad?"

There was a chorus of "yeses", "uh-huhs" and "heck yeas."

"Well being late is just like that." Dad began to explain. "When you agree to be somewhere at a certain time, it's like you've agreed to pay someone. But instead of paying in cash, you're paying in time and respect. When you're late, you're taking away that time and disrespecting them." Then he added, "And a good Boy Scout...or Christian for that matter... doesn't do that. Okay?"

There was the hint of agitation lingering in his question. Once again everyone agreed. Then he purposed the question. "What's the Boy Scout's Law everyone?"

Like brainwashed cult members, we all shouted in unison, "A Scout is trustworthy, loyal, helpful, friendly, courteous, kind, obedient, thrifty, brave, clean, and reverent."

"And which of those laws are you breaking when you're late?" Dad completed his lesson.

We mentally went down the list and one by one and called out our replies. "Trustworthy, loyal, helpful, friendly, courteous, kind, obedient." There was a pause and then Dirk Howard, the Scout Master's son shouted. "Thrifty, because you're wasting time." Then he

proudly added. "And reverent because you're
breaking a promise and God doesn't like when
you break promises."

We looked one another amazed that one
little act of being late could cause you to
stumble down a staircase of so many broken Boy
Scout Laws.

It was so out of character for dad to behave
so publicly purposeful and poignant. He was
always the quieter and more laid-back father
who was there to help set up tents and build
fires. He wasn't there to guide or teach. That's
why his lesson on punctuality stayed with me
all my life.

Over the years, it became ingrained into my
head to respect others by always being on
time. And I expected others to do the same. My
attitude was: Here's the time. Now be there. If
you're running late, then communicate that to
me. But don't tell me you'll be there at 2 p.m.
and show up at 2:30 p.m. without calling. That
will piss me off. Instead, tell me you're going
to be there at 2:30 p.m. and be on time. My
obsessive punctual nature eventually got me
labeled as a "Time Nazi" by my friends and
especially my co-workers.

And so, it was that particular morning, the Time Nazi himself was
running late. I was hurrying my ass through the crunching snow about
to break, not only my own personal rule but the Boy Scouts Laws all
to hell. And if that wasn't bad enough, I started stressing that if I was
too tremendously late, Amanda might call my house to make sure
everything was all right, like she did the night of the vodka watermelon
dream. If that was the case, I was totally screwed. Mother Nature must
have been reading my racing thoughts because the snow, which had
started slightly sporadic, was now heavy and somber.

I went from a hurried walk to a full jog down the street. Then I got
the brilliant idea to forgo the bus stop and keep running down

Bellefontaine. It would probably be faster than waiting for the bus and all its stops before it finally got to Steak 'n Shake.

I wrapped my scarf around my face, not so much to keep me warm but to hide my identity. The last thing I wanted was to get back in school and have someone say, "Hey Chris I saw you running down the street last snowday, what was that all about?' I would have to make up another lie. It seemed ever since I met Amanda, I was constantly telling little fibs and sometimes bold lies. But the worst part was, the lies weren't only to my friends and family. I was also lying to myself. That made me think about the song *Lies and Alibies*. I began singing it in my head over and over like a motivating mantra as I picked up my pace to win the friendship, trust and hopefully capture the heart and vagina of Amanda Marrow sitting at Steak 'n Shake.

She sits by the phone and cries
She's on the verge of suicide
Nowhere to run. Nowhere to hide
Her life is nothing but lies and alibies,

Twenty minutes later I arrived. Ten minutes late.

CHAPTER EIGHTEEN

I took off my hat in the lobby of Steak 'n Shake then walked inside. The restaurant was warm. The smell of coffee and bacon wafted around the room. I loved the smell of frying bacon. We never ate it at our house. It was on mom's taboo food list. But on those occasions when I would spend the night at Grandpa and Grandma Hayes' house there was always bacon at breakfast. Grandpa Hayes was raised on a farm. Eggs and bacon were as much of their standard diet as Rice-A-Roni was ours.

One long inhale. I was back to being a kid again waking up to the smell of fried bacon at my grandparent's house. Other than the long, cold jog there, the day was starting off excellent. First, the snowday and sleeping in. Now an olfactory high and meeting Amanda. Life could be worse. I could be committing a felonious academic crime.

Amanda was tucked away in a corner booth with her feet up on the bench reading a book. She was too nose deep in the story to notice I was there. I made my way through the tables looking around to see if I could pick out which waitress was Lucy. For a snowy Tuesday morning, the restaurant was surprisingly busy. I saw only one waitress, a middle-aged black lady standing next to a table of construction workers hurriedly writing down their order.

As I walked towards Amanda, I studied her beauty. To my utter amazement, she was dressed extremely simple and conservative. A pair of tennis shoes. Blue jeans. A grey long sleeve knitted sweater that clung tight to her thin shoulders and small frame. No skirt or heels. An old denim newsboy hat sat on her head. A burgundy crocheted muffler mingled with her hair and cascaded down covering her chest.

No makeup. No pretentious anything. She didn't look like the Freshman Fire that had sexually and psychologically hogtied me four days ago with all her sexiness and charisma. In her place was someone different. Another Amanda plucked out of time. A bohemian artist perhaps, lost in a literary world. One who didn't give a hoot's ass about makeup, style or any outer beauty she may possess.

Could this be her true sixteen-year-old self? I wondered. A suppressed inner nerd that radiated intellect and literary savvy. Her true character that she sported around the house when there wasn't an audience of eyes constantly upon her. It was an entirely different look. It didn't make her less beautiful. Matter of fact, it made her even more enchanting.

She sat against the canvass of a large window with winter's white snow falling in the background. Like a masterpiece in the museum of my mind. A living visual of a vagabond beauty that only books and movies are made of.

On the table in front of her was a steaming cup of coffee. She raised her eyes from behind the book and smiled.

"I'm soooo sorry I'm late." I profusely apologized.

It didn't matter that I ran my ass in the snow for a couple of miles. The fact was, I was late. My guilt negated any kindness I may have felt.

She rolled her eyes, "Whatever. Don't worry about it. Look at you! You're covered in snow." Then the reality set in. "Did you...walk here?"

I humbly shook my head yes and added, "More like ran. I'm one of those Time Nazi's that hate to be late." I took off my coat and hung it on the hook next to the table.

Amanda scooted over and patted the seat next to her. I sat down. "Oh my God. I can't believe you did that. Now I feel horrible. I am going to have warm you with sexual favors in the bathroom." She grinned. I blushed. She couldn't tell because my face was already red from running my ass twenty minutes in the snow.

"I just embarrassed you again didn't I? Your red face got even redder."

I looked over at the book she was reading. "What are you reading?" I tried to change the subject, which is easy to do with an ADD person.

"Well since I'm a Missourian now," she spoke the sentence with a slightly bitter aftertaste, "I thought I'd read some Mark Twain." She turned the book over and showed me the cover. Her eyes sparkled. "Oh my god, I love Twain! The way he beautifully paints his characters with witty words and delightful dialects. Last week I read Tom Sawyer. Now I'm reading Huckleberry Finn." She continued her praise. "Can you imagine hiding on an island all by yourself with nothing but a runaway slave to keep you company? Then seeing a house float by on the river and climbing into it, only to discover there's a dead body inside!" The pitch of her voice rose with every word. Then she shut her eyes, smiled, and added in her own logosistic way. "It would be the epitome of excitement!"

I took the book from her hand and examined it. "You know, Hannibal is only about an hour away from here." Her eyes widened as she bit her lower lip and cupped her hands together. Thrilled. Elated. "A couple of Forth of July's ago my family and I took a day trip there to attend their annual Tom Sawyer Days." I was attempting to impress her with my literary trip. "It was pretty cool. We saw Injun Joe's cave and rode on a riverboat. They had frog races and a white-wash fence painting contest."

"That would be so totally awesome!" She smiled and reached over and put her hand on my arm.

I was beginning to realize Amanda was one of those people who loved to touch you when they talked to you.

It reminded me of Mrs. Grant, an old lady at church, who would always hold your hand when she talked to you. You'd be walking down the hall and she'd walk by and say "Oh Chris, you're getting so big." Then she would reach out and take my hand in hers and cup her other hand over it. She would say "And how's school going?" We would have a short little conversation. She'd let go and smile and tell me to tell my parent's she said Hello. It was like she was holding me by the chains of her hand and I had to listen.

As I got older, I've learned that not only does touching make a person pay more

attention to you by anchoring your words; it
also breaks down an invisible wall of distrust
that people naturally build around
themselves. That's why so many car salesman
and politicians are so quick to shake your
hand and pat you on the back.

Human touch, even in the vaguest and
simplest manner, draws two people together
like an invisible spiritual thread.

I didn't mind Amanda touching me. She
already had my thoughts intertwined with
hers. She was slowly wrapping me around her
little finger. It felt almost natural to let
her bind me with her spiritual threads.

"I want to go!" Amanda let out an excited plea. "I'll drive." She
picked up the book again. "We'll make it an adventure like Tom and
Huck. But I get to be Tom Sawyer because he's the one that says all
the funny shit and Huck's more of the quiet and shy one, like you."

No, YOU get to be Huck. He was the hoosier
who liked to drink and smoke and skip school.
Mom would point that fact out on our trip to
Hannibal. And why was she calling me quiet
and shy? I was NOT quiet and shy. Ask anyone
in the world who knew me. No one would ever
use those two adjectives to describe me.

Just then Lucy came to the table. A feeling of uneasiness fell over
me, heavy and strong.

Was she the mysterious eavesdropper who
listened to our midnight phone conversation
the other evening? And did she know I was
really masturbating on the other end of the
line?

"So this is Chris, the best big brother in the world and the Vodka Watermelon White Knight?" Lucy smiled warmly without any signs of accusations. She held out her hand. I shook it.

"Nice to meet you," I said.

There was no doubt at one time Lucy was beautiful. Her sandy blonde hair hid streaks of brown beneath the improvised bun she worked in. Like Amanda, she was small, almost too skinny with a smile that radiated a hidden hurt that kept it from being a shade or two from glorious. Her dark eyes were lined with heavy eyeliner to match her cherry red lips. She had a raspy, almost harsh tone to her voice that smokers often acquire after decades of the addiction. When she held out her hand, I notice a tattoo of three moons on her right wrist. Something Cher or Janis Joplin would have sported in all their sexiness during the sixties and seventies. I could easily picture the picture on Amanda's wall. The hippie activist.

"You looked like a snowman when you came in." Lucy smiled and glanced at Amanda, "I *surmise* your parents wouldn't let you take the car?" She gave her daughter a playful wink. My heart began to beat faster. Surmise? Why did she use that particular word? And why was she winking? I nodded. "Unfortunately, no."

"Bellefontaine and the other main streets weren't that bad," Lucy explained. "But the side streets were still pretty treacherous." She looked out the window. "This was the part of St. Louis I didn't miss," she said in a reminiscent voice.

"You've lived in St. Louis before?" I asked surprisedly.

"Yeah, I grew up on the south side by Bevo Mill. But we moved away when I was about nineteen. My dad was in the military and stationed at Scott Air Force base."

"Really? What high school did you go to?" I asked.

Lucy laughed. "Of all the places I've lived, only in St. Louis does everyone ask each other, What high school did you go to? I went to Roosevelt High. Matter of fact, I went to visit my cousins in Florida to celebrate my high school graduation and that's where I met Amanda's dad," Lucy looked over at Amanda. "Or sperm donor, however you want to call him." She added. "We fell in love, got married and I stayed there. But when Bud, that's his real name, went to prison, I decided to make the move away from the Sunshine State and maybe try to re-grow some roots back here in St. Louis." Lucy took the menu from behind the condiment stand and handed it to me. "So I'm used to all this." She pointed at the snow falling outside. "But Amanda and Sara have never seen snow…at least not *in the wild.*"

Amanda's face lit up "I already told him the 'in the wild' story."

Lucy pushed Amanda's hat down on her head and fixed the scarf around her neck. "Poor girl's going to freeze her nipples off if we don't get her some winter clothes."

Amanda looked at me with the expectation that her mom's words were once again about to embarrass me. But it didn't happen. It wasn't the words "freeze her nipples off" that froze in my brain. It was the words that followed "get her some winter clothes" that sent my thoughts soaring south.

Was it possible the reason Amanda dressed so scantily and sleazy was because she didn't have anything else to wear? She was born and raised in Florida. You don't need a winter wardrobe there. Hmmm. Ruth already said they didn't have any money. That is why Amanda had to get a job at the bookstore. Was I stereo-truthing this girl as being a bigger hoosier then she really was?

I looked over at Amanda. For the second time, it was as if she knew what I was thinking. I had figured out part of her secret life and by doing so, I had chiseled away a piece of the wall she had built around herself. But that was just one single snowflake epiphany in a blizzard of mystery called Amanda Marrow, the Freshman Fire.

"Could I have another cup of coffee, please?" Amanda slid her cup towards Lucy.

I looked down at her empty cup and made an unpleasant face. "You drink coffee?" I said. Not really surprised.

"Yep, been drinking it since I was a baby."

"You can blame that one on me." Lucy chimed in, then stopped and looked at Amanda. "Did you tell him this story?"

"No, Lucy, this one's all yours." Amanda rolled her eyes.

"Well, I know this is going to be hard to believe." It was Lucy's turn to roll her eyes. "But Amanda was a loud and noisy baby. Always crying and begging for my attention."

Really? Amanda the attention magnet, a loud and noisy baby? Go figure.

"One morning she wouldn't stop crying. So I went to give her her bottle to quiet her down. However, we didn't have very much milk. So I poured the last of it in her bottle and filled the rest up with coffee. Then I added a couple of spoons of sugar." She reached over and patted Amanda on the shoulder. "The sweet, warm coffee calmed her down and shut her right up. She's been drinking it like that ever since."

"But it doesn't shut me up anymore. It just calms me down." Amanda tapped her hands on the table in nervous excitement. "And sometimes it doesn't even do that."

Coffee was also on mom's list of taboo food. Too much caffeine wasn't good for the stomach or the nerves. I had probably taken three sips of coffee my entire life and found each one bitter and nasty. But they were all pure black coffee. Not the kind Amanda enjoyed.

Lucy took a pad of paper and pen out of her black apron. "Can I get you a cup of hot coffee and something warm to eat before you head back out into that cold blizzard?"

"Well, I don't normally drink coffee, but what the heck." I shut the menu. "I'll have a cup of coffee just like hers and an order of bacon."

I wasn't skipping school or committing an academic felonious crime as we had initially planned, so my conscious was pretty clean. Why not dirty it up a little by partaking of a couple of items on mom's taboo food list.

Lucy took my order and returned right away with two cups of coffee and set them down in front of us. Amanda took it upon herself to take out exactly eight packets of sugar and poured them, along with a hefty glob of milk, into my coffee. She picked up my spoon and stirred like a professional coffee bartender. Or perhaps, like a witch stirring a cauldron of magical love potion. Or poison? She pushed the cup towards me. I took a slow sip.

"Mmmm. That's really good!" I licked my lips. "It's like a hot, milky, toffee, thingy drink."

Amanda beamed with pride. "Stick with me Christian Hayes and I'll open you up to a whole new world." She chuckled and, in a whisper, repeated to herself. "Hot, milky, toffee, thingy drink," as she took a sip of her coffee.

We spent the next fifteen minutes talking about school and snow. How she had gotten her driver's permit months ago and that Lucy let her drive all the time as long as she was in the car. She promised she was a very responsible driver and was confident she would pass the test. However, she was a little concerned with driving on snowy streets. She had never done that before. Snowy streets!

"Holy crap, do you think the DMV is even open today?" I said in a panic. "Or do they have governmental snowdays?"

"No worries." Amanda put her hand on my arm once again. "I called them right after I hung up with you and they're open."

We sat there for another half an hour, watching the snowplows go by and the falling snow slowly taper from a frenzied flurry to nothing. We drank our hot, milky, toffee, thingy drink. People stared at us because we were young and Amanda was loud and beautiful. She was happy and excited because it was her birthday. She was going to get her driver's license. I was happy and excited because it was a snowday and Amanda was happy and excited. Which made me even happier and more excited knowing that I was part of her reason for being happy and excited.

I asked Lucy for the check, but she refused to give it to me. Breakfast was on her for taking Amanda to get her license. I tried to argue but was shut down by both the Marrow girls. Amanda and I began to put on our coats. Lucy gathered our cups and plates on a tray and started wiping off the table.

"After all that coffee, I need to go the bathroom" Amanda gave me a smile, then turned and shot Lucy a worried stare as she patted her stomach and walked away. She didn't think I saw. But I caught her face in the window's reflection. It was an uneasy, nervous look. Like she was telling her mom, "I don't feel so good."

Lucy just smiled, picked up the tray, and leaned over to me and said with a smile. "Well at least this time, she's doing it in private."

My face flushed as red as her cherry lips, but she had already turned to take the tray back and didn't see it.

Holy crap! Was Lucy the midnight phone conversation perpetrator?

Amanda's potty trip took a little longer than expected. I waited and pondered on the possibilities of why she looked at her mother like she did. When she came out of the bathroom, I tossed a twenty onto our table. If I couldn't bribe my way to Lucy's redemption, then maybe it could go towards a pair of winter pants for her daughter. Amanda met me at the door with her mom following behind. Lucy handed me her car keys and then hugged Amanda. "Now, Chris, this is one of my most valuable possessions," she said as she kissed her daughter's forehead. "So be careful out there."

I assured her I would and held out my hand and said, "It was nice meeting you best eavesdropping mother in the world," But of course, I left out the words *best eavesdropping mother in the world.*

"It was great meeting you too." She looked at Amanda. "Happy Birthday baby, love you rivers deep and mountains high and good luck on the tests."

"Love you too!" They gave another one last hug.

CHAPTER NINETEEN

Lucy's four-door Impala was buried in snow. She had no snow scraper, so we brushed the windows off with our arms and hands. I opened Amanda's door.

"Well thank you, Sir Hayes the Vodka Watermelon White Knight. You are such a gentleman."

"My Lady." I bowed and closed the door behind. The pungent smell of smoke quickly assaulted my nostrils as I sat in the driver's seat. I looked around the interior of the car. I was pleasantly surprised to find that, besides for the smell of stale cigarettes, it was relatively clean for a hoosier's car. After a few failed cold attempts, the old engine finally came to life. We made our way out of the parking lot and onto the adventures of the Hoosier Girl and the Vagina Hunter.

Amanda turned on the radio. The Beatles were in the middle of singing, *Lucy in the Sky with Diamonds*.

"I love this song!" She held an imaginary microphone to her mouth and began singing with the enthusiasm of a rockstar. "This is my mom's song," she said as she held the microphone up to my mouth. "Come on Christian, sing it with me! 'Lucy in the Sky with Diamonds.' Bum. Bum. Bum."

I didn't sing. I just laughed, shook my head, and let her continue her crazy antics. The milk and coffee might have calmed her down as a kid but at this moment the sugar and caffeine were kicking in and heightening her already hyper-activeness.

Amanda opened her *Anne of Green Gables* purse and took out her pack of cigarettes and a lighter.

"Can I ask a favor?" My words stopped her. "My mother has a nose like a bloodhound." I nodded to the pack of cigarettes. "She'll be able to smell smoke on me the moment I walk in the door and wonder why I smelled like smoke when I was supposed to be shoveling driveways."

"Sure, no problem." Amanda put the cigarettes back in her purse. "I'll wait until we get to the DMV." She pulled out a little blue book with the Missouri state seal on the cover and the words: "Getting Your Driver's License" beneath it.

"What's your mom's name?" she asked as she opened the book.

"Rosemary," I replied.

Amanda got a horrid look on her face as she reached over and tightly grabbed my bicep. "Your mom's name is *Rosemary*?" The reflective fright in her eyes and vice-like grip told me I was about to step into some uncharted, crazy story that Amanda had written and kept hidden in her notebooks until it was the perfect time to tell. I was also quickly learning she was a master storyteller and anytime was the ideal time to tell one.

"Yeah. Why? You don't like the name Rosemary?"

Amanda let go of my arm and leaned towards me as a parent often does to their inattentive child. I turned my head and gave her my momentary attention. "Have you ever seen the movie *Rosemary's Baby*?" she asked.

"No. I'm not into horror movies."

Rosemary's Baby, along with the long list of other Satan-driven movies that followed such as, "The Exorcist," "Damien," and "The Omen" were what Rev. Monty once referred to as 'The Devil's Porn.'

Unlike normal porn like "Hustler" and "Penthouse," which excited your sexual organs and caused you to physically sin, The Devil's Porn seduced your soul into eternal damnation. I was a big fan of the first, and an adversary of the latter.

"Well, my sperm donor was." Amanda began telling her story with the intensity of radio war correspondent caught in the midst of a battle. "One summer before first grade, dad took me to Ben Franklin to buy school supplies. I was excited and picked out a box of Crayons and some pencils. I remember wanting this cool little pencil box in the shape of a school bus with all the Peanuts characters on it. But there was also a Partridge Family lunch box and I loved watching The Partridge Family."

"I forgot all about the Partridge Family." I interrupted.

"I think I love you, so what am I so afraid of?" Hmmm...let me count the reasons.

"Yeah, well, dad yanked the lunch box out of my hand, put it back on the shelf and snapped, 'We can't afford both of those, goddamnit!' She imitated her sperm donor dad with her brow furrowed, mouth turned down and a voice that compared to Jack Nicholson's. Then she continued in her beautiful Amanda Marrow manner. "I was, like, totally, bummed-out because I really wanted the Partridge Family lunchbox. But I didn't complain because I still got the cool Charlie Brown pencil box.

Anyway, as we're leaving, dad noticed the movie theater across the street was having a classic horror movie marathon. They were showing scary movies all day long and you could watch as many as you wanted for one price."

Amanda crossed her legs in the seat and turned her body towards me. Her short story was turning into a verbal tomb. "As I said, my dad was a big horror movie fan, so we walked over to the ticket box and he asked what movie was playing next. 'Rosemary's Baby,' the cashier said. I'll never forget in a million years what happened next. Dad bent down, looked me in the eyes, and said, 'If you swear never, ever to tell anyone, especially your mom, that we watched this movie, I'll buy you the Partridge Family lunch box'."

Amanda paused as a tow truck drove by. "Praying Mantis!" She yelled and pointed to the truck. I gave her a puzzled look. "Sorry, it's a car game Sara and I play." She apologized and continued. "Soooo, I told dad he'd have to buy the lunchbox first. Even though I was only, like, six, I was already learning my dad wasn't your normal, trusting, nice guy like Grandpa Marrow."

"Or me." I smiled.

"Yes, or you." She smiled too. "Well, we went back to Ben Franklin, bought the lunch box, and went back to the movie theater. Now, you have to know, we were poor and I had only been to the movies once before in my life to see Chitty Chitty Bang Bang. I was totally psyched and excited. I mean, the movie was about someone's baby. How bad could that be? Dad even bribed me more and bought me a soda and popcorn."

She stopped and gathered her thoughts. "I should have known something was up. He was being waaaayyy too nice. I remember the ticket-taker asking him if he thought it was a good idea to let me watch a movie like that." Amanda imitated her dad by waving her hand. "Ahh, she's too young to understand it,' dad said. Well, that was the wrong thing to say. I took it as a challenge to understand it." Amanda took off her hat and ran her fingers through her hair. "Boy, was I in for a fucking psychotic surprise." She put her hat back on. "Do you know what it's about?"

"Not really," I said. No. Satan. Porn.

"Well," Amanda's eyes got big. "It's about this lady who gets pregnant by Satan."

"Hold on." I interrupted. "You knew who Satan was at six years old?"

I was surprised someone so young and so heathen would be aware of Satan.

"Duh. I knew who the devil was." Amanda looked at me incredulously. Like she couldn't believe I would even ask such a question. "I may not have gone to church, like you Chrisssstian Hayes. But I watched cartoons and went trick or treating every year." Then she had a commercial break in her brain. "Remind me to tell you the story about how my neighbor went out trick or treating dressed like Jesus Christ one Halloween. It's hilarious."

A trick or treating Jesus Christ? Now that's a story I want to hear. Ruth and I were never allowed to go Trick or Treating. The idea that children learned about Satan through Saturday morning cartoons and Halloween was an interesting revelation. Like finding God in the Charlie Brown's Christmas special.
Hmmm?

"I admit it was over my head, but at the same time I understood words like, "dead baby" and watched Rosemary take off her clothes and you could see her tits. There was also a scene with a dead lady lying on the sidewalk with blood all around her because she jumped out a window. This was pretty heavy shit for a six-year-old."

"Uh, yeah. What was your dad thinking?"

"That was one tiny slice of why my father was such an asshole pie. He always only thought about himself." She continued. "I really wanted to watch all of the movie, but it's like over two hours long. So as hard as I tried to stay awake, I eventually fell asleep. I woke up at the end when Rosemary realizes the devil worshippers and witches have taken her baby and they tell her that Satan is the father. She looks inside the crib and screams. They never show the baby. Which made it even worse because I imagined it as having hoofs for feet and claws for hands." Amanda held up her hands and curled her fingers into ravenous claws. "Now *that* movie scarred me for life." She let out a deep sigh.

I tried to lighten the mood. "I thought the fuckin flying monkeys from the *Wizard of Oz* scarred you for life?"

Amanda smiled. "Compared to *Rosemary's Baby*, the fuckin flying monkeys of Oz were a playful walk down the yellow brick road."

"I don't think I've ever watched a movie that scarred me for life," I said as a passive thought. "Thank God." Then I suddenly remembered. "Although I have to admit when the shadow of death came creeping around in the movie *The Ten Commandments*, that freaked me out! All the screaming and weeping when the first-born were dying. Scared the crap out of me. I was first born." I looked over at Amanda. She was still deep in thought. The master storyteller had finished her story, but the narrative voice never stops. It just keeps whispering in your ears. "Did you ever tell anyone that your dad took you to see *Rosemary's Baby*?" I asked.

There was a slight hesitation. I watched Amanda's expression change from master storyteller to a tentative teen. "Have you ever wondered why I'm only a freshman and I'm sixteen years old? Most freshmen don't have their driver's license in ninth grade."

The question took me by surprise. I thought about when I first took my driver's test. I was a sophomore. Our birthdays are only three days apart. I turned eighteen. She turned sixteen. "Wow, now that you've said something, what are you doing getting your driver's license as a freshman?"

Amanda switched back into her master storyteller mode. "Fast forward about a month later. It's my first day of first grade. I get off the bus and walk into class where I'm greeted by Miss Howe, this sweet, short-haired, blond lady. Hmmm…" Amanda tapped her chin in thought. "She sort of looks familiar but I don't give it a second thought because I'm excited and busy showing off my new Partridge Family lunch box. Well, about an hour into class, another teacher sticks her head into the door and says something like, "Rosemary, Principal Patterson would like for you to stop by his office at lunch." Amanda took a long deep breath and her eyes grew wide with terror. "I swear Christian, I almost pissed in my pants. Literally." Miss Howe looked just like Mia Farrow in *Rosemary's Baby*." She stopped her story momentarily so that I could mentally digest it.

"Wow! That's totally freaky. So…?" I cued her to continue.

"So, I wanted to get up and run out of the fucking room but instead I froze in fear! Remember, I'm only six years old but in my little hyper-imaginative brain I'm thinking, 'This lady isn't some sweet, pretty, young teacher. She's Rosemary and she's married to the devil." Amanda's tone got desperate. "I couldn't say anything to anyone because that would have meant telling that dad had taken me to see the movie. And if I did that, I was afraid dad would whip my ass and take my lunch box away."

Amanda raised her hands and held out her palms as a sign that her story was coming to an end. "Well, to make a long and emotionally traumatic story, very short, I withdrew into myself during school. I didn't listen or participate. I was afraid that she would cast a spell on me like the other witches did in the movie and something bad would happen to me—just like the girl in the movie who jumped off the building and killed herself." Amanda shot an inquisitive look over to me. "Isn't it weird what your mind thinks when you're a kid? In class, I was this silent, timid and very standoffish little girl, but I'd come home from school and be my loud and obnoxious self. I was like Sally Fields in the movie *Sybil*. Did you ever read that book or see that movie?"

I shook my head no.

"She had, like, a dozen different personalities. I watched that movie too. I was about twelve. Another bad movie choice for a child." Amanda shook her head in an agreement with her own conclusion. "I once read that art imitates life. That's bullshit. Life imitates art. I'm proof. Watch fucked up movies and you become fucked up." She picked up her purse. "Thank God for *Anne of Green Gables*. If she didn't come along when she did, I'd probably be in a mental asylum brain deep in that depressive horror shit by that whacked out author, Stephen King."

"One of my co-workers loves Stephen King, he's read all his books and has seen *Carrie* and *The Shining*. He comes into work and tells me about them. Yeah, I agree. That man's mind is messed up."

"Totally." She nodded in agreement. "Anyway, where was I? Oh yeah, *"Rosemary's Baby"*. By the end of the school year, my grades were horrible. I got an F in "Plays well with others." She laughed. "Can you imagine, me, Miss Gregarious, getting an F in "Play's well with others?" She put the words in finger quotes. "I didn't want to play with others. I just wanted to be left alone in my imaginary world of ..." Amanda began humming the theme to *The Partridge Family.*

Hello, world, here's a song that we're singin', c'mon get happy.
A whole lotta lovin' is what we'll be bringin', we'll make you happy

"Yeah, I just wanted to be happy." Amanda smiled. "But instead, I had to go to the fucking school shrink every Wednesday and play with pictures of happy children and sad children and angry children. Which I loved because I was out of Mrs. Satan's class and Mrs. Gavin, the school's shrink, gave me candy for talking to her about all those goddamn children in the pictures." Amanda bit her lip and pulled a past confession out of her psychological purse. "I almost broke down once and told Mrs. Gavin about seeing *Rosemary's Baby*. But I decided against it. School was almost over and I'd be out of Mrs. Satan's class forever."

A passing ambulance went by with its sirens blaring causing the Master storyteller to pause her story. She wanted to make sure I heard every little detail.

"The last week of school, Lucy and the sperm donor were called into Principal's Patterson's office. He told them that because of my grades and behavior he was unable to move me into second grade." Amanda spun her head in a slow circle. "Oh my God, that's when the shit hit the school fan. My dad kicked over a coffee table and threatened to kick Principal Patterson's ass if he didn't promote me. They had to call the police. Lucy was screaming and crying. By the end of it all, dad was in my fucking face yelling at me for being a stupid little dipshit." Amanda smirked, tilted her head sideways, and blinked her eyes. "Yeah, that's what he called me, stupid little dipshit."

Stupid. Little. Dipshit. Wow. The worst
thing my father ever called me was,
"Sleepyhead." We were running late to a church
picnic where dad was in charge of setting up
the tables and chairs. I had overslept because
I didn't hear my alarm go off. Dad wasn't very
happy at all. Time. Nazi. When we arrived, they
were almost done setting up the tables and
chairs. Dad immediately started to help and
apologized profusely. "Sorry for being late."
He shot me an angry stare. "Sleepyhead over
there didn't hear his alarm go off."

"You know what I did?" She didn't wait for me to answer. "I started
bawling my eyes out and I ran and got my Partridge Family lunch box
and I threw it at the asshole, as hard as I could. I told Lucy the entire
story. How dad took me to see *Rosemary's Baby* and bribed me with
the lunch box and how Miss Howe looked like Rosemary and that's
why I acted like I did in class. I was so pissed Christian. I didn't care if
I got an ass whipping or lost my Partridge Family lunch box. Just don't
call me a stupid little dipshit," she said defiantly as she uncrossed her
legs and sat upright.

"Well, Lucy stopped talking to the sperm donor. The sperm donor
went on a drinking binge. He got fired from his job. We had to move
to another house in another neighborhood. I started first grade all over
again at a different school.

But this time Mr. Bryant was my teacher and he looked like Hoss
on *Bonanza*. But only a smart Hoss and he smelled like Old Spice. I
loved Mr. Bryant because he said he had a niece that I reminded him
of that was smart, funny and animated just like me. I didn't know what
'animated' meant. He explained I was like a character in a cartoon or
in a book." Amanda beamed proudly and stared at me.

Add one more characteristic to Mr. Bryant's
description. Hoss. Old Spice. Prophetic.

I waited for her to continue. But she said nothing. "Are you done?" I asked.

"Yep. The end," she said and opened her purse, took a Cotton Candy Lip Smacker and put it on her lips.

"That," I paused and shook my head in utter amazement. "is one of the craziest and tragic stories I've ever heard."

As pathetic as the story was, it was marvelous to hear. I wondered how many other guys in school knew this hidden piece of knowledge. This was precisely the kind of bonding I wanted to do with Amanda Marrow.

"Yep. I should be in tenth grade, but because of my sperm donor and *Rosemary's Baby*, I'm not."

"Man, Amanda, that's terrible." I tried to sound genuinely sincere, which I was, without being too pitifully sympathetic. "I'm really sorry to hear that." I paused, and then, to verify our mutual bonding that had just taken place by her telling me her deepest darkest secrets, I asked. "I take it you haven't told many people this story?"

"Are you fucking kidding me? I love telling this story. It's like one of my top ten favorite stories to tell."

Fuck. Me. Master Storyteller.

Amanda tossed the Cotton Candy Lip Smacker back into her purse. "You reap what you sow." Her expression got brighter. "My asshole father is in prison and I'm living the dream being driven to get my driver's license by Chrisssstian Hayes, the best big brother in the world and the Vodka Watermelon White Knight." It was my turn to beam proudly. "You want to know what's really weird about the whole thing?"

"What?" I was afraid to ask.

"Shortly after Roman Polanski directed *Rosemary's Baby* his wife, Sharon Tate, who was pregnant at the time, was murdered by Charles Manson's cult followers." Amanda rubbed her forehead. "Now that's some freaky shit."

"Yeah, that's freaky." I agreed.

"But do you want to know what's even freakier than that?" Amanda asked.

"What?"

"When you think about it, you're Rosemary's baby."

CHAPTER TWENTY

I could tell Amanda was jonesing for a cigarette. She kept doing things with her fingers. Putting on lip gloss, playing with the clasp on her purse. Flipping through the driver's test manual. Like a horse chomping on a bit, ready to run. I pressed down on the gas pedal to speed up the car and shorten her suffering.

"Why do you call your mom Lucy?" I asked.

"Because she's more than my mom. She's my friend and my confidante and she loves me more than anything in the world. And I love her more than anyone in the world." Her words were warm and heartfelt. As an afterthought, she added. "Mom is such a lame and boring three letter word to give someone who gets stretch marks all over their tits and stomach and stretches out their... you know what... while suffering massive amount of pain just to give birth to you" There was a connecting pause and she reached over and turned up the heat. "And works two jobs so you can have food on your table and clothes on your back ..."

"So you don't freeze your nipples off." I thought.

"...So you don't freeze your nipples off." She laughed and looked to see if she had embarrassed me, unaware that she had just miraculously verbalized my thoughts. "M-O-M." Amanda spelled the word. "How unoriginal and totally uncreative. Lucy is so much juicier and more delicious of a name than M-O-M." She giggled at her wordplay.

"That's funny. I often thought calling God by the name of God was a little obscured."

Of course, I had never told anyone that. A good Christian doesn't go around complaining about God's name. It felt good to share one of my many heretical thoughts with Amanda.

Although, I didn't want to get into another theological discussion. It's just that when your entire childhood and adolescence revolves around the Son, it's hard not to keep bringing God or religion into a conversation.

"Oh, my God. I totally agree!" Amanda laughed. "It's, like, whoever decided to call God by the name God, should be hung by his testicles. And speaking of testicles, why does God have to be a He? That's so unfair and sexist. So God has a penis? Because a penis is the only thing that makes something masculine, isn't it? And if God has a penis, it must be one gigantic penis because God is everywhere." I think she was enjoying tossing the word "penis" out in our conversation. She was about to reveal to me another epiphany. "Maybe this earth is one of God's testicles and we're like little STD crabs on the balls of God."

There was a pause — a regrouping of thoughts. An imaginary 'but,' she often used. "And earthquakes and tornados are God scratching His balls!" She burst out in a fit of laughter so loud, one would have thought she had told the funniest joke in the world. I laughed too. The image of a hairy, bearded God standing in space and reaching down and scratching the earth, like it was his left testicle flashed in my mind. How could I not laugh? Watching the antics of this creative beauty at her best was delightfully dumbfounding.

"Where in the hell do you come up with stuff like that?" I shook my head and asked.

"I don't know. It just pops in my head." She shrugged her shoulders like it happened all the time. "My mind constantly goes a zillion miles a minute and I sometimes go along for the ride."

"Sometimes?"

"Yeah. Sometimes." She gazed out the window. "Other times, I stay here and look normal and sane as if I'm paying attention to reality." Although she said it in jest, I could hear a steel edge in her words that cut to the truth. Reality and imagination were both her playground and her battlefield.

CHAPTER TWENTY-ONE

The sun was melting holes into the clouds and bursting through like golden columns that stretched across the horizon. The streets, while still slushy and messy, were getting better with each pass of the city's snowplow. We pulled into the DMV and there were only two cars parked in front.

Amanda scanned the parking lot. "Do me a favor and park over there." She pointed to the side of the building. I did as she said and turned off the car.

"Well good luck!" I said as I started to get out of the car.

"Hold on." She reached around to the back seat and pulled out a brown paper grocery bag. She opened the bag and removed a short denim skirt. Without missing a beat, she began taking off her shoes. "You always want to get on the good side of the driving examiner officer." And with that, she unzipped her pants and pulled them off exposing the sexiest pair of blue silk panties my stupid, sex-starved, eighteen-year-old eyes had ever seen. I did not attempt to skirt my stare as she slipped her pants off and her skirt on.

My Vagina Hunting hormones were racing to my lower extremities, thus leaving my cheeks with a shortage of blood making them blush bright red.

Amanda continued to slide her skirt up her tanned, slender legs and over my trophy hidden behind a wall of silk a mere millimeters thick. I watched in wonderful delight as she buttoned up her skirt and put her tennis shoes back on. When she was finished tying her laces, she looked at me with a content, almost satisfying look.

"I hope you enjoyed that." She nodded as a stage magician would after thrilling his audience with a great act of trickery. "I did it just for you. I could have climbed into the back seat and changed there. Or put the skirt on first and then took off my pants. Or told you to close your eyes, but I didn't." She gave me a devilish smile, took a cigarette out of her *Anne of Green Gables* purse, put it in her mouth and got out of the car.

Although she didn't come right out and say it, everything in her eyes and expression told me I had just received some type of payment for the deal we had shaken hands on yesterday at school.

"Ok, then it's a deal. Skip school with me and take me to get my driver's license and I promise, cross my heart and hope to die, stick a needle in my eye, that I'll return the favor in some non-sexual capacity."

I don't remember the next couple of minutes. I think I got out of the car or melted in a euphoric sludge that slipped out of the exhaust pipe. I can't recall if the sixty-second non-sexual sex show was enough to bring my spear to full attention or the cold winter air calmed its war call. It all became a blue silk blur.

I kind of remember walking past her and saying. "I'll be inside where it's warm while you stand out here in the cold killing yourself with that poison stick."

And I think she said. "OK best big brother in the world, I'll be right in after I ingest this anti-freeze into my lungs." Don't quote me as any of that being fact. It's just my mental hearsay brought on by the circumstances.

CHAPTER TWENTY-TWO

It took the drab décor and stale smell of the DMV to shake me back to reality. I walked past the empty lines and around a row of empty chairs to be the only person standing in an empty room. There was a picture of Governor Teasdale hanging on the wall. He was looking down at me and smiling like he was happy that I was there and proud that I didn't commit an academic felonious act to get there. I sat down. A door to one of the back offices opened in unison with the front door. In the first door came an overweight thirty-something male whose eyes grew twice the size of his already bulging belly when he saw what was coming in the other door—a smoking hot sixteen-year-old looking like a scantily dressed snow nymph in a bad Broadway Christmas musical.

"Can I help you?" The clerk asked. I waited in bated anticipation for him to wipe the drool from his Vagina Hunting slobbering lips.

"I'm here to take my driver's tests." Amanda gave him that smile that makes every guy think she's paying more attention to him than she really is. He was fooled like every other guy, including me. I didn't hear everything they were saying. I wasn't sure I even wanted to hear everything they were saying. He asked for the proper credentials, wished her a happy birthday, and escorted her towards another room. She looked at me and gave me a thumbs up.

I returned the thumbs up and yelled "Good luck!

I'm quite confident that had it not been Amanda Marrow, the Freshman Fire that walked into that test room but some other normal, old or ugly person, the DMV man, whom I labeled as DMV Tubbs, would have let them take the test in their own solitude. But since it was Amanda Marrow, the Freshman Fire, he sat in the same room in a chair directly across from her and pretended to be reading a magazine. Through the glass window that separated the two rooms, I watched and prayed to God that she wasn't doing to him what she had done to me at Aloha last Saturday night. Tantalizing him with an up-skirt peek, just to pass the test.

After the jubilant high, I had just experienced with her sixty-second non-sexual show, the hormone raging buzz was slowly wearing off. It began to sink into my stupid, sex-starved, eighteen-year-old brain exactly what she was doing. She was using her legs, her smile and her entire petite beautiful self as a box of donuts to bribe the uniformed examiner officer into "getting on his good side." What that meant exactly, was left up to her hoosier interpretation. But it didn't sit well with me. As I sat there feeling unwell, I rethought the entire epiphany of her not having a winter wardrobe and had another epiphany that trumped the first one:

The truth was she liked to look slutty.

Her sexuality was her crutch to help her walk through a life of despair. It was the one thing she controlled. She mastered and manipulated her sexuality towards Vagina Hunters as she did the words of her stories.

A writer creates her characters; telling them what to say and how to act. And because the character is newly created, he has no past and no idea of what his future will be. So he slowly comes to life and believes she is his god.

Guys are drawn into Amanda's world by her beauty and sexuality. They have no past with her, so she creates them and molds them into the image that she desires. The DMV officer was going to be one that makes sure she passes her driver's test, no matter what happens. I was the one to get her to the DMV at the risk long term repercussions.

And how was she getting all these characters to play her parts? The answer to that question is a juxtaposed irony. By giving them the impression there's a possibility to play with her body parts. A part for a part. It was all quite sneaky and seductively

simple. And the worst part of it was, I was the main character in this story.

Several minutes later, Amanda got up and handed DMV Tubbs her test. He scanned the paper then pulled out a red marker and wrote something on it. Amanda clapped her hands in excitement and held the test up for me to see through the window. The red letters read '100%'. She came out of the room smiling like she was the first man on the moon.

"I got a perfect score!" She ran over and hugged me. Her arms around me acted as an exorcism casting out the spirit of jealousy and accusations of darkness. I was suddenly back to my senseless Vagina Hunting self.

"Officer Tumblet will be right out to give you your driving test." DMV Tubbs said and went into another room. Seconds later he came out followed by a lady who looked about the age of my mother. She wore a khaki state uniform with a big gold badge on her right chest. On her left chest was her black name plate that said "L. Tumblet". She looked as if she had been a kindergarten school teacher in another life. Amanda and I looked at one another and giggled.

"Well, I guess since you're the only female in this waiting room, you must be Amanda Marrow." Officer Tumblet read the sheet on her clipboard.

"Yes ma'am, the one and only."

"My name is Officer Tumblet and I'll be giving you your driver's exam today." She looked out the window. "I hope you have a four-wheel drive and the roads aren't too treacherous."

'Actually, I have a military tank and no the roads aren't that bad."

Officer Tumblet looked Amanda up and down. "What are you doing wearing a skirt like that on a day like today, young lady?" And before Amanda could make up an excuse, Officer Tumblet answered her own question. "I suppose trying to get on the good side of the examiner." She walked from behind the desk and put on her coat. "Well, drive safe and get me back here in one piece with no accidents and you'll get on my good side." She motioned for Amanda to follow her to the front door. I could only watch with mild trepidation as they walked outside and got into Lucy's Impala.

DMV Tubbs gave me a courtesy smile and disappeared back into his office probably to have an HMS with Amanda being the star of the show.

I sat alone in the lobby and used the reflections of the DMV windows to reflect on the morning. The snow had stopped and now everything appeared sunny, but still cold and translucent. A bus raced by followed by a cloud of black exhaust that hung in the air like black crepe paper floating up and down behind it. Up. And. Down. I watched as it dissipated into nothingness and wished my thoughts could have done the same.

Instead, they became thick and heavy. Thick with the lessons that I was learning that I didn't know I was learning. Heavy with answers that were being given without me knowing the questions.

Images of Lucy and Amanda saying goodbye and telling each other they loved one another and genuinely meaning it. It was not some tripe, meaningless, obligatory act between family members that were so common in my zoo life.

A mother, a hoosier mother, for that matter, that lets her hoosier daughter smoke in the house and doesn't mind that she curses and skips school and yet she works two jobs and puts in overtime for money to put food on the table and warm clothes over cold nipples. "She's not just my mom. She's more than my mom, she's Lucy."

What's wrong with this picture? Could it be that in the midst of hoosier families there's a role reversal that takes place? Instead of functional dysfuctionalism that fills my zoo, it's reversed and called dysfunctional

functionalism. Where craziness turns into normality and the improper becomes pragmatic?

Fifteen minutes later Lucy's Impala pulled back into the parking lot. I watched as Amanda drove to the corner of the lot where there were four orange traffic cones set up as an improvised parallel parking spot. Officer Tumblet got out of the car and moved the cones further apart to accommodate Lucy's tank-size car. She motioned for Amanda to parallel park as she stood and watched the cones. Amanda slowly worked the car back and forth until she was safely between the fluorescent orange cones. It took a little time, but time wasn't a penalty, only touching one of the cones with a bumper resulted in immediate failure. Officer Tumblet gave her the thumbs up and Amanda once again tugged back and forth and pulled out of the spot. Officer Tumblet got back into the car and they drove up to the office.

I could see Amanda was somewhat frazzled when she got out of the car, but she held tight to her air of confidence and gave me a relieved look, followed by the sign that she was going to remain outside and have a smoke. You know the motion, it's like the universal blow job sign where the hand moves back and forth in front of your lips but instead of a cupped fist, it's a peace sign. Officer Tumblet walked into the DMV.

"Well I'm alive and we didn't have any accidents." Officer Tumblet smiled as she unbuttoned her coat and put it on the back of a chair.

"How'd she do?' I asked.

"Just between you and me..." She looked out at Amanda who had her back turned to the cold and was huddled against the building. A fountain of smoke formed above her head. "She did awesome, but don't tell her. I'll be right back." She went into the office and shut the door.

Several seconds later Amanda walked in the door. "Oh my God, it's freakin' cold out there." The bitter wind had turned her cheeks bright red and she looked childish. The fact was, she was childish but now standing there with her rosy cheeks, skimpy skirt, tennis shoes and newsboy hat, she was elementary childish. She stood there for a second shivering. "Where did she go?"

I pointed to the door. "She walked in there and said she'd be right back."

"Did you see me parallel park, Christian Hayes? I didn't hit one cone." She boasted as she took off her hat and shook her head to fix her hair and caress the coldness out of her cheeks.

"Yeah, but it took about six hours." I looked at my watch.

"Oh, bullshit!" She playfully punched me in the arm. "Besides, when do you ever parallel park in Spanish Lake anyway?"

Officer Tumblet came out of her office with a yellow piece of paper on her clipboard. "Congratulations Miss Marrow, you're now an official Missouri driver." She handed Amanda the yellow piece of paper.

Amanda jumped up and down and hugged both Officer Tumblet and me.

"Take this over to that counter," she motioned to the other side of the room. "and Matt with take your picture and give you a temporary license until you get yours in the mail in about a week or so." Officer Tumblet gave her one last warm grin. "Drive safe." Then she looked Amanda up and down. "And try to dress a little warmer, Miss Marrow. Remember you're in Missouri now."

Amanda nodded in compliance. "I'll do that Officer Tumblet and thanks." She turned, grabbed my arm and we hurried to the counter.

CHAPTER TWENTY-THREE

"Shit, I totally forgot that I was going to have to get my picture taken," Amanda said as she took off her hat, shook her head, and fluffed her hair. Then she opened her purse, took out her compact, and brushed powder on her cheeks and forehead. She spent five more minutes fixing her shirt, putting on lipstick and doing everything she could to look like she had just stepped out of a limousine and onto a red carpet instead of Lucy's beat up Impala and the DMV. Finally, she gave herself a quick spray of Heaven's Sent.

"You have to smell good to get your picture taken?" I asked.

"No," she giggled. It's just a girly habit." She took one last look at herself in the mirror. "Well, this picture sure in the hell isn't going to look like the one I gave you on your birthday." She rolled her eyes and stepped on the X on the floor in front of the camera. DMV Tubbs gave me a jealous look that said, "And exactly what kind of picture did she give you for your birthday?"

"You know, I just had an epiphany." I smiled. "Theoretically, I'm giving you this picture for your birthday," I motioned to the camera in front of her. "In exchange for the picture you gave me on my birthday."

"Theoretically," Amanda gave me a naughty grin. "You need to stop talking like that in public, young man," she chastised. "Or I'm going to have to you-know-what." She posed. The camera flashed. Once again, her beauty was eternally captured for prosperity.

I wondered if DMV Tubbs had the ability to keep the pictures he had taken of every female he found attractive. And if he took those pictures home and had his own HMS with them. It was my turn to be jealous. Prick. He had her picture and I didn't. But then I smiled. A glorious, joyful, and elated smile. Pants. Brown bag. Car. It was cold outside. She would want to change back into her jeans. Hopefully. God. Please.

DMV Tubbs signed a little grey card and handed it to Amanda. "Use this temporary permit until your license comes in the mail."

Amanda thanked him with one last, "You're the man of my dreams." smile and we walked towards the door. "Hold on. I want to use the restroom. Oh, and I promised to call Lucy when it was over." Amanda turned towards the lady's rest room.

"I'll be in the car," I said.

"Ok but I'm driving home."

I went out to the car and sat in the passenger's seat, reached over, and put the key in the ignition and started it. As the morning grew later and the sun melted more of the clouds away, I could feel both the external temperature around me and the internal temperature that warms one's heart, begin to rise. The birds were now out in full force chirping happily in the nearby trees. I felt their merriment and watched as several swallows bantered back and forth over a lonely berry on holly bush until a cardinal came and pirated it for himself.

I had accomplished what I had set out to accomplish. I helped Amanda Marrow, the Freshman Fire, get her driver's license. In the process, I got to peek into the crystal ball of her past and gaze upon her cloudy, fucked up childhood.

I saw sparks of insanity and flickers of functionality. I watched her disrobe down to a pair of silk panties. That alone was enough fuel to fire this Vagina Hunter's HMS machine for many months. And yet, through it all, I remained a Good Guy...

My thoughts were abruptly interrupted when Amanda jumped into the car. She was no longer smiling. "Let's get the fuck out of here." Her voice was distressed and angered. She tossed her purse in the back and quickly put the car in reverse. "Oh my God, Christian, you're not going to believe what happened while I was taking the driver's test." She shook her head in disbelief as she looked in the rearview mirror.

"What happened?" I reached over and touched her arm. "Is everything all right?"

"No, not really." She put the car in drive and sped out of the parking lot. "You wouldn't believe what that cunt," She paused. "Sorry, that's a repulsive word that I seldom use, but that cunt Officer Tumblet, just sexually molested me while I was taking the driving test."

"No. Freakin'. Way." I was in shock.

"Way!" Amanda said as we drove down the road. "I told her how nervous I was about the parallel parking part of the test. She started talking about what a pretty young girl I was. And then Christian, out of nowhere, she put her fucking hand on my leg and started caressing it" Amanda put her hand on my leg and moved it up and down. "So I'm driving down the fucking road trying not to freak out and kill us both. Suddenly she runs her hand up my skirt and touches my..." She gave me a paused, panicked stare. "...my pussy and says if I was good and didn't tell anyone she would make sure I passed the test even if I failed the parallel parking."

Holy Shit! But it's all your fault for pretending to be a box of donuts and trying to get on her good side and making that dyke examiner want your box. That's what happens when you dress like a sleazy hoosier.

"Holy Shit! What did you do?"

"I told her my boyfriend's dad was an attorney for the City of St. Louis and if she didn't quickly remove her boney-ass fingers from beneath my skirt, she would NOT have a job tomorrow."

I grabbed my head with both hands "Are you kidding me!!!"

"Yeah," she said.

And without another word, she reached over and turned on the radio. Pat Benatar was signing *Heartbreaker*. Amanda joined in...

You're a heartbreaker
Dream maker, love taker
Don't you mess around with me

"Oh, my freaking G-O-D, I can't believe you just did that!" I screamed into her face.

"I told you I'd get you back." She continued to sing as she surveyed the traffic around her. "Now hand me my pants and hold this steering wheel while I put them back on." She motioned to her jeans laying on the floorboard. "I'm freezing my little ass off and if you want to enjoy the view go right ahead but don't crash because it's almost Christmas." She reached down and unsnapped her skirt. "I don't want to come back like Marley's ghost in *A Christmas Carol* and haunt your ass for killing me right before Christmas," she threatened.

And without another word, she slid her skirt down to once again show me her blue silk panties.

CHAPTER TWENTY-FOUR

Christmas morning.

To my bitter disappointment, besides for a couple of casual run-ins with Amanda during lunch and in between classes, the rest of the week following the trip to the DMV was uneventful to say the least. We were both busy with end of the semester exams and getting ready for the holidays. Hello. Status. Quo.

However, something unusual did began to happen since the two, sixty-second, non-sexual paybacks, I began remembering my dreams. It was like seeing Amanda in her panties kick-started my nocturnal memories. Or perhaps up until that point in my life I never dreamed of anything good enough to recall. That changed dramatically. I was now incessantly dreaming Vagina Hunting storylines. Some included Amanda. Others had random classmates, church girls and even strangers as my sexual starlets.

"Wake up Christian. It's Christmas!" Ruth cheered as she bounced up and down on the side of my bed and promptly woke me up.

"You're supposed to knock before you come into my room!" I hissed through the pillow. Fortunately for both Ruth's and my sake, I was sleeping on my side with my back facing the door. I was sporting a morning Woodie that would have been impossible to hide had I been lying on my back.

"Come on Christian. It's time to get up and open presents."

"Ok!" I pushed her off my bed. "Get out of here. I'll be down in a minute."

"OK, Grinch." Ruth barked back and promptly slammed the door on her way out.

I looked at the clock. 8:17 a.m. We had been up late the evening before to attend Christmas Eve church service. I was looking forward to a morning of sleeping in late. It was going to be a long, busy day. Christmases at our house were always long, loud, and busy days. For the past ten years, the Hayes house was the gathering place for most of the family to celebrate Christmas.

I laid in bed pondering how the day's events were going to unfold while waiting for my Vagina Hunting spear to go back its dormant state. For a second, I thought about having a quick HMS which would have taken the edge off the stressful day. But being Christmas morning and having everyone waiting for me, I decided against it.

There was a knock on my door.

"Come on Christian. Time to get up. It's going to be a long day."

Oh my God. Mom was now hurrying me along. Holy crap. The added pressure only increased the blood pressure in my spear.

"OK mom, I'm getting dressed. Be there in a second." I threw on a pair of jeans, a sweatshirt, and listened at the door until mom was gone. Silence. I darted directly across the hall to the bathroom.

Every male knows that you can't stand up and pee like a man with a morning woody. You have to sit down on the toilet like a girl.

I thought about previous Christmas mornings. Even as a kid I never understood why other kids woke up at the crack of dawn and raced wildly to the Christmas tree to rip open their presents. Were they afraid someone was going to steal their gifts if they slept in a few more hours? Ruth and I had never been crack-of-dawn, Christmas morning risers. Mom and dad would let us sleep in, which meant they could sleep too. Everyone awoke Christmas morning rested and ready. It was all part of my functionally dysfunctional upbringing.

In our zoo we were trained Christmas wasn't about decorating the tree, Santa bringing gifts and opening presents. It was a celebration of the birth of Jesus Christ. Each Christmas morning before opening presents, dad would take the big, worn and battered, family Bible off the bookshelf and read the Christmas story.

Afterward, we would say a prayer of thanks for both the birth of Christ and all the gifts that were under the tree. Those religious rituals had to take place before we were allowed to open even one present. Which was not only functionally dysfunctional but purely hypocritical because while I was incredibly thankful for the birth of Christ, I was only thankful for about twenty percent of my Christmas presents. The other eighty percent were gifts of necessity like clothes, cologne, and umbrellas.

That is why Ruth and I were never excited like most kids when it came to Christmas morning. Our family put Christ in Christmas but in a manner that was ritualistic and sterile. And by doing so, we left out the merry part of Merry Christmas.

My Christmas presents that year were as follows:

-A stocking with a plastic candy cane filled with M&M's and a little tin that looked like a book filled with a variety of Lifesavers. It was the only annual junk food ordained by my parents as permissible to eat because it was a holiday. To go along, or should I say, to counteract the tooth decaying effects of the M&M's and Lifesavers, were the traditional stocking stuffers: toothbrush, floss, and mouthwash. The three Wise Men of dental hygiene.

-A book titled, *"Christian Co-eds: How to be Christ-Like During College."* Never mind that I hadn't read a book on my own free will since third grade.

-A short sleeve, burgundy, velour shirt to go with the new Jordache jeans I got for my birthday. No complaints. Ruth picked it out.

-A red sweatsuit that reminded me of something The Six Million Dollar Man would wear while Vagina Hunting the Bionic Woman.

-The Annual Big Gift: A set of three leather suitcases that fit into one another like Russian nesting or matryoshka dolls. It was a very nice gift. I was going away to college and my current vinyl suitcase had bit the dust years ago. These would come in handy.

-A cool pair of Foster Grant sunglasses from Ruth. Ruth and I had developed a sibling skill of knowing what to get one another for birthdays and Christmas. Throughout the year we'd listen to what each other showed an interest in. Sometimes we'd make comments like, "That would be a good gift." while we were at the mall or in a store. When Christmas or birthdays came around, we always knew we would enjoy one another's gift.

On my eighth and ninth birthdays, besides my normal gifts, mom and dad gave me an extra ten dollars. I could not spend this money on myself. I was to buy everyone Christmas presents with it. This was to teach me how to budget my money and use it wisely when spending it. They did the same with Ruth when she turned eight.

At ten-years-old, we were given household chores like doing the dishes, taking out the trash and folding the laundry. In exchange, we earned a small weekly allowance. From that weekly allowance, we learned to take ten percent of it and put it in the tithing envelope in Sunday school. Another ten percent went into our savings account that mom and dad had opened for us at their bank. The rest of the money we could use for our own pleasure. Like buying Bomb pops from the ice cream man or mercury head dimes for my coin collection.

At sixteen, I was expected to get a part-time job and the allowance stopped, but the tithing and saving didn't. Each was taken out of my paycheck and put in the proper place. It was part of the work and financial disciple training Ruth and I received.

Out of everything my parents taught me, financial management was the second most useful and important lesson in life that I learned. It ranked right below the first and greatest lesson. The Golden Rule:

Do unto others as you would have them do unto you. Luke 6:31

I handed Ruth her present from me. Last spring when we were at the hardware store Ruth had stumbled onto a display of birdhouses with clear plastic backs that attached to a window with suction cups. She thought they were the first man on the moon. You could see inside the birdhouse and watch the birds nest, lay eggs, and raise their little birdies. The next time I was at the hardware store I picked one up. It had been hidden in my closet for the past six months.

"Yay!!!" Ruth screeched as she opened the gift and gave me a big hug. "Thanks, Christian. I forgot all about this."

Just then the doorbell rang.

We looked at one another with a strange, almost sacrilegious stare. Who would be ringing the doorbell this early on Christmas morning? It was too soon for the relatives to arrive; they weren't expected for several hours. We got up as a family and moved to the front door in one motion. Dad looked out the peephole.

"There's no one there," he said.

He opened the door. The morning sunshine reflecting off the glittering snow momentarily blinded everyone. Through squinted eyes, I saw the faint glimpse of a white Impala disappearing over the crest of the hill. Sitting on the welcome mat was a present. Ruth bolted out the door before mom could stop her and in doing so, committed a major hoosier faux pas causing mom a slight panic.

Only hoosiers went out in public in their pajamas.

Ruth brought the box in the foyer and read the tag on top: To the Hayes, Merry Christmas. There was no signature.

"That's Sara's handwriting!" Ruth heralded to everyone. "She spells her y's just like that with a long tail. And I know she loves gingerbread houses." She pointed to the side of the box. The wrapping paper was festive gingerbread houses of all sizes. "She said if she was ever really rich, she was going to build a life-size gingerbread house. I could come over and spend the night. If we got hungry and wanted a snack, we could just take a bite out of the bedpost." Ruth laughed at the thought as she took the box into the living room and sat it on the coffee table.

"It smells like cigarettes," Mom noted out loud.

But even through the smell of the cigarette smoke, there was a delicious potpourri of spices and other scents permeating out of the box. You couldn't miss the odor. Ruth didn't ask for permission to open the box. She tore into it with the passion of a normal kid opening a Christmas present at the crack of dawn. She reached in and pulled out a Santa Claus made from a deliciously, deep red and colossal apple. Ruth sat him on the table. We gazed at him in curious wonder.

His apple tummy was about the size of a softball and shined like a new Buick. His head, arms, and legs were large fluffy marshmallows spiked to his tummy with toothpicks. At the end of his marshmallow arms were two sugar-coated red gumdrops that acted as mittens. His boots were black licorice gumdrops. Stretched around his waist was a twisted and spun cotton ball that became his belt held on with a buckle of clove. From his marshmallow chin hung another piece of pulled cotton. His mouth and eyes were cloves. On top of it all, sat another red gumdrop toothpicked to his marshmallow head as his very own Santa's hat.

"Oh, my word, isn't that just the cutest thing?" Mom said as she helped Ruth get the other three out of the box. "And there are four of them, one for each of us. How sweet."

Ruth couldn't contain her joy as she danced around the living room, putting the Santa apple to her nose and inhaling its delicious aromas.

"This is totally awesome!" she beamed.

I could tell dad was even delighted by the way he looked at the Santa apple with a twinkle of Christmas spirit in his eye. I thought those Santa apples R-O-C-K-E-D. They were the first functional Christmas presents the Hayes household had ever experienced. And even though they weren't religious or about Jesus' birth, they were incredibly creative, sweet and even healthy. They embodied all the smells and sights of the holidays. But most importantly, they possessed one other reason for the season; giving from the heart. These weren't sterile store-bought gifts made in China. They were fresh, handmade, jolly little sweet gems that took someone's time and genuine care to create.

"Ohh...." Ruth sighed in disappointment as she set the Santa apple back on the coffee table. "I feel bad because we didn't get them anything."

"We'll get them something," Mom said. I could only imagine what mom would give the hoosier Marrow family for Christmas. Maybe a post-Christmas, seventy-five percent off pine scented candle to cover the smell of cigarette smoke in their house. Or a "Jesus is the Reason for the Season" ornament.

"You know what Sara says?" Ruth sat her Santa apple on the coffee table. "She said that she believed in Santa Claus up until she was in third grade. Third grade!" Ruth rolled her eyes and continued. "She also said that they didn't leave milk and cookies for Santa. Do you know what they left for Santa? You'll never guess what they left for Santa." Ruth had the entire family's attention and she leaned towards us as the serpent may have leaned into Eve to tell her it was OK to partake of the forbidden fruit of the Tree of Knowledge. "They left a bottle of Budweiser and some peanuts. Imagine that! A bottle of beer and some peanuts on the coffee table right next to the Christmas tree."

Dad and mom looked at one another with horror. Ruth leaned back on the couch satisfied that she had caused an emotional stir with the parents. It was especially delicious because it was Christmas. She tossed in the side note. "But you know her dad was...or is...an alcoholic and that's why they did that. Can I please call her and thank her?" Ruth begged.

"Make it quick. We have to eat breakfast and get ready for today."

My thoughts briefly flew away and landed on Amanda. I wondered what her, Sara and Lucy were doing on this holy day. How did they celebrate Christmas in their heathen and hoosier way?

How tremendously thoughtful and kind it was to make the Santa apples, then to get up, get dressed, and drive over in the cold Christmas morning to deliver them. They didn't put on a proud and pretentious show, like some of my religious relatives would often do when presenting gifts around the tree. They just anonymously dropped off their gifts and drove off into the morning sunrise. Somehow, I was beginning to think that a hoosier Christmas may not be that bad of a Christmas at all.

Making these "Marrow's Merry Christmas Santa Apples", as we named them, and anonymously giving them as gifts became a yearly Christmas tradition in my family.

CHAPTER TWENTY-FIVE

What. A. Bitch.

I expected some kind of communication from Amanda during our Christmas break. A phone call, a relayed message from Ruth, or *any* word from her. It didn't matter if it was beautiful, fancy or not. I just wanted some type of confirmation that she hadn't forgotten about me and my act of kindness. I hoped that maybe she now considered me more than just an academic acquaintance. I mean, we talked and bonded for hours that morning of her birthday.

She may not have opened the gates to her soul and poured out her deepest, darkest secrets, as I hoped she would. But she did open the shutters and let me peek into not only her past, but at her panties too. Didn't that mean something?

Or was that just SOP (Standard Operating Procedure) for a sleazy, hoosier girl? Until personally meeting her, I had no experiences with hoosier girls. I didn't associate or hang out with them. I definitely had never dated one. As far as I knew, her silence could be a hoosier girl's way of showing some sort of interest in a guy.

Chuck and I had a Three-Day Rule that meant we always waited three days before calling a girl after she gave us her phone number. It was part of what we called "playing a girl off." Whenever we met a female we were interested in, it was our SOP not to immediately call her or show any interest in her. We surmised that by playing her off, it would make her want us more. Hard. To. Get.

Maybe a week of not speaking to a guy—after he had shown you kindness and you had shown him your panties (or more)—was a hoosier girl's way of "playing him off."

I tried to convince myself that she must have been too busy at work. With Christmas returns and everyone being off school, it had to be hectic and crazy at the mall. That's why she was unable to pick up the phone or tell Sara to tell Ruth to tell me Hi. Nothing. Silence. Every night at Aloha, I waited like a daddy in a delivery room hoping to see her enter the doors. She never did.

I was used like a doormat in Steak 'n Shake.

On the other hand, our younger siblings were becoming the best of buddies. Ruth was constantly calling Sara and vice versa. I admit I was jealous. It pained me to no end to watch their friendship blossom. And there I was, no further along being Amanda's friend then when we first met. I pretended to be unaffected by the entire situation. When Ruth begged me to take her to Jamestown Mall to meet Sara, I refused.

I knew she would try to drag me into Waldenbooks to say Hi to Amanda. Even though every part of me wanted to see her, the prideful part told me to stand my ground. She needed to be the one to take the initiative to reach out to me. It was, after all, friendship I had shown her. I didn't have to take her to the DMV and risk parental punishment from a snowday scam. I took all the risk that day. She only took a couple of drivers tests. Now, she's basking in the glory of being a Missouri driver while I'm feeling slighted, rejected and a little pissed because of her silence. As the days went by my pissfullness skyrocketed. I'm not sure there is such a word as pissfullness. If not, then it was my turn to make one up, pissfullness: **verb**: *the emotional state of being consumed by anger, hurt, hatred or frustration. Often brought on by the scorn of love or lust.*

Example: His *pissfullness* had escalated to its boiling point because he felt he was taken for a ride by giving her a ride.

When I woke up New Year's Eve morning, I had resigned to myself that the gloves were now off. My New Year's resolution was that I was no longer going to be Mr. Nice Guy. I was going to be a full-fledged Vagina Hunter. And Amanda Marrow, the Freshman Fire, was my number one trophy.

I had asked Mr. Abernathy for the night off the same day Chuck told me his parents had given him the green light to have his New Year's Eve party. Mr. Abernathy agreed. I had been looking forward to it for weeks. It helped me take my mind off Amanda.

Chuck's family went to our church and was of the religious sort. Not to the level of my parents but still pretty high on the radical charts. It would be a safe party. Safe in the sense there wouldn't be any smoking, alcohol or drugs. But as far as promiscuity, one never knew. It's hard to tell what'll happen when you corral a bunch of vaginas into a basement with a herd of adolescent Vagina Hunters. Even under the watchful eyes of protective parents or the All-Seeing eyes of God, things are bound to happen. However, there was one guarantee— Amanda wouldn't be there. She would be at a different kind of party. A hoosier party. Where there was lots of booze, drugs, and sex. I was in the middle of mentally picking out who my prey might be at Chuck's party when the phone rang.

"Chris, I'm feeling a little under the weather." Mr. Abernathy's voice was tired and weak. "I've been fighting it all day here at the rink. But I just took my temperature and it's 102. I feel it's just going to get worse." He paused. "I really hate to ask you this at the last minute, but can you run the show tonight?"

Mr. Abernathy had only missed about three nights of work the entire three years I been there. I knew he had to be pretty sick if he was calling and asking to take the night off, especially on New Year's Eve. I was the only one who knew his closing procedures. I was also the only one he trusted to collect and count the money and do the night's receipts.

"Um…I…guess." I couldn't hide the disappointment in my voice. "But would it be OK if I just closed and left without doing the after-hour chores? Chuck's having his New Year's Eve party and I really wanted to go. I can come back first thing in the morning and make sure everything is cleaned and put away."

"That would be fine." Mr. Abernathy almost moaned. "I appreciate it. I'll see you when you get here. Hopefully, a good night's rest will kick whatever's butt is ailing me."

"I'm sure it will." I hung up the phone.

Sometimes it totally sucked being trusted and reliable.

CHAPTER TWENTY-SIX

As a rule, Aloha stayed open thirty minutes after midnight on New Year's Eve. It was just long enough for the hundreds of parents who used the skating rink as their babysitters to come back and pick their children up after their parties were over. Tonight was an unusually wild night. There were two fights, three kids got caught smoking in the restrooms and one boy was busted trying to bring in a bottle of "Boone's Farm Strawberry Hill" in his skates.

I desperately tried to get Amanda out of my mind and much of the time, it worked. However, on the occasions when she did pop into my thoughts, she popped with the fury of an M-80 firecracker. Loud. Disturbing. How many lucky guys would be kissing her when the clock struck midnight? Which one would be winning her trophy after midnight?

I once read in that plethora of sexual knowledge magazine called *Hustler* that New Year's Eve and prom night were the two biggest nights of the year that girls lost their virginity. The article suggested that alcohol consumption among teens were at its highest on those two nights. Everyone knows when you have an increase in alcohol intake you have a decrease in moral judgment.

I tried diverting my attention to something more beneficial. Like motivating my staff to start cleaning up early and clearing out the kids ASAP. By 12:50 a.m. everyone was gone. I was alone. Twenty minutes. That was an Aloha record. I went into the office and called Chuck.

"I'm about five minutes from walking out the door. Is anyone still there?"

"Yeah, there are all kinds of people still here, so hurry up," Chuck yelled over the loud noise in the background.

"I told my mom I'd probably be spending the night because I didn't know how late we'd be staying up. I hope that's cool?"

"You know it is."

"OK, see you in about fifteen minutes," I hung up the phone.

I quickly counted the cash from the night's receipts. It was a lucrative evening. I thought how nice it was that one could be at home as sick as a dog and still make a bank bag full of money. Maybe banking wasn't my best future career option. Owning a roller-skating rink looked pretty profitable.

A flash of headlights suddenly hit the front window and caught my eye. I watched a car pull up to the entrance. A dark hooded figure stepped out and stumbled to the front door and started banging on it.

Bang. Bang. Bang.

My view through the cashier window and the darkness of the lobby blurred the silhouette that looked to be holding something in his hand. Sometimes people forget coats and keys and come back and we let them in to look through the Lost and Found. But tonight, I was by myself. The thought of getting robbed immediately crossed my mind. The banging continued. I tossed the fat bank bag into the safe, shut it, and spun the dial. It was now locked and I didn't have the combination. If I were robbed, he was only going to get some skates, candy, and stale popcorn.

Bang. Bang. Bang.

I picked up Mr. Abernathy's golf putter, turned on the lobby lights and cautiously walked to the door.

"Can I help you?" I asked as I tried to make out what the figure behind the hood looked like.

"Yeah you can ffuckin' let me in." She pulled back the hood covering her face.

"Holy crap, Amanda! Are you OK?"

I immediately opened the door. Amanda stumbled in and waved at the waiting car. It slowly pulled away. Her hair was disheveled and tousled. She smelled like alcohol and sex. There were scratches across her face and her arms were beginning to show signs of bruises.

"I am nnnow that I'm out of the ffuckin cold!" she said. I helped her through the lobby and into the concession area. She was shaking and sobbing.

"What the hell happened?"

"I went to a party and got into a fffight." Her words were drawn out and slurred. She was totally wasted. She sat down at a bench and tossed her *Anne of Green Gables* purse on the table in front of her. "This prick was making me look like a worthless piece of shit. Right in ffront of everybody at the pparty."

She put a cigarette in her mouth and fumbled with the lighter but couldn't get it lit so she took a drag off it anyway then suddenly jumped up off the bench.

"So I ppunched him! Yep, as hard as I could, I ppunched him right in the ffucking eye." She threw her fist in the air, reenacting the punch. Then continued her story in her inebriated slurred speech. "He went fflying backwards over the table against the wall. "BANG!" she yelled. "He hit the wall. And then you know what I said, Christian? I said, Don't mess with me motherffucker. I'm the antagonist your English teacher warned you about." She giggled at her wordplay. "Did you hear that Christian? I said, 'Don't mess with me motherfucker, I'm the antagonist your English teacher warned you about.' I thought that phrase up all by myself. Well not the, 'don't mess with me motherffucker' part, that came spontaneously but the, 'I'm the antagonist your English teacher wwarned you about.' I made that up all by myself and I always said one of these days when I write a book, the eevil bitch antagonist is going to say that to the ggood guy."

She took another hit off her unlit cigarette.

"But I ddidn't have to wait to write a book. I used it tonight." She paused and looked at me with a sign of wanting approval. "But I'm not an evil bbitch. Am I an evil bbitch Christian?"

"No." I helped take her coat off and sat her back down on the bench. She relaxed and laid back and in doing so, her legs fell wide open exposing a full-frontal view of her crotch. There were no ands, ifs, or buts, just all crotch and hers was covered with sheer black lace panties.

"Well right after I said, 'Don't mess with me motherfucker, I'm the antagonist your English teacher wwarned you about.' His evil bbitch girlfriend jumped on my back and we had it out. Christian, I've been in ffights before, but we really had it out. We ffought like guys, punching, scratching and pulling hair. Two girls ffighting and one with a skkirt on. I'm sure I gave them all a good show and it would have gone on all night. They all just sstood there and laughed until his mother heard the commotion and came down and they ppulled us apart."

She put her feet on the bench.

"Can you ssee my panties, Christian?" She spread her legs and raised them into the air and laughed. "Everyone saw Amanda Marrow's panties but you can bet your ssweetaass by the time the story gets out, I won't have any underwear....or a bra...on. But I have a brra and underwear on isn't that rright Christian?" She spread her legs once again and pulled up her shirt to expose her matching black laced bra-covered breasts.

"I told Kimberly who I came with I wanted to leave but ssshe didn't want to leave because Mike Burgmiester was flirting with her and that pissed me off too. Mike Burgmiester may be a great football player but he'zz a prick and can I tell you something Christian," She motioned for me to come closer. "You promise not to tell anyone elze?"

I nodded my head.

"Ssseriously Christian you can't repeat this to anyone...." She grabbed my arm and shook it.

"I promise, it'll be our secret." I held my hand up like I was swearing on the Bible in court.

Amanda's face went blank and I could tell she was gathering her thoughts. She suddenly changed her mind.

"No, I can't tell you Chrissstian..." She shook her head back and forth. "...SSsorry".

"I promise Amanda," I gave her my most trusted look. "I cross my heart, hope to die stick a needle in my eye, I won't tell a soul," I said then smiled.

"Oh, I believe you Christian, I don't think you'd tell anyone, but I can't tell you because I sswore to Mike that I wouldn't tell anyone." She mustered a look of pride. "And if I told you then that would make me an untruztworthy piece of sssshit like him and I'm not like him at all. I personally think he's going to grow up to be an alcoholic, wife-beating, Vagina Hunter." Amanda smirked and assured me. "That's not anything I was supposed to keep secret, it's just my opinion. Yep, Mr. Popppular, Homecoming King, Football star quarterback, that all the girlz want will make one fucked up terrible husband."

Amanda suddenly stopped and stared into the darkness of the skating rink. She was having a conversation or maybe an argument with herself as she recycled the secret she knew about Mike Burgmeister around in her head. She shook her head and with it went the thoughts of Mike Burgmeister.

"Anyway...that douchbagette Kimberly wouldn't give me a ride home so Kyle Bently, you know who he is right? One of thoze nice church going boys like you, offered to take me home. So we got into his car, but I didn't want to go home. I was crazy mad and drunk Christian and I don't like Ssara to see me like that, so I asked if we could stop at Denny's for ssome coffee. He thought that was a good idea but when we drove by here, I saw your car in the parking lot and told him to pull in here." She took one last drag off her unlit cigarette, looked at it funny, then put it back into the package. "And here I am."

"That's just freaking nuts!" I looked at her in both amazement and pity. "Do you want some coffee?" I pointed to the concession stand.

"Oh my God pleazz, with lots of cream and sugar. Thatz how mom put it in my bottle when I was little."

I made a fresh pot of coffee.

"I gotta go to the bathroom!" Amanda announced and got up and stumbled to the restroom. I watched her sway back and forth as she mumbled to herself along the way. When she reached the door, she turned and yelled, "Remember that ffirst night we met and you called me in the middle of the morning and I peed on the pphone?" She burst out laughing, "I mean...I... didn't pee on the actual pphone, I peed while on the pphone and you heard me." She opened the door. "You aren't going to listen to me now, are you Chrisstian?" And without waiting for my response, she went in.

I jumped up and down, threw my hands in the air and did a stupid, sex-starved, eighteen-year-old victory dance. I looked at my watch. 1:07 a.m. I called Chuck and told him about the miracle that just happened. How Amanda Marrow, the Freshman Fire, just dropped out of the heavens and into my lap. OK, maybe not exactly into my lap. But she stumbled into the front door, drunk as a skunk and wearing a short skirt with black lace panties. He gave me a verbal high five and I imagined a universal sign for a blow job. Then he swore I had to give him the full details after we "did the dirty" as he liked to call it. I took out a piece of gum and tossed it in my mouth. I wanted to have fresh breath for my first kiss with my Vagina Trophy.

No. More. Mr. Nice Guy

I went over to the skate counter, leaned against it, and waited. I was about to prove if *Hustler Magazine's* theory was right.

$$NYE+AC^2-MJ=S.$$

Whereas the NYE is New Year Eve, the AC is Alcohol Consumption, MJ is Moral Judgement, and the S is Sex. If so, my hunt was about over. The capture was about to take place. As drunk as she was, it was going to be a breeze, like hunting a deer in the zoo. I almost felt a little guilty. So I imagined her spreading her legs and seeing her sexy black lace panties. Guilt. Poof. Gone. I looked at my watch once more. 1:15 a.m. Seven minutes to take a pee?

I got an idea. Why wait for her to come out of the bathroom? She had already more or less peed in front of me on the phone. Maybe she needed help wiping or pulling up her panties. One might as well find out. I walked over and stuck my head in the door of the lady's bathroom.

"Amanda, you OK?' I called into the room. There was no answer, so I stepped in.

A stall door was open. Inside, Amanda was on her knees heaving and vomiting her guts out. She didn't hear me come in. I could see her skirt was pulled up around her waist and her panties were partly pulled down. Leaving me with a birds-eye view of her bare, beautiful, ass each time she bent over to puke. Never before in life had I seen anything so pathetically sad, yet so breathtakingly gorgeous. And had she not been puking her brains out, my spear would have been at full attack mode. However, she was puking and crying and a part of me, the goddamned Mr. Nice Guy who I didn't want to be, wanted to go over, pull her skirt down, and help hold her hair back. Like best girlfriends do in books and movies and all. But I wasn't sure if that would help or only embarrass her. I quietly closed the door and went back to the concession stand and waited.

The angel on my right shoulder and the devil on my left were warring with one another like it was the apocalyptic end-times. And to be totally honest, the devil was winning by a wide margin. I had played my hand as Mr. Nice Guy and it got me nowhere. That was all about to change.

I took my pack of gum and held it in my hand. I didn't want to kiss a girl right after she vomited. There are certain lines stupid, sex-starved, eighteen-year-olds won't cross. After an uncomfortable five more minutes of moral tug of war, she came out. She faked a smile and stumbled back to the concession area, sat down in the booth, and put her head on the table.

"What a great ffucking way to start out 1981, eh Christian?"

"Well, the night's not over yet." I gave her a smile that looked friendly but reeked of seduction. "Let me get you that coffee..." I paused. "...the kind with lots of milk and sugar, like your mom used to put in your bottle when you were a baby."

She picked up her head and said with a surprised look. "How did you know that?"

"You and Lucy told me at Steak 'n Shake on your birthday when I took you to the DMV to get your driver's license, remember?" I went to the counter and poured her a cup of coffee.

"Oh yeah, thaz right." Her head slid back down to the table. "That was one of the nicest thingz anyone has ever done for me," she paused. "without wanting some puuussssy in return." She looked up again. "Opps, I just said the ppeee word? I hope I didn't embarrass the birthday boy." She giggled and then shut her eyes.

Well, if you treat everyone who does nice things for you like you treated me, it's no wonder we all act like Vagina Hunters towards you. I looked at my watch. How much time did I have to hunt this Vagina?

I sat the cup of coffee in front of her and placed my pack of gum next to it. That should help kill any nasty vomiting tastes.

She raised her head and took a long, slow sip of coffee. "Yum... thaz one good hot, milky, toffee, thingy drink." She licked her lips. We both smiled.

"What time do you have to be home?" I asked.

"I don't want to go home Christian. I already told Lucy and Sara I'd be spending the night at Kimberly's house. I don't want Ssara to see her big sister wasted and beat up. I don't want to go home." She looked around the room. "Can I spend the night here? I'll find some place to crash in the corner." Then she got another idea. A sinister and seductive look suddenly took over her demeanor.

"Why don't you sspend the night with me Christian? Just you and me. We'll have a good'ol time here tonight all by ourselves." She spread her legs and looked at me as I imagined David looked at Bathsheba as he watched her bathing on the top of the building. "I'm all yourz tonight Christian Hayz."

"That sounds totally awesome!" I almost shouted as I reached over and took out a piece of gum and offered it to her.

She took it and put it in her mouth. "Thankz," she slurred.

No. Thank. You. The hardest part of the hunt had just been won.

"I'll be right back." I winked and went into the office and called Chuck once more. I told him part two of God's miracle was about to take place and asked him to cover for me if my parents asked if I spent the night. Amanda and I were about to "do the dirty" all night long at Aloha. He assured me he would. I once again vowed to give him all the delicious details in the morning.

I went to the Lost and Found and gathered all the sweaters and coats and spread them all over the floor behind the skate counter and made a comfy make-shift bed. I went to the stereo and found the "couple's skate music" cassette tape and popped it in and pushed the play button. Then I turned off all the lights except for a rotating colored wheel. This was going to be my night with Amanda Marrow. I walked back to the concession area. Her hands were supporting her head up in almost a brace-like manner and her eyes were closed. She still hadn't finished her coffee, so I picked up her cup and held out my other hand. "Your bed awaits, my Queen."

She opened her eyes and took my hand. "Why Christian you sly fox you. Romantic muzic, dimmed lights, don't let that name fool ya girlz, he's a Vagina Hunter." She put her arm around my waist and we stumbled to the skate counter. She suddenly stopped.

"Can I smoke a cigarette before we do this?" Her eyes begged. "I really need a cigarette."

"Nope, sorry." I continued to guide her towards my make-shift Vagina Hunter's Lair.

"Then put some poison antifreezzz in that coffee so that I can forget all my regrets tonight." She laughed and fell into the bed of parkas and long forgotten shirts and sweaters."

All. My. Regrets.

Like Dick Clark's New Year's Eve ball that falls in Times Square, the three words crashed into my skull.

I sat her coffee on the bottom shelf and fluffed the faux fur jacket beneath her head.

"You don't have to worry about getting me pregnant or anything Christian. I'm on the pill. I've been on it since I was Ssara's age."

"Ssshhhhh" I put my fingers to her lips and laid down next to her.

What were all her regrets and why has she been on the pill since she was thirteen? The thought of Ruth having sex with a boy was unfathomable.

I began slowly running my fingers through her hair. She shut her eyes. I could feel her body relax heavy against mine.

"That feels really good Christian. You are a master of sseduction aren't you?" I continued to run my fingers over her head and then down her neck and around her warm cheeks still red with scratches. I gently stroked her shut eyelids and ran the back of my hand softly over her lips. And then I repeated the entire process. Over and over. She let out a tender sigh.

All. My. Regrets.

"I got you figured out Christian, you're like one of thoz girls who act all goody goody around everyone but the moment you get them in bed...or behind skate counters," she laughed. "They're the wildest and craziest fuckz in the world."

She spread her legs once again showing me her black lace panties but this time she wasn't laughing.

"I'm not like that Christian. What you see is what you get. I'm a wild and crazy fuck on the streetz and in the sheetz," she chuckled at her world play. Then she got a puzzled look as she ran her fingers across my cheeks. "Why don't you have a girlfriend Christian? You're a good looking, nize guy."

"I guess I just have too high standards."

"You need to find yourself a good little Christian girl." Her hand moved from my face down my chest to my manhood. She started caressing it. I reached over and moved it away.

"Oh, playing hard to get... excuz the pun." She burst out in loud laughter. "Get it, hard to get? That's good Christian. Girlz like boys who are hard to get."

We lay in the darkness with the red, blue and green lights passing over our heads reflecting off the metal skate rack above. Listening to the music. Caressing. Comforting.

The song *My Tiny Treasure* began playing over the speakers.

"You like this song?" I asked.

"I absolutely love this song," she replied.

"Have you ever listened to the words?"

"I'm a logossist, Christian, I listen to the wordz of every song."

As the lyrics of the lullaby filled the air, she began singing along...

I watch you
as you sleep
my tiny treasure
and wonder if
you'll ever know

you're more precious
then the air I breathe
Rarer than a million
Michelangelos

I consecrate the day
You were born
wept when I held
you in my hands

oh my tiny, tiny treasure
we are atoms

intertwined will
you ever understand

"Consecrate. Thaz such a beautiful word. You should know what that means, Christian?"

"It means to make something sacred or holy." I've heard it in church many times. Reverend Monty consecrates the little white wafers and grape juice when we take the Lord's Supper.

I would fight an army
of immortal foes
and sacrifice my
eternal soul to hell

and should you
ask for the moon
in heaven
I would give it
To you as well

"You fought the fires of hell in my dreamz, Sir Hayz." She looked me in the eyes and for a brief moment I saw the creation of one of her beautiful epiphanies. It was magical. "Did they write this song about uz, Christian? Because if you say they did, I'm going to start crying right now. And I haven't cried since I was six yearz old when I threw my Partridge Family lunch box at my fffuckin father."

I looked past her troubled past and into her soul as I ran my fingers slowly across her temples, over her forehead, around her eyes and down to her mouth. I caressed her messy hair that smelled of smoke and sin and rocked her back and forth until she shut her eyes and sank closer to my heart. Physically. Emotionally. Then I continued to stroke the one part of her body that no boy's hand had ever touched. The part that needed it the most. Her mind.

All. My. Regrets.

"Yes, Amanda Marrow, they wrote this song about us" And then I began softly whispering the words into her ear...

I consecrate the day
you were born
wept when I held
you in my hands

oh my tiny, tiny treasure
we are atoms
intertwined will
you ever understand

Amanda rolled over and gently kissed me on the cheek and buried her face into my chest and started crying. I didn't know why she was crying. I was eighteen and stupid. I didn't know whether they were tears of sadness, happiness, or regret. I didn't know if she would even remember that she was crying come morning. I just let her cry, imagining maybe those tears were her inner child. The one she never knew. Five minutes later she was asleep.

slumber soundly
mon petit trésor
cradled in my
arms and God's
nocturnal shrine

I will rock you
gently til morn'
and love you
until the sun
runs out of shine

CHAPTER TWENTY-SEVEN

Morning.

There was a loud slam and when I opened my eyes, Mr. Abernathy was standing over us. He was pissed. I threw the parka blanket off us and jumped to attention. The clock over the concession counter said 7:47 a.m.

"Come with me, young man." He gave me a stifled look, turned and walked towards the office. I followed. As we walked through the concession area, he pointed. "Coffee maker wasn't turned off. Lights and music were left on all night. Heat wasn't turned down...."

"I'm really sorry Mr. Abernathy." I paused. "I take it you're feeling better this morning?" I tried showing some concern for him even if it appeared I hadn't shown any for his roller skating rink. His reply was a look of pure accusation. "I swear we didn't do anything but sleep on the floor." I motioned towards Amanda who was now on her feet gathering up the coats and sweaters. "She partied a little too much and got in a fight and didn't want to go home. She asked if she could spend the night here because she didn't want to get into trouble at home and I didn't want to leave her alone."

Ok, it wasn't because she would have gotten in trouble at home, it was because she didn't want her little sister to see that she was wasted and beat up, but that was too long and difficult to explain, so I lied. Forgive me, Lord. I had just acted like a perfect saint the entire evening; I was allowed one little white lie.

When we got into the office, he shut the door behind us. "I didn't think it would hurt anything." I continued. "As I said sir, we didn't do anything. I swear to God." Mr. Abernathy shot me one final, Please don't swear to God, glare. "If you want to dock my pay for leaving on the coffee and lights and things, I'd have no problem with that."

"What would your parents say, Chris?"

"They'd have a conniption fit and kill me, sir," I said as I bowed my head and stared at the floor. "Probably ground me until I went away to college."

Mr. Abernathy opened the safe and took out the fat bank bag I had set in there hours previously. His building had been violated now he wanted to make sure his revenue hadn't. Hopefully, the busy night and fat bank bag would have a positive impact on his attitude of an ugly situation.

"I don't appreciate my skating rink being used as a cheap hotel."

"I know that sir and it wasn't." I looked him straight in the eyes. "You might say it was more of a sanctuary." If he only knew how true those words had rung.

"She's a pretty girl, Chris," he frowned. "But your mom wouldn't want you to hang around a girl like that. I've seen her around here. She's always leaving with guys and going to smoke and do other things in the parking lot. She dresses like a streetwalker and has a mouth like a sailor. She's just bad news, son."

I stood there not knowing how to respond to his true statement.

"You smell like smoke and if you keep hanging around her, more than the smell of her smoke will rub off on you. Do you understand what I'm saying?"

I nodded.

"Did you tell your parents you spent the night here with her?"

"No."

"So you lied to them?" He furrowed his face. "See, she's rubbing off on you already."

"Well sir, I haven't told them anything yet. But in all fairness, she's a lot different than the rumors you hear about her. And..." I played the God hand. "...didn't Jesus befriend the adulteress?"

"You aren't Jesus!" Mr. Abernathy shouted. "You are a teenage boy and she's a beautiful teenage *hoosier* girl. Those two combinations don't equal salvation. They equal sin. I know, Chris, I was a teenager too." He walked over to his desk, moved some papers around until he found what he was looking for. "I suppose you're the one who dropped this." He handed me Amanda's school picture.

"Yes, sir." I took it and slid it in my back pocket.

"Now go turn off the coffee maker, clean out the pot and take that young..." He paused for the best words. "...so-called lady home and don't ever do anything like that again." He unzipped the fat bag of money and began taking it out and stacking it on his desk. "You're a great kid, and you've been a wonderful employee, Chris, and for that, I will give you this one error of judgment. I hope you learn from it and don't repeat it."

"Thank you so much, sir, I will...I mean, I won't...I mean...I'll learn from it and not repeat it."

"Don't worry about me saying anything to your parents," Mr. Abernathy's voice softened. "As I said, I was a teenager too." He looked me directly in the eyes. "However, if they ask me anything, don't expect me to lie to them for you. Because I will not do that."

"Yes, sir." He began counting the money as if to say, "You're dismissed."

I walked out of the office. Amanda had turned off the coffee maker and cleaned the pot. I turned off the music system and lights and together we put the coats, shirts, and sweaters back into the Lost and Found. We left quietly without saying goodbye to Mr. Abernathy. It wasn't until we pulled out of the parking lot when Amanda broke the silence.

"Are you in big trouble?"

"Thank God, not yet." I sighed. "He promised not to say anything to my parents. I told them that I was spending the night at Chuck's house. I was supposed to go there after work for his New Year's Eve party, but then you kind of interrupted that game plan. So I called him and told him what happened and I asked him to cover for me. Now let's pray his parents don't talk to my parents."

"I'm sorry, Chris." It was daylight and she was sober. I had gone from Christian to just Chris.

"I feel like shit." Amanda opened her purse and took out a box of breath mints and tossed one in her mouth then offered one to me. "You want a piece of candy little boy?"

I held my hand out and she dropped one in it. She took out her bottle of Heaven Scent and squirted it on her to hide the previous evening's sinful scent of alcohol, cigarettes, vomit, sweat, and sex. None of which involved me.

"To tell you the truth, you look like shit," I said with a brave smile.

But even at your worst, you are the best my eyes have ever beheld.

"I know. God, I went into the bathroom. I looked like a whore on dollar day. But that's not what I meant when I said I feel like shit. I meant I feel like shit because I don't want to get you in trouble." She turned the rear-view mirror towards her and powdered her face and fixed her hair.

"Well, I guess we'll just have to pray and see what happens." But I knew that asking God to cover-up your deceptive lies was like asking the same God to nourish your body before you sat down to a meal of greasy fried chicken and French fries—*She* didn't appreciate those kinds of prayers.

"So how much of last night do you remember?" I wondered out loud.

"I pretty much remember a lot of it but in a foggy, surreal kind of way. You know, like when they show someone dreaming in a movie. How it's all clear in the middle of the screen but fuzzy around the edges. I remember going to this party and getting really drunk because Mike Hamilton kept giving me shots of tequila. I remember Tony asking me if I wanted to get high, but I don't do that stuff because it's illegal."

Like drinking shots at sixteen isn't illegal?

She got slightly embarrassed then immediately angry. "I remember that asshole, Dirk something, being a prick to me and then punching him in his face."

"Dirk...Howard?" I looked surprised. "How was he a prick to you?"

"Don't worry about it." And by telling me not to worry about it, I immediately started worrying about it. I knew Dirk Howard. He used to be a nice guy. Matter of fact, we were in the same Boy Scout troop growing up. But then his mother got cancer and died three months later. Dirk got angry at God and went from an exemplary Boy Scout to an exemplary juvenile delinquent; drinking, smoking, shoplifting, skipping school and getting into fights. My dad still talks to his dad on occasion. Mr. Howard said when his wife died, it was like he lost his son too.

I remember saying "I'm the antagonist your English teacher warned you about." She chuckled at her wordplay. "Did I tell you that I said that to him?"

"Yes, and how you made that line up and you were going to put it in one of the books that you write."

"Yeah, I am," she said confidently as if it was a great piece of literary art or a famous quote that someone would have tattooed on their arm or inner thigh.

"But it all starts to become discombobulated and fuzzy after he fell backward over the table. I know I got into a fight with Dirk's douchbagette girlfriend, Gina, and kicking her ass. Then Kimberly telling me she didn't want to go home because Mike Burgmeister was flirting with her. Bitch. Then, someone, I don't remember who, drove me to Aloha. I remember throwing up and you giving me some coffee before you threw me to the ground behind the skate counter and rapaciously raped me."

"I…WHAT?" I looked at her in shock which caused her to burst out laughing.

"I'm just kidding." She gave me a friendly punch in the arm. "I remember it was Kyle that drove me there." She continued to laugh.

I shook my head and rolled my eyes. "Don't even joke around about that." My words were stern and strict. "You should be the first to know how rumors get spread around."

"I'm sorry, Chris. You're absolutely right." It was her turn to become serious. "You were a perfect gentleman last night. You did something I don't think any other guy at Hazelwood East would have done." Her voice was now soft and her stare was appreciative. "You did nothing."

We drove in silence as we reflected on what did and didn't happen last night. She did try to entice me into having sex with her. I didn't do it. Did she remember opening her legs and giving me approval to hunt her Vagina?

And did I refuse because I was really a Mr. Nice Guy or because it wasn't really hunting? Hunting requires an unwilling animal who

runs, hides and fears for their life. One can
never hunt, that which lays down before you
and says take me. That is called either a
sacrifice, as in the case of Christ. Or in her
case, a regret.

We turned down her street and pulled into her driveway. She leaned
over and kissed me. A long, wet kiss on the lips. I wasn't expecting it,
so I just sat there frozen with fish lips. Cold. Puckered. By the time I
was able to react, it was over.

She pushed the rearview mirror back and opened the car door.
"Thanks a lot," she said as she got out. She turned around and looked
me in the eye. "I appreciate everything you did...and didn't do." She
started to shut the door before I reminded her.

"Please make sure you tell Sara not to tell Ruth I dropped you off.
We don't want our secret getting out."

CHAPTER TWENTY-EIGHT

Our little secret didn't get out. It remained locked deep within my soul to ferment with the hops and barley of emotions that slowly brewed into an intoxicating addiction. Mr. Abernathy was true to his word and never said anything to my parents. My parents never said anything to me. My purely platonic naughty-less night with Amanda Marrow was now a just a memory that required no immoral guilt or confession. There was also no residual embarrassment that often plaques two hormonally charged teenagers that come crashing together in a bittersweet situation. It was a nice feeling. No, it was better than a nice feeling. It was a normal feeling. The kind of normality I had known prior to my eighteenth birthday. For the first few days of the new year, I was caught up and swept away by this fresh and free feeling.

Then suddenly, without notice or warning, an emotional earthquake rumbled all the normality out of me. It was a new semester, which meant new classes. I walked into my third-hour Current Events class and there was Dirk Howard slumped in his seat with his feet on the back of the chair in front of him. His wrestling jacket was bunched into a ball behind his shoulders making him look almost hunchback. His smug, bully smile hung on his face like a jailer's key to an inmate.

Just the sight of him set me teetering between two slopes. On one side was pure hatred and on the other side was impure hatred. The difference between each being those two letters I and M which secretly symbolized, I'M now part of his miserable world. He wasn't aware that our lives were once again going to be intertwined, but he would soon find out. A nauseating feeling set about my stomach as I found a desk as far as I could away from him. The only pleasure to that miserable morning was witnessing the black eye he was sporting like a badge of honor inflicted by his antagonist and my courageous little nymphet.

"What the hell happened to you?" Someone yelled from across the room. Everyone turned to look at Dirk who moved his head proudly to the side so everyone could see the damage done to his face. Mr. Cortez, our teacher, hadn't come into the room yet.

"That freshman slut, Amanda Marrow, nigger-punched me at a New Year's Eve party." Dirk tossed a daring glance to the two black guys sitting together in the back of the room. His prick reputation and "I dare you to say something" stare was enough to smolder any rebuttal from them.

Everyone knew there had to be more to the story. Few people liked Dirk Howard anymore. He was a cocky, smartass, trouble magnet. He was an average wrestler on the wrestling team who liked to use his skills as a weapon to intimidate those would let themselves be intimidated. Other wrestlers, the really good ones, the state finalists like Tim Joplin and Johnny Barker, didn't have to prove to anyone they were bad assess. Their wrestling stats, trophies and patches said it all. But guys like Dirk Howard wore the wrestling jacket as an excuse to start shit and try to prove they were tough. One time he and his buddies started some trouble with one of the rink guards at Aloha and Mr. Abernathy had to kick them out. I was off that night, but I heard all about it. The next Monday Dirk caught me at school.

"Tell your guard buddies that I ain't scared of them." He stopped me in the hall and threatened.

"I'm sure they are not scared of you either," I pleasantly said correcting his bad grammar.

Up until New Year's Eve, I had no ill-will towards Dirk Howard. On the contrary, I felt sorry for him. I knew the source of his Dr. Jekyll/Mr. Hyde personality was watching his mother die of cancer. As much as my mother and I disagreed on things and her religious righteousness seeped out of her pours and dripped on me like acidic rain, I would never want to watch her, or anyone I loved, slowly die of cancer. It had to have a harrowing and psychologically debilitating effect on an only son. Therefore, I understood his brash and bully behavior and even made excuses and forgiveness for it.

But now Amanda was part of the picture. My hidden feelings for her overpowered any pity I had for Dirk. In the short time I had known Amanda and attempted to read her untold story, I knew no matter how many adjectives you added to her tattered and tarnished reputation, violence and aggression weren't two of them. They weren't part of my personality either but as I sat there staring at the asshole across the room and listening to his words my palms began to sweat.

I could feel the demon that usually danced on my left shoulder dive into my heart and stoke to life the embers of violence and aggression. Dirk had no idea I was the one Amanda came stumbling to that violent, yet blissful, evening. I was one who wrapped my arms around her and held her. I wiped her tears away and caressed her beat up body and abused mind to sleep.

Amanda was tight-lipped with the details of her altercation that night but now it looked as if Dirk were about to unravel the story for the entire school to hear. Of course, this was Dirk's side of the story and one had to wonder how much truth, if any, was mixed into the plot. One also had to wonder exactly what it took to offend a sexually wild girl like Amanda, who, by her own confession said she didn't ever get embarrassed. What would make her snap as she did?

"So Dirk, Amanda just randomly punched you, unprovoked?" My words accused him of more.

Did you try and Vagina Hunt her behind your girlfriend's back and she rejected you? Or perhaps, you were one of her Vagina Conquerors and this was some kind of remorseful battle that each of you waged on one another. Oh, please don't tell me she slept with you because that would surely sour my desire for her.

"Yeah, pretty much." Dirk shrugged his shoulders. "She punched me because she farted." Dirk's face got a disgusted, animated look on it. "She walked by and farted right next to me. It was bad too, like lima beans and bratwurst." The class laughed. "I called her on it and she denied it and got all psycho and started yelling at me to take it back. I told her to fuck off and the bitch just punched me." He motioned his fist towards his eye and jerked his head back.

"That's when my girlfriend jumped on her and started beating her ass. It was crazy." Dirk shook his head and flung his arms wildly about. "The best part was watching Amanda because she didn't have any panties on under her skirt!" He smiled big and bobbed his eyebrows up and down at all the boys in the room.

"That's a lie!" I screamed from across the room. Dirk jerked his head my way.

"It is not." Dirk sneered and tried to give me his bully look, but I had known Dirk for too many years for it to have any effect on me.

"It is too!" I tried to remain calmly in my chair. "I saw her right afterward at Aloha and I know for a fact she had panties and a bra on." I meant to say it like an attorney who had undeniable evidence and was pleading his case before a trial of his student peers, but the words came out like I was a Vagina Hunter bragging about my conquest. Dirk and everyone in the room turned a surprised stare in my direction.

"Well, whatta know, Christian Hayes—the Eagle Boy Scout—is dipping his walking stick into the well-charted waters of Amanda Marrow." Dirk clapped his hands to congratulate me while others snickered and whispered to one another. I could feel my face flush with anger. A host of heavenly angels could not restrain me from the verbal ass-kicking that I was about to unleash. I jumped up from my chair.

"I didn't touch her, you lying...."

Just then Mr. Cortez came into the room. He must have seen my red face and the rage in my eyes because he quickly walked in front of me and put his hand on my shoulder.

"Everything OK, son?" he asked and looked around to see what the cause of my angered state could be. Everyone, including Dirk Howard, seemed to be in a normal, pre-class state of mind. I took a deep breath and nodded my head yes then sat down and relaxed back into my seat giving Dirk Howard one more "fuck you" look before Mr. Cortez instructed us to take out our books.

The next fifty minutes passed and I'm sure there were valuable lessons to be learned about what was happening in the current affairs of our world, but the current affairs of my mental lobes were steaming and scheming.

Are you prepared to fight for her? Is she worth a potential ass-kicking and being sent to the office and having to explain it all to mom and dad? Am I to believe that Amanda punched him because he accused her of farting? That's ridiculous. Why would that upset someone, especially a hoosier someone, to the point of violence?

Breathe Christian, just breathe and when the bell rings leave.

The dismissal bell rang and I left. I didn't want to look at anyone and I didn't want anyone to look at me. I just got out of my chair and headed to the door praying that Dirk, nor anyone else for that matter, said a word to me. No one did.

I immediately hunted Amanda down to tell her what had just transpired. Unsurprisingly, I found her in the student smoking area; a covered patio just outside of the shop classes. I had never stepped foot there before. I felt like a butterfly in a beekeeper's hive with all the smoke in my face and my brain still abuzz. Amanda got a surprised smile on her face as I walked up to her.

"Got a second?" I leaned over and whispered in her ear.

She nodded to her court of mostly males standing around her and then stepped away with me.

"Guess who's in my Current Affairs class?" I asked.

"Dirk Howard," she said. The flabbergasted look in my face made her laugh. "Yeah, I heard all about it."

"How could you hear all about it? The class just let out five minutes ago and I walked straight from there to here."

"Oh..." Amanda slowly waved her hand in the air like a witch casting a spell, "I have ears and eyes all over the school."

No, it's more like the school has ears and eyes all over you.

"Well?"

"Well, what?" she replied.

"He's telling everyone you punched him because he said you farted by him." The words pierced her spirit and she tried to hide her angered embarrassment, but her eyes went briefly wild.

"It's true." She took a frustrated and hard drag of her cigarette.

"You punched him because you farted by him?"

"No! I punched him because I DIDN'T fart by him, but he was making it look like I did." She looked away and I watched her bottom lip curl tight against her teeth. She began nervously nibbling on it. "I may have a mouth like a sailor and a reputation of a slut, but flatulating...," she said the word as if it stunk coming out of her mouth. "...in public, is something I absolutely don't do. Sober or drunk. It's against my moral fiber."

Oh. My. God. You'll fuck a guy's brains out and let every vulgar vernacular spill out of the orifice on your face but farting in public is against your moral fiber? How messed up is that?

"I know what you're thinking Christian Hayes. You're thinking I'm lying and there has to be more to the story." She tossed me a slight smirk. "I'm starting to read you like a book." She dropped her cigarette on the concrete ground and stepped on it. We both watched it smolder and die. Then her stormy amber eyes moved up and looked at me. "But the fact is, I'm not lying." She paused and her voice got snippety. "And yes, there is more to the story but it's not a story about Dirk Howard. Or you. Or anyone else in this school. It's my story." She tapped her forehead with her finger. "And that story remains here until I decide when, or even if, I tell it."

We both stared at one another. She, in a state of tug, and me in a state of war. It lasted a mere few seconds but in reality, it was a lifetime. Her lifetime. Hidden. Repressed.

What do I have to do to get you to tell me your story, Amanda Marrow? Can't you see I'm crushing on you? Crushing in the sense that I'm standing at the tip of the pit of love. I'm tossing stones of kindness down into the darkness, trying to determine its depth and discovering it's a lot deeper than I thought it was. Do I dare dive in not knowing if there's a well of water to save me or a heart of stone that will kill me?

For the first time since she skated into my life, it slowly began to make sense. Her past was filled with wounds and she used her gorgeous self and beautiful words as a wall to hide those ugly memories. It was going to take more than just a few fucks or several acts of kindness to penetrate the fortress she had built around her heart. I slowly nodded my head. I didn't realize I was nodding my head, it was an outward manifestation of an inner realization, but Amanda picked up on it because, after all, she was beginning to read me like a book.

"Is there something you have to say?" she asked.

"Yeah," I smiled. "I just had an epiphany" Then, without a care in the world of whose eyes were upon us or what scandalous lies would sling around the school, I leaned over and kissed her on her forehead.

"Craziness is contagious," I said and turned and walked away.

And because I was now starting to read her, I could tell she wasn't mad or embarrassed or that it had any effect on her at all.

"I appreciate you attempting to stand up for me, Sir Vodka Watermelon White Knight." She yelled as I walked away. "And telling everyone I had panties and a bra on!" Her words were loud and echoed with a tone of true appreciation as they flew over the clutter and clatter of all the kids slowly killing themselves with cancer sticks. Some of the students even looked at her and laughed.

CHAPTER TWENTY-NINE

January started off blustery and cold with scattered clouds of conflict between Dirk and me, but I was slowly warming up to the Freshman Fire.

"Did you know that January is named after Janus, the Roman god of new beginnings and transitions?" Amanda enlightened me at my locker before first hour. "The Latin word for door is ianua since January is the door to the year." Her words radiated with excitement.

"And you're telling me this why?"

"Well, Christian Hayes. I just added the word ianua to my word collection and I thought I would share that with you."

"That's awesome," I said in a tone to match her excitement. Which made her even more excited because I was excited that she was excited. She looked in my status quo, clean, and organized locker. "By the way, when are you going to hang my picture on your locker "ianua?" She asked pointing to the inside of my locker door.

"When you open this "ianua" to me." I pointed to her chest.

"Are you referring to my shirt or my chest?" She smiled. We both knew the first ianua led to her tits and the other one led to her heart.

"Yes," I said. Leaving it at that.

Whether she knew it or not, Amanda was slowly opening her "ianua" to me. The fact that she shared her beautiful new word with me was proof. It wasn't like we were now the best buddies in the world, but there was a definite budding of something between us.

It wasn't a rose relationship with deep hues of caring and love. Nor was it of the timid and shy tulip type. I would say it was more like a sunflower relationship. Glorious golden petals surrounding a dark center.

Janus, the god of new beginnings, had moved me from being an outsider, into a regular attendee of her queen's court. Life around the Haye's dysfunctional functional house and Hazelwood East was a little easier.

And yet, as honored as I felt, when all was said and done at the end of the school day, it wasn't enough. I wanted more. I wanted what my little sister had with her little sister—best buddy status. Sara and Ruth constantly talked on the phone.

Through laughs and whispers, they plotted, played and planned. Amanda and I, on the other hand, didn't call one another. We only conversed between classes and at lunch. We often laughed, but rarely did we ever whisper. It was the whispering that I wanted. The middle of the night telephone tete-a-tetes spent whispering beneath the blankets. We spent more time together, but it wasn't quality time. Quality time is in whispering and whispering is when two people really get to know one another.

Sara had even come over to our house on several occasions to hang out with Ruth. Mom and dad thought she was a very nice little girl but...

"She eats with her mouth open." I heard mom telling her friend after church. "And they have a bed sheet over one of their front windows!" They both looked at one another shocked and appalled as if mom had announced that the Marrow girls had one of the Old Testament plagues.

"If there was one sign that the people inside the house were hoosiers, it was sheets, blankets or newspapers over a window. You never see that in a decent neighborhood." Mom would say each time we drove down a street and witnessed one.

Yes, to the utter jubilation of Ruth, mom had given her pious approval that Sara could come over to our house. But when it came time for Ruth to visit Sara, that's where the goodness of her heart ran out. Mom would not allow it. Ruth begged to know why.

"Because her mom is never home and there is no one to supervise you two." Then mom added. "And Sara smells like an ashtray every time she comes over. I can't image what that house smells like and I don't want my daughter to smell like a nasty old ashtray."

Even though mom saw blatant examples of hoosier-ism running through Sara's personality veins, she wasn't ready to write her off as a lost soul just yet. Sara was bright, personable and young. The perfect candidate for recruitment into our cult called Christianity.

Mom and dad were now taking turns shuttling Ruth back and forth to our house, but they still had not met Amanda yet. This, I felt, was a good thing. I really wanted to make sure I was there to witness the event. Something told me there needed to be some kind of spiritual buoy between mom and Amanda. A religious referee you might say.

"Looks like Sara is going to spend the night over at your house tomorrow night." Amanda surprised me with the news as we set down to lunch that Friday. "She's beside herself with bliss. It's her birthday so they're meeting at the mall tomorrow afternoon and then they're going back to your house." Amanda picked up one of my celery sticks and pretended to smoke it.

"Why don't you spend the night too?" I said. In the wake of our new budding relationship, I was finding a greater boldness to feed that inner fire of desire by flirting.

"In your dreams...." She bit the celery stick and began chewing it with her mouth open and lips smacking.

Funny how, with enough alcohol, you're ready to spread your legs and show me your world but once the buzz and bruises are gone and life goes back to normal the possibility is merely "in my dreams".

Saturday morning came and mom assigned me to pick the girls up from the mall and bring them home. A task I gladly accepted because I knew Amanda was working.

I walked into Waldenbooks. There was an older man in a tweed jacket with suede elbow patches leaning against the magazine rack reading *Architectural Digest*. I secretly watched him as he secretly watched Amanda sitting behind the counter lost in her world of reading. She was conservatively dressed in pleated tan pants with a pink Polo shirt that had its collar popped up. She was wearing glasses and had her hair pulled tightly into a bun. She was your perfect oxymoron poster librarian girl. Nerdy. Beautiful. Sexy. Studious.

"Whatcha doing?" I said.

She jumped. "Oh, hey Chris...just sitting here reading." She looked up at the clock. "I'm off in about five minutes." I looked at the book in her hands. *Kane and Abel* by Jeffrey Archer.

"I didn't know you were into religious books."

She laughed. "It's not a religious book. It's a best seller. One of my favorite customers said it was a must read. It's a rag to riches story about a wealthy American banker named Kane and a poor Polish immigrant named Abel. I'm only about six chapters into it and I can't put it down. I love rags to riches stories. They really inspire me." She closed the book and walked over to a bookcase at the front of the store. The man in the tweed jacket watched her every move over the top of his *Architectural Digest* magazine. "That's the great thing about working at a bookstore. You get to read books for free and then you can just put them right back onto the shelves," she said placing the book back on the shelf.

"I didn't know you wore glasses?" I nodded towards the unfamiliar face accessory at the end of her nose.

"I don't. They're fake." She pushed them back to the top of her nose. "But I think they make me look sexy and intellectual. What do you think?"

I shrugged my shoulders.

You're asking a bias person that question. Amanda Marrow, the Freshman Fire. I think you'd look sexy in sackcloth and ashes.

"I have to do something to look sexy since I have to dress like a fucking homogeneous librarian." She motioned to her outfit as she curled her lips in fashion torment and took a look at herself in the reflection of the store's front glass. "You should see the way all the nerdy old Vagina Hunters come in here and look at me." She glanced over at the *Architectural Digest* guy who immediately raised the magazine to hide his stare. She rolled her eyes and smiled. "Like I'd be a goddamn prize trophy to hang over the fireplace. I love it."

Why is it always about looking sexy when it comes to you, Amanda?

"Why's it always about looking sexy?" I bravely asked.

"Because it pleases me," she said without hesitation. "And a girl is all about pleasure. Matter of fact, I had an epiphany the other day that everything we do in life is to make us feel better. Every choice we make and every action we take from the womb to the tomb is merely to please us."

"That's crazy. Everything we do isn't meant to please us. I don't go to school every day because it pleases me. I go because I have to go."

"No, you don't *have* to go," she insisted. "You can stay home and watch TV all day. But it pleases you more to please your parents and school officials by going than it pleases you by not going. Two choices or options but one is the worst of two evils."

"I go to school because I don't want to feel the wrath of my parents" And then I added. "Or be a loser drop out."

"So, there you have it. It basically pleases you more to go to school then enduring your parent's punishment or the thought of being a loser." The *Architectural Digest* man left leaving the magazine on the best seller table. Amanda picked it up and put it back on the rack. "So the truth is, it pleases you to go to school."

I thought of other examples. "What about soldiers who have to go to war and die? Or mothers who sacrifice their lives for their children? Where's the pleasure in that?"

"As I said, nobody ever has to do anything. They choose one option over another but the fact that they're choosing the one gives them a slightly greater sense of pleasure. Even if the two options are horrific like war and even suicide. Does that make sense?" She walked back to the counter. "Everyone who commits suicide finds more pleasure in killing themselves then staying alive." She added a dramatic tone. "Thus, the thought of death is more pleasing to them than facing the cold, cruel world."

I shook my head. "No, that doesn't make sense. We do things all the time that we don't want to and it doesn't give us pleasure."

"No, we don't." She got more determined in the argument. "Why do you wash your hair, brush your teeth, take a shower or wear what you are wearing?" Amanda asked. "You don't have to; you do it because it pleases you?"

"No, I do it because I want to look nice and decent. I don't want to look a *hoosier*." The word came out of my lips and fell flat in the conversation in an embarrassing stumble. As the word "amputee" would awkwardly sound while talking to a man with one arm.

"A what?" Amanda inquisitively furrowed her brow.

I hesitated and repeated softly. "A hoosier."

"Hoosier? I have never heard that word before." The thought of her stumbling upon a new word in a conversation at the mall with one of her male peers made her eyebrows rise.

"Oh my God, you're a self-proclaimed logosist and word collector but you don't know what a hoosier is?" I said, thinking she was patronizing me.

"Hoosier?" Amanda walked over to the reference shelves and pulled out a paperback dictionary. I followed her. "How do you spell that?"

"H-O-O-S-I-E-R." I spelled the word. Like a prospector sifting through a pan of rock and dirt in search of a glimmer of gold, I could sense the excitement in her fingers as they scrolled through the pages hoping to discover a new word to add to her collection. When she came to the definition, she read it out loud.

"Hoosier, a native or inhabitant of Indiana." She looked at me confused.

"Go on," I said.

"That's it?" She replied and turned the book towards me. I took the book from her, read the single definition, and looked at the cover. Pocket Oxford American Dictionary. I put it back on the shelf and picked up the six-inch thick massive hardback Webster's Dictionary and searched for the H's.

"Hogwash...hooligans...here we go...hoosier..." I cleared my throat and began in a loud, purposeful voice, "Slang or nickname. A resident or native of Indiana." My eyes then frantically continued to scan further. "What the hell..."

IT WASN'T THERE! My breathing became drawn and short. Dizzy. Distraught. I suddenly felt as if I were Alice in a wordless wonderland. There was no definition of hoosier as being a low-class, trashy and uncouth person? One with low morals who had unbridled sex, vulgar language and destroyed their health and happiness by drinking, smoking and doing drugs?

I was stunned. Amanda must have seen my bewilderment.

"Are you OK, Christian?"

"No." I walked over to the bench in front of the magazine rack and sat down. Amanda followed but a young mother pushing a baby stroller stopped to ask her where she might find a book about the Great Flu epidemic of 1918. Amanda gave me a concerning look and then motioned that she had to help the women. I nodded her along.

Hoosier. I had grown up on that word. It was as common to my vocabulary as Rice-A-Roni was to my nightly cuisine. And now, at the age of eighteen, I'm suddenly discovering it's not a real word? Was it a figment of my parent's imagination? A metaphor created by mom to repel a repulsive society that she didn't want me to be a part of. That was impossible. Mr. Abernathy used it. Chuck used it. I've heard all kinds of people use the word hoosier.

Or did I? Yes, I know I did. I specifically remember the time when I went with my grandfather to Burger Chef. Two Western Auto mechanics were sitting next to us and as they got up to leave, one of them let out a loud, obnoxious belch that echoed across the restaurant. They both laughed and I was about to also, but Grandpa shot me a scathing stare that I remember to this day. "Don't ever do that in public, it's hoosier-ish." He said it in a tone that I imagined Jesus would have used when clearing the money changers out of the temple. And it was carved into my memory.

Amanda came back and found me still in a muddled state.

"The weirdest thing in the entire world just happened to me." I walked over and put the Webster Dictionary back on the reference shelf. "I had been raised with that word my entire life. Mom and dad used it as religiously as their religion. Now I realize that it doesn't have the definition I've come to know it as in the dictionary." I shook my head.

"Just because it's not in the dictionary, doesn't mean it's not a real word." Amanda attempted to encourage me. "There are thousands of slang and regional words that never make it into the dictionary. When I lived in Florida, we always used the word "pop" for soda, but no one ever calls that here. Matter of fact, I have an entire notebook of words that I use that aren't in any dictionary because I made them up." Her encouraging words weren't helping and she knew it, but she continued. "Have you ever heard anyone other than me used the word "douchbagette"? Nope. Because I made it up. Or how about the word "trith"? You won't find that in any dictionary either, but I use it all the time."

"Trith?" I asked.

"Yeah, trith is used before listing three things. For example, that woman was looking for a book about the flu. So we looked in trith the history, reference and medical sections of the store. It's like using the word "both" but when there are three things to list. There wasn't a word that preceded three things, so I invented it. "I am trith a reader, word collector and logosist." She smiled at her cleverness and somehow her eagerness to pull me out of my funk made me a little happier. I smiled too.

"What's your definition of hoosier?" she asked.

I picked my words gingerly so as not to seem too critically descriptive.

"A hoosier is kind of like a subculture of people who are low class, trashy and uncouth." I tried to think of a book or movie character that had a stereotypical hoosier that she could relate to. "Think Huckleberry Finn." I continued. "He was poor, lazy and uneducated. He smoked and wore dirty, raggedy clothes. His father was an abusive alcoholic hoosier too."

She was tossing the definition about in her brain like a literary salad.

"I wonder what a hoosier is?" She asked to herself more than to me. "I mean why are people who live in Indiana called Hoosiers? Is it a type of person? An animal? Maybe a hoosier is like a backwoods, country hick with no class or sophistication and that's how your definition came about. I'm going to have to research that one."

"Please do and let me know what you come up with." I regressed. "Remind me again why we got on this subject?"

"You were arguing with me about my epiphany that everything we do is for our self-pleasure. I asked you why you wash your hair, brush your teeth, take a shower or wear what you're wearing? And you said because you don't want to look like a "hoosier.""

I tried to pigeonhole the conversation in a different direction. Away from me and towards her. "That's correct," I said. "I don't ever want to come off as being a hoosier." It was time to turn the table. "And you wear the things you wear because it pleases you and makes you feel..," I drew the word out. "Sseeexxxyyy."

"Yes, I like to be noticed. It makes me feel special."

"But what happens when you think you look sexy but other people think different?" I turned my gaze to the middle of the mall where a group of teens dressed in tight mismatched clothes was standing next to the fountain. Some had colored spiked hair and some, both boys and girls, had make-up on. "Like those punk rockers over there. They think they're cool but I think they look pretty silly."

"It's all a matter of tastes. And tastes, my friend, is what makes the world go around." Amanda picked up a random book off a table. "Imagine how dreadful the world would be if there were only one kind of book? That's why we have trith mysteries, horror, and sports." She pointed to each section of the store as she called out their genres. "And travel and children's books. Each has their own group of readers and together they make up," she raised her hand to the air and spun around like a fairy princess, "Everything that's around us."

She took her *Anne of Green Gables* purse out of the cabinet beneath the cash register, took off her fake glasses and tossed them into it.

"I guess when it comes to tastes or judging a book by its cover, I'm reference and erotic fiction and you, Christian Hayes are over there next to the bathrooms in the religion and self-help sections," she smiled then looked at the clock once more time.

"Well, I am now officially off for the day," she said just as an older lady with salt and pepper hair fixed firmly in a ponytail came into the store and walked behind the counter and said Hi to us. She was wearing a long flowing bohemian style skirt of burgundies and blues, leather sandals with socks and a sweater blouse. I judged her to be a book that belonged in the poetry section.

CHAPTER THIRTY

We left Waldenbooks and headed towards the Aladdin's Castle Arcade to pick up Sara and Ruth who were spending the day at the mall celebrating Sara's birthday. As we passed The Merry-Go-Round, a clothing store favored by every fashion-conscious teen, Amanda stopped and stared at the female mannequins in the front window. One was sporting a stone-washed denim jumpsuit. The other had on a t-shirt bursting with neon colors, a pastel blue blazer, and a yellow mini skirt. Spring was just around the corner, or so the merchandising people wanted you to think. Amanda pointed to the last mannequin. This one had big hair and even bigger breasts with nipples that poked through the purple spandex jumpsuit it was modeling.

"That is, like, so Pat Benatar-ish. I love it!" She ran her fingers over the mannequin's pink legwarmers. "God, I'm glad I work in a bookstore and not here. I can borrow books and put them back when I'm done. But if I worked here, I'd have to let them keep my paycheck every week because I'd spend it all on new clothes."

We moved to the next display window where a mannequin wore a more conservative, salmon-colored, dress with a fat shiny black belt that resembled something a weightlifter might wear. "That reminds me. I need to find a dress for the Sweetest Heart Dance."

"That's right. I heard you were nominated for freshman Sweetest Heart court over the intercom yesterday. Congratulations," I said and wondered how many other girls had ever been nominated to such a popular status in such a short time.

"Yeah, I've had three guys ask me and I keep putting them off because I don't know which one to go with," she said. Her dates were like her dress option. Eeny. Meeny. Miny. Moe.

"Are you going?" she asked.

"No, I'm going to sit this one out." I didn't want her to think I was a loser, so I defended my statement. "I'm just not into Sweetest Heart dances." Then I lied. "A couple of girls hinted that they wanted me to ask them but..." I stopped mid-sentence and shrugged my shoulders like I had no interest in ever going to any Sweetest Heart dance.

"But what?"

But I don't want to go with anyone but you. Because if I did, I would just be thinking about and watching you all night.

Fortunately, another outfit captured her attention, so we walked over to it. She took the dress off the rack and held it up to her. It was hot pink, sleeveless with a high cut skirt and very low-cut chest.

"What do you think?"

My face must have conveyed my disapproval.

"You don't like it?"

"Well, to be totally honest..." I was stopped mid-sentence by Amanda putting her hand over my mouth.

"Ok Chris, you HAVE to stop saying that!"

"Saying what?"

"To be totally honest". You say it all the time. Please take that sentence out of your vocabulary. It's such an ugly phrase. It gives people the impression you're normally a liar or you have this bad habit of not telling the truth. But right now, just for this moment, you're going to be totally honest. Used car salesmen and attorneys use that phrase. Please don't ever prep a sentence with those words, just say what you have to say."

I pondered on the little proper grammar lesson she had just given me and, not surprisingly, it did make sense. "OK, I think that outfit is kind of..." I was slowly picking my proper word. "Well, it's...." I paused and caught myself once again wanting to say, "Well truthfully," but I didn't. I did what she told me to do—say what I had to say. "...it looks hoosier-ish?" It was the only word I knew to describe it.

"Excuse me?" She got an indignant look about her. "So you're basically calling me a hoosier?".

"No, I'm not calling you a hoosier. I'm calling that dress hoosier-ish."

"But I like this dress. I would wear this dress. So, therefore, I'm a hoosier?"

"That's not what I meant."

"Then what did you mean?" She put her hand on her waist and waited.

"I meant, that we all think things that don't necessarily come out in our words." I put my hands up in frustration. "I don't want to get into it again, or you'll go off on one of your philosophical epiphanies again."

"No, please. Do tell, Christian Hayes. Do you actually think I'm a hoosier?"

"I don't know you well enough to say you're a hoosier." I lied. "All I'm saying is that I think you tend to dress in a manner where people pre-judge you to be something or someone that you may not be."

"They can judge me all they want. I don't give a fuck what they think." She put the dress back on the rack and we walked out of the store.

"That's bull crap!" I said following her. "You just said that you liked to look sexy and it made you feel good. So don't tell me you don't care what others think about you."

"I care about what I feel makes me sexy." She pointed to herself. "What pleases *me*. Not what they feel is sexy. There's a difference."

"And what's the difference? How do you base your sexiness?"

Amanda gazed down the mall, pondering on the question.

"I guess I base my sexiness on...the way I..." She paused and started over. "I think I'm sexy when...I" She paused once again. "...when..." She stopped in front of the fountains and we watched a little girl toss a penny into the water. "OK, maybe you're kind of right. My sexiness is based on how people look at me. How they're attracted to me. But that doesn't mean I live my life for what others think of me."

"It's not how people look at you, but how guys look at you." I let the accusative words roll. "And you've said it with your own mouth that all guys are nothing but Vagina Hunters. I don't mean to offend you Amanda, but if you keep looking like a vagina wrapped in tight sexy clothes and heels, then that's exactly what you're always going to attract: Vagina Hunters. Guys that just want a piece of ass and don't respect you or think you have any intelligence. And those are not the type of guys you want in your life."

Oh my God, I was sounding like my mother.

"Oh my God Chris, you're sounding like my father. I..."

But then she stopped. And I could tell by her demeanor she was having another epiphany realizing that her father had probably never once given her any good fatherly advice because, well, to be totally honest with herself, he was a hoosier who drank and abused.

She continued walking down the mall avoiding eye contact with me and everyone we passed. I could tell I was stroking a raw nerve. I was making her think beyond her normal scope and she wasn't enjoying it. And while I felt she wasn't exactly warming up to what I was putting out on the table, she wasn't rejecting it either. I tried to bring the conversation back with a positive twist.

"How about instead of sounding like your father..." I walked in front of her, turned, and began walking backward as we continued the conversation. "...it's more of an older brother just trying to save his little sister from a lot of future pain and heartache." I smiled to help ease the tension. "I'm sure you do the same thing with Sara."

"I appreciate that Best Big Brother in the World, but don't think I'm going to change the way I am just because of your advice. Everyone knows Chris, change doesn't come from without, it comes from within. If I ever change in any way, it'll be at my own choice."

"You're absolutely right." I stopped walking backward forcing her to stop right before me and stare into my eyes. "And don't get me wrong, guys like their girlfriends to look nice and sexy but not slutty. It's nice to leave things to the imagination." She tried to walk around me, but I moved in her way. "Do you know what you have, Amanda, that most girls don't have?"

"Yeah, I have a word collection that no other girl has and a gregarious personality that maybe a dozen other girls in school have." She stepped to the left and I stepped in front of her.

"Yes, you have those things. But you also have something way more valuable and desired than those."

She held up a fist. "I also have a right hook that someone's going to feel if they don't get out of my way," she said, half in jest and half seriously.

I stepped out of her way and we continued.

"Well, you have that, but more importantly you have your— beauty," I emphasized the word. "Do you know what other girls would give for that? You could wear sackcloth and ashes and still look better than any other girl in the entire school." I nodded and bashfully, bowed my head. "At least in my humble opinion."

"Sackcloth and ashes." She chuckled at the wordplay. "What are sackcloth and ashes?"

"It's what people in the Bible wore when they were mourning. It's like wearing a potato sack and rubbing ashes all over you."

"Sackcloth and ashes. I like that phrase." She repeated it. "Sackcloth and ashes. Sounds like a clothing designer. "Come see the latest sackcloth and ashes fashions at Saks Fifth Avenue." Amanda quickly acted as if she was a runway fashion model and turned and struck a poise.

"Are you paying attention to me? Or do you just want to change the subject?" I asked.

"Yes, I'm paying attention and yes I want to change the subject. You're still subconsciously trying to get me to change the way I dress because you..." She poked her finger into my arm. "...think it makes me look slutty. And just because you..." She poked me in the arm again. "...think that, doesn't mean that I am, or that others think that. Can you see how wrong or unfair it is to ask that of me?"

I once more defiantly stood in front of her and stopped her.

"Well, to be totally honest," I let the phrase fill her thoughts to get the full impact of what I was about to say. "I guess it's like someone asking you to remove a certain phrase out of your vocabulary because it makes you appear like something that you're not."

We stood there and smugly looked at one another, both wondering what the hell was going on in each other's mind. I could tell she was beginning to see where I was coming from.

"Touché," she said.

We walked silently down the mall and as we passed by Sears, Amanda stopped. In the front display window was a poker table and spread out across the table were playing cards. Two male mannequins were sitting at the table and behind them were two female mannequins. Each was dressed in Sears latest spring fashions. At first, I thought Amanda was admiring what the women mannequins were wearing but when I looked over at her, she was staring at the cards laid out on the poker table.

"Stay right here. I'll be right back." She walked into the store and gave the Vagina Hunter working behind the desk a few smiles and they exchanged words. Then she walked over to the poker table and sorted through the cards and picked one up. She tossed another flirtatious grin to the Vagina Hunter and waved thank you and walked out.

"What was that all about?" I asked incredulously.

She smiled a smile that screamed she was up to something. She took my arm and we began walking once more towards the arcade. There was a cockiness in her stride and a snootiness in her tone as she handed me the playing card and said, "See that?" She pointed to the card. "What kind of card is it?"

"A shoplifted jack of spades," I said sarcastically.

"I didn't shoplift it!" Her eyes got innocently big. "The guy said I could have it. Now I want you to take a good look at jack of spades. Because it's not just any jack of spades." She took the card out of my hand and held it up. "It's a one-eyed jack of spades. The ugliest card in the deck according to my sperm donor." She pointed to the one eye, tapped it several times and then handed it back to me. "I want you to take this home and put it right next to the picture of me I gave you." She handed the card back to me.

"And why would I do that?" I took the card.

"Because whenever you..." She poked me in the chest. "...are able to change this ugly one-eyed jack." She pointed to the card. "Into something more valuable and pretty like...say...a queen of hearts. Then you..." She poked me once again. "...will be able to change the girl next to it." She pointed to herself. "Into something you perceive as more valuable and pretty. Until then, Chrissstttiiian Mathew Hayes, always remember, the card you're holding in your hand, is, and will always be, nothing more than what you see at face value, a one-eyed jack of spades." She smiled her glorious smile and started singing like Doris Day. "Que Sera, Sera. What will be, will be." As she turned and walked away. The conversation was over.

I stood there staring at the shoplifted, one-eyed jack of spades and shook my head. Not only was she beautiful, but she was also almost genius-like. I was starting to see where she was coming from. I put the card into my pocket and ran after her.

CHAPTER THIRTY-ONE

Amanda and I arrived at Aladdin's Castle Arcade together. Ruth and Sara ran out and greeted us.

"Hey, Amanda!" They gave her a big hug.

Ruth took Amanda's hand and pulled her to the Galaga arcade game. "Guess what?" She began with an excited deep breath. "I got to the second challenge stage in Galaga and I was the tenth highest score and I got to put my initials on the screen. And we found three tokens in the air hockey game and those three boys over there." She pointed to a group of young Vagina Hunters that were sheepishly staring over at Ruth and Sara, "They gave us their tickets. So all together we have a total of 157 tickets. I think we should get the bald guy thing with the magnetic hair..."

Sara attempted to break into the conversation. "...but I want the stuffed smiley face and since it's my birthday I think I should get my way..."

Amanda put her hand on Ruth's head. "I love how Ruth rattles on and on. She's so loquacious. She reminds me of Anne Shirley with sandy brown hair."

Ruth looked at Amanda inquisitively. "Anne Shirley? Who's that?"

"Sara looked at Ruth like she was stupid. "You know, Anne Shirley, from *Anne of Green Gables*?" She pointed to Amanda's purse. Amanda held it up and Ruth admired it.

"I think I've heard of it, but never read it," Ruth replied.

Sara put both hands to her heart and donned a sad face. "That's just tragically wrong. It makes my heart weep with bitter sorrow to know that a kindred spirit like you has yet to read *Anne of Green Gables*." She smiled. "That's how Anne Shirley always talks in the books. You need to read them. There's a whole series. You'll love them. Amanda read them to me a million times when I was little and I've read them a million times since then."

"Well, if you say so," Ruth said. But her attention was quickly snatched away by a bolt of loud laughter. We turned our stare to the corner of the arcade which sat a sizeable inflated house. Its walls were bright orange rubber with giant square gaps that acted as opened windows. Air-brushed green ivy ran up the walls to circle the words Bouncy House painted above the door. It bustled back and forth with kids flinging themselves against the floors and walls and springing up and down with shrieks and screams of laughter.

"Speaking of being little, Christian, can we do the Bouncy House! Oh, how I so loved jumping in the Bouncy House when we were little." Ruth begged.

I looked at the Bouncy House and then at our two little sisters who stood enviously staring at the younger kids playing inside. I too remembered how fun it was. "Well, since its Sara's birthday." I smiled and reached into my pocket. "I'll pay for the tickets." That earned me a hug from both girls as they giggled and clapped their hands in excitement.

"But you and Amanda have to bounce with us too!" Ruth insisted.

Amanda immediately held up her hands. "Oh no! I don't do Bouncy Houses," she protested.

"Oh Christian, please talk her into it while we go to the bathroom." Ruth turned to Sara. "You don't want to have to go pee while you're in the Bouncy House; it'll bounce it right out of you." They ran off to the restrooms.

Amanda sat down on a bench that faced the Bouncy House. "You go ahead. I don't like going into those things."

"How could you not like going into a Bouncy House and flinging yourself to and fro?" I sat down beside her and coaxed her.

"No, thanks. I'll sit this one out," she said defiantly as she diverted her stare away from the Bouncy House. We were a mere ten feet away and it jostled with activity and laughter, yet Amanda refused to look at it. Disregarded. Ignored. Like a beggar standing on a corner at a traffic light. I couldn't tell if she was still a little miffed from our previous conversation or if there was something else that was bothering her.

"You all right?" I asked.

"Yeah," she forced a smile. "Sorry. I don't mean to be a party pooper." I could tell she was balancing a thought on her brain. Something she wasn't sure if she wanted to share or not. "I had a bad experience in something like that when I was a kid and ever since then, I've hated them."

I didn't want to press the issue. I sat there quietly and watched a little girl and her brother skip by on their way to the putt-putt golf course.

There was an uncomfortable vibe. Amanda opened her *Anne of Green Gables* purse, took out a compact, and looked at herself in it. She flicked her bangs with her fingers. Checked her make-up. Then she put the compact away and gave me a resigned stare. "I don't know what it is about you, Chrissstian Hayes, but, I'm about to tell you a story I've never told anyone." Her tone said I was to tell no one what I was about to hear.

"Is this a true story or an Officer Tumblet made up story?" I smiled. "Because I didn't want to get too emotionally involved only to have you say, "Just Kidding!""

"Oh, it's true alright. I wish it weren't though," she sighed.

Amanda sat upright, took a deep breath. "One time when I was about ten. We went to a state fair and they had something like that." She pointed to the Bouncy House. "But it had tunnels and slides and all kinds of other things attached to it. Mom and the sperm donor thought it would make a great babysitter. So they let Sara and I play in it, while they went off to find their own fun at the beer garden.

'We'll be back in fifteen minutes,' dad said. 'And keep an eye on your sister.' Mom added. Well, Sara and I were in kid heaven. We crawled through the tunnels and bounced and climbed. But, just like Ruth said, all of a sudden I had to take a piss." She subconsciously crossed her legs. "I didn't want to leave to find the bathroom by ourselves, so we kept waiting and waiting for mom and the sperm donor to get back. I had to go so bad that I kept putting my hand 'down there' to try to hold it in." Amanda slid her hand between her crossed legs and let it rest there. "As I was looking around waiting and watching for mom and dad, I noticed this older man, dressed in a nice suit with a tie staring and smiling at me."

Even at ten years old you had guys eyes upon you.

"At first, I figured, he worked there; the way was dressed and how he kept smiling and looking at me. Like he was the boss watching over everyone. I thought, well, maybe he could show me where the bathrooms were. But every time I looked at him, I realized, he wasn't watching everyone, just me. I started to freak out a little, but I wasn't really that scared because he looked friendly. Besides, I was in the middle of the kids play area and mom and dad were bound to be back at any time." Amanda paused. "You know, when someone's watching you, you can almost feel it and you don't want to look over, but you just have to?"

I nodded my head.

"Well, I looked over at him and he started walking to the other side of this big generator or something." She mimed a big wall next to her with her hands. "Suddenly he unzipped his zipper, pulled out his dick and started jacking off. I was so shocked that I couldn't turn away. I didn't know what he was doing at the time. All I knew, he was playing with his privates and privates weren't supposed to be out in public, that's why they call them privates. But nobody else could see him hidden behind the generator."

Amanda's pace hurried. "So there I was holding my privates staring at this man playing with his privates and I realized he probably thought I was playing with my privates too. So immediately took my hands off myself and started to turn, but just as I did, I watched him shoot this white stuff into his own hand. When I looked at his face, he was no longer looking at me and smiling. He was shaking and squinting with his mouth open and he looked like he was in pain." She stopped for a second and shook her head at the past tragic thought. "I freaked out and immediately crawled through the tunnels to get Sara so that we could get the fuck out of there. I found her playing in the pit of plastic colored balls. I jumped in with her and as I landed, I accidentally started peeing. I tried so hard to stop, but I couldn't. I pissed right there on the bottom of the play pit of plastic colored balls."

Her face flushed be she didn't seem to notice or care. She was skiing through a landslide of suppressed emotions. "I was so embarrassed and humiliated. I wanted to cry but I didn't want to bring any attention to myself. I crawled out of the ball pit and found some kid's jacket sitting there and wrapped it around my waist so no one could see my pissed stained shorts and yelled at Sara to get the hell out of there. We had to leave."

Amanda reached out and touched my arm and through that physical act became an emotional connection that passed between us. I could feel all that she felt. Terror. Dread. Anxiety.

"I couldn't stay there any longer," Amanda continued. "I didn't know where I was going, but I had to leave. I grabbed Sara's hand and we shot out of there and just as we left, mom and the sperm donor came walking in. They're arguing and everyone's looking at them because my dad's drunk and 'motherfucking' my mom and my mom's yelling back at him.

And all the while, neither one notices the stolen jacket around my waist or the fact that they were gone for about an hour or that I fucking pissed in my pants." Her words were sharp and bitter. She finished the secret story like she had just run a marathon of bad memories and was now somewhat mentally fatigued, but at the same time satisfied that she had accomplished the feat. Then she forced a smile. "And that is why I don't like those things." She nodded towards the Bouncy House.

"Wow." I wanted to say more but I didn't know where to begin, so I just left it at "Wow."

Pervert. Pissing. Public. No child should have to endure that.

"Yeah, pretty crazy eh?" She looked at me, not for sympathy or compassion but for more. She wanted stability or maybe courage.

I took her hand and pulled her reluctantly to the Bouncy House and stood her in front of the window. "But that was long ago, a different miserable place, a different fucking bad time." I explained. "But now you're living in Spanish Lake, Missouri and hanging out with the best big brother in the world." I tried to make my smile as bright as the pinball machines that surrounded us. For the next few seconds, we watched the kids bobble and bounce as they laughed and screamed with excitement. I used their joy as an emotional elixir. As gradual as her disturbing memories ebbed, I waited and watched for them to wane.

I was beginning to realize that Amanda Morrow carried her emotional baggage like guns at a policeman's ball. You may not be able to see them, but you knew they were there. All

around you. Ready to protect one moment or possibly hurt the next.

Sara and Ruth came bouncing out of restroom towards the Bouncy House.

"So did Christian talk you into doing it with us?" Ruth took Amanda's hand and begged. "It's so fun. Please. Please. Please."

I wanted to reach out and silence my little sister to save Amanda from the struggle of rejection but to my utter amazement, she said: "Yes he did." And then Amanda looked at me as an angel would look at God upon being asked to enter the gates of Hell. Uncertain. Fearless. "But let me go to the bathroom first." She tossed an appreciated glance my way. "If I'm going to be bodaciously bouncing my bladder all over the place" Amanda giggled at her wordplay. "I better empty it first."

Over the next two hours, I spent about a week's pay dropping quarters into video games, buying tickets for the kiddy rides and paying for putt-putt golf. But, to be totally honest, a phrase I don't use anymore, I didn't give a hoot's ass. Watching those three girls having the time of their life was worth a king's ransom or Vodka Watermelon White Knight's paycheck. I could tell Amanda was enjoying playing with her kid sister and regressing into a childhood that she may have never known. We made one more trip into the Bouncy House before it was time to go. Amanda flung herself upon the walls and flipped and fell and laughed and leaped. When the attendant stuck her head in the window and announced our time was up and unzipped the front door, we all rolled out onto the floor mats that were painted to look like a front porch.

"That was about the most fun I've had with my pants on for I don't know how long!" The words came out of Amanda's mouth, and she didn't even realize she said them until she saw the shock on Ruth's face. She attempted to play it off. "I mean...things are always more fun when you don't have your pants on. You know, like when you're in your PJs or swimming suit or sometimes just running around the house bare butt naked."

Ruth gave her another horrid look. "I could NEVER run bare butt naked around the house." She crinkled her face. "Mom would have a conniption fit. Not to mention, dad and Christian..."

"Well, when there are three girls and no boys in the house, there are always bare butts running around naked," Amanda assured her.

Oh, to be a fly on the wall of the Marrow's house. Or a sheet hanging over a window.

Ruth and Sara put on their shoes and ran playfully off to the cashier to redeem their tickets. Amanda and I sat on the bench in silence putting our shoes back on.

"Thank you, Chris Hayes." She turned and hugged me. "That was a wonderful thing you did this afternoon." She stood up and said. "You know I just had another epiphany?"

"Do I even want to ask?"

She pointed to the Bouncy House. "This morning when I woke up, I despised those things." She sighed in satisfaction. "I based it all on one bad experience. But today, I remember how fun and enjoyable they can be." She smiled. "When you think about it, in some small, esoteric sense, I changed today. And while I was the one that forced that change." She pointed to herself. "You…" she poked me in the chest. "…were the catalyst to that change."

Stick with me, Amanda Marrow. Trust me. Your whole world will change for the better. She had confided in me a story that she had never told anyone. If that wasn't proof we were becoming best buddies, I don't know what more proof I needed. But was "best buddy" a good status or a curse?

Was I walking into that world that guys often walk into with girls where they become too good of friends to ever want to date? Or worse, have sex with?

CHAPTER THIRTY-TWO

While most Friday the 13ths are said to be unlucky, Friday, February 13, 1981, turned out to be an extremely lucky day for me. It was the day before Valentine's Day. I decided to ask Samantha Brown to our school's Sweetest Heart Dance. It wasn't that I wanted Samantha Brown to be my Sweetest Heart or that she was even someone I even remotely considered dating. It just so happened that her locker was several down from mine and in between classes we would often make small talk. That morning my lucky conversation went something like this.

"I'm so bummed out. My cousin, Eddie, is in the band that's playing at the Sweetest Heart dance tomorrow night." Samantha said matter of factly. "I really wanted to go and hear him play, but no one has asked me. And I think it'd be weird showing up by myself" I could hear the disappointment in her voice.

Samantha was one of those ghost girls who walked down the halls unnoticed and invisibly intelligent. She was not popular, but at the same time, she wasn't unpopular. She was simply there. Like a fire extinguisher who sits quietly on the wall, but by doing so, she gives a certain amount of comfort in the form of safety. One could talk to Samantha or ask her questions and they felt safe she would know the right answers or that she wouldn't say anything to anyone because, again, she was a ghost girl.

"What does he play?" I continued the conversation.

"He's the bass player and I've wanted to hear him play for a long time but they're always at clubs where you have to be over twenty-one to get in." She took a big pink plastic comb out of her back pocket and ran it through her long, straight, brown hair.

"Who are you going to the dance with?" she said, not so much in a suggestive manner but in a way that she had presumed I was already going.

Several weeks earlier, Principal Perry announced over the intercom the eight girls who were nominated to the Queen's court of the Sweetest Heart Dance. Unlike prom and homecoming, where the students vote the courts and are generally based on popularity, the Sweetest Heart Dance, Queen's court was nominated by the school staff and administration. Each January, the teachers, principals, counselors, secretaries, and even the school nurses and janitors nominated two girls from each class whom they felt represented Hazelwood East Sr. High's best and sweetest personalities. Each nominee was then required to write a one-page reason on why they should be the Sweetest Heart Queen. These essays were then re-typed without the author's name and given to twelve staff members to read prior to the dance. On the night of the dance, the twelve judges gathered and voted that year's Sweetest Heart Queen based on the best anonymous essay.

Amanda Marrow and Cynthia Rhodes were the two freshman class nominees. Before Amanda's nomination, I had no interest in going to the Sweetest Heart Dance. I had been to two others and didn't find them too exciting. But after her name was announced, I wanted to go. I felt it was no longer merely a Sweetest Heart Dance, but more of a celebration of Amanda's sweetheart. And that was something I didn't want to miss. At the same time, I had massive hesitations about going. I knew I would spend the entire evening mentally and emotionally stalking Amanda. That wouldn't be fair to my date or my mental state. I decided to bow out. I knew I'd hear all about it afterward.

Immediately after the Queen's court announcement jealous rumors flew around the freshman halls that Amanda had only been nominated because she flirted with all the male teachers. It was even suggested, probably birthed by the mouth of Dirk Howard, that she was screwing several of them with Mr. Wilson, the chemistry teacher, being the number one Vagina Hunter conqueror.

Mr. Wilson was slender to the point of athletic, fashionable and sported long, wavy, sandy blond hair with puppy dog eyes and a brilliant, white smile. The girls said when he put on his glasses, he looked like a nerdy, but still sexy, Leif Garrett. On several occasions, I had witnessed Amanda and Mr. Wilson's out-of-class interactions. The way they joked and were overly friendly with one another sometimes seemed to cross the unprofessional line. But that was my opinion and my opinion was slighted and bias. I felt Amanda perpetually played on the other side of the unprofessional line. It was her playground. My opinion was also that Mr. Wilson's eyes were not those of a puppy dog, but those of an older, experienced Vagina Hunting hound dog.

But now, out of the blue and almost like a heavenly gift from God or Cupid, Samantha Brown was subconsciously coaxing me to escort her to the Sweetest Heart Dance. I took it at face value.

"Well, to be totally…" I stopped midsentence because the fact was, I wasn't being totally honest and besides, I hadn't totally removed that phrase from my vocabulary yet. "…I didn't plan on going but if you need someone to go with, I'll go with you," I said with a sprinkle of outer mercy and a wheelbarrow full of inner joy. "We can go stag, but I'll drive if you want."

"Oh my God, Chris Hayes, you'd do that for me?" Her plain eyes sharpened and beamed with excitement. Then she got calm and serious. "I mean, it wouldn't be like a date, date. It'd just be two friends going to listen to a great band."

"Exactly," I assured her.

We quickly hashed out the details of the non-date then Samantha gave me a hug and thanked me. I immediately went over to Chuck's locker and told him the news.

"I've decided I'm going to the Sweetest Heart dance. Do you think Pete can take over as rink manager tomorrow night?"

"It's Valentine's night we're going to be packed." He took a small glass vial of Polo cologne out of his pocket and dabbed it on his neck. "If you and I aren't going to be there and Pete's playing rink manager, who's going run the skate counter?

"I'll ask Jim to jump over to the skate counter and then I'll see if Frank can be a floor guard. If not, Pete's little brother has been begging me for months to be a floor guard."

"I thought you said Sweetest Heart dances were for losers." He reminded me as he put the Polo sample back into this pocket. "Who are you going with?"

"Samantha Brown," I said and defensively added. "We're just going as friends. Her cousin is the bass player in the band." Chuck smiled, bobbed his eyebrows up and down and gave me the international sign for a blow job. I rolled my eyes.

"Do you want to double with Debbie and me?" Chuck asked.

"Nah, that would be too much like a date. We'll just meet you there." I turned and started towards economics class.

Chuck's little blowjob sign had me thinking. Having sex with Samantha Brown had never crossed my mind. But was it possible? My Vagina Hunting instincts slowly stirred into action. "We're just going as friends". Her words echoed in my ears. How many marriages, affairs and one-night stands all began with those five words? I wondered.

Then I wondered even more if the plain ghost girl, Samantha Brown could be one of those good girls on the street but a sex freak behind the door, or however Amanda like to put it.

Lunchtime came and I sat down across the table from the queen who was busy taking bites of her square piece of pizza and telling her court the events of the morning. She chewed with her mouth opened showing the now masticated white dough and red tomato sauce as one would watch clothes spinning in the dryer at the local laundry. No one seemed to notice but me.

"I wish you were going to the Sweetest Heart Dance, Christian, so you can see my new dress. It's so sweet and yet incredibly sexy." She motioned how the dress was cut innocently high across her chest but then it followed tightly down her hips and ended mid-thigh with two zipper slits in the front and back that could be raised or lowered for whatever mood she may be in that evening.

"It's the one I showed you in the display window at Merry-Go-Round." She took another bite of pizza. "But too bad you won't be there." She made a sad face.

I wondered if she was saying that as an obligatory gesture from a Queen to one of her court members. Or could it be that maybe she did want me there?

"Well, I will be there," I announced.

She stopped chewing and closed her mouth just long enough to display a look of delight. "Really? Who are you going with?

"You don't know her. She's just a friend."

CHAPTER THIRTY-THREE

Valentine's evening.

The previous night, I had a Vagina Hunting dream about Samantha Brown. I couldn't remember the exact details but what I remembered was more than enough to alter my thoughts about Samantha. If Amanda was free to play in the hunter's field per se, why couldn't I? I could turn this evening into a Samantha Safari. It would take my mind off Amanda during the dance. But most importantly, my own night of vaginal venery might help me forget what Amanda was doing after the dance. When all the eyes of school weren't on her and she was alone in the backseat or bed of a non-Mr. Nice Guy, Vagina Hunter.

I met Samantha at our agreed spot—the parking lot of Sambo's Restaurant. We made our way to school discussing our favorite music and classes. The conversation came easy and I was surprised at how, with a little make-up, tight black leggings, pink heels and an oversized ripped sweatshirt covering what looked to be her bra-less breasts beneath a pink t-shirt, the ghost girl turned into an apparition of mild beauty. We walked into the school gym which had been officially transformed into "The Palace of Love".

Reflective red hearts with pink and white crepe paper dangled from the ceiling like crinkled stalactites. Giant cupids, drawn by the art club, were scattered about the front of the folded bleachers. Red and white mums sprinkled with heart shape confetti acted as centerpieces to the dozens of tables that were now covering the gym's ultra-modern rubberized floor. At the end of the tables was the empty dance floor speckled with little white lights reflecting from a three-foot mirror ball hanging from the center scoreboard and spinning its hypnotic, magical powers.

A crowd of students and staff lined the front near the entrance and filled the tables. The band was in the midst of their version of *September* by Earth, Wind and Fire. Samantha and I quickly found Chuck and Debbie sitting at a table next to the dance floor.

We said our hellos and then Chuck grabbed Debbie's hand and pulled her unwillingly to the dance floor. An empty dance floor begged Chuck's dancing soul like a merry-go-round to a child. He immediately put on the white boy lip bite and started jerking and gyrating to the beat.

Samantha and I walked over to the side of the stage where the sound man was tweaking out the music. Her cousin Eddie was on the little stage lost in the groove, strumming his guitar strings with his eyes shut and his head bobbing up and down. His denim jean vest covered in patches perfectly matched his patched pants. When he opened his eyes, Samantha was there smiling like a proud parent. He returned her big smile and nodded his head. I asked her if she wanted to sit down but she had found her own groove and said she wanted to hang out there for a while. Our contractual agreements were now complete.

I covertly scanned the crowd looking for Amanda and immediately found her amongst her crowd within a crowd standing near the refreshments. I walked over.

"Hey, handsome," Amanda said. She fixed my tie and leaned over and hugged me. I immediately smelled alcohol on her breath. The average person couldn't smell it, but I inherited my mother's hound dog nose and when one is never around smoke or alcohol they have a propensity to smell even the smallest scents. I reached into my pocket and took out a piece of *Freshen Up* gum.

"Here, you need this," I said and handed it to her.

She immediately covered her mouth. "Is my breath bad?" she said slightly embarrassed.

"No, it smells like booze."

She got a guilty look that relaxed into a sinister smile. "Mark and I had a couple of drinks on the way here to relax us and get us in the mood." She unwrapped the piece of gum and tossed it in her mouth. "Yuumm! This is that cum gum that squirts in your mouth when you bite into it." She bobbed her eyebrows up and down. "I love it."

The alcohol was already seeping its way into her moral fibers causing them to loosen and be sexually stretched and making her wet with seductiveness.

"So whatta think?" Amanda spun around showing me her dress and stuck out each foot to showcase her shoes. "And see the zippers." She unzipped the front of her skirt so high I got a glance of her pink satin panties. "Oops, went a little too far." She teased as she zipped it back down.

I ignored her flirtations and immediately looked around to see who else had just gotten a free peek at Amanda's pink panties. Mr. Wilson and my eyes immediately met. He gave me an uncomfortable smile. I pretended not to notice it. "Well, it wouldn't be my first pick to wear to a Sweetheart dance but..." I shrugged my shoulders as if to say, "That's your hoosier choice, not mine."

"See you can do it!" She slapped me on the shoulder. "I knew you could. You made a completely honest statement without prepping it with...to be totally honest." She laughed but I could tell her laughter was a subtle disguise to a mild hurt I imposed upon her by implying she had made a hoosier choice.

I'm reading YOU like a book now, Amanda Marrow.

"Where's your date?" She looked around.

"She's over there in the pink shirt." I pointed to Samantha who was standing next to the stage dancing by herself. "Her cousin is the bass player."

Amanda looked over at Samantha and then look at me with a serious, almost pensive stare. "Soooo..." Amanda donned a discovering smile. "...it's a courtesy date. She needed a date to watch her cousin play and you needed a date to watch me play." She giggled at her wordplay. "Remember, Chris Hayes, I can read you like a book."

I tried to hide my embarrassment and prayed to God the darkness of the room hid my flush face. "In your dreams." I quickly countered.

"You just never know what's in my dreams, Sir Vodka Watermelon White Knight."

Just then Amanda's date, Mark Forrest, came over with two cups of punch in his hands and handed one to Amanda.

"Hey, Chris. How ya doing?" We both gave each other smiles and Mark reached out and shook my hand. Over the course of four high school years, Mark and I had several classes together and we always got along. Mark was the Senior class president whose popularity was based on his determination to become a politician. His great grandfather was the mayor of St. Louis many years ago. A fact everyone knew and if they didn't, he'd enlighten them with the knowledge. But what he didn't let people know, was Great Grandpa Mayor Forrest was asked to step down after eight years in office because of several bribery charges brought against him. Mark had been the class president of every class he was in since ninth grade. He was handsome, sported a head of hair that never seemed to get out of place and was a master at conversation. During our freshman and sophomore years, he was a regular at Aloha. I recall one time a wheel came off his skate and I fixed it for him right on the spot and I didn't charge him for it. He seemed to be genuinely appreciative and it struck me that someday he probably would be a senator or congressman and I was glad that I did it.

I wasn't glad however that he was Amanda's date to the Sweetest Heart dance. I was even less happy about the pre-dance drinks "to loosen them up and get them in the mood." Of all the Vagina Hunters in the school, Mark was probably the most dangerous. He was ambitious and his career compass pointed towards a life of success and perhaps even power. And what Queen, or any other female for that matter, didn't desire a handsome, wealthy and powerful man who could give her a life of luxury and security. But as far as Mark knew, I was just another one of Amanda's fans, part of her daily court.

"Who you here with?" Mark asked as he sipped his glass of punch.

I pointed over to the band. "Samantha Brown. That's her cousin playing bass in the band."

"The Boogie Boys is a great band," Mark commented. "We sneak into Cagney's Bar sometimes when they're playing there. My father knows the owner, so he lets us in. I really like ... "

"Holy Fuck!" Amanda words suddenly broke our conversation. Mark and I followed her stare to the front of the gym. Dirk Howard had just walked in with his girlfriend, Gina, on his arm. They were making their way towards the dance floor. Dirk was all smiles. When they got to the dance floor, they started dancing extremely erotically, grinding and kissing all over one another. It wasn't hard to tell they were both wasted. But it wasn't until one of the disco lights hit Gina's dress that we quickly discovered the depths of Amanda's Holy Fuck. It was the same dress Amanda had on.

There was no question that Mark had heard about the fight between Amanda, Dirk, and Gina. If she hadn't told him herself, it was the hottest gossip of the first week of school until Peggy O'Connor disappeared. Rumors said she was pregnant by Mr. Wilson, but come to find out Peggy had wrecked her dad's car and decided it was better hiding out at her boyfriend's house than going home to her angry father.

"She's wearing the same fucking dress!" Amanda grabbed my arm and pulled me in front of her to shield her from Dirk and Gina's view. "That dress looks like shit on her." Mark and I agreed and both voiced the same agreement. "She looks like a...like a...hoosier." Amanda said the word and then shot me a "don't say a fucking thing" look.

Dirk and Gina's eyes finally found trith Amanda, Mark and I standing in front of the refreshments. Gina got a look of embarrassing horror upon her face and then leaned over and said something to Dirk who then gave all three of us an evil look and flipped us his middle finger.

"I'll be back in a second," Mark said and then we watched him walk over to Principal Perry and motion to Dirk and Gina.

"Congratulations!" Mr. Wilson yelled over the band as he greeted us from behind with his Leif Garrett looking smile. He leaned down and whispered something into Amanda's ear. Her character quickly changed. She politely smiled and excused herself. I watched as they walked behind the bleachers and into the coach's office and closed the door behind them.

What the hell? Please tell me they didn't have the audacity to do that right in front of me. Did she think I was so stupid that I wouldn't know what was going on? A handsome young teacher and a beautiful slutty student don't disappear into a private room to talk about grades and homework in the middle of a school dance. He was capturing her vagina; I was sure of it.

I may be part of her Queen's court, but I am not the court jesters. Every iota of my existence wanted to walk over to that door and

fling it open and expose them for what they were...but I couldn't talk myself into doing it.

I went back and stood next to Samantha and pretended to listen to the band play Little River Band's *Reminiscing*. I watched Mark finish his conversation with Principal Perry and then he looked around the room for Amanda, but she was nowhere to been seen. Our eyes met and then I motioned to the back of the bleachers towards the coach's office. Mark knew her reputation and must have been thinking the same thing. Even in the darkness, with all the disco lights flashing, I could see the anger and concern on his face.

As much as it pained me to stand there and watch the secret sexual escapades of the woman that I wanted, a weight was also being lifted from my shoulders. I held my breath and watched as Mark walked towards the coach's office. I wondered how it was going to play out. Would Mr. Wilson and Mark get into a fight? Would Mr. Wilson get arrested for sexual molestation and would Amanda have to leave Hazelwood East in shame? My heart beat to the point of explosion as he neared the door. But just as he reached the bleachers it opened, and Mr. Wilson and Amanda stepped out. Both smiling and laughing.

And following behind Amanda and Mr. Wilson was a group of eleven staff members all filing out from the same door.

Thank you, Jesus.

A wave of relief swept through my soul almost causing me to collapse into the chair next to me. Amanda left Mr. Wilson talking to the other teachers and found her way back to Mark who had seen everything that I had just seen. She showed him her purely whites with her smile and said something to ease his anger, then grabbed his arm and they walked over to a castle made of cupcakes sitting on a table next to the refreshment counter.

When the band finished playing they took a break. Samantha introduced me to her cousin and then I left them to talk alone. I sat down with Chuck and Nancy who were sitting at a table happily conversing with Nancy Clemens and an older man sitting next to her. I soon found out, the older man was her father, Mr. Clemens. They both had the same slightly pointed ears and big smiles.

I had known Nancy Clemens since she first
moved into Spanish Lake when I was in third
grade. Nancy was the first "special" person I
had ever met. She walked with a bent leg that
caused her to teeter back and forth as she
strolled down the halls and she talked in
slurrish mumble. She had mild Cerebral Palsy.
I knew nothing about it. As third graders, it
freaked us out. We would be gathered around
the teacher or librarian and Nancy would sit
there drooling and not even notice it.

I came home and told mom about Nancy one
day. Mom reminded me about other "special"
people in the Bible like the man with leprosy
whom everyone rejected because of his terrible
skin-rotting disease. But Jesus didn't reject
him. He did just the opposite. Jesus touched
him and the leper was healed.

And there was the story of the adulteress,
who was "special" too in her own way," Mom said.
"Everyone rejected her and wanted to stone her
to death. But instead of following the crowd
and rejecting her, Jesus forgave her and saved
her life."

God doesn't make mistakes." Mom assured me.
"There was a reason Nancy was that way. You
shouldn't be afraid of her, you should be nice
to her, just like Jesus was nice to the leper
and the adulteress."

So the next day I volunteered to be Nancy's
reading buddy. I quickly discovered to my
utter amazement that she was an excellent
reader. I would be less than halfway finished
reading a page while she was already done and
ready to move on. The words and stories of the
books clicked inside her brain. She just
couldn't outwardly convey it like the rest of
us.

As the years went by, I watched as Nancy grew out of her slobbering special kid stage and with therapy and braces, she slowly morphed into a trendy teenager. What she lacked in normality, she made up with clothes that were always fashionable.

But more important than her outer appearance, Nancy knew she didn't have the exterior package—the walk or the talk of everyone—but she had a heart and brain unlike everyone and she was determined to use those God-given gifts.

She had a 4.0 grade average and helped tutor students who were behind in their studies. She also volunteered at sports events, socials dances and school plays. Her popularity was based, not on her outward appearance, but on the kindness she showed towards others.

That's why she was nominated to the Sweetest Heart court by the school's staff all four years of high school. Sadly, she had never won Queen. This year, being her last year at Hazelwood East, she brought the love of her life and her number one fan. Her. Dad.

While the band was on break, Principal Perry called for all the court nominees and their escorts to come to the dance floor. We congratulated Nancy and her dad and wished them luck. I watched Amanda and Mark join the rest of the court in front of the stage. Then Principal Perry proceeded to read from various teachers ballots why each girl was nominated to the court as their date escorted them from the stage, down the middle of the dance floor to stand next to a gold-encrusted throne that was used for every homecoming, prom, and Sweetest Heart dance since long before I ever started Hazelwood East.

When Principal Perry called Amanda Marrow's name, she and Mark began their walk down the promenade. Principal Perry read how

Amanda's sharp wit and gregarious personality acted as a welcome mat to friendships with fellow classmates and teachers.

As they passed Dirk and Gina, Dirk made a thunderous farting noise that sent some students into a burst of loud laughter. Mark ignored it all. But Mr. Wilson and several other staff members quickly walked over to Dirk and Gina. Moments later they were escorted out of the dance. But not before Dirk made a few more explicative remarks towards Amanda who stood there smiling. She wasn't going to let Dirk ruin her moment in the spotlight.

Principal Perry introduced Mr. Wilson to announce the winner. As he walked to the microphone several girls whistled and made catcalls. He faked a flash of embarrassment.

"Ladies and Gentlemen, just minutes ago in the coach's office the staff voted this year's winner of the 1981 Hazelwood East, Sweetest Heart Dance." He took a piece of paper out of his shirt pocket. "Upon this paper is the name of this year's queen." He unfolded it and held it up. "Drummer roll please," he said jokingly but the band was still sitting in their places, so the drummer did a loud drum roll causing everyone to laugh. While the rest of the crowd was watching Mr. Wilson, I was watching Amanda, who strangely kept staring over at Nancy. "And this year's Queen is..." Mr. Wilson gave one more dramatic pause, "Nancy Clemens!"

The entire place went wild with applause and cheering. Nancy jumped up and down in her special way and hugged her dad.

"After four years Nancy, Lady Luck was finally on your side." Mr. Wilson congratulated Nancy. The crowd cheered once more. The band began to play Neil Young's *Heart of Gold* as Mr. Clemens walked Nancy to the throne. She sat down with a smile on her face as big as her heart. After a few pictures from the school's yearbook staff, she and her father took to the floor for the customary slow danced. Seconds later, they were joined by the other court nominees and their dates. And while nobody else in the room noticed, I watched Mr. Wilson give Amanda a wink as he looked over at the other judges who were all smiling too. Several of them even had tears in her eyes.

It was then I realized, Amanda had really won the vote. But being the truly kind-hearted person she was, she probably told Mr.

Wilson, that if she did win, she was going to pass it on to Nancy.

Amazing. The modern-day adulteress had secretly given away her queen's crown to the modern day leper so that she could live, if only for a song or two, a happier life.

Even though Amanda didn't believe in them, to me, it was a tremendously unselfish sacrifice. My mom was right. "No, God doesn't make mistakes. There was a reason why Nancy was born that way." To teach this stupid, sex-starved, eighteen-year-old Vagina Hunter that even a hoosier girl can have a heart of gold.

CHAPTER THIRTY-FOUR

Easter.

My stomach was twisted and tied like the braided bread served upon this special holiday. The previous night of attempted sleep was just that—attempted. As soon as I dozed off into a semi-slumber, my conscious kicked my body back awake. Tomorrow mom and dad were finally meeting Amanda Marrow.

February flew by and Amanda dodged all the arrows of love that Cupid had sent her way at my request. March came in and marched out with no more luck from the leprechaun than Cupid had given me in my quest to win her affections.

It seemed that Mark Forrest was just like her other social dance dates. Rumors always followed, but whether her vagina had been captured or not remained a mystery. They were now nothing more than friends. Even less maybe. She had been his arm candy and he had been her escort. Popular. Political. Puppet. Now they barely spoke to one another.

Samantha Brown and I went back to being locker neighbors who chatted every once in a while. After the dance, on the way back to Sambo's Restaurant she was a little flirty causing me to believe I could have had some type of success in the Samantha Safari. But by the end of the night, after witnessing what I had witnessed, the interest had waned.

But most importantly, the gravitational pull between Amanda and I continued to strengthen. We walked to classes together and laughed at lunch and it didn't hurt that both our little sisters were best of friends. And that is how Amanda came to go to church with us that Easter morning.

I wanted so much for Amanda to make a good impression on my parents, especially Jesus' other judge, my mother. I begged her to wear something sweet and conservative and not to smoke beforehand, lest my mother and her hound dog noise would smell it and complain about it for weeks. Cussing was absolutely forbidden. Amazingly, she agreed.

Easter morning was crisp. The sun was sparkling. The sky was cloudless and blue. Dad pulled up in front of Amanda's house. Ruth jumped out and went to the door and knocked. The door opened and Amanda and Sara came out. Lucy was at work. Sara was all smiles in her angelic white dress with its pink belt that matched the ribbon in her hair. Amanda looked like a vintage Sunday school postcard. Her dress was frilly and sunflower-yellow and flowed just below her knees. She wore white patent leather princess shoes. Her hair was pulled back into a ponytail tied back with a pink carnation ponytail holder. Mom got out to let Ruth get into the front seat.

"Mr. and Mrs. Hayes, this is my sister Amanda." Sara did the introductions.

"Nice to finally meet you face to face." Mom smiled. "I've heard a lot about you."

"And nice to meet you, too. I've also heard a lot about you." Amanda innocently smiled and shook mom's hand. She said hello to my dad as she climbed into the back seat and sat next to me. She leaned over and whispered in my ear. "Well, you finally got me in the back seat of your car." She grinned and I prayed that nobody had heard.

"You both look beautiful!" Mom said as Ruth climbed into the front seat between her and dad and Sara climbed in the back seat and shut the door.

Sara held up a little Easter basket filled with green plastic grass and several eggs. "It looks like the Easter Bunny left something at our house for the Hayes," she said. Ruth immediately turned around. Sara reached into the basket and took out a colorfully died Easter egg. Painted in pretty pinks and lavenders were three gothic crosses on the egg. "This one's for you Mrs. Hayes because you like going to church so much." She leaned forward and handed it to my mom.

"Why, isn't that just the most precious thing." Mom admired its artistic beauty. "Thank you, Sara."

Sara reached into the bag once more and pulled out another Easter egg painted to look just like a football. "And this one's for you Mr. Hayes because you like to watch football." Ruth took dad's football egg and showed it to him while he was driving.

"Thank you, Sara," dad said. "You should be an artist when you grow up."

Sara smiled at the thought and the compliment as she pulled out the third egg. "And this one is for my best friend who loves seashells."

Ruth reached around and took her egg. "A Junonia seashell!" she screamed. Her egg had been meticulously painted with brown spots spirally down its side to a white split that looked just like a seashell. "I finally have a rare and lucky Junonia. Thanks, best friend in the world!" Ruth kissed her egg.

"And last, but not least, is the Sir Christian Hayes Vodka Watermelon White Knight egg." Sara stately announced as she pulled my egg out and handed it to me. True to its name, it looked just like a little green and white watermelon with a sword painted on one side. I was thoroughly impressed. "That's awesome!" I said and showed it to Ruth and mom who had turned around to take a look. There was a suppressed look of shock on mom's face.

"The what knight?" Mom suspiciously asked.

Amanda spoke for the first time. "The first night I met Christian, I had this whacked-out dream that my father was throwing watermelons filled with vodka all over the rink at Aloha. They burst into flames and Aloha started burning down and Christian ran in and saved Sara but when he went back in to get my school picture, the entire place blew up. It was horrible. That's why I called so late that night." Amanda made a quick narrative of the entire night.

Mom slowly nodded as she remembered the call. I could see she had several more questions but before she could get them out, Amanda quickly changed the subject.

"Ruth, did you get anything good in your Easter basket?" Amanda asked.

"We don't do Easter baskets." Ruth began. "It's about Christ rising from the dead. Not a bunny that leaves baskets full of candy that rots your teeth and makes you fat." Ruth replied in a manner that led one to believe she was a brainwashed zombie in a cult. She shot a look towards mom that said, "Isn't that right, mommy dearest?" I think mom didn't like the guilt of being blamed as the one who robbed us from the sweet satisfaction of finding candy-filled Easter baskets on this special day, so it was her turn to change the subject.

"That's a beautiful perfume you're wearing Amanda, what's it called?"

I pointed to my nose, leaned over and whispered. "I told you, a nose like a hound dog."

"Heaven Scent," Amanda answered.

Mom smiled radiantly. "Ahh, driving to church on a glorious Easter morning in a car filled with the beautiful fragrance of heaven's scent," she proclaimed and then added. "Praise Jesus!"

Amanda chuckled at my mother's wordplay. "That was beautiful Mrs. Hayes."

"Amanda collects words, Mom." Ruth proudly boasted. "Like I collect seashells. She has all kinds of notebooks filled with funny, fantastic, and foreign words." Ruth chuckled at her own wordplay.

"Well, word collecting sounds like a very fine hobby," mom said. "Do you know what the Bible says about words?" She posed the question to the entire car. My mind scanned my scripture bank, but nothing immediately registered. "How about John 1:1? Come on Christian you know this." I was under pressure and couldn't perform my Bible verse memory challenge. After more silence, mom continued. "In the beginning was the Word…." I can't believe you can't remember that verse." She criticized me like I had forgotten that Jefferson City was the capital of our state.

"Oh, yeah," Ruth repeated. "In the beginning was the Word, the Word was with God and the Word was God."

"Very good Ruth. So, if you're collecting the true Word," Mom preached to Amanda. "You're really collecting parts of God."

I watched the idea sink into Amanda's mind and could tell, while her body was sitting next to me, her thoughts were outside the car, past the buildings that zoomed by and still even further beyond what my eyes could see.

In the beginning, was the Word, the Word was with God and the Word was God.

Like Moses coming before the burning bush and being filled with supernatural wisdom, Amanda became more enlightened. All the beautiful, vintage and made-up words she had been collecting throughout her life represented, not only who and what she was, but that entity which created her-God.

Everything had a word attached to it. If it wasn't expressed in a word, it didn't exist.

And while other collectibles like coins
and cars, rust and die, words were eternal. The
same words we speak here on earth are going
to be the same words we speak in heaven, or
hell if that was her destiny. And even if we
speak a different language in the afterworld,
it was still words of a different language.
And even more profound, if we didn't verbally
speak in eternity at all, we merely
communicated with only thoughts; what are
thoughts but non-verbal words?

Without words, there would be no thought
and without thoughts, one didn't exist. So yes,
In the beginning, was the Word, the Word was
with God and the Word was God.

CHAPTER THIRTY-FOUR

Bellefontaine Baptist Church was usually a couple of hundred people strong on an average Sunday morning, but on Easter and Christmas, those numbers swelled to the point where deacons had to line the ends of the pews and the back walls with extra foldout chairs.

We arrived just when Deacon Jones, dressed in his circa 1975 powder-blue leisure suit, was unlocking the front doors. He greeted us with a big Easter smile and handshake. We made our way through the Big Church, so called because it was the "big" sanctuary where everyone gathered for sermons. We went through the Fellowship Hall and down the corridor to the "Little Church" where all the Sunday school classes were held. Mom and dad went upstairs to the adult Sunday school classes while, Amanda, Ruth, Sara and I went downstairs to the youth department. We separated even further as Sara and Ruth went to the Jr. High department at the end of the hall. Amanda followed me to the big open room at the other end of the hall called the High School Spirit room.

As we entered, several boys turned to stare at Amanda. This caused some of the girls to do the same. More heads turned, then eyes got bigger and soon there was chattering between one another as art critics do while discussing the latest artwork hanging on a gallery wall. Mrs. Underwood, the Sr. High leader, rushed over to Amanda and greeted her with a sincere smile. She escorted her to the guest sign-in table. One could feel the spiritual battle stirring around the room. Some of the same guys and girls that were bad mouthing and belittling Amanda in school where now being hypocritically forced to put on a fake smile and act as if they were happy she was there.

As Amanda signed into the guest registration, Kyle Bentley, the guy who drove her from the New Year's Eve party to Aloha, pulled me over to the side. "What is she doing here?" He motioned toward Amanda like she was a rotten egg in an Easter basket. "Are you two an item?"

"No, we're just friends." I waved off the idea. "She's only been to church like three times in her life. Ruth invited her and her little sister to come with us."

"Amanda Marrow in church. Wow." Kyle shook his head in amazement. "Well, I guess that makes another miracle that happened on Easter Sunday."

"Why is that such a miracle?" I questioned.

"Oh, come on Chris, you know she's one of the biggest sluts in the school. Nobody really likes her besides for her little "click" and a few teachers and guys who just want to get down her pants." He tossed me an accusing stare knowing I fit two of those descriptions. "She likes to party too much. She's got the mouth of a pirate and dresses like a whore." He gave a righteous pause. "But to be totally honest, I don't really know her." He shrugged his shoulders. "I'm just surprised to see her here, that's all."

Kyle's condescending expression rubbed me like spiritual salt on an emotional wound. His judgmental tone that reverberated in my ears was the same tone my mother used over and over to the point that I despised it.

I wondered for a long second if Kyle had other motives that evening as he taxied Amanda from the party to Aloha. More motives than just being a good Samaritan. Could he have wanted to try and capture her Vagina while she was in her sleazy and susceptible drunken state?

I was pissed to think that no matter where Amanda went, even in the supposed sanctuary of Sunday school, she still wasn't shielded from scorn and ridicule.

"It makes me sick how people are so quick to spread all her sins, but nobody ever says anything about her virtues." I verbally blasted him.

"Virtues? What virtues does Amanda Marrow have?" Kyle took mom's interrogating stance.

"Did you know she comes from a very abusive, alcoholic and dysfunctional family and yet she gets almost straight A's? She practically raised her little sister. She reads more books in one year than we've probably read our entire lives." I continued counting her virtues on my fingers as I went down the list. "She works part-time to help support her single mother. And as much as she loves sex, she doesn't cheat, lie or steal. Have you ever heard that gossip going around?"

Ok, I tossed in those last few virtues to pump up her image, but he deserved it.

Kyle's stance relaxed and his stare lowered. I could almost see the guilt begin gnawing on his nerves. "No, I didn't know that."

"I'll tell you what, Kyle. I'd give her greater odds getting into heaven based on things hidden in her heart, then half the other girls in this room who act like two-faced Pharisees." I nodded my head towards several girls who were now welcoming Amanda. "And if by some miracle, I'm there on the day of her judgment and she is cast into the fiery pits of hell, then I'm jumping in the flames right behind her. Because I'd rather live in eternal hell with an honest, kind-hearted, heathen, hoosier slut like her." I pointed to Amanda across the room who was looking at me with a "help" expression on her face. "Then spend a day in heaven with those cold-hearted, Christian hypocrites over there."

I turned and walked away leaving Kyle speechless and made my way to Amanda who was putting a "Hello My Name is: Amanda" sticker on her dress.

"It smells funny in here," Amanda said, then she wrinkled up her nose. "Like mothballs...and...fried chicken."

I couldn't help but laugh a little too loud and a little too hard. Mothballs and fried chicken? Nobody had ever described our Sunday school room as smelling like mothballs and fried chicken.

I took a deep breath and realized she was right. The senior citizen classes were above us. I've caught the pungent scent many times in the corridors during the Fall when coats and jackets came out from hibernating in mothball protected closets.

Across the street, next to the insurance
building and just beyond the car wash, was a
Kentucky Fried Chicken. You could often smell
the Colonial's famous secret recipe wafting
about in the wind when we left God's house and
went home.

I had been attending Bellefontaine Baptist
Church my entire life and had never noticed
the two odors cumulating in our class. I had
become desensitized to its mothballs and fried
chicken fragrance.

I wondered if there were other things about
this room and the people in it that I had also
become desensitized to.

"It's the virgins in the next room getting ready to be sacrificed." I
joked.

"Well, that's one ceremonial act that I won't ever have to worry
about." She gave me a smile that was a little too naughty to be in
Sunday school.

Mrs. Underwood motioned for everyone to take our seats. We sat
down and she welcomed the half a dozen or so visitors. Amanda
delighted in the attention and while all the visitors were asked to stand
and give their name, Amanda went one step further and thanked
everyone for being so warm and friendly.

Afterward, we worshipped by singing a few hymns while Mrs.
Underwood played the piano. There were a few announcements and
then we were divided once more into smaller groups based on our high
school grade. The senior students went into one room while Amanda
and all the other freshmen went into another. I wished with all my
might I could have snuck a supervisory glance into her room for fear
that she might do or say something that would only add fuel to the
gossip fire.

A half an hour later, when we all came back to the Senior Spirit
Room, to my great relief, her Sunday school teacher and fellow
freshman were wearing smiles and merrily inviting her to come back
next Sunday. Like usual, Amanda triumphed over her adversaries with
her wit and charm.

After Sunday school, we meet mom and dad in the lobby of the Big Church. As we were standing, making small talk, waiting for Sara and Ruth, the front doors opened. A chilly breeze blew in, followed by Mr. Abernathy and right behind him was Mrs. Abernathy—a short Asian woman who looked to be at least 10 years younger than her husband. Her coal, black hair was pulled into a bun and kept in place with a band of small, delicate white roses. She wore a white, silky sundress adorned with purple and pink specks. She was petite, even shorter than Amanda but her red lips and radiant, almond-shaped, eyes reflected a personality that was intelligent and proud.

"Amanda!" Mrs. Abernathy called out in surprise as she walked over and gave Amanda a big hug. "How wonderful to see you," she said in a barely noticeable Asian accent. Amanda returned the warm welcome. "What are you doing here?" Mrs. Abernathy asked.

"My little sister and Ruth Hayes are best friends, so Ruth invited us," Amanda answered.

She threw her hands into the air and turned to Mr. Abernathy and smiled. "My Lord, what a small world!"

Needless to say, all other parties standing there were in a mild state of bafflement.

"So how do you two know one another?" My mother asked.

Amanda put her arm around Mrs. Abernathy. "Claire is one of my favorite customers at work. She has fine taste in books and even better taste in clothes." Amanda motioned to Mrs. Abernathy's dress.

"And Amanda helps me find books for my research at work." Mrs. Abernathy countered. "She's so intelligent and friendly. I already have her on my intern list at the university when she turns eighteen." Amanda's grin widened. Mrs. Abernathy's eyes looked Amanda up and down. "You look stunning," she said. Amanda moved her hips back and forth causing her sunflower yellow skirt to swing around. "Yes, that's better than all those drab librarian clothes you wear at the bookstore." Mrs. Abernathy had an additional thought. "You know we're about the same size. Maybe we could give each other our hand-me-downs." She smiled.

The thought of his wife wearing Amanda's hand-me-downs made Mr. Abernathy suddenly choke and me to chuckle out loud.

Amanda turned to the choking Mr. Abernathy and held out her hand. "Glad to officially meet you," Amanda said. "I see you at Aloha but you're normally busy in the office." Mr. Abernathy accepted her hand and bowed his head and returned her Hello.

After a few more minutes of church chit-chat between the Marrows, Hayes and the Abernathy's, the lobby soon filled with an Easter parade of people followed by Sara and Ruth.

Mrs. Abernathy looked at her watch. "Well, it's about time for the service to begin." She gave Amanda one more hug. "I hope to see you back here." She turned and looked at me and then looked at Amanda. "And just for your information, I've known this young man almost his entire life and he's one of the finest young men you'll ever meet." She winked at Amanda and Amanda gave her an approving nod. My face went a little red. However, my mother's eyes grew big with fright.

How incredible. Three miracles on Easter Sunday.

Mom, dad and the Abernathy's went to the front rows of The Big Church where the deacons and their wives sat. Amanda, Ruth, Sara, and I went to the balcony where all the young people sat, talked, and mostly didn't pay attention to the sermon.

The organist began a rousing version of "How Great Thou Art."

"I know this song!" Amanda grabbed my arm with both her hands and shook it. "Lucy has an Elvis record with it on it. I love it." She began to hum along. She and Sara exchanged smiles.

Our Pastor, Reverend Don Monty, had the face of a gardener and the soul of a saint. And if that wasn't enough to make him preacher worthy, he loved the color lavender and spoke as sweet as the flower with the same name. That Easter morning, he greeted everyone with a glorious spring smile and immediately started in on his traditional Easter sermon. From Good Friday to Christs' Resurrection, he spoke of Jesus' trials and tribulations. And when he preached about God's all-knowing and all-seeing powers and used words like omniscient and omnipotent, Amanda paid exceptionally close attention. She even took the Bible from my hands and followed along. When Rev. Monty read *Matthew 23:27-28* out loud and said the word, sepulcher, she tapped the word on the page and made what seemed to be a mental note.

Woe unto you, scribes and Pharisees, hypocrites! for ye are like unto whited sepulchers, which indeed appear beautiful outward, but are within full of dead men's bones, and of all uncleanness.

Even so ye also outwardly appear righteous unto men, but within ye are full of hypocrisy and iniquity. Matthew 23:27-28

Amanda was learning that church wasn't only a place to feed the soul but where one could stumble upon a sepulcher of beautiful words. Reverend Monty read a few more verses and then closed his Bible. The lights suddenly dimmed and a spotlight lit up two young girls, dressed as Mary and Martha coming to the Jesus' sepulcher to discover it was empty. Sara sat mesmerized as the reenactment of Christs' resurrection continued. Amanda, however, was still busy looking for other beautiful words in the Bible.

After the short skit was over, the lights came back up and the curtains covering the baptismal opened. Rev. Monty, now dressed in a dark robe, stepped down into the water. Amanda turned to me and inquisitively asked, "What the hell's that?" She pointed to the baptismal tank.

"Well that actually keeps you from going to hell," I replied then explained that, what looked to be the lateral view of a huge hot tub stuck in the middle of the wall, was what Baptists call a baptismal tank. "It allows the congregation to witness when a person gets their sins washed away. Just like Jesus did when John dipped him in the Jordon river." I could tell it wasn't quite clicking with her yet. "Just watch," I said.

A small boy about ten years old was the first to walk down into the tank. On his way down, the boy's black baptismal choir robe filled with air and was now floating up obstructing his entire nervous face. Reverend Monty smiled and pulled the boy's robe down into the water so the entire congregation could see the boy's face. "Josh Kizca, has made a public confession that he accepts Jesus Christ as his personal savior. Is that correct Josh?" Josh grinned and nodded his head yes. Then, just as they had rehearsed prior to the curtains opening, Josh put one hand over his mouth and the other over his nose. Rev. Monty placed one hand on Josh's hands and the other behind his neck. "In the name of the Father, Son, and Holy Ghost I baptize thee." Josh leaned back and Rev. Monty immersed him completely under the water and raised him back up. The congregation applauded as Josh smiled and walked out of the water, a Born Again Christian.

Amanda watched wide-eyed as three more Christian converts followed after Josh. Each was making their public confession of accepting Jesus Christ as their personal Savior and then being baptized. Four re-births. It was a rejoicing day for Jesus and Rev. Monty. There was a momentary pause in the process and many of us thought it was over. But then, the biggest black lady I'd ever seen in our church in my eighteen years of attending, stepped out from the curtains and slowly made her way down into the baptismal tank. With each step she took, the water crept higher and higher until it got dangerously close to the top of the glass.

Amanda leaned over and whispered to me as if I was Helen Keller and she was narrating a tragic news story. "Two more steps down and that water is going to cascade over the top and into the choir," she said.

And just as she finished her sentence, several choir members whose backs were to the baptismal must have noticed the fearful looks on the congregation's faces, so they turned around to see what was so shocking. One soprano, Mrs. Germanotta, saw the water level tipping towards the top of the tank and she got a look of fright on her face like those people wore when running down the street to flee from the "The Blob" or "Godzilla." That sent the congregation in a suppressed laughter that sucked half the oxygen out of the church.

Amanda saw the look on Mrs. Germanotta's face too. I guess because she had never been to a Baptist church before and didn't know that church wasn't a place of fun and laughter, she started laughing out loud. That caused Sara to laugh, which caused Ruth to laugh, which caused me to laugh. Together we unleashed a dam of more laughter that flowed over the balcony down through the pews and up to the altar. Until it got to Rev. Monty, who stood there with an embarrassed and extremely nervous look on his face. He was in a predicament. Then, like divine intervention, the big black lady stopped and spoke in a thick southern accent so loud one could almost hear it in Texas.

"Ya'll better just splash some water on my head, Rev, cause' I don't think you can hold me up and if ya'll drop me, half dem choir singers are goin' to get baptized too!"

The ENTIRE congregation including all the deacons, their wives, the choir members, the ushers and especially Rev. Monty burst into a hilarious roar that I can still hear echoing in my ears all these years later.

After the service, dad asked Amanda and Sara if they would like to join us for lunch at The Heritage House Smorgasbord Buffet. Sara jumped at the chance to spend more time with Ruth and I secretly jumped on the opportunity of increasing my odds of jumping on Amanda.

The morning had gone exceptionally well. Praise Jesus. No embarrassing incidents. No fatal faux pas'. I knew dad would take an immediate liking to Amanda. Guys are naturally drawn to her by her beauty. Even old guys like dad. But mom could care less about Amanda's physical sepulcher. It was what was inside her, that acted as a litmus test to mom's approval.

CHAPTER THIRTY-FIVE

The Heritage House Smorgasbord Buffet restaurant was packed. We filled our plates and found our way back to our table. By the look of Amanda's plate, one would have thought she hadn't eaten in days. It was piled high with French fries, fried chicken, macaroni and cheese and mashed potatoes. Like she had purposely piled the top four fattening foods of the buffet on her plate. She sat her dish down and then went to get her drink. I was alone at the table and actually tried to build a wall between her plate and mom's view with the condiments and little table tents they had sitting in the middle of the table. It was the first embarrassing thing Amanda had done that morning. And to be totally honest and fair with Amanda, to most people, it wouldn't have mattered.

But I knew the moment mom sat down and saw the pile of junk food sitting on Amanda's plate that she would be judging and expressing her adverse verdict when we got home. But that embarrassment would be lost in my mom's mind forever upon Amanda's first conversational words.

"Do you really think God is all-knowing or omniscient?" Amanda tossed out her new word as she dipped her French fry into a pile of ketchup and then stirred it into another pile of ranch dressing, she had concocted on her plate.

"As sure as you're sitting in front of me," mom said.

Oh! No! She! Wasn't! Going! There!

"Well, if God knows everything then God would know that Jesus wasn't really dying." Amanda paused, "Well, he may be dying to our mortal eyes, but God would know that he would come back to life because that was Jesus' purpose." She dipped one more fry. "And that's not a real sacrifice."

I loved watching my mother being challenged. But the last thing I needed was for Amanda to be that source of confrontation. Mom's pure disapproval of Amanda would mean that I had two fronts to fight. I was already struggling with the first but seemed to hopefully be making some kind of headway. But the battle against my mother's dislike of her would be arduous, to say the least. Joan of Arc-ish to say the most.

Mom's face grew rigid with horror, but Amanda was too busy trying to convey her latest epiphany. She continued.

"A real sacrifice would require not knowing that Jesus was coming back. I mean, let's say I wanted to sacrifice a virgin to the gods by throwing her into the volcano." Amanda moved the burning candle sitting in the middle of the table closer to her. "It's only a sacrifice because I'm losing her forever." She acted like she dropped something into the candle. "That's what makes it a sacrifice. But, if I tossed her into the volcano knowing she'd come walking out three days later, then it's not really a sacrifice, is it?" Amanda gave a satisfying smile that she had purposed such a profound idea.

Mom was still trying to choke down the mouth full of broccoli she had ingested during Amanda's first blasphemous question. Still, Amanda continued, not realizing she was stirring a pot of theological poison of apocalyptic proportion.

"And if God's is all-knowing or omniscient." She smiled upon saying her new word twice now. "Then He...or She for that matter...would know that Adam and Eve were already going to eat the apple. So why would He tell them not to eat it, when He knew they were going to eat it anyway? That's just silly."

Mom could not hold back her defensive verbal daggers any longer. "It's called free will. Amanda. God made us with minds to make our own choices. Not like puppets who have no choice in the matter of their own lives." Mom preached with a mixture of piety and anger. White and Red. Ketchup and Ranch dressing.

Amanda took a bite of her greasy fried chicken and chewed it with her mouth open while chewing on what mom had said.

Ruth and I just kept our heads bowed and silently ate our meals. Dad began moving restlessly around in his seat. Sara sat with a prideful smile on her face. She had seen her sister in the same situations many times. Resisting. Rebelling. Revolting.

"But when you really think about it, free will doesn't matter with an all-knowing or omniscient God." Amanda moved her plate to the side. "OK, pretend God is the referee of life and we're all the players. You have your black team. The sinners who are going to hell." She picked up the pepper shaker and gave it shake. And the team wearing the white are the Christians who are going to heaven." She held up the saltshaker.

"We're going about playing the game of life and yes we can make all the plays and pass the ball and do everything we want with our 'free will.' Amanda held up her two quotation fingers and then moved the salt and pepper shakers about in front of her. "But in the end, since God is omniscient and knows everything, then He already knows that the black players are losing and going to hell." Amanda set the pepper shaker next to the burning candle. "And his white players are winning and going to heaven." She put the saltshaker on top of a folded napkin. "So, in reality, free will doesn't mean a hoot's ass. As someone might say."

She leaned over and poked me with her elbow. Like we were on the same theological tennis team and she had just aced her serve. I was afraid she was going to shoot me the high five sign and thus seal my fate of forever living in the imaginary dungeon of the Hayes' house. I could see metaphorical flames began bursting forth from my mom's nostrils and her eyes went blood-red with rage.

Just as I thought I was about to witness the first fist fight mom had ever had, Mr. and Mrs. Lucas, friends of ours from church, came over to the table and gave everyone a robust and jolly, "Happy Easter!"

Mom immediately did her Doctor Jekyll, Mr. Hyde personality change and switched from scathing conquistador to cheerful Christian with the snap of a spiritual finger. And to act as holy water sprinkling on a forest of hell and brimstone fire, trith me, Ruth and dad quickly tossed out some pleasantries to entice the two to stay around a little until mom had cooled down.

"And who are these two beautiful young ladies?" Mrs. Lucas asked.

"This is my best friend Sara, and this is her sister, Amanda," Ruth replied as Sara and Amanda smiled. Everyone exchanged greetings.

It was time to make my break and pull Amanda away from the table and off the theological wrestling mat. As much as I sadistically enjoyed the confrontation between the two, I feared nothing good could come from it.

"I think I need another glass of tea," I said specifically to Amanda even though my glass was half full. "You want to come with me and get another soda." I raised my eyebrows and held my smiling stare so that she would get the hint to come with me. She caught the clue. "Sure," she said. We excused ourselves and made our way to the refreshment fountains.

"What are you trying to get me crucified?" I said half-jokingly with a trace of trepidation. "Questioning our religion and getting in a theological debate with my mom?"

"Well, first of all, I will always question anything I don't understand or doesn't make sense to me," she said matter of factly. "I'm not going to apologize, because that's just the way I am." She filled her cup with soda. "And secondly, I wasn't debating with your mother. I was simply speaking my thoughts on the subject." We walked over to the salad bar and began refilling out plates. "I didn't mean to get your mom's religious panties in a bunch."

Did she just say, "My mom's religious panties in a bunch? The thought of trith mom, religious and panties all used in the same sentence caused me to trip, which sent my salad sailing all over the back of Amanda's dress. Fortunately for both of us, there was no dressing on it yet. So the leafs of lettuce, tomatoes, carrots and celery just bounced off her back and landed on the floor. She quickly spun around, looked at me, then looked at the foliage mess on the floor. There was a second of uncertainty but then, like two mischievous children who accidentally broke a valuable vase, we burst out in a belly of laughter and quickly left the scene of spilled salad.

By the time we got back to the table, the Lucas' had gone, and everything seemed to have settled down. Mom was merrily talking to Ruth and Sara about the beautiful tulips that had popped up all over her flower garden. Dad was busy eating his baked tilapia. Amanda and I scooted back into our seats like nothing ever happened. Mom's attitude mellowed as she spoke in sweet tones of her daffodils and her love of her vegetable garden. Amanda listened intently and watched as mom finished her green beans and then moved on to her corn.

"I absolutely adulate gardens too." Amanda gracefully entered the conversation. "One of these days when I'm a rich and famous, I'm going to have a garden just like the one in the book *The Secret Garden*." She closed her eyes and imagined what it would look like. "It's one of my favorite childhood books," she added.

"That's one of my mom's favorite books too!" Ruth exclaimed. "Well, next to the Bible." She shot mom a repentant stare. "We've both read it a million times. Like you and Amanda read *Anne of Green Gables*." Ruth looked at Sara. "I just loved Mary and Robin Redbreast!"

"Me too!" Sara agreed. "But I like Dickon the best. Oh, how I wish I could meet a real boy like Dickon."

For the next ten minutes, all four ladies sitting around the table talked about what a wonderful story *The Secret Garden* was. I was happy to witness another Easter miracle. Everyone was in a unanimous agreement about one subject.

I think mom was moved by the fact that Amanda "absolutely adulated gardens" and placed *The Secret Garden* high on her favorites list of literature. Somehow, I got the impression that she felt that anyone who loved *The Secret Garden* couldn't be that bad. However, had Amanda said she "absolutely adulated" the Bible. It would have made her marrying material in my mother's eyes.

Ever since I can remember, mom had the habit of eating meals, one particular food at a time. She would typically start with vegetable and then move on to her starches like her pastas or Rice-A-Roni. And once she systematically ate her veggies and starches, she completed the meal by eating her meat. She rarely ever ate desserts but when she did it was in the same process. Cake first. Ice cream second.

I don't know why she did this. Maybe because that's how her mom fed her. Or perhaps it was the organized and proper way to clean her plate. Whatever the reason, her functionally dysfunctional eating habits had often caught the attention of others at holidays tables and church dinners. Occasionally friends and family would point it out.

It was now Amanda's turn.

"Why do you eat one thing at a time?" Amanda asked.

"I know, isn't that strange?" Ruth chimed in. I was thankful she used the word "that" and not "she."

Mom shrugged her shoulders. "I don't know. I've just eaten that way my entire life." She took another bite of her corn.

"Oh, come on, Mrs. Hayes. How boring." Amanda's manner became animated. "Your taste buds want to explode with a variety of flavors." She took a fork full of macaroni and cheese and then dipped it in her mashed potatoes and then ate it. "Let them dance and play with your jaws in the garden of your maws," she said, without waiting to swallow her food or keeping her mouth shut.

It was Sara's turn to talk. "Yeah, when we go to Burger Chef, Amanda even puts her French Fries on her hamburger." She made a yucky face. Mom made the same yucky face.

"I think that's the way God made food to be eaten." Amanda tossed the sentence in as her seal of approval.

"That quite possibly could be." My mother agreed to everyone's amazement. "But He also designed it in such a way that it should be done in the privacy of your own *oral entry*." She paused at her own wordplay and then finished her two-line poetic rhyme. "And not shared by everyone else around the table to see." She smiled. Not so much a smile of condemnation or belittlement, but one of satisfaction that she had gotten one over on the logosist.

Amanda quickly put her hand over her mouth.

"I'm sorry. Was I eating with my mouth open?" She bulleted an embarrassing stare my way. "That's so …hoosier-ish." She apologized.

For the rest of the meal, and for the rest of her life, Amanda ate with her mouth shut.

Just like that, The Hoosier Girl changed in a small manner and lost one of her hoosier ways. Did that change come from the inside or the outside? Or does change come from both the inside and the outside? I wondered.

And as far as mom? Well, she still eats one food at a time.

CHAPTER THIRTY-SIX

Amanda stuck her head around the corner of my locker. Second hour had just finished and I was unsuccessfully trying to get my gym shoes into my already overflowing book bag. I had a big chemistry test next hour and had worked two double shifts on Saturday and Sunday which had cut my study time to nearly nothing. I was up late the night before. Tired. Troubled. Her smile acted as aspirin to the headaches and worries of the morning. "Congratulations!" She smacked me on the back.

"For what?" I looked at her with suspicion hidden beneath a layer of interest; the normal feelings one felt when Amanda came to you with new and undisclosed information.

"Well, not only are you the Best Big Brother in the World, but I just found out you won "Best Smile" in the senior superlatives and you've also been nominated for Senior Prom court!" She clapped her hands and hugged me.

"And how do you know this?" I said with barely a tinge of emotion.

"Oh, you know, I have my spies and eyes all over school."

One more forceful shove and the heel of my tennis shoe bent just enough to fold into my gym bag allowing me to zip the zipper. I closed my locker and clicked the lock shut.

"Great. I guess that's what three years working at a roller-skating rink and eighteen years of daily brushing and flossing your teeth get you." I was still holding back my excitement. I tossed my gym bag over my shoulder and started down the hall.

Being voted with the "Best Smile" in the senior superlatives didn't really matter to me. I was not a fan of anything that involved the popular vote. If I were to travel forward in time, I would see that Scottie Miner whose

long flowing blonde hair that made many
girls insanely envious, would win the senior
superlative "Best Boy's Hair." And then lose it
and be almost entirely bald by our ten-year
reunion.

Jenny Kobalt, the personable, yet often
somewhat snobbish and bitchy, cheerleader
who was voted "Best Looking Female," carried
her beauty crown away to college and got
caught up in partying and too many pizzas. It
took her five years of marriage and three
kids, or roughly twelve years, to go from the
"Best Looking Female" in Hazelwood East to
look like the little, fat, haggard cook that
dished out the mushy peas and carrots in the
lunchroom.

Matter of fact, most of the popular slim
cheerleaders and trim jocks were sporting
spare tires around their waists and life's
fatigue on their faces by our fifteen-year
reunion.

And then there was Kevin Whitehead, the
industrious boy who had four guys on his
grass cutting company payroll while he was
still a senior in high school. He was voted
"Most Likely to Succeed," but ended up finding
greater happiness in suicide than dealing
with life.

I was friends with Kevin even after high
school. His is a tragic story. He had two
beautiful little girls and his grass cutting
company turned into a thriving landscaping
business with over thirty employees.

One cold Thanksgiving morning, he woke up
to the music of the Macy's Thanksgiving Day
parade blaring away on the TV in the living
room and the moaning of his wife, Gretchen,

being screwed in the garage by their
neighbor--a single and suave car salesman.

Like a faithful husband and loving father,
he tried to save the marriage through
counseling but six months later he found her
fucking the neighbor again—this time in
their bed. Gretchen filed for divorce on the
grounds that Kevin was never home. He was a
workaholic and she and the kids were
neglected. Kevin defended that he worked so
hard specifically because he loved her and
the kids and wanted to give them all the
comforts of life.

Gretchen didn't have to work. They had a
beautiful big two-story house, an in-ground
swimming pool, a finished basement that had a
pool table and a half a dozen pinball machines
in it. Their three-car garage contained
Kevin's old Dodge Ram pickup, a new Cadillac
and mini-van bought specifically for
Gretchen from the piece of shit car salesman
next door.

The day the divorce papers were served,
Kevin must have felt he had done everything
he could to make his wife happy, but it was to
no avail. So drove to the parking lot of the
Sears Automotive and put a bullet through his
brains.

I was shocked at the news of Kevin's suicide.
But more than shocked, I was angry and pissed
at both him and his douchbagette, cheating
whore of a wife, Gretchen. I watched her at
his funeral as she sat crying with their two
beautiful girls at her side. All I could
mentally muster was how she was now free to
do whatever she pleased. She would get the
insurance money, the big house would be paid
off, and she wouldn't have to go through an

ugly, drawn-out divorce. What Kevin meant as a revenge suicide was, in reality, a free lucrative lottery ticket for Gretchen to marry the scum bag car salesman neighbor.

The only losers in the entire situation where the two little girls who no longer had a loving and caring father. They had to live the rest of their lives trying to hide the fact that their dad had killed himself and wondering if he had some mental disorder or incurable depression that would one day make them do the same thing.

Five months after Kevin's body was buried, Gretchen and the neighbor got married. Less than a year later the scum bag car salesman was caught taking one of his lovely, young customers for a test drive in their bedroom. Gretchen immediately divorced him.

I ran into Gretchen a few times over the course of several years following Kevin's suicide. She looked like shit. Weary. Defeated. Ten years older than she was. Karma's a bitch baby. Kevin Whitehead, the senior voted "Most Likely to Succeed" was proof that prom courts, dance queens and voting contests like senior superlatives were just petty popularity contests that had no value to the meaning and purpose of life once you tossed up that graduation hat and got into the real world called Adult Life.

Poor Kevin Whitehead. A truly successful man would have stayed alive and made his wife's life pure hell by finding a better woman and a happier life. A greater level of happiness and lots of success is always the ultimate revenge.

As I said, I didn't give a hoot's ass about being voted with the best smile in the Senior Superlatives. But being nominated to prom court was an entirely different situation. It mattered. Only because it meant that I would have to take the night off at Aloha. Rent a tuxedo. Buy tickets. Order a corsage. Buy pictures and maybe rent a limo. But ultimately it meant I would have to find a date.

Now that Amanda and I were getting to know one another I hadn't paid much attention to other females. My Vagina Hunting scope had been set on one particular trophy. Why settle for ordinary skates when you can have the pretty pink leather ones, was my metaphoric philosophy. There was only one girl in my world who was worthy of all those prom expenses. Only one girl that would make my senior year prom the most incredible night of my life and she was standing in front of me.

"Did you know that this Friday will be exactly four months since we met?" Amanda asked.

And my life hasn't been the same ever since.

"And your life hasn't been the same ever since," she added as she nosed around my locker.

Mental Flash. The day our worlds collided. The excitement of it all. Her contagious smile that melted my heart. The purple panties that turned out to be skater's shorts. And then there was...the picture...

"You know, there's something I've never been able to figure out about the first time we met." I stopped mid-sentence, turned and put my hand on her shoulder. It was my turn to capture her attention and hold it with my touch. "Why did you give me your picture? I mean, you didn't even know me."

"I..." She started to say something but stopped. Then she stared at me for a microsecond before looking away. But in that microsecond stare, I read an entire book of thought. Thoughts she longed to share. Stories she wanted to tell. Secrets she yearned to disclose. But for some reason she rejected the idea and started walking down the hall again but this time with a little more silliness in her step. "It's a secret that I might share with you one of these days."

We walked through the stares and up the stairs to The Commons watching kids quickly stop at the vending machines to grab a soda or candy bar to snack on between classes. Above the Dr. Pepper machine was a handmade poster that read: "The Best of Times" and beneath it was the details about prom. Ticket prices. Place. Time. This year's prom theme was "*The Best of Times*" based on one of my favorite rock group, Styx's, hit song.

"Amanda." Someone yelled out and shortly several girls surrounded her. A little brunette with purple eyeshadow and too much mascara asked her if she had a cigarette she could borrow. Amanda opened her *Anne of Green Gables* purse, took out a pack of Marlboro Lights, pulled one out and gave it to her. "Thanks," she said taking the cigarette. "Are you going to the smoking area?" The purple-eyed girl asked motioning to the door outside and ignoring the fact that I was standing right next to her and we were in mid-conversation.

"No, don't have time." Amanda smiled and with her smile, she dismissed the girls. We walked away and continued our discussion.

"So, it wasn't just a random gift because it was my birthday? Or a thank you for giving you the pretty pink skates? There was an actual reason or purpose for it?" I pressed.

"Of course, there was a reason." There was a discerning sound of indignation in her voice at the thought I would even suggest that she had given me her picture—just because. "That wasn't just any picture. It was one of the only two big ones that came in the package. Yes, there was a purpose for it." And then she tried to change the subject. "I don't think you've ever told me what you did with it after Mr. Abernathy gave it back to you, *that day*." And by saying "that day" we both knew she was referring to the day after "that night."

"It's taped to the ceiling above my bed." I lied. "You're the first person I wake up to and the last person my eyes fall asleep seeing."

Amanda rolled her eyes.

In reality, it was in the safest place in the entire house. It was next to my bed buried deep within my Bible. Everyone in our family had our own Bibles, not to mention the other half dozen that was scattered about the house.

There would never be any reason why mom, dad
or Ruth would ever want, or need, to use my
Bible. If mom were to go snooping around my
bedroom for signs of sin, she'd look in the
closets, dresser and under the bed, but she'd
never imagined in her entire pious life that
I would put something as sacrilegious as a
picture of a beautiful, sexy, hoosier girl in
my Bible. I felt no sense of guilt or
condemnation. What better place to put a
picture of a word collector, than into God's
Word?

I continued to push the issue. "What purpose?"

"I told you, it's a secret and one day when..." She paused and
recalculated the statement. "...Or if ever, the time is right; I'll share that
secret with you."

"The time is right? What does that mean? How is that accomplished
or determined?" I tried to censor the censure in my voice with a slight
smile. "Do I have to run into a burning building to save your picture?
Or maybe commit an academic felonious crime and have my parents
disown me?"

I believed that I had proven my worthiness
in many ways and now it was time for some
payback. I wasn't asking for sex or any kind
of commitment. I just wanted a few simple
answers and maybe some returned favor.

"Those are good starts of worthiness," Amanda smiled.

"Amanda..." I said and then took a deep breath.

I'll never forget it because it was one of those monumental
moments in life. The kind that burns an indelible impression on your
brain and it doesn't matter how many times the earth traipses around
the sun and causes days to turn into years and years into decades, you
never forget it. I was standing with my back to the soda machines
looking towards the administrative offices. Natasha Krieger, the most

unusual and strangest girl in the senior class just skated by in her "Pop Outs" clog shoes that turned into roller skates with a click of a button.

Amanda was wearing a stone-washed denim skirt that came to just above her knees with slits running up both sides exposing her thin, sexy thighs. She had on a white belt and white heels with leather straps. Her top was tight and yellow with a mint-colored triangle that started at about her naval and wrapped around her back. Her hair was pulled into a ponytail tied by a yellow ribbon and it sat on the right side of her head. My palms began to sweat. I could feel everything inside my body begin to twist and tighten causing my lungs to stifle the output of air and leaving me with a shortage of breath. And then, before I changed my mind or lost my nerve, I asked.

"How would you like to have the honor of attending prom with the senior guy who has the best smile?" Then I faked the biggest nervous smile I could muster.

Her face lit up like a charismatic lightning bolt. "I thought you'd never ask!" And for one majestic moment, my heart was ready to swim with the dancing dolphins in a sea of happiness. But then, just as quick as a lightning bolt lasts, she changed her composure and looked away. "But I can't." Her stare fell firmly to the ground and my heart and happiness followed it. "I already told someone else I'd go with him." When she looked back up, she must have seen the hurt in my eyes and how her rejection smacked the fake smile off my face because she came over and gave me a consoling hug. "Sorry."

FUCK. Why did you do that? Why wouldn't you probe the issue first and see if she already had a date? And why would you think she wouldn't have a date? She's Amanda Marrow. The Freshman Fire. She's probably been asked to prom by a dozen guys months ago before we even officially met.

But no, you're caught up in the excitement of being in the Queen's court and thinking she favors you. And somehow or some way, she's going to finally give in and see you're the guy she needs in her life to lead her down the path of righteousness and cure her of her

hoosier ways. And you foolishly think that in
return, she's going to give you her body to do
whatever you want with it as a reward for
your kindness. What a stupid, sex-starved,
eighteen-year-old you are Christian Matthew
Hayes.

"Who?" I wanted to know what classmate would rein at the top of
my hate and envy list because he would be having The Best of Times
conquering the Vagina of the love of my life on prom night.

She started to back slowly away as she gave me a hesitant smile.
"Oh, come on, where's that award-winning beautiful smile, Christian
Mathew Hayes?" I felt as if she was holding a secret that had to be told,
but by doing so, someone was going to be hurt. She gave one last
parting smile and started down the Freshman hall.

"Who!" I raised my voice, partly out of angered frustration and
partly out of necessity as she got further away. Several classmates
turned to see who I was yelling at.

"Your friend." She yelled, shoving the knife deeper into my heart.

"Who?" I didn't want to know any more, but it was as if I was
watching my own train wreck and I couldn't turn my head or stop my
lips. I needed to know how this nightmare was all going to end.

She was almost out of sight and sound but above the cacophony of
kids that surrounded her I could see her face as she turned around with
a smile as big as the sun and screamed at the top of her lungs, "Sir
Vodka Watermelon White Knight Hayes!"

I didn't catch what she meant at first because I was still dazed and
numbed by the previous rejection. But then, true to Amanda's ways, I
realized she was being her usual obnoxious self and making me
mentally suffer one minute only to come to my climatic rescue the next.

"Is that a yes?" I don't remember the words coming out of my
mouth, just the euphoric feelings coming into my soul.

"No, it's a Mais Oui Mon Ami! See you at lunch." She screamed at
the top of her lungs, turned and I watched her disappear down the hall.

"Thank you, Jesus!" I jumped up into a cloud of happiness and
high-fived the sun.

And so it came to be, like a biblical miracle, that I asked Amanda
Marrow, The Freshman Fire, to prom and she accepted. I felt as the
blind man must have felt when Jesus lifted the darkness from his eyes

and gave him sight. Rapturous. Heavenly. My feet carried my body towards Chemistry class, but my mind was miles away. I wanted to skip class and find Chuck and tell him the unbelievable news but more than that, I wanted to run to Principal Perry's office and flip the switch to the school intercom and shout into it.

"May I have the entire school's attention? Amanda Marrow is going to prom with Chris Hayes!"

I found myself once again on the verge of being tardy as I walked in a trance-like state to the senior side of the school. Ask me if I gave a flying fart? Nope. I could fail, not only the test but the entire chemistry class and I wouldn't have given a hoot's ass. Christian Hayes, the boy with the Best Smile, plastered upon his face, was going to prom with Amanda Marrow. Nothing in the world could ruin the ecstasy of the moment. I rounded the corner busy with pulling my chemistry book from my gym bag and suddenly...

BANG!

We collided like atoms in a black hole which sent an echo down the hall and into my ringing ears. I felt my body fall backward as I attempted to juggle my chemistry book and gym bag back into my arms. But my hands instinctively abandoned the book and bag to brace myself from crashing ass first to the ground. I followed the backward falling momentum and when I hit the floor, I tumbled into a back roll. Three hundred and sixty degrees later, I quickly jumped up and landed on my feet. The entire scene must have taken about five seconds and looked like a clown act in the Barnum and Bailey Circus.

When I finally finished, I was standing face to face with Dirk Howard. His books were scattered on the floor, his eyes filled with rage and the veins in his neck were sticking out against his tightened skin. Then, before I could even gather my senses, with all his might, he shoved me into the lockers causing another crashing noise down the chemistry corridor.

"Why don't you watch where you're fucking going Hayes!" His daring and evil stare pierced my prom bubble as he waited with clenched fists for me to say something so he would have an excuse to launch into a fight with me.

Little did I know at the time, Dirk had thought I was the one who told Principal Perry that he was drunk at the Sweetest Heart Dance. Don't get me wrong, I would have told on him if he kept harassing Amanda, but I didn't. It was Mark Ferris who went over and said something to Principal Perry. One of Amanda's spies said that Dirk would have gotten expelled, but his dad came to school and pleaded mercy for him on the grounds he was still grieving the loss of his mother. So Principal Perry only gave him a three-day suspension. Ever since then Dirk Howard hated me and I didn't even know it. We were no longer in any classes but whenever our eyes met around the lunch tables or in the halls, he would always hold his stare. As if to say, "I'm going to get you, Hayes." I figured he was carrying a grudge against me because I was now part of the Queen's court—a queen that had blackened his eye and reputation and lived to tell about it.

Now those same eyes were staring at me and I was sensing something terrible was about to happen as dogs, chickens, and cows sense earthquakes before they happen. Fast. Frightening. I looked around to see if any teachers or staff were there to witness whatever was about to take place. But we were alone and the bell was about to ring. Just like it does at the start of a boxing match.

DING. DING. DING.

CHAPTER THIRTY-SEVEN

"You got something to say Preacher Boy?" Dirk took one step closer and I could feel his breath on my face and see that he longed to hurt me in his eyes.

I was scared. I'm not afraid to admit it. Dirk was a wrestler who liked fighting as much as Amanda loved rare and beautiful words. The odds were definitely in his favor. But even though I was scared, I didn't fear him. There's a fine line between being scared and having fear. I learned that lesson when I was a kid in Sunday school through different bible stories like David and Goliath and Daniel in the Lion's Den. I was taught that one can be scared, yet still be fearless.

It was written on a wooden plaque that hung on our foyer wall that I'd seen every day of my entire life. I can quote it.

The Lord is my shepherd; I shall not want.
He maketh me to lie down in green pastures:
He leadeth me beside the still waters.
He restoreth my soul:
He leadeth me in the paths of righteousness for his name's sake.
Yea, though I walk through the valley of the shadow of death,
I will fear no evil: for thou art with me;
Thy rod and thy staff they comfort me.
Thou preparest a table before me in the presence of mine enemies:
Thou anointest my head with oil; my cup runneth over.
Surely goodness and mercy shall follow me all the days of my life:
And I will dwell in the house of the Lord forever.
Psalm 23

Dirk Howard was evil. He had turned into a bully who enjoyed bringing misery into the lives of others because misery had entered his

own life with the loss of his mother. Evil
loves misery. Misery loves company. Both are
the best of friends. And even though I was
scared and thought he would probably kick my
ass, I wasn't afraid of him.

I just wasn't ready to fight him. And when I
say I wasn't ready; I mean I wasn't ready on two
levels. The first being, school wasn't the
right place for a fight. It didn't matter who
was in the right or wrong, school fights went
into those academic records that followed you
to your grave.

I had a squeaky clean academic record. I
wasn't about to blow it weeks away from
finishing secondary school forever.

My second reason for un-readiness was the
fact that I wasn't sure it was the right time
for such a fight. My heart hadn't wholly
convinced my head if Amanda was worthy of
such a battle.

After all, Dirk wasn't fighting me; he was
fighting Amanda, through me. By hurting me,
he was avenging himself. Was I important
enough to Amanda to allow myself to be her
whipping boy?

No, I wasn't quite ready to take on Dirk just yet, so I simply bent
over and gathered my books back into my gym bag and walked away.

"You pussy," Dirk yelled down the hall.

If there was any amount of compassion for Dirk Howard as a
former friend or fellow Boy Scout left in me, it was now completely
sucked empty and the void was filled with seething hatred. I went to
chemistry class riding a rollercoaster of emotions. Ecstasy.
Embarrassment. I couldn't concentrate. My mind was caught up in that
bullshit game you play with yourself after a sucky situation when you
replay the scenario over and over in your mind and you think to
yourself, "I should have done this or said that." And of course, the
things you think to say and do after it's all over when your mind is a

little less muddled are amazingly more wonderful then what you actually said and did. And so you mentally beat yourself up once again and sometimes it's even worse than the mental beating you received in the sucky situation. I was so emotionally black and blue while taking the chemistry test I wasn't able to answer something as simple as:

What's the common name of the chemical compound Fe_2O_3?

Everyone knows that answer. It's Iron III Oxide or Hematite one of the most abundant minerals on Earth's surface. But all I could come up with was an imaginary Choice D. "Why didn't you smash his face with your fist?" When the dismissal bell rang I still had a half dozen questions unanswered. I took the test up to the teacher's desk and despairingly dropped it off. Then I walked out of the class.

I felt as if the weight of the world or at least every personal problem I had was heavy on my shoulders and it pressed down on my entire being prohibiting me from walking fully upright and normal. I walked slumped shouldered down to The Commons to meet Amanda. I didn't even stop at my locker to get my lunch. I felt as if everyone was looking at me slouching down the hall. I knew they weren't, but that didn't stop the angel on my right shoulder telling me I did the right thing. I was being mature and Christ-like. While the devil on my left shoulder was having a hell of a time calling me a pussy and a coward and whispering that everyone around me knew it.

I didn't feel it was necessary to tell Amanda about the confrontation with Dirk. How I had pussed out when I should have smashed his face, even if it meant I would have still got an ass kicking. I figured she would already know. Her spies would have a heyday with this one.

I went straight to the Common's cafeteria, walked over to the lunch line and got a piece of pizza and a Dr. Pepper. It was a quick fix, a temporary vice for a boy who ate healthily and didn't drink, smoke or do drugs. Pepperoni Pizza and a Dr. Pepper would become my go-to comfort food to wash away my woes for years to come.

"Are you all right?" Amanda felt my forehead. "I've never seen you have pizza and soda for lunch before."

"The chemistry test took it all out of me." I semi-lied. I took a bite of pizza and gnawed on its greasy cheesiness waiting for her to say something satirical or severe about the sucky situation that took place just an hour earlier, but to my utter amazement, she didn't say anything. I wasn't sure if she didn't know about it or was taking the higher road and not saying anything to save me some embarrassment. I faked a sense of relief. I watched her walk up to the food line followed by a flock of friends and come back and cheerfully start eating her chicken fried steak sandwich with her mouth closed.

"Ok, I was thinking about us going to prom together." She slid her chair closer to mine and lowered her voice so all the prying ears around the table didn't hear. "And I've decided that we have to set some ground rules beforehand."

Those four words—going to prom together—slowly soothed my slumped self out of the funk I was currently residing in. It was like waking from a nightmare and realizing it was all just a dream. But in this case, I was waking from a nightmare and realizing I was in the dream and—going to prom together—with Amanda Marrow. Scattered in the midst of all those emotions and buried deep behind the elation and the agony of the morning, I also had an agenda of my own and ground rules that I felt needed to be discussed.

"I agree," I said and took a sip of soda.

"First, you can't think that we're a couple. Just friends."

"I know that we're just friends." I rolled my eyes and assured her that rule wasn't something she needed to worry about. Yes, I longed to be more than just mere friends with her, but I wasn't about to admit to it. It was my turn to toss out a ground rule.

"You can't drink or smoke the entire night," I said.

She didn't react like I thought she would. I figured she'd veto that request or we'd have to work out some compromise where she could only have a few drinks, but not get drunk and she could smoke but only if I wasn't around to smell it. But to my utter amazement, she put her fingers to her lips and played it like a piano then turned her stare into the air and thought about it for a couple of seconds. Then shook her head and agreed. I don't know why, but somehow, I got this strange sense that she was finally settling on some kind of self-improvement solution. Like a person who looks in the mirror and realizes they're out of shape and decides to say no when the lady at the drive-thru says, "Would you like fries with that sir?" The light comes on in their brain. The time had come to cut out the junk food and get on an exercise program but in Amanda's case, she was cutting back on those hoosier-ish vices. But then she took the ground rules one step further.

"You can't expect to have sex with me." She grinned as she played her Vagina Hunter trump card.

I threw my hands up into the air and shrugged my shoulders. "What?" Well then never mind." I pushed away from the table. "That was the only reason I wanted to go with you in the first place." I got up and started walking away only to turn back and see her sitting there with a "you're so full of shit" look upon her face. I sat back down at the lunch table and immediately dished out another one of my ground rules.

"Ok, I agree. But you can't wear anything..." I paused to make sure she completely understood what I was saying. "...hoosier-ish."

"Wait a minute." She got slightly indignant. "You're telling me what to wear to prom?"

"No, I'm not telling you what to wear, I'm asking you politely to wear something sophisticated and sexy. Not slutty. We've had this conversation before."

"Ok, but you can't preach to me about anything. Just enjoy the evening." She tossed in one final rule.

"Preach? I don't preach."

Just as her feelings were hurt with the not hoosier-ish dress request, my feelings were hurt with the preaching accusation. I didn't like it when my mother preached at me and yet, there I was being accused of doing the same thing. To me, it wasn't preaching; it was just more of suggested guidance in a better direction of life.

Oh my God, that sounded exactly like something my mother would have said to defend herself against my accusations of her preaching to me.

"Agreed. But you can't fart all night." I tossed that out to be funny, but it caused her almost to spit out her chicken fried steak sandwich. Her face turned red and she shot me a piercing look."

"That's not fucking funny at all."

"I was just kidding! Geez, why are you so sensitive about that?"

"I just find that parlously repulsive."

I had no idea what the word parlously meant but repulsive was simple. It meant there was a line that even a hoosier girl draws in her personal beliefs that she refuses to cross lest she considers herself rude and crude.

One could drink themselves into a disgusting stupor or smell as vile as a skunk by smoking; they could talk as trashy as a sailor or dress like a lady of the night, but exhibiting the natural body function of releasing stomach gas from your anus (at least publicly) was a hoosier's hoosier line.

Very interesting.

Parlous: *Adjective*: *Full of danger; perilous*
   Adverb: greatly or excessively

CHAPTER THRITY-EIGHT

Costello Tuxedo's in Jamestown Mall looked like an army recruiter's office. Dozens of high school boys were standing around in nervous anticipation waiting their turn to pick up their tuxes. I decided to wear the white-on-white tux with the baby-blue cummerbund and tie to compliment Amanda's dress. The manager was busy in the back stock room looking for a pair of ultra-shiny, white, patent leather shoes. The scene was chaotic. It seemed like every school in the St. Louis area was having prom that weekend. Chuck and I had just finished visiting Amanda at Waldenbooks and were waiting like the rest.

"I can't believe you're going to prom with Amanda Marrow," Chuck said with an underscore of jealousy. He had known for weeks, but as the date drew nearer, it was starting to settle into his doubting skull. "I mean you're not a jock. You're not even what you call that popular. You're very average looking." He shrugged his shoulders. "Oh, you've got a great smile going for you, I'll give you that. But how or why you got Amanda Marrow, The Freshman Fire, the hottest chick in high school, maybe in the entire Spanish Lake area, to go to prom with you is a mystery to me."

Memento Homo. It's said that when the Roman military leaders, like Caesar Augustus and Octavian, rode in their Triumphs (parades celebrating their military victories), they would have a slave standing behind them whispering the words, "Memento Homo" or "Remember, you are only human," into their ears to remind them that even with all their success and victories, they were not gods or immortal. They were still frail and faulted mortal human beings.

You have to love having a friend who, in their own loving and innocent way, whispers "Memento Homo" into your ear at the height of your glory.

"I think you should get her drunk and do-the-dirty in the hotel so I can watch." Chuck's expression got sexually sinister.

"We're just friends." I waved Chuck's conquer by association away. "And besides we made an agreement that she can't smoke or drink the entire night and I don't expect any sex."

"What! Are you flipping crazy? That's not an agreement, that's pure stupidity on your part. Let her drink, smoke and then expect something sexual." He made the universal blowjob sign. "I wouldn't care if she tasted like an ashtray and got so drunk she vomited all over me if it meant we were doing-the-dirty." Chuck then did the universal sex sign with the hips and the fist thrusting opposite one another.

"You're a sick puppy. Charles Kobalt"

The manager of Costello Tux came out from the back room wearing a cloth measuring tape around his neck and a frazzled look on his face like he wanted to be hung with the same tape.

"Here ya go. I think it's the last pair of white patent leather shoes in the entire St. Louis area." He handed me a bag with the shoes in it and I thanked him. He took Chuck's receipt. "I'll be right back." He disappeared into the back room.

"You know I once read somewhere that New Year's Eve and Prom Night were the two biggest nights of the year that virgins lost their virginity," Chuck informed me.

The manager returned with Chuck's tux and shoes and guided us to the checkout counter and proceeded to ring us out.

"One never knows with Amanda Marrow. She might like the fact that you're a virgin and she'd be the first to deflower you." He gave me a curious look. "She does know that you're a virgin right?" The manager paused before taking Chuck's change out of the register and turned his glance towards me waiting for my answer.

"NO!" My face flushed and my threatened stare cautioned Chuck to keep his voice down. "I don't know how she would," I whispered. "I wouldn't volunteer that information and I expect it to stay that way."

The manager handed Chuck his change. "Thank you," he said with a slight grin. I paid for my tux rental and as we turned to leave, the manager leaned over the counter and said in a fatherly tone. "I've been doing this job for seventeen years and let me warn you, in the umpteenth thousands of tux return conversations I've heard, prom night is the biggest night of the year to lose your virginity. So be wise and take precautions."

This wasn't Hustler magazine hearsay, this was pure fact, straight from the mouth of the tailor. Chuck and I gave him an awkward appreciative smile and left the store.

"I can't promise that I'll keep your virginity secret from Amanda." Chuck jested. "I might accidentally let it slip out." He paused. "Of course, if you were to offer your best friend a bribe, like a visual show or pair of panties if something did happen, I could guarantee my silence."

I can't say the thought of something sexual happening between Amanda and me wasn't at the tip of my cerebral cortex.

As a stupid, sex-starved, eighteen-year-old, sexual thoughts sat on my brain like a gargoyle sits on the architectural end of the Notre Dame Cathedral. Watchful. Threatening.

CHAPTER THIRTY-NINE

"I don't like the thought of you renting a hotel room for a post-prom party." Mom cornered me with her words as I walked into the kitchen. Ruth was up in her room and dad was outside. How she ever found out I was the one who was actually renting the room, I'll never know. But she did and now she wanted to broach the subject alone. Dad may have tilted his opinion to the side of letting me enjoy my last high school social event of my life. And Ruth, well, she was always ready to take my side. Other than our family vacations and youth camp, I had never spent the night in a hotel room without mom and dad supervising from an adjoining room.

"Mom, we don't drink, smoke, or do drugs." I opened the refrigerator and took out the carton of milk. "And nothing is going to happen between Amanda and me. We're just friends. What else could possibly happen?"

"Well if none of that is going to happen, why do you need to rent a hotel room? Why don't you all just come over here? I'll have snacks and soft drinks and you can talk and play board games until the sun comes up." She motioned to the window where the spring sunshine was pouring in through the parted drapes. "At least I know you'll be safe and sound."

Safe and sound from what? Drunk drivers? Bullies? A red-headed, demon-possessed girl named Carrie?

"Safe and sound?" I asked. "Mom, snacks and soft drinks don't sound too safe and sound for my health and physical well-being."

She knew I was patronizing her. She also knew I knew it wasn't my health she wanted me to be safe and sound from. It was my morals.

Her fear was of me making unwise and unChrist-like choices. But there was even a greater fear-a beautiful, brown-eyed Hoosier girl.

"Come on mom, how could you not trust me? Have I ever behaved in a manner that would lead you to think you couldn't trust me?"

She rolled her eyes. "It's called peer pressure and it can be more powerful than willpower." Then to stir the pious religious pot, she added. "It was peer pressure that sent Jesus to the cross."

"Oh, brother!" It was my turn to roll my eyes. "I thought it was God's Will that sent Jesus to the cross. Now you're telling me it was peer pressure?"

I couldn't believe my ears. My mother was using Jesus' crucifixion as a means of hijacking the enjoyment out of my prom night? Someone must have told her that prom night was the biggest night of teenage fornication and it was chewing on her parental conscious like a hungry piranha.

"It's true!" She reached over to the Bible sitting on the counter and flipped through the pages until she found the passage:

"*And they cried out again, Crucify him. Then Pilate said unto them, Why, what evil hath he done? And they cried out the more exceedingly, Crucify him. And so Pilate, willing to content the people...*" Mom stopped reading and looked me in the eyes. She continued. "*...released Barabbas unto them, and delivered Jesus, when he had scourged him, to be crucified.* Mark 15:13-15." Mom shut the Bible with the air of Moses tossing the Ten Commandment tablets at the Israelites. "Now if that's not peer pressure, I don't know what is!"

Here was a perfect example of mom Bible-beating me. Bible-beating is when one uses the Word of God to habitually control the actions of another. Like a whip to a disobedient slave.

However, Bible-beating doesn't leave physical scars. It leaves something worse. Mental and emotional trauma. It lacerates the brain and impedes better judgment that lasts a lifetime.

In many instances, Bible-beating is birthed out of kindness. But when it is used consistently as a form of manipulation and power, it becomes unscrupulous and evil.

The result is hatred and spite in its victim; forcing one to fight and rebel in the hope of causing emotional (and sometimes physical) pain to the Bible-beater. This gives the victim a sense of gratification and revenge.

Ask any preacher's kid (or PK). They're the biggest recipients of Bible-beating.

I grabbed the Bible and found my own ammunition in this war of Holy Words.

"You believe the Bible to be the perfect word of God?" I asked.

"Absolutely."

"And there are no mistakes. It's all the absolute Truth?"

"I would lay my life down on it."

I paged through Proverbs until I found the verse I wanted. "OK, let me read a few words of Truth." I cleared my throat. "In the sixth chapter of Proverbs David says, *"Train up a child in the way he should go: and when he is old, he will not depart from it."* I looked her in the eye. "Did you train me up in the way of God?" I asked.

"I tried to the best of my ability."

"Then according to God's Perfect Truth." I pointed to the verse. "I will not depart from it." I closed the Bible and almost sacrilegiously tossed it back onto the counter.

"First of all." Mom took her defensive stance. Which is like her interrogative stance but instead of only one of her hands on her hip, they're both on her hip. "You're not *old*. You're just a teenager. And secondly, it's not you, I'm so much worried about." Her voice rose argumentatively. "It's your peers. Your friends. Those you associate with that can pull even the greatest man of God into the depths of sin and depravity."

"Well you've never had any qualms with Chuck being my best friend for eight years, so I'm presuming you have some Godly ax to grind with my choice of who I'm taking to the prom?"

The was a long silence as we stood defiantly starring at one another.

"Amanda is a very attractive young lady." Mom began in a softer, more rational voice. "She seems to be very smart and personable, but…"

"But she's a hoosier."

There I said it. I spotlighted the white elephant in the room with a single word. Hoosier. And there I was again about to defend Amanda's hoosier-ness.

"Yes. She's a hoosier!" Mom spit the nasty "H" word out.

Once upon a time when I was about 13-years-old, a couple of Jehovah Witnesses women came knocking on our door. I was in the living room watching TV. I could hear a constant banter between my mother and one of the ladies at the door. I snuck into the hall to listen.

As I said, I love watching anyone stand up to my mother. This woman was doing a good job countering mom's accusations that the Jehovah Witnesses were nothing but a cult. You could almost see flames flowing from my mother's nostrils as she tossed scripture after scripture at them only to be defended by another shield of scriptures.

Finally, after about five minutes of this folly, the Jehovah Witness asked my mom…

"Ma,am, is there anything I can say or do that would make you change the way you feel?"

"Nope." My mom replied and promptly crossed her arms and waited for her next rebuttal.

"Then my time would be more wisely spent talking to someone else. God bless you." And with that, they turned and started to walk

away but before they stepped off the porch,
each wiped their feet on our door mat.

It was so strange because you usually wipe
your feet before you go into someone's house.
Yet, these ladies were wiping their feet upon
leaving our front porch. Like they had
stepped in dog shit or something.

I'll never forget it. Especially the
reaction mom had on her face. It was as if they
were giving her the finger in some Biblical
way. The incident had a lasting impression on
me.

That Jehovah Witness lady, had the wisdom
and sensibility to understand that all the
arguing in the world, wasn't going to persuade
my mother to change her opinion, so why waste
time and breath doing it?

One Sunday morning about three years later.
I was sitting in church when Rev Monty began
reading from the book of Matthew....

"And whosoever shall not receive you, nor
hear your words, when ye depart out of that
house or city, shake off the dust of your feet."
Matt. 10:14

I remembered the Jehovah Witnesses
incident and realized those two ladies were
doing exactly what Jesus told them to do. In
their minds, they were doing the Will of God,
just as much as mom thought she was doing the
Will of God by calling them out as being a
cult.

That little incident planted a tiny seed of
doubt in my mind. It made me seriously
question the "Truths" and "Beliefs" of
organized religion. Prior to Jehovah
Witnesses, I was like a puppy dog that followed
along on the leash of religious loyalty.
Happy. Content. Trusting.

And then I met Amanda. We openly talked about the dogmas, hypocrisy, and all the contradictions of Christianity, Catholicism and other organized religions. It felt amazing being able to speak honestly from my heart and not be condemned or judged.

Little did I know, I was coming out of the closet of closed-mindedness.

I also found it incredibly strange that even though Amanda and I were worlds apart in our moral and spiritual upbringings when we tossed out all the rules and regulations of organized religion, we had the same ideologies and beliefs. Love. Kindness. Peace. Truth.

My mother and I were about to start our own argument over her deep-seeded hatred of "Hoosierism." I knew she loved me and wanted the best for me. She was attempting to keep her (Christian), Christian away from a girl, a hoosier girl to be exact, that made terrible choices. One who cursed, smoked, drank, and was promiscuous.

Yet, ironically, even with all her faults that I hated and wanted her to change, it was Amanda's good characteristics that spoke the Words of Christ louder and more powerful than a lifetime of reading the Bible and going to church. Amanda's truth, kindness, compassion, and forgiveness magnified the existence of God in my eyes.

But I doubted, because of her religious radicalism and hoosier phobia, that mom would ever see Amanda as anything other than a heathen, hoosier girl. It was pointless to argue.

I silently said to myself, "All the arguing in the world, wasn't going to persuade my

mother to change her opinion, so why waste time and breath doing it."

For the first time in my life. I looked at my mother and at that exact moment, I realized I was becoming an adult. A truly mature human being that could see the difference between piousness and prejudice. I was not mad. I was filled with more pity for her than anger. I could only think of one thing to say. So, I said it with a smile. "Que Sera, Sera. What will be, will be." And with that, I went upstairs to shower and get ready for prom. When I got to the top of the stairs, I wiped my feet on the carpet.

CHAPTER FORTY

Set way back in the corner of Spanish Lake, hidden by farmer's fields and woods, was a mysterious place to many locals called the Pipefitter's Recreational Complex. In addition to having grand ballrooms where local schools held proms and couples had wedding receptions, there were also meeting rooms, an apartment complex for retired union pipefitters, a golf course, and a humongous swimming pool. Supposedly the second largest privately-owned pool in the country. The entire complex was surrounded by a ten-foot-tall electric fence topped off with two rows of barbed wire and an armed guard at the front gate entrance. It was the home and headquarters to a branch of alleged organized crime. Several of its residents were even survivors of car bombs that plagued St. Louis during the previous decade. Giving St. Louis the notorious title of the top car bombing city in the country during the 1970s.

During the summer, Pipefitters, as it was called, was an aquatic retreat for its privileged patrons. Its five diving boards and two poolside cocktail bars were reminiscent of a rather large Las Vegas resort, minus the scantily clad poolside servers. It was what we called the "Face Place" of North County. Where local, and sometimes even national, celebrities were seen swimming and schmoozing with politicians, police chiefs and other powerful people. I lived in Spanish Lake my entire life and had never once been beyond the front gates. Tonight would be the first.

The excitement of the evening was almost paralyzing. I drove into the Pipefitters with Amanda Marrow, the Freshman Fire in my passenger seat and Chuck and Nancy in the back. So far the evening had gone literally picture perfect. We posed for pictures at Amanda's house. Lucy and Sara were as excited as the rest of us as they clicked the camera's shutter button and put us in various poses. I wished Ruth was there to experience the fun too. Amanda had decided to wear a long white taffeta dress with ruffles that ran horizontally from her hips to the ground completely covering her slender sexy legs. Flowing from the top of her beautiful petite breasts up towards her neck and down the lengths of her arms was a sheer white satin lace in a floral pattern then ended with a baby blue taffeta collar and matching cuffs. In one word she looked—*pure*.

"Doesn't she look like Sandy in Grease?" Sara asked. You could see the pride of her sister's beauty shining in her eyes.

"Besides the fact that Olivia Newton-John is tall with blue eyes and blonde hair and I'm short with brown eyes and long brown hair…"

"And you can't sing," Sara added.

"Yes, I can't sing." Amanda agreed.

"You look stunning," I assured her. Chuck and Nancy both agreed.

But something inside my conscious sort of bothered me. She looked too virtuous. She was covering everything sexy about her. Now that I was the one that was going to be walking in the room with her, I wanted her to be more revealing. Not slutty, mind you, but sexual in a sinister sort of way. I wanted her to set the stares of all the other Vagina Hunter's ablaze with lustful envy. It was a strange and hypocritical feeling. Demonic. Possessive.

They say that power corrupts. If it's true, then attention and vanity are its bastard siblings.

While Lucy and Sara were busy taking Chuck and Nancy's pictures, Amanda leaned over to me and whispered. "Not that you're ever going to see them, but beneath this dress is the hottest sheer laced bra and pair of crotch-less white satin panties." Her fingers flowed down her dress to guide my eyes. "With French garters and matching thigh-high stockings." They stopped just below her crotch.

I shut my eyes and tilted my head back in sexual frustration. "Now why in God's creation would you ever tell me that? Knowing full well, it was going to drive me crazy all night." Her wicked ploy had worked. "You are a cruel little vixen, Amanda Marrow."

"And no matter how much of a good friend, nice guy or Best Big brother in the World you are…" She continued our secret conversation.

"You are still a Vagina Hunter deep inside. You can't fool me Chrisssstian Hayes." She lobbed a condescending smile and a teasing stare right at me. Then, without warning hit me with, "I'm just kidding." She spun around and her dress widened with the wind. "With all this taffeta over me and the fact that we're not going to do anything tonight, I purposely put on a pair of ugly white granny panties and a stupid boring white padded bra."

Sara turned her attention back to Amanda and me and walked over to where we were standing. "You're probably not going to see Amanda too much after tonight." Sara put her arm around her sister. "As much as mom spent on the dress and she spent on her lingerie she's going to be working a lot of over time." Sara laughed.

Amanda put her hands over Sara's mouth. "You little shit tattletale." Then she walked away smirking and singing… *"Look at me, I'm Sandra Dee, lousy with virginity…"* She gave Lucy and Sara one last hug and we left.

When we pulled up to the guardhouse at the Pipefitters there was a line of cars about seven deep. We waited as the guard checked each car to make sure they were filled with high school prom attendees and not mafia hit men. When it was our turn, the middle-aged guard who was wearing long sideburns, a space between his two front teeth and an authoritative attitude stepped up to the driver's side of the car. I rolled down the window and he politely smiled and poked his face in to look around.

"Hey, Steve!" Amanda smiled and waved.

"Hey, Amanda!" The guard returned his surprise.

"I didn't know you worked here. I thought you did Elvis impersonations." Amanda said.

"Well I do Elvis mostly on the weekends, but that doesn't pay the bills." He leaned on the car as to start a casual conversation. "Yep, been doing this for four years." He stuck out his chest so Amanda could see the gold security guard badge with his name inscribed on it. "Busy night. Looks like it's going to be a lot of fun."

"Steve, these are my friends, Chris, Chuck, and Nancy. It's our first prom, so we're all excited."

Steve greeted us with a tilt of his head and turned his attention to me, "You're a lucky man, my friend," he said in his Elvis' voice and gave the right side of his upper lip a nervous twitch. "Don't be cruel to her. She has friends who carry guns." He backed away from the car and gyrated his legs. We all laughed.

He seemed to remember something suddenly. "Hold on." He ran inside the guard house and quickly returned with a book in his hands. "I'm halfway through *Gorky Park* and it's fabulous, thanks for the suggestion."

"I thought you'd like it." Amanda beamed with pride. She was becoming a master literary matchmaker connecting a certain book with its perfect reader.

"Have a fun night kids," Steve tapped the door as a sign that he approved our visit. I was just about to roll up the window when he popped his head in once more. "The pool will be opening Memorial Day." He nodded to Amanda. "Come on up whenever you want. You have a friend with connections." He did one last Elvis trademark, "Thank you, thank you very much."

He looked at me with an envious smirk that reeked of the realization that Prom night was the biggest night of the year for virgins to lose their virginity and he'd rather be in my driver's seat then singing Jail House Rock in the guard's house.

"How totally awesome is that?" Amanda turned to Chuck and Nancy who were both beaming with excitement.

"I presume he's a customer at Waldenbooks?" Nancy asked.

"Yeah, he's a regular who likes to read books about spies and crime stuff. I knew that he did Elvis impersonations because we had talked about it. He even gave me his impromptu version of "Love Me Tender". It was a little embarrassing, but he did a good job and the other customers in the store enjoyed it."

I sat there wearing my Senior Superlative winning smile. But on the inside, my heart frowned with frustration. First, Love Me Tender sang to her by a middle age man in the middle of the mall? Really????

Secondly, I had lived in Spanish Lake my entire life and had never once been into Pipefitters. Mom and dad had marked it as a den of thieves where gangsters and criminals hung out. A place where God-fearing, good

Christian folks wouldn't be seen. Which made me want to go there even more.

Sadly, I had never known anyone who had access. But now, the Queen had been given VIP access by the King. The gatekeeper himself!!! Oh, how this harlot would be welcomed into Pipefitter's giant pool of popularity. She would soon rule the pool, just as she did school.

We passed a row of limousines rented by the wealthier students and parked the car. As we made our way into the building, we couldn't help noticing all the smartly dressed men standing around the parking lot suspiciously gazing about. It was the Pipefitters version of the Secret Service.

My excitement built with each step we took towards the doors. There was only one thing that could spoil the evening and I didn't want to think about it, lest it might jinx the evening. But as she so often does, Amanda voiced my thoughts.

"I'm thinking." She motioned to several security men standing by the door who looked notoriously like a couple of characters from *The Godfather*. "If Dirk were to show up here and start trouble, he'd be beaten up, dragged off and tossed into the Mississippi with a pair of concrete shoes." The visual gave us both a sense of satisfaction and security.

We walked into the ballroom and, to give kudos, where kudos are due, it looked just like the theme said, "The Best of Times." The walls were filled with large black and white posters that were pictures taken from the past three yearbooks and made to look like the front pages of the newspaper. Every sports championship, academic honors, and other school awards were displayed in giant picture frames hanging from the ceiling. And of course, the previous prom kings and queens and other popular kids had another fifteen seconds of fame as a slide projector flashed their faces in full color upon one of the walls. Nick Gaimen, the Senior Class Vice-President, whose father was a big shot at the St. Louis Post-Dispatch, acquired several cases of old newspapers and they used them as table clothes. It gave the entire room a perfect touch.

As usual, every eye was on Amanda as we entered the room. Some of her court came to greet us. Since this was not a date, date, I didn't hang around to chit-chat with her court. I followed Chuck and Nancy and we found an empty table near the dance floor. Go figure. The DJ sat at the side of the stage and was busy filling the room with the sounds of the past four school years.

Dinner was served up in three courses, each as elegant as the next. Caesar Salad. Prime Rib and baked potato. Turtle cheesecake. The table was lively with lots of laughs and comraderies. After dinner, everyone danced and during the song *We Are Family* we gathered in a semi-circle on the dance floor and watched one another strut their moves down the middle, just like they did on that late night TV show, Soul Train. When it came time to announce the prom King and Queen. All the members of the court were asked to come up front and stand next to the stage.

"I'm so excited and nervous," Amanda said biting her nails. "I need a cigarette."

"Go ahead and smoke one," I said as I motioned my head to the back door where the smoking area was located. Amanda looked at me surprised.

"Really?" She furrowed her brow. "You wouldn't mind?"

"It's not that I wouldn't mind; it's just that our agreement would be off."

It suddenly dawned on her and she grinned. "Oh, hell no and then the Vagina Hunter will start sexually stalking me." She pinched my cheek. "Nice try but I'll just stick to biting my nails, Chriisssstian Hayes." She gave me a good luck hug and I walked out and stood with the rest of the court nominees.

Fortunately, the Prom King and Queen coronation didn't last long. Morgan Frezman, a 6'3" black, All-state basketball player won the title of king. Patty De Laurentiis, the gymnast, Honor Student, and varsity cheerleader was crowned queen. They both well-deserved their titles. Each was extremely smart, friendly and well-liked without carrying the chip of snootiness upon their shoulders. When the DJ turned down the lights and called for the Queen and King and the rest of the court and their dates to come dance, Amanda met me on the dance floor. Then the night's theme song, The Best of Times, began to play.

"I hope you don't mind dancing with a mere prince of prom?" I said as we wrapped our arms around each other and began slow dancing.

"Well, to be totally honest," she smiled, "You're better than a prince in my book. You're Sir Christian Hayes, the Vodka Watermelon White Knight. I'll take a knight over a prince any day. Princes are prudish and prissy." She giggled at her wordplay. "Knights are rough and tough. They protect the innocent and defend their Maids of Honor." She paused then added. "And run into burning buildings to save pictures from the pyres of hell."

"Well, Lady Amanda Marrow of Spanish Lake," I spoke in my best British accent. "We've banned the expression "to be totally honest" out of the royal court. Instead, we use the phrase, "truth be told". Therefore, truth be told, being at this royal ball and having your arms around me during this dance makes this humble knight feel as if he's King of the World."

She put the back of her hand upon her forehead and acted as if she was wooed to dizziness. "Oh Sir Haye's, I bet you say that to all the Ladies in the land." Her British accent was better than mine.

The Best of Times is one of those awkward songs that starts slow and then builds in speed. What began as a slow dance suddenly turned into a fast dance. Many of the prom court and their dates separated and started dancing apart. Soon others joined in on the dance floor. Amanda made no attempt to stop slow dancing. She held me in her arms and we swayed back and forth to the beat. Then she leaned her head against my chest and I held her close. It wasn't just the best of times. It was heaven.

"Do you want to know a secret?" She leaned her head back and looked up to me.

Amanda Marrow my Queen, I've been wanting to know all your secrets since I first laid eyes on you.

"It's not really a secret, secret. It's more of a confession," she added.

"You know you can tell all your secrets and confessions to Father Chriisssstian." It was my turn to draw my own name out. "And they'll be safe."

"And please don't take this personally." She prepped her confession. "But I didn't think I would have as much fun as I'm having tonight." She saw the mild offense in my face "No, it's not you. It's me. I didn't think I could relax and be myself without drinking or smoking."

"Well I've lived my whole life without drinking and smoking and I've never had a problem having a great time." There was no piety in my words. "That's a fact, Jack."

Amanda smiled. "And I've lived my whole life with most of my great times somehow linked with drinking and smoking and..." She stopped mid-sentence and stared at the mirrored globe above the dance floor and watched it spin around and around. Her thoughts seemed to be doing the same. I knew what laid on the other side of that last "and".

It was the reason she had her reputation. She didn't bother to finish her thought. She laid her head against my chest once more and we continued to slow dance.

Once again, she was in my arms. But this time she was sober and instead of trying to seduce me in the privacy of Aloha, she was confessing her secrets in the middle of the dance floor. I really wanted to run my fingers through her hair and caress her head just like I did "That Night" at Aloha. I felt she needed it.

But I refrained. This was not an official date, date. Just two friends enjoying an expensive dinner on one friend's behalf. I didn't want to put her on the spot and I sure in the hell didn't want to start the rumor mill running.

"'It's nice being out with a friend like you," she said in a loud sigh. "I don't have to worry about any hangovers." She smiled and added. "Or have any regrets." She slowly began to caress my back as one would caress a child's back.

Why in the hell was she doing this? Was she purposely trying to mess with my mind? It's not like she didn't have every eye on her, to begin with. Then, toss in the fact that we were

the only ones out there slow dancing while
everyone else was fast dancing. Now she's
caressing MY back.

I know I should have just gone with it and
started caressing her in return, but
something inside continued to tell me to take
my time. I had the entire night to play her
game.

"I feel safe and sound with my White Knight."

"Yep, safe and sound," I assured her.

The Best of Times slowly faded out and Michael Jackson's *Don't Stop Until You Get Enough* started playing.

"Thank you." She pulled me down and kissed me on my cheek. My face went flush but I didn't care.

"You better stop doing that…" I pointed to the DJ's speaker and smiled. "…or I'm not going to stop until I get enough." Amanda rolled her eyes and we walked off the dance floor. Chuck and Nancy meet us at the table.

"Sorry, you didn't get voted king," Chuck said without an ounce of sorry-ness in his voice. But I took no offense. We both knew to be there with Amanda as my date was better than getting voted prom king any time. Chuck looked at his watch. "It's time for this party to be over." His face grew with excitement. "And the real party to begin!"

CHAPTER FORTY-ONE

Sitting in the trunk of my car, next to a cooler filled with soft drinks and several grocery bags filled with snacks, was our evening's entertainment: Monopoly. Sorry. Battleship. Chuck's Atari 2600, a stereo boom box and a case of cassettes.

Was it enough to entertain Amanda? I fretted it wasn't. She liked to Party with a capital "P". Loud music. Lots of booze. And people doing either illegal or "R" rated activities. I was offering her a rated "G" walk through Mr. Roger's Neighborhood. This is what I was wondering as we made our way around the banquet hall saying our goodbyes. Several of Amanda's court friends gathered around, telling her where the best parties were.

"Which one are you going too?" one of them asked. I was standing off to the side talking to Chuck, but still in earshot to the conversation.

"We're still deciding," Amanda answered.

"Still deciding? I've spent several hundred dollars on tickets, tux, hotel room, and party supplies to make this night special and she's telling her friends "She's still deciding?" What the hell is that all about? Why didn't she say we were having our own party?

Was she leaving her options open, just in case she really couldn't stand partying in Mr. Roger's Neighborhood with Mr. Nice Guy? She could act like she wanted to go home and call it a night when in reality she'd call one of her court and go have some real fun at her Parties with a capital "P".

Once a hoosier. Always a hoosier. I was so pissed. The entire joy of the evening was slowly seeping out of my senses punctured from what she had just said.

I was trying to hide my anger and disappointment when Amanda walked over.

"Just in case anyone asked what we're doing afterward, please don't tell them?" She leaned over and whispered in my ear.

"Why not?" I snapped a little too fast and a little too harsh.

"Because I don't want certain people to show up at your party and ruin it."

She placed a plug back into my senses and it once more began to inflate with joy. It made perfect sense. She wanted an evening free from hangovers and regrets. Once the word got out, people would automatically follow in her footsteps and show up with their "R" ratings activities. She was, after all, Amanda Marrow, the Freshman Fire.

We got to the Red Roof Inn and parked in the back where several of our other friends were hanging out waiting for our arrival. I had never had a hotel party, so I wasn't sure how to sneak everyone into the room. I voiced my concerns out loud.

"Here's what we'll do." Amanda immediately took charge, as if she was a veteran hotel party general who had strategized these plans many times.

"Chris, you and Nancy go check in like you're a couple. You're both over eighteen and you have reservations, so there should be no problems. If there is, take out a $20 and hand it to the desk clerk and tell him it's his tip. That should resolve any issues." Amanda surveyed the hotel. "Once in the room, Nancy you wait there ready to open the door while Chris, you come to that back entrance." She pointed to a dark door at the end of the hotel. "We'll meet you there with everything. We'll take the back steps up to the room." There were four floors to the Red Roof Inn. "Hopefully, we won't get a room on the first floor because that'll make it easier for management to notice there's a party going on. And we don't want the fourth floor because I don't want to have to carry all this shit up all those steps." Amanda motioned to my car trunk filled with party supplies.

Nancy and I walked into the lobby and were shocked to see twenty or more high school teenagers dressed in tuxes and evening gowns waiting to be checked in. The hustle and bustle about the place seemed more like the platform of a train station than a hotel lobby. Students came in carrying boxes, bags, and coolers. One boy, dressed in a black tux with matching lavender bow tie, vest and shoes, wheeled in an entire stereo system complete with two gigantic Bose Speakers. I recognized some of the faces from school, but most were from other high schools also having prom that evening. It was evident by the calm and unconcerned attitude of the manager; his Red Roof Inn was about to become an apartment of prom parties. When we finally made our way to the front desk, I told the clerk my last name. She found the reservation and asked for a credit card.

"A credit card?" I looked at her puzzled. "No one said we'd need a credit card. I was going to pay cash."

The clerk donned a cocky smile and pointed to a big sign behind her.

CREDIT CARD REQUIRE WITH CHECK-IN.
ALL DAMAGES TO THE ROOM, IT'S PROPERTY, OR ANY
PART OF THIS HOTEL WILL AUTOMATICALLY BE
CHARGED TO THAT CREDIT CARD.

It was one of the reasons why the manager wasn't too worried about having a hotel full of parties. Credit cards on file were their property insurance. Neither Nancy nor I had a credit card. For a brief second, I felt as if I were about to fail miserably and have to return to the parking lot and tell everyone we were going to have to move the party to my house. My heart sank into a quagmire of embarrassment and loathing. No, we wouldn't move the party, we would just crash another party. I was not going to give mom the righteous satisfaction of having our Mr. Roger's neighborhood party in her domain where she could play Jesus and invisibly watch over us making sure we all behaved like good little Christians.

Just then, the little devil on my left shoulder kicked the angel on my right shoulder in the balls. And as the little devil was hysterically laughing at the angel curled over in pain, he whispered in my ear. "Chuck has a credit card his parents gave him for emergency uses."

"We'll be right back," I told the clerk. "I have a friend outside that has one." She rolled her eyes in frustration and set the reservation to the side.

Nancy and I walked back out to the car and told everyone what was going on inside. How the lobby was packed and we didn't have to sneak in. "We need your credit card to check in the room, though," I said to Chuck and held out my hand.

He hesitated. "No way." Chuck shook his head. "Are you kidding me? My parents will kill me if I charge this to their credit card."

"Here's fifty-bucks." I handed him the money. "That should be more than enough. The room is only twenty-five dollars per night."

Chuck stood there shifting his weight from foot to foot evaluating the dilemma. It wasn't until Amanda put her arms around him and in a little too overly flirtatious tone said, "You only get the chance to throw a prom party once in your life, Chuck. It will go into your album of memories along with your marriage and children's births as one of those life events you'll never forget." Chuck opened his wallet and relinquished the card.

We walked in the front door of The Red Roof Inn. Of course, all eyes turned to Amanda. Several guys tapped their buddy's shoulder. Pointing. Staring. Lusting. A couple of girls who weren't part of her court but still knew her, walked up and greeted her like they were old friends. Jealous. Two-faced. We quickly checked in and went to our room #222 Just like the television show.

Chuck immediately went about setting up the Atari game console, while Amanda and Nancy took out the snacks and refreshments. I plugged in the boom box and put a cassette of Fleetwood Mac *Rumors* in. Chuck and I had invited about twenty people to the party. Mostly our good friends, guys who worked for us at Aloha, and a few people whom I had recently befriended with my new popularity. We explained to them all that it would be an alcohol-free party and we were going to provide the soda and snacks, but they were welcome to bring any Atari or other games they liked to play.

When Billy Powers walked in carrying a game of Scrabble, Amanda scream so loud everyone in the room looked her way.

"Oh, my God. Someone brought Scrabble!!!" She grabbed the game out of Billy's hands and hugged it. "This is going to be the best party ever!" Amanda exclaimed in the excitement of a little girl having a pony at her birthday party. She quickly cleared off the bed and opened the box and spread the board out.

It wasn't exactly the game I would have preferred to play on the hotel bed. But the night was still young.

CHAPTER FORTY-ONE

The party was going perfectly. I was busy playing party host. Between Atari, Scrabble, music, and munchies everyone seems to be enjoying themselves. Amanda had just won her second round of Scrabble when I meet her at the table with all the snacks.

"So, Lady Amanda of Spanish Lake, are you having a good time?"

"Totally." There was a sincere sense of appreciation in her smile. "You don't understand how much I love Scrabble. The only time I get to play it is with Lucy and Sara." She switched to her British accent, "And truth be told." She switched back. "They're not that good. Although, Sara is getting better." She grabbed a can of Pringles and poured some out in her hands. "I've got some good competition over there." She motioned to Billy Powers. I looked over at him and he quickly turned his head to hide his stare away from Amanda.

You can hide your stare, Billy Powers. But I still see your Vagina Hunting fangs. Foaming. Drooling.

"He's really good." She added. I was immediately jealous. She leaned over and whispered. "Do you want to know another secret?" But before I could reply, she continued. "It's not hard to please a woman's pussy." She giggled at her wordplay. "But it takes a real man to stimulate her mental clit." She tapped the side of her forehead with her finger and smiled. Then she walked over to the soda cooler.

Mental clit. The two words were as opposite to me as night and day. The first pertained to the invisible intellect, the latter was the button to pure physical pleasure. But here was the logosist combining the two to make the

perfect expression for stimulating a woman's mind to the capacity that it turns her on, not so much in a sexual capacity, which it quite possibly could, but more so in an intellectually stimulating manner. My jealousy of Billy Powers quickly evolved from envy and then to hatred. Mental clit.

Scrabble was to Amanda what a Hustler Magazine was to a Vagina Hunter. Why it never dawned on me to bring this game was totally asinine on my part. I made a mental note: Start mastering my vocabulary and learn to excel in Scrabble. A game of words. The perfect decoy for my own Vagina game. But was I too late?

"We were almost out of ice," Amanda said as she opened the cooler.

"I'll run down to the lobby and get more," I was the host and it was my duty to make sure my guests were well supplied with their party needs.

"No. I'll do it." Amanda volunteered as she picked up the ice bucket sitting on the bathroom counter. "My brain needs a rest." She put her hand on her stomach and rubbed it. "My belly also needs a rest from eating all this junk food," she said with a "blah" and walked to the door. "I'm going to skip this game." Amanda announced to everyone sitting on the bed playing Scrabble. I watched Billy Powers watch her leave. I walked over to the bed and, like a good host, asked if everyone was having a good time. There was a choir of "yeps" and "yeses". Moments later, Billy pulled me to the side.

"So what's the story between you and Amanda?" His eyes flashed as he said her name. "She said you two weren't dating and that you're just friends." He paused and looked at me with an expression like he was a kindergartener standing at the recess line waiting for the playground monitor to give him permission to go play.

At that moment I wished I had never invited Billy Powers to my prom party. He was a longtime friend who lived up the street. We

were best buddies for about three years of our
elementary lives. We played in parks and
creeks and climbed trees together. But then
in fourth grade, his dad got a promotion and
they started sending him to Our Lady of
Loretto, the private Catholic school.

Soon we both acquired new friends from our
different schools. I also started spending a
lot of time at Aloha, so we seldom spoke.
However, we would still see each other
occasionally on the street as we passed one
another's house and wave and sometimes stop
and catch up.

Billy was a nice-looking guy. During our
childhood, he was chubby to the point of being
fat but over the years he lost the pounds and
now he was slender, with radiant blue eyes. He
wore a constant crew cut that made him look
a little military-ish and tougher than he
really was.

Ever since I can remember he wanted to be a
teacher, just like his grandmother who urged
him to read a lot. Back then I thought it was
so strange how sometimes he'd stay inside to
read when he could be out flying kites or
collecting cool milkweed pods with me. (But
now, who's the strange unread one?) And even
though we seldom ever spoke, I still liked
Billy. He could be somewhat self-centered and
had a habit of always bringing the
conversation back to himself. Boasting.
Bragging. But he was a sincerely nice guy.

That is why, when I drove by his house
several weeks ago and saw him out washing his
dad's car, I stopped to talk to him. I told him
about my nomination to prom court and all
about Amanda. It was my turn to boast a little.
Not surprisingly, he had heard about her.

What exactly he had heard, I didn't know. He
said his prom was the same night as ours, so I
suggested that he and his date stop by the
party. I explained that it was an alcohol-free
party and we'd be playing games and just
hanging out. He accepted the offer
surprisingly quick, leading me to believe
that he had no after-prom plans. But when I
drove away and thought about it for a sec, I
wondered if Amanda's reputation was the real
reason for his expedient response. Beautiful.
Smart. Slutty.

Yes, before that moment, I really liked
Billy Powers. Now I loathed him. I had known
Amanda for 120 days, 3 hours and 14 minutes
(not that I was counting or anything). I froze
my ass off for her. Almost committed an
Academic felony for her. I verbally fought
for her and even lied and sacrificed for her.
And now, within an hour of meeting her, he
was already stroking her mental clit.

Fuck. You. Billy. Powers.

Instead of confirming that Amanda and I were only friends, I
answered his question with the same kind of questions.

"Aren't you and Martha an item?" I pointed to the pretty brunette
wearing a yellow silk dress sitting on the couch amid several guys
playing Atari.

"We were," he said matter-of-factly. "But we decided it just wasn't
working out. So we broke up." He took a hand full of M&M's from the
snack table and tossed them in his mouth. "But we promised to remain
friends." He leaned over and whispered. "With benefits." He poked me
in the stomach with his elbow and winked at me. "We had already made
plans to go to prom before the break-up. She had bought the dress and
I had the tickets and tux, so we agreed to go and see how the night
played out." He paused. "Just like you and Amanda."

I wanted to take offense at Billy for inquiring in his own Vagina Hunting way if she was fair game. But I didn't. If Billy wanted to believe that Amanda and I were friends with benefits, so be it. Unless he had a bottle of Tequila and some shot glasses hidden in his jacket, it was going to take more than some mental clit stimulation from a couple games of Scrabble for him to capture her vagina tonight. How sad and pathetic that I felt that way about her. Billy was bringing out the worst in me.

Suddenly, Amanda burst back into the room and slammed the door behind her with a loud BANG!

"Fuck!" She leaned against the door, shut her eyes, and banged her head against it. Everyone stopped what they were doing and turned their stares her way. Amanda's hands were shaking. The ice bucket was still empty.

CHAPTER FORTY-TWO

I ran over and put my hands on Amanda's shoulders to settle her down. "What happened?"

"I just ran into fucking Dirk Howard in the lobby." She let out a frustrated sigh and then walked over to the coffee table and sat the ice buckets down. "I don't know if he saw me or not. I got right back in the elevator and came up here. But when the door opened, his bitch of a girlfriend was right there." She shook her head back and forth and then sat down on the arm of the couch. "Fuck. Why? Why? Why?" Of all the places that asshole could be partying tonight, he's here?" She looked at me because she knew we shared the same sentiments about Dirk Howard. Everyone in the room had known about the incident, except Billy and Martha. They went to Rosary High were there weren't any rumors of Dirk Howard.

Chuck was the first to try and ease the tension and set the course back to fun and games. "He's not going mess with us." He waved the idea off with his right hand. "He's too busy partying." He picked up the joystick and went back to playing Atari. Several minutes later, everyone resigned that he was right and they relaxed. The Scrabble game resumed. I could see Billy was asking Nancy what it was all about. She pointed to Amanda as she explained what had happened.

But both Amanda and I knew better. If Dirk was partying, he was drinking. If he was drinking, he was getting more belligerent. It was the perfect recipe for trouble.

Then there was a pound on the door. The room went silent except for the Space Invader's electronic beeps echoing from the TV and Billy Joel now singing on the boom box.

Before I could decide what I was going to do, Billy jumped off the bed.

"I'll take care of this," he said assuredly as he motioned his hands for me to stay where I was. Then he walked over to the door. He tossed the security latch on its catch and then opened the door. He had about two inches of safe eyesight. "Can I help you?" he said with an air of authority.

"Tell that slut and her fag friend to come out here." Dirk's words seethed and slurred. "I want to kick their asses for getting me suspended." One could almost smell his cigarette and beer breath breathing through the crack from across the room. Then Dirk punched the door causing the screws on the security latch to creak and a booming echo rolling down the hotel's hall. Billy's character quickly changed from cocky to almost cowardly upon seeing Dirk's muscular size and his drunken rage.

"You must have the wrong room." Billy's voice went almost falsetto with fright. He then went to shut the door, but Dirk shot his hand inside and grabbed Billy's bow tie.

"Look you douchebag. If you don't open this door, I'm going to beat your ass too." Billy attempted to pull away, but Dirks' fist refused to let go. I ran over to the door and threw my body weight against it. Dirk let out a loud, "Fuck" as the door smashed his arm causing him to let go of Billy and pull his hand out the door. Billy slammed the door shut. "Someone needs to call security." His face was now ashen.

Amanda picked up the phone and called down to the front desk to tell them about the situation. Meanwhile, Dirk continued beating on the door and making threats of bodily harm to everyone who was in the room. They knew Dirk's reputation. Everyone sat there in silent fear.

"I can't just let him keep doing that." I walked towards the door.

"Chris, don't let him ruin this fabulous night. Let security handle it."

"Security isn't always going to be there." I tried to explain my thoughts. "Don't you see, Amanda, if security, or the police for that matter, takes him away, then he's going to be even more pissed and harbor an even greater grudge." I paused. "It's time to make a stand against this asshole or he'll just keep disrespecting and bullying us."

Dirk then started making loud farting noises at the crack of the door. Had it not been Dirk and our violent history with one another, it would have been funny. But with each flatulent sound that he made, I could see Amanda's face flush with anger.

The last time Dirk called me out I failed to answer his threat. Not so much out of fear but because of my unreadiness. But now I was ready.

We were no longer on school property, so I couldn't get into any academic trouble. And the fact that out of all the other hundreds of guys at Hazelwood East who would have given their left testicle to go prom with her, she chose ME. It didn't matter if we were just friends.

Or maybe it was because I realized we were actually friends. And real friends didn't just sit there and let others verbally abuse them or threaten to harm them physically. True friends stood up for one another. They fought each other's foes.

What's the worst that could happen? I could get my ass kicked. Big deal. Life would go on. I wouldn't have this constant bully hanging on me like a booger that you can't flip from your finger.

It was time. No more Christian Hayes, Mr. Nice Guy. I was Sir Hayes, the Vodka Watermelon White Knight about to defend my Lady Amanda of Spanish Lake.

I walked over to the door and took the chain off the lock.

"If you open that door, Christian Hayes, I swear I will fucking leave this party and never speak to you again."

Not exactly the words I was expecting out of the mouth of my fair maiden. I could see the fear and anger in her eyes. She was trying to save me from getting an ass whipping.

"I thought fair maidens were supposed to support their knights and kiss them before they went off to battle?' I said half in jest and have to take my mind off of what was about to happen. Amanda turned her head and said nothing.

Dear God, please don't let me get my ass kicked too bad. Please give me supernatural strength to defend myself and the honor of this beautiful fucked-up, hoosier girl who,

**to be totally honest to you and myself, I think
I've fallen in love with. Amen.**

I took a deep breath, turned the doorknob and threw open the door.
"Why don't you get the fuck out of here?" I met Dirk's bloodshot eyes
and raging temper.

"Why don't you make me? Pussy." He smirked.

With the might of a team of mules, I pushed Dirk backward. He
flew against the wall and a picture of a wheat field came crashing down,
spilling glass all over the floor. In a flash, he came back at me like a
bull wrestler who was ready to take revenge. I crouched down to meet
his attack hoping I could grab his legs and toss him over my head like
I had read in a self-defense magazine. But he knew the tactic and
instead, he used his right knee as a fist that hit me in the nose, sending
a shock of excruciating pain through my skull. I fell back, but on my
way, I saw an open shot right at his face. I shut my eyes and swung my
fist in its direction as hard as I could. It met with flesh and made a
smacking sound. But it didn't seem to deter Dirk from wanting to kill
me. The last thing I wanted, I thought in my deep despair, was Dirk to
use his wrestling skills to pin me to the ground so he could beat me to
a pulp. So I just kept kicking, punching and struggling in the hope that
some divine miracle would save me from a complete annihilating ass-
whipping. Off to my left, I heard Amanda screaming and looked to see
if she was all right. But as I turned my head, I watched in surreal slow
motion Dirk's fist grow in size as it came from behind his back and
made direct contact with my face.

CHAPTER FORTY-THREE

KNOCK. KNOCK. KNOCK.

The beating on the door woke me out of a nightmare. I tried to lift my head and look around to see where the incessant sound was coming from, but only managed to raise my eyelids. Darkness. Pain. A firefly-like glow from the clock caught my attention. I witnessed one of those rare moments in life when you literally watch time pass as one of those little time-keeping scorecards within the workings of the clock flipped from 11:12 to 11:13. By the light permeating from around the room-darkening curtains, I surmised the 11:13 was from the AM side of the day. My head ached. My face throbbed. And within my throbbing face, my waking eyes slowly began to adjust to the darkness of the room. I recognized a form to be an Atari game console on top of a television. To its immediate left was a cooler and behind it, some sort of picture tilted sideways on the wall. Beneath the picture was a nightstand. I was in the hotel room. The tragic scene where the nightmare before the nightmare took place.

I lay there and replayed the entire folly in my fractured mind. The perfect dinner. The incredible dance. The fabulous rated "G" party. Dirks fart sounds at the door. Opening the door. But the doors of my memory seemed to slam shut the moment after I watched Dirk's fist slowly grow in size before it made contact with my face. I strained to recall what happened after that painful instant. But it was as if a part of my memory was clipped from the timeline of my life. Like my dreamless sleep before I met Amanda. A black void of time. I wasn't sleeping. I was awake. Fighting. Defending. Or was I? I laid there in a Rip Van Wrinkle world attempting to recollect that which wasn't collectible. For those of you who have never lost a piece of memory, it's an unsettling experience to say the least. Disturbing to say the most.

KNOCK. KNOCK. KNOCK.

There was that fucking sound again. Then came the sound of keys jingling. Then came the sound of a door opening. Then came the sound of someone standing there. The fluorescent light from the hall flowed into the room creating a silhouette of a plump female figure standing in the doorway. Behind her was a rolling cart filled with towels, sheets, cleaning supplies and a tub of little shampoo bottles. She flipped on the light and quickly realized two guys were sleeping in the same bed.

"Ahh!!!" she screamed, fumbled her keys, and they fell to the floor. I couldn't see her shadowed stare, but I imagined it to be pale, freaked-out and somewhat pissed off as she picked up her keys, apologized profusely and immediately shut the door. I once again looked over at the clock but this time I missed the moment. 11:14. Checkout time was 11:00 am. Chuck's credit card was about to be charged for another day. I would have gladly paid the extra $25 dollars for another day just to lay there trying to remember what I had forgotten and forgetting everything that I remembered, but I was scheduled to work in one hour and sixteen minutes.

I slowly and methodically crawled out of bed. Think. Galapagos. Lizard. I limped into the bathroom, flipped on the light, and looked in the mirror to witness a victim of a bad beating. My poor right eyelid was swollen, squinted and bright red. A semi-ring of blue, almost purple-ish black flesh hung beneath it. Around my head was a loosely wrapped Ace bandage. I wondered if it was the shock of two barely clad guys sleeping in the same bed or my appalling appearance that alarmed the maid and made her drop her keys and slam the door. I then pissed the longest piss I think I ever pissed in my life and stumbled out of the bathroom. Chuck was still dead to the world wrapped within the cheap starchy hotel sheets. I slapped his foot and sat down on the edge of the bed.

"Wake up" I grumbled. "We gotta get out of here before they charge us for another night."

Chuck slightly stirred and turned over, exposing a morning woody that created a tiny teepee in the sheet wrapped around him. If I weren't in so much pain, I would have enjoyed the pleasure of snapping a Polaroid picture with the camera sitting on the coffee table. Instead, I just bounced up and down on the bed.

Nothing.

I shook his shoulder.

Still nothing.

Frustrated, I reached over and flicked his hard-on and he let out a girlish squeal and immediately sat up bright-eyed and bushy-tailed holding his penis. "What the hell you do that for?"

"Let's go, man, it's after 11:00 if we're not out of here ASAP, they're going to charge your parent's credit card for another night."

Chuck immediately jumped out of bed making no attempt to hide his hard-on bulging from his boxers as he ran to the bathroom to girl piss. We had been buddies for years; morning hard-ons were as common as...well... morning hard-ons.

"I don't remember anything from last night past Dirks fist coming towards my eye in slow motion," I yelled at Chuck through the bathroom door.

"Yeah, it was a pretty fucked up night," his voice echoed back.

I opened the curtains. In the parking lot below was a van with all its doors opened. Airbrushed on the side of the van was a very bosomed blonde in a string bikini surfing a wave. Its stainless-steel wheels were polished to the point they became mirrors reflecting the hot morning sun directly into my aching eyes. The guy in the black tux with lavender accessories from the lobby last night was slowly and cautiously putting his stereo system into the backseat. Tired. Hungover. I watched as his date, who also looked a little weary and disheveled, helped him put the two giant Bose speakers in the back. It appeared I wasn't the only one who had a rough night. They climbed into the van and slowly pulled out of the parking lot. The bathroom door opened. Chuck was now wide awake. The sunshine filled the room.

"Holy Shit! I thought you looked bad last night," Chuck said shaking his head and taking a closer inspection of my face. "But you took a real ass whooping." He smiled and gave me a brotherly pat on the back. "But I have to say, Christian Mathew Hayes, I'm proud of you for standing up against that prick..." He paused. "...even though you got your ass kicked."

"So what happened?" I stood there waiting to hear a story in which I was the protagonist. Yet I had no recollections of my actions. I couldn't tell if the tale Chuck was about to tell was fiction or non-fiction? The scene was esoteric.

"You still don't remember?"

"I swear to God," I held up my hand as if I were testifying on the Bible. "I don't remember anything after getting hit by Dirk!"

"Well, thank God for Martha and her dad, Dr. Laird."

"What do you mean Martha's dad?" My confusion continued. "As in Billy's date?"

"Yeah, after the fight me, Nancy, Billy, Martha and you went looking for Amanda and you kept saying "What happened and where's Amanda?" We thought you were joking at first, but you had this dazed look on your face. So we'd tell you everything and then you'd nod your head like you understood. But five minutes later you were like... "Where's Amanda and what happened?" Chuck put on his shirt on and bundled up his tie and cummerbund and put them into a plastic bag. "Martha's father is a pediatrician. Martha wants to be a doctor too. She looked at your pupils and saw they were really dilated and said she was afraid you might have suffered some kind of brain damage during the fight. Well, I know how your parents are." Chuck shot a stare at me with big crazy eyes. His look summed up years of being my best friend and experiencing the over-zealous, radical religious, hoosier-phobia, dysfunctional-function, zoo I was raised in. "I knew there was no way I was going call your parents or take you to the ER without them finding out. So Martha called her dad and told him what had happened and we took you over to her house and he examined you."

"Bullshit! You're making all this up." I shook my head and rolled my eyes.

"Swear to God!" It was Chuck's turn to raise his hand and gave me the best buddy no-bullshit stare while swearing to God. "Marth's dad, Dr. Laird, checked you out and asked you questions, 'Like what day of the week was it?' And you didn't know. He said that you didn't appear to have any skull fracture or anything serious. But you did have a minor concussion. We put an ice pack on your head and he wrote a prescription for some pain medicine that you'll probably need. He also told us to keep you awake for another hour and keep asking you questions to check if you're back to normal or not." Chuck picked up a piece of paper off the nightstand and handed it to me. Sure enough, it was a prescription by a Dr. Laird. "So, we went to Denny's and drank coffee for an hour."

"That's why I just pissed like a Russian racehorse."

"Yeah, we asked you all kinds of questions too. It was so freakin' hilarious!! Nancy asked you your mother's name. You got this weird look on your face and said, 'I think it's Satan or some movie title.' Chuck burst out laughing. "I asked you how many HMS's you had a day? You took a sip of your coffee and said something about a hot, toffee, thingy drink and then proudly smiled and exclaimed 'Eight!' Oh my God, if I could have recorded that conversation so you could have seen it."

"Well, I wish you could have too." I folded Dr. Laird's prescription up and put it in my pocket. "And I'm glad I was able to entertain whoever was at the table…"

"Oh, it was only me, you and Nancy. Billy and Martha stayed at Martha's house. I took Nancy home after Denny's and then we came back here and crashed."

"So no one called my mom and dad?"

"Hell no." Chuck assured me.

A sense of relief crept within the folds of my other numbed senses. In the madness of the morning, I hadn't notice Chuck was sporting his own skinned chin and red cheek. There was blood on my tuxedo's jacket. That would cost me. The entire evening was going to cost me.

"So what happened?" I said as handed him his tux pants and motioned for him to hurry up. "And where's Amanda?" I didn't want to phrase it like that, but those were the two subjects foremost on my mind.

Chuck shot me a "you have to be fucking kidding me" look. I assured him I was no longer in a whacked-out state of mind. "It's 11: 34 am on Sunday, April 19th, 1981. My name is Christian Mathew Hayes, your name is Charles Robert Kobalt and last night was one of the best and worst nights of my life."

"You were getting a pretty badass whipping so Billy and I and a couple of other guys jumped on Dirk to try and pull him off you. That's when Gina slapped me right in the head." He pointed to a spot on his right cheek as red as a strawberry. "And she jumped on me. Next thing I know, Amanda's pulling that bitch off me and they start fighting. Some of Dirks drunk buddies from the party down the hall heard the commotion and ran down and jumped on us." Chuck ran both his hands through his hair and shook his head. "My God, it was like something you'd read in a book or see in a movie. A big bad-ass brawl with everyone punching and kicking and trying to defend themselves."

Chuck disconnected his Atari game, put it in the box and continued. "The hotel manager called the police, but by the time they got there, Dirk, Gina and everyone else was already gone. We explained to the manager what happened and that we didn't do anything and we weren't drinking. He was ready to kick us out until Nancy and I took him into the room and showed him there was nothing but soda and chips. So he let us stay. You were in the bathroom with Billy and Martha trying to get your nose to stop bleeding. But Amanda was nowhere to be seen. She just disappeared while we were talking to the manager."

Chuck set the Atari game on top of the cooler and gathered his bloodstained tux accessories and put them in the box with the Atari. "So you and I went looking for her throughout the entire hotel, but we didn't find her. Came back to the room and everyone had pretty much gone, except Nancy, Billy, and Martha, who were cleaning up." He pointed to the blood on my tux shirt. "You don't remember any of this?" He looked at me with pity and amazement. I shook my head no. "The entire time you kept talking crazy. That's when Martha called her dad."

I looked on the coffee table and there was an ice pack. Beside it was a trash can filled with bloody tissues. "Wow." I pointed to the trash. "Was all that from me?"

"Yep. Your nose wouldn't stop bleeding. We had to put one of Nancy's tampons up your nostrils to finally get it to stop." He laughed out loud.

"Are you fucking kidding me!" I was embarrassed by the thought.

"Yeah."

"You bastard." I picked up the ice pack and threw it at him. He ducked and it slammed into a bright brass wall sconce. The glass shade fell out and crashed to the floor into three pieces. "Fuck!"

"That one's going to cost you," Chuck said as he picked up the glass pieces and put them back into the sconce.

I realized that everything about last night was going to cost me. From the extra charge for the blood on my tux to the tale I was going to have to tell mom and dad.

"If you open that door, Christian Hayes, I swear I will fucking leave this party and never speak to you again."

I had a headache. But worse than the pounding in my brain was the uneasiness in my consciousness and a stabbing in my soul that pained me more than any damage that Dirk Howard could have done to me. I wanted to call Amanda right then but thought it would be best to wait until I got home. We could talk in private.

"No, it's going to cost you. You're the one with the credit card," I said with a smile.

We picked up our belongings and walked out of the room. On the way down the hall, we passed the maid that we had shocked earlier. I stopped, reached into my pocket and pulled out a $20 and handed it to her as an apologetic bribe. "That's for room number 222. Sorry about the mess." She accepted it with a giant grin.

The drive back to Chuck's house was quiet and reflective. Both of us replaying in our minds the bizarre events that took place the night before.

"Well, at least there's no broken bones." Chuck tossed the thought out from nowhere as proof we were both on the same mental wavelength.

"Praise Jesus." The words made me think of my mom. "If I get home quick enough, I can shower and leave before Mom and Dad get home from church and delay the drama until later this evening." I dreaded the thought.

"To be totally honest," Chuck started his sentence in a bad way. "Before today, I envied you for taking Amanda to prom. But now, you couldn't give me anything to be in your shoes right now."

"Why?" I said. And then answered my own question. "Because Dirk probably still wants to kill me? Or Amanda hates me and doesn't want anything to do with me? Or because my mom and dad are going to toss me in our imaginary dungeon and ground me for life?"

Chuck shook his head. "D. All the above."

We pulled into his driveway. It was nice to see his parent's car wasn't there. They were still at church. Hopefully, my parent's car wouldn't be in ours either. Chuck opened the door to leave but then stopped and stayed seated.

"You know Amanda was right." I gave him a befuddled stare. "We will never forget last night's prom party. It will go down in the albums of our memories with our wedding day and our children's births." He quoted her verbatim. Then his face lit up and he held his hand up for a high five. "Fuckin A!" We slapped hands and both went our ways knowing we had created a story we would one day tell our grandchildren.

CHAPTER FORTY-FOUR

I got home and dad's car wasn't in the driveway. Thank. You. Jesus. Everyone was at church. But when I walked into the kitchen from the garage door and heard the TV blasting away in the living room, I froze. Two seconds later Ruth came running in. She suddenly froze when she saw my face...

"Oh my God Christian!" She gave an appalling stare. "Are you OK?" She hugged me with the might of a prodigal mother.

"What are you doing home?" I asked. "Why aren't you at church with mom and dad?"

"I had to lie to them, Christian, and tell them I was sick." She got a guilty look on her face. "It wasn't a real bonafide lie because I really was sick. I called Sara first thing this morning and she told me that there was a big fight at prom last night and you and Amanda were in it and some wrestler guy beat you up." She took a quick breath and continued. "Amanda called Lucy and she picked her up from 7-11. Her dress was torn and bloody and she was crying. I got sick to my stomach because I didn't know what happened to you. I didn't want to tell mom or dad because you know..." She didn't have to say it. We both knew how they would have reacted. "So I told mom I was having terrible stomach pains and begged her to let me skip church. I knew if you were alive, you'd come home before they came home from church so you wouldn't have to talk to them and I was right and Oh my god, Christian your face looks horrible. Tell me what happened." Ruth ceased her one-sided conversation and sat down on the kitchen chair. Wondering. Waiting.

"I have to get in the shower and get ready for work." I tossed my keys on the counter. "Make me something to eat for lunch and I'll give you the details...," I paused. "Well, what I remember... when I get out of the shower."

"What details you remember?" she said curiously.

"Yeah, I got a concussion and I don't remember half the night."

Ruth jumped out of the chair and gave me another big hug. "This was the best trouble you've been in...ever!" She could hardly contain her excitement.

I showered and dressed and came down to trith, a bowl of tomato soup, a PB&J sandwich and a little sister sitting at the table with a look of fascination on her face. I gave her the details of the previous prom night. Her eyes got big when I told her about the Pipefitters complex and they filled with rage when I recalled the fight. She "Awww"ed when I told her about Amanda and I being the only ones slow dancing on the dance floor while everyone else fast danced. And she laughed so hard she snorted when I told her mom's name was Satan.

"I really don't want to tell mom and dad it happened at prom." I took Ruth in my confidence. "You know mom. She'll say she was right and that I shouldn't hang around a hoosier girl like Amanda." Ruth knew I was right. She had seen mom's prejudice against Sara's older sister on several occasions. "Maybe I can say it happened at work." But the thought stopped there. "Mr. Abernathy would not cover such a bold-face lie."

"You mean a black and blue face lie." Ruth corrected me. "I called Sara and told her you were all right and that I'd call her back and give her your side of the details." I stopped her right there.

"What do you mean, my side of the details?" Is Amanda saying something different?" I was eager to hear her side of the story even if I had to listen to it through the filter of two little sisters.

She turned her head to the side and gave a contemplative thought. "No, she pretty much said the same thing." Then she continued. "Sara said that Amanda's really mad at you and says she doesn't want to talk to you ever again. I told her she was just mad and she'd get over it, but Sara said she knew her sister and she was as stubborn as a two-headed mule and she didn't make idle threats." Ruth picked up my plate and took it over to the sink and began rinsing it off. "I wouldn't try to talk to her for a while. Let her cool down. Maybe she'll see how bad you got beat up for her and change her mind." She turned off the water and turned and gave me a sisterly stare. "You really do like her don't you Christian?"

Like her? I got my ass kicked for her. Of course, I more than liked her. I just didn't understand why she was so pissed.

Was she mad because her album of eternal
memories was now stained and tarnished with
the spilled blood of a bad-ass brawl on prom
night? Did Gina give her an ass whipping and
now she's blaming and hating me? Perhaps she
was embarrassed because drunk Dirk kicked
her Vodka Watermelon White Knight's ass?

I began second guessing the entire decision.
Once again, mentally beating myself up,
thinking about the sucky situation of being
physically beaten up.

Maybe I should have let security handle it.
I could have drove over to Dirk's house the
next day when he was sober and confronted him
man to man. Try to talk and reason with him.
Maybe even used the "old friend" card and
attempt to rekindle that friendship that we
once had.

Perhaps I should have done what I was
trained to do in my radically religious zoo—
heaped some coals of kindness on his head—
instead of wanting to punch him in his head.

*If thine enemy be hungry, give him bread to
eat; and if he be thirsty, give him water to
drink. For thou shalt heap coals of fire upon
his head, and the LORD shall reward thee.*
Proverbs 25:21-22

Love and forgiveness towards your enemies.
That's the true way to win any battle. Victory.
Champion.

It was Jesus' purpose on this earth and he
was a great example. I was named for the man
and was raised with the title and label. Yet
there I was a stupid, sex-starved eighteen-
year-old Vagina Hunter, trying to be Vodka
Watermelon White Knight.

"I plead the fifth," I said and left for work.

Mr. Abernathy caught me at the front door. He was bending down picking up some trash off the floor. When he looked up and saw my face full of scrapes, bruises, and a black eye, he gasped. "Good God Christian Hayes! What happened to you?" Mr. Abernathy was always in a constant state of subtle confidence and coolness. His worried reaction caught me off guard and reminded me how bad I looked.

"Got in a fight last night at my prom party." I helped him pick up a couple more pieces of trash off the lobby floor. "Same guy that Amanda got into it that night we accidentally spent the night here." I hated to bring up an already sore subject, but I wanted him to know there was some sort of justification for what had happened.

Mr. Abernathy wasn't the kind of person to say "I told you so," but I could read it all over his face, or maybe I was using his face as a mirror to my own conscious. He just nodded his head and stared at me. Which made me feel even more uncomfortable. "What did your parents have to say?"

"I haven't told them yet. They weren't home from church when I got home this morning."

He continued to stare and nod like he was listening. Yet, somewhere in his thoughts, he was deciding whether he should give me advice or keep it to himself. "Supposed you thought about telling them it happened here?" He went down the advice road. "So they wouldn't be so hard on you." Then added. "And her."

"I really don't like to lie, especially to my parents," I said and waited to see if he had any other wisdom he wanted to toss my way.

Mr. Abernathy gave me a pensive look and then nodded for me to follow him. We walked over to the concession counter and he poured two cups of coffee and handed me one. I put lots of cream and sugar in mine and waited for what he had to say. He took a sip, gave me another long contemplative stare and then leaned against the counter.

"One time when I was in the Navy and stationed in San Diego. I had this beautiful girlfriend named Stella." Mr. Abernathy paused and reflected. He began unfolding his story. A story that I was quite confident hadn't been told very often, if at all. "She was the love of my life. We met at a USO dance. Boy, could she dance. And she was smart and witty as a whip. She would come to visit me and we'd spend hours together." He stopped and looked me in the eye. "Just talking and getting to know one another. Well, one night we talked a little too late and ended up falling asleep right there on the couch in her parents living room. I was supposed to be on the quarter deck watch at 1:45 a.m. But I was sound asleep. Something woke me up at about 4 a.m. I rushed out and got back to the barracks but when I went to get back into my bunk, my Chief Petty Officer stopped me and asked where I was coming from so late." Mr. Abernathy took a long sip of his coffee. "Well I didn't want to tell him I had fallen asleep at my girlfriend's house, so I told him I was out playing poker with some buddies and we lost track of time."

Mr. Abernathy reached over and placed his right hand on his left bicep and held it there. I knew beneath his sleeve was a tattoo of a mermaid sporting a Navy sailor's hat. I had seen it on several occasions. When I first inquired about it, he passed it off as being "the result of too much tequila and not enough will-power." But as he stood holding his arm like an amulet, I knew there was more behind his sailor's story.

"The next morning, I was sent to the Captain's Mast and was written up. It seems the Chief Petty Officer did a little investigating and none of the other guys who I was supposed to be playing poker with had any recollection of the event. So I confessed to the captain what truly happened. I lost a week's pay, a rank and 30 days of my liberty." Mr. Abernathy tilted his cup from side to side and watched his black coffee move back and forth. Forgotten. Sea. Wave. "The Captain said it wasn't that I had missed the deck watch that cost me so much. It was lying to a superior. "Hell," he said, "we've all fallen asleep or lost track of time, that's a physical flaw. But lying, well, that's a moral flaw and that's going to cost you more." Mr. Abernathy stared out over the skating floor. "But I lost something more than that. That lie cost me the love of my life. Since I was unable to leave the base for 30 days, Stella didn't want to sit at home all alone every weekend. So she continued to go out dancing and she met and fell in love with someone else." There was heartache in his final words.

"Man, Mr. Abernathy. I'm sorry to hear that."

"I'm not finished." Mr. Abernathy's composure suddenly changed. "Time went by and I met another woman. A little Asian woman." He paused and smiled. "Now she couldn't dance as good as Stella, but she was more beautiful and smarter than Stella ever was. She could sweet talk a sunken ship right back to the surface of the ocean and then convince its drowned crew she was their admiral and lead them to victory." He boasted. And then a grin came to Mr. Abernathy's face bigger than any that I had ever seen in all the years I had known him. "And she's been the best thing to ever happen to me."

He looked me in the eye once more. "So that lie, as wrong as it was, may have brought me to the real love of my life." Mr. Abernathy swallowed the last of his coffee and as it went down, he reverted to his normal cool, calm and collected self and said, "I'm not telling you that it's Okay to lie, Chris. I'm saying, you never know what God has planned for you. But as sure as this tattoo on my arm, you can rest assured, it's always for your absolute best. You may not realize it at the time because you only write the individual daily pages of your life. But God has already read and published the entire book called "The Life of Christian Hayes." He turned and tossed his coffee cup into the trash can. "And if you always try to make the best choices in life, I think you're guaranteed a best seller."

I know that Mr. Abernathy threw that analogy in because he knew Amanda was a book worm and that I was falling madly in love with her.

"But how do you know if the decisions your making are the best? What if you think it's a good choice but in God's mind it's not?"

"Trust your heart because that's where God lives and speaks directly to you. Not in your head or other parts of your body." He tossed a fatherly look. "And if you make a mistake, well, that's where God comes in and edits your mistakes and sets you back on course to become a best seller." Mr. Abernathy then turned and walked into his office. Leaving me all alone with just my black eye and blue demeanor.

So God is the Great Editor of our lives? I never read that one in the Bible. The Word was God. And God was the Word. It made perfect sense. God is all things and everywhere. She could be an editor too. I couldn't wait to pass this epiphany on to Amanda.

I worked the rest of the afternoon trying to listen to my heart but all I kept hearing were the "ohs", "aahhs" and other reactions made by everyone who saw my face. As much as I wished I could disappear like Peggy O'Connor from school did when she wrecked her dad's car, I knew I couldn't avoid my parents forever. I had to face the firing squad sooner or later.

I got home that evening and put the biggest Senior Superlative grin on my face to hopefully offset the ugliness of the beating and walked into the living room where mom and dad were watching "CHiPs".

"There you are. How was prom..." And when mom looked up from watching Erik Estrada straddling his shiny police motorcycle and saw the shiner on my face, she let out a blood-curdling scream. "Oh my Lord, Christian Mathew Hayes!!! What happened??" She jumped off the couch and ran over to examine my injuries. I looked over at dad who got a very rare, disturbed look on his face. Ruth faked a surprised scream and came over and stood next to mom.

"Well, I got into a little fight after prom last night. It was no biggie. Some drunk guy tried crashing our party and we got into it."

"No biggie? No biggie?" Mom always repeated herself when she was overwhelmed. She looked over at dad who by now had stood up and walked over to do his own examination. "You look like you were beaten with a baseball bat!" Mom waited for dad to agree with her.

"He pushed me. I punched him. He tackled me and, in the process, I took a knee to the face. Chuck and Billy Powers broke it up." I pointed towards Billy Powers house. "And everyone went their merry way and we had a fabulous fun time afterward." I lied.

"Were there any charges pressed?" dad asked.

"No. He left before the police got there."

"Police!" Mom shrieked. "Does this "he" have a name? Do you know him? Did anybody try to follow him and get a license plate or anything?"

"No." I let out a frustrated sigh. "Really mom, it was no big deal. If I hadn't taken a knee to the eye, you would have never known it happened."

And then it finally came. I had been waiting for it since I woke up and looked at my miserable self in the mirror. "See." Mom shook her head in agreement with her own frazzled self. "That would have never happened if you would have had the party here."

Ruth just stood there behind mom and dad with a shit-eating grin on her face thoroughly enjoying all the trouble she was getting into through osmosis of me. But any time mom or dad looked her way, she'd switch to her pathetically sad, over-dramatic, my-dog-had-just-

died, look. Like one of those plastic clown rings you get in the bottom
of a Cracker Jacks box. Right. Happy Face. Left. Sad Face.

CHAPTER FORTY-FIVE

I counted the number of days left until high school was over forever. Forty. How ironic. The same amount of days Jesus spent in the wilderness being tempted and tested by Satan.

"Are you hungry?" Satan asked Jesus. "Then turn those rocks into bread and eat it." And what was Jesus' reply?

"Man shall not live on bread alone, but on every WORD that comes from the mouth of God." Matt. 4:4

There was that damn word again, WORD. I couldn't escape it. I had lived the entire eighteen years of my life on a daily diet of God's WORD. And yet, I was still empty and hungry — both spiritually and physically. I didn't know it at the time, but I was entering my own desert experience. And while Jesus fasted from food and was tempted by the Devil, I was doing my own fasting and being tested. Amanda. Finals.

I downed the Dr. Pepper and pepperoni pizza at lunch the first day back to school after what I now called "Amandageddon." The caffeine blast and warm greasy dough helped ease my physical hunger leaving me now only spiritually starving. I needed some divine intervention to make it through the next 40 days of high school.

I decided to abolish both their names from my vocabulary. Thinking in some grand, esoteric way that, without those words in my life, what they represented would disappear from it too. Dirk and I were both sporting black-eyes, while Amanda continued to wear her black, cold heart.

Rumors flew around the halls, lunchroom and smoking area as wild as the night itself. Some were saying Amanda was drunk and she was coming onto Dirk. Others were saying I was drunk and flirting with Dirk's girlfriend, Gina. Being ostracized out of her inner circle only added fuel to the gossip fire. But no matter how the stories began, they always ended the same way—I got my ass kicked. Disgrace was the cloak of misery I was wearing when the week began. I spent the first few days with my head down to hide my black-eye but mostly to avoid the possibility of making eye contact with either one of them.

But then a strange thing happened. God edited my life. My story could have gone something like this...

I went back to school that next Monday after prom. As I walked down the halls, everyone looked and laughed at me. "That's the guy who got his ass kicked by Dirk Howard." Pointing. Staring. "What a loser" Their whispers exploding in my brain like hand grenades.

I couldn't hide my shame. Soon I went into a deep depression and what followed were thoughts of suicide. Amanda was right. I found more pleasure in killing myself than having to deal with all the drama in school and religious dogma at home...

But it didn't happen that way. As the week went by and I walked down the halls and into my classes and lunchroom people began to…it's hard to find the right word…I want to say… notice me…but it went beyond noticing me. They nodded their heads, smiled and acknowledged me. They started conversations with me out of the blue. Even teachers seemed to treat me slightly differently. I ran into Mr. Howell, my English Comp teacher in the parking lot and he shook my hand and said,

"Ah, there's the metaphoric David who stood up to the Goliath bully. Congratulations."

I didn't get it at first, but then it finally dawned on me. Standing up and fighting Dirk Howard got me an ass-kicking. It earned me a black-eye. But instead of my peers ridiculing me, they began to respect me. This gave me a mild boost in popularity. By the second week back to class, I was no longer bowing my head in shame. Instead, I was walking with my head held high proudly displaying my black-eye and my award-winning smile.

THANKS FOR THE EDIT, GOD. I REALLY APPRECIATE IT.

But life wasn't all hunky-dory. I seldom wandered from the senior floor and stayed far away from the areas in school where I might run into either one of my anonymous nemesis'. Smoking Area. Lunchroom. Library. To my amazement, I never physically encountered either one. However, I couldn't escape the mental and emotional post-party bouts that played in my mind. Hurt. Anger. Frustration. And there was only one person I could blame for it.

Me.

Oh, if I could only edit my own life. I would have done things a lot different. But the absolute worst part was the self-inflicted guilt. Like I had done something wrong, when in fact I hadn't. On the contrary, I did the right thing. That was my problem. I was always doing the right thing. I should have validated that fact that I was a Vagina Hunter and fucked her eyes out that night she stumbled into Aloha, drunk and sprawled out, inviting me to partake of her pleasures.

Once I captured her vagina, I should have taken her home and not called her ever again. She probably would have fallen madly in love with me. Girls like guys who treat them like shit. Why is that?

Because girls are stupid, that's why. Somehow though, I don't feel Amanda would have acted like most girls. She would have gone her merry, slutty, hoosier way. I would have been just another one of her Conquered Cocks sitting on a shelf with all her other regrets in life.

Oh, the trials and tribulations of teens. How earth-shattering and traumatic they are at that time.

And then, like mental manna from heaven, I came home from school one day to an envelope sitting on the kitchen table addressed to Christian Hayes. Praise. Jesus.

CHAPTER FORTY-SIX

It was a Letter of Admission from the University of Kansas, Lawrence.

"Wow. I are now a college student." I joked to myself. By the end of the summer, I'd be 284 miles away from Spanish Lake. Away from her. Away from my radically religious mother.

We had a celebration dinner at Ponticello's Italian restaurant. A Spanish Lake culinary institute. To my mother's horror and my own need for some physical self-flagellation, I ordered a Dr. Pepper and pepperoni pizza. Ruth and Dad just watched, as one would watch a cockfight where both cocks had their feathers ruffled and were ready for the other to strike. Fortunately, we both stayed in our corners and only clucked. I could see in Ruth's countenance that she wanted with all her heart to test mom's patience by taking a piece of my pizza too, but she faltered and declined. She still had several years to live in the Zoo. I, on the other hand, had a passport that was going to allow me my freedom to experience a new and exciting wild kingdom called college. It was like my official papers to Manhood with a capital M.

The weeks went by and I buried myself into my books and studying for finals. When I wasn't working or going to school, I was fantasizing about the start of a new life, more liberties and the pursuit of some kind of happiness independent of—her. By the last week of school, life was beginning to melt back into my normal functional dysfunctional world. My new popularity was causing a spike in my social life. Chuck and I had counted at least a half a dozen graduation parties that we could pick from. Thursday was the senior's official last day of school. Our graduation ceremony was Friday evening. Saturday would be the night of social mayhem in the form of P-A-R-T-I-E-S. My biggest fear would be that I would run into one of the dysfunctional duos.

Our graduation ceremony was normally held on the football field, but it was moved into the gym because the local meteorologist had predicted bad thunderstorms rolling in all evening. By the time we pulled into the packed parking lot at Hazelwood East Senior High, the morning rain had dispersed and the sun was shining through scattered clouds heating the blacktop causing it to let off a subtle steam. It was too late to move all the chairs, stages and such back outside so Principal Perry and a gang of teachers guided parents through the Commons and onto the bleachers of the gym while all the graduates went to the auditorium to don their gowns and get instructions on the procedures.

Burgundy and gold banners, along with Spartan effigies hung from the steel rafters like piñatas at a Mexican child's birthday party. Cathy Neville, our class valedictorian, gave her speech. I sat and watched it. I would have liked to say that I heard it or even listened to it. But to be totally fucking honest, my mind was somewhere else. Three speeches and six hundred and twenty-three students later, I was an official high school graduate. Mom took pictures of Chuck and me in front of the school marquee that read: Congratulations Seniors of 1981.

My blackeye had all but disappeared, but I still hurt. When we drove out of the parking lot, I looked back and said goodbye. In a couple of months, I would be far away, meeting new friends and Vaginas in Lawrence, Kansas.

CHAPTER FORTY-SEVEN

The next morning I got to work early and worked the afternoon shift. I was looking forward to having the night off so I could celebrate the closing chapter of high school and the beginning of the last summer in Spanish Lake before I went to college. Chuck and I had surveyed and mapped out the list of parties. We were for sure stopping in at two of them. And, depending on how our Vagina Hunting options played out, we might hit a couple more. It was going to be a night to remember.

Rumors had gotten back to me that Samantha Brown had told someone, who told someone, who told someone that she had secretly wished I would have made a move on her after the Sweetest Heart dance. I was too busy thinking about the Anonymous One that evening to even ponder on any other Vagina Trophy. Well, tonight will be different. Should Samantha cross my Vagina Hunting path, I will take full advantage of her wishes. Prom night may be the night when lots of teens lose their virginity, but graduation night had to rank up there with Valentine's Day and birthdays as other special dates for deflowering. The image of Samantha Brown and I passionately making love in the back seat of my car was playing in my mind when I walked into our front door.

"Sara is spending the night tonight," Ruth yelled from the top of the stairway as I went into the kitchen. "Mom said you have to pick her up." I immediately noticed that it wasn't a polite request. It was an order. That's why she tossed in the "Mom said" part. Ruth knew I hated picking up Sara. I was forced into doing it once since that tragic night and hated every moment of it. I felt like I was crossing a mental restraining order and violating my inner principals as I reluctantly drove there.

As I turned onto their street, a wooziness swept over me at the thought that Amanda might be outside washing Lucy's car or hanging with some friends. It was the same nauseating feeling one gets when stepping off Tom's Twister, the notorious amusement ride at Six Flags.

Spinning. Queasy. I'd be forced to look at her or acknowledge her presence and she'd have to do the same. Something told me she probably wouldn't. She'd ignore me. Act like I wasn't there and that would piss me off even more and make me feel like a piece of shit. I prayed every inch of the way. Please God in all your glorious mercy I don't want to see Amanda. Amen. Fortunately, my plea was heard and Sara was waiting by herself on the front porch. The drive back was awkward and mostly silent for both of us.

"NO!" I protested. "I don't have time. I have to be at Chuck's by seven. Why can't mom or dad pick her up? Or have Lucy drop her off?" Notice the "A" word didn't come up in any part of this previous paragraph.

Sara was becoming a permanent fixture in our house. I think Ruth was subconsciously looking for someone she could use as a mental crutch to take my place when I left for college. My parents liked Sara to be around too. She was a possible Christian convert, but more importantly, they were trying to withdraw the hoosier-ness out of her. Just as I wanted to do with her nameless sister. There was one big difference between the two Marrow siblings. Sara wanted and welcomed the change. She enjoyed being around us.

Yes, we were a functionally dysfunctional family, but it was still a nuclear family unit made up of a mother and father. We weren't a hoosier family. There wasn't any major arguing or drama. We had actual window curtains that were made of floral material and purchased at Sears. You wouldn't find any hoosier-ish dingy white sheets thump-tacked to the wall to cover our windows. The smell of cigarettes didn't hang in the air and yellow the walls or repulse the olfactory. Mom made sure the house always smelled fresh with those hockey-puck shaped "Stick Ups" air fresheners hidden under the cabinets, alongside the toilet, and over the range.

And then there were the ever-present homemade repetitive Rice-A-Roni meals served at a table with chairs that had plastic covers over the cushions. But in those chairs were people. Adults. Security. That's what Sara liked best about our house. She didn't have to be alone the entire day. Sure, Ruth was always around to talk on the phone, but it went deeper than that. It was a nice feeling knowing that there was an adult presence to scare away the imaginary spooks or real-life robbers, should either come calling. Ruth and I took mom and dad's omniscience for granted and sometimes even hated it. But for a little hoosier girl like Sara Marrow, the Hayes house was a haven of safety and security.

I was the only family member who wasn't thrilled with the presence of Sara in our house. Don't get me wrong, she was an awesome young lady. Smart. Talented. Funny. But every time I looked at her, she became an anchored memory of the beautiful world of what used to be. There was an uncomfortable vibe that passed between us. Ruth must have told her that I absolutely abolished Amanda's name from my vocabulary and she was expected to do the same. The A-Word never came up in conversations.

Or maybe it was the Anonymous One's doing. Perhaps telling her sister not to bring me into any conversations in the Haye's household. There was never a "How's your sister?" spoken from my lips nor an "Amanda says hi" from her lips. But there were times when Ruth and Sara would stop their conversations when I walked into the room. I felt as if they liked the idea of their two older siblings liking one another and they were always up to something secretive. They whispered a lot and looked at each other as two spinsters would, watching a poor, lonely widower walk by.

"Mom and dad are at a dinner at church and Lucy's working," Ruth said still hidden up the stairs. "Sara's getting in the shower, so go take a shower and then she'll be ready by the time you get there."

I took a shower and dressed, all the time hoping and praying that mom and dad would come home to take this potential cup of suffering away from me. But it wasn't my Will, it was His and they never came, so I reluctantly got in the car and left.

When I got to the Marrows, I thanked Jesus for not letting Amanda be outside and then I thought, 'Sara probably told her I was coming to pick her up,' so she probably would avoid me. And that thought made me feel a little better. I sat in the driveway and honked the horn. Nothing. Fuck. Maybe she was drying her hair. I waited some more. Honk. Nothing. Double Fuck.

I was going to leave but then thought of coming back home to a crying sister was enough to cause me to sit there several more minutes. Damn. Ruth said she was getting in the shower. She had to be out by now. I didn't want to make the trip again. I quickly jumped out of the car and banged on the front door. Against my better judgment, I stayed there and stared at the window that had the sheet hanging over it. There were flickers of lights from the inside.

Then I heard the sound of footsteps coming to the door. Not just the normal footsteps of a thirteen-year-old in tennis shoes but the high-pitched sound of heels tapping against a ceramic floor.

My hands began to tremble. I couldn't catch my breath.

The door opened.

There Amanda stood, dressed exactly like she was on prom night. Same dress. Same shoes. Same hair. In her left hand was a gift-wrapped package.

CHAPTER FORTY-EIGHT

"Hi."

She said in a tone that was meant to calm
the disturbed look on my face. Like a verbal
pat on the back from a friend who could sense
I was emotionally staggering at the sight of
her and she was there to help me with her
heroic "Hi". To stabilize me. Hold me up.
But instead, it acted as a bullet to my
brain and even though my body remained
upright and in the standing position, my
stomach crashed to the concrete below and
without anything else holding it in place, my
heart floated up through my throat so that I
was rendered a mute, retard. Speechless.
Nauseated.

After an eternal second, I said. "I'm here to pick up Sara." I forced
the six words from my cold lips and turned and started to walk back to
my car. I didn't need her help to hold me up.

"Wait." She came to me. The storm door slammed with a loud crash
behind her. It was the delayed sound of the bullet piercing my brain.
My body was flesh and weak and I wanted to stop but I didn't. I
continued back towards the shelter and safety of the steel-skinned car.

"Sara's not here." She paused. "She's already at your house." Her
words pierced me from behind.

"What?" I turned angrily around. "What the fu…" but before I
finished the word she spoke.

"I asked the girls to trick you over here because I wanted to talk to you. So that I might..." She lowered her stare to the driveway. "apologize...to you."

You could speak a million beautiful words of apology, but it's all verbal fluff if your actions don't back up those words. Its actions that reflect your attitude and for the last month you have rejected me, avoided me and hurt me deeply.

"OK so apologize," I said stoically. "So I can leave. I've got parties to go to." I specifically said "parties" as in plural, knowing that as a logosist she'd catch the implication. Did she know that I had become more popular and that she, in some negative sense, was the reason for my new popularity? "But to be totally honest, I really don't want or need your apology," I turned and said.

I lied, but the last thing I wanted was for her to think that I was miserable because of her. Or that I was just another one of her court jesters that she could manipulate like a Vagina Hunter puppet.

"You want me to be totally honest with you." She threw the gift to the ground. It made a loud THUD. Her voice got suddenly loud and brave. She stepped closer and pinned me with a pensive stare. "You scare the fuck out of me, Christian Mathew Hayes! And that is why I haven't talked to you."

Oh my God. Did she just use my full name like my mother does when she's angry?

"Scare you? What have I ever done to scare you?" I continued to walk to my car. My voice escalating with each step I made. "I've treated you better than anyone's ever treated you. I respected you and defended you with my words when people criticized you and talked bad about you. I even jeopardized my own physical well-being..." I opened the car door and paused letting my words and my pain fall heavily upon her. "…and got my ass kicked for you and you act like I deserved it! You erased me out of your life like I'm one of your fucking fancy and pretty words" My voice was now filled with weeks of suppressed anger. "Do you know I can't even fucking remember what happened that night? And, to be totally honest," I said sardonically, "I wish I couldn't fuckin remember anything about you since you roller skated into my life." I got in the car and slammed the door.

Amanda quickly ran up to my opened window and shoved her face in. "You want to know what happened that night, Chrisssistian?" She yelled in my ear.

I started the car. "I know what happened. Chuck told me everything!" I stared straight ahead, not wanting to look at her beautiful face so close to mine, lest I fall under her Medusa spell but instead of turning to stone, I should melt or turn to putty.

"No, Chuck didn't tell you everything because Chuck didn't know what happened to *me*." She flung my car door open and stood there defiantly pointing to her chest.

"I ran down to 7-11 and called Lucy and had her come pick me up. And while I waited, I hid in the shadows of the side of the building shaking and shivering with blood all over my dress." She pointed to her prom dress where, if you looked closely, one could still see the faded remains of red stains... "But that's not the only reason I was hiding." She suddenly stopped talking. I waited for her to continue as I stared straight at the steering wheel. After several moments of silence, I turned and looked at her. She swallowed and her eyes began to blink repeatedly as she fought back her emotions. "I didn't want anyone to see me…"

And as she said the word "cry," she released a torrent of tears that poured forth that caused her entire body to shake and shiver. Then she covered her face with her hands and continued through her sobs. "I couldn't stop crying. Christian." She took her hands away from her face and looked at me. "That was the fucking greatest, kindest, and most romantic thing a guy has ever done for me."

"But I guess because I got my ass kicked you figured I wasn't worthy of you." My stare showed she had hurt me with her rejection and silence.

"*Especially* when the knight gets his ass kicked." Her words came broken now. Through deep breaths of air and between waves of tears she struggled to verbalize her thoughts. "Fighting for a fair maiden…

SNUFFLE… when you know you can win… GASP… well….that on the scale of brotherly love… BREATH…but fighting for a fair maiden…INHALE…knowing you're going to lose the battle, well that's...that's..." She stuttered in search of the right words. "That's the kind of love that books and movies are made of."

Her eyes were now red as wine and her voice had lost its boldness and defiance and was now just a quivering mess. She attempted to stop the tide of tears but failed. "But…I'm not ready for that kind of love, Christian. I'm too young." She shook her head. "I don't know if I'll ever be ready for that kind of love." She once again hid her face behind her hands, but this time she didn't attempt to stop her emotions. She had finished talking. She had said what she wanted to say and the rest was her show of sorrow.

Her words hit me harder than Dirk's punch. Was it possible? Amanda Marrow, the Freshman Fire was fighting against herself to love, or not to love—me. No. She didn't say that. She said she wasn't ready for the kind of love that I was willing to give her. At no time did she say she loved or wanted to love me. I didn't want to read too much into her words.

But still, it sounded like she was scared, not of me, but of herself. If I took her meaning right, she was fighting her own emotional battle not to love me. I wondered which is the noblest war. To battle external foes like Dirk Howard or inner fears of love and commitment?

Both battles as brutal and deadly as the other. Yet victory over one acts as an allied force to help conquer the other.

I could no longer watch her stand there weeping without acting as her own allied force to come to her rescue. I took her hand and pulled her into the car and onto my lap. She came willingly and put her arms around me and squeezed me until every atom of my existence did the happy dance.

We sat there in my car; the Hoosier girl and the Vagina Hunter and I didn't give a hoot's ass if every neighbor on the street was watching. Which I'm sure they were, because, after all, she was Amanda Marrow, the Freshman Fire. Soon her sobs slowed to mere sniffles and she pulled back and looked into my eyes.

"I'm so sorry Christian will you ever forgive me?"

I wiped a falling tear from her face, smiled and nodded my head.

There were those two words again. Forgive. Me. Spoken so effortlessly from her lips that drew me towards her in the first place. She was asking for my forgiveness and by doing so testing me with life's hardest task— forgiving the undeserving. But she wasn't undeserving. She was merely a little misguided and, as usual, misjudged.

Amanda stepped out of the car and picked up the gift from the ground and handed it to me. I could tell from the torn paper it was a book. "Here's a graduation gift from Lucy and Sara."

I unwrapped a hardback copy of *Kane and Abel,* the book she was reading the day I went into the Waldenbooks and talked to her. The same day we bounced with Sara and Ruth in the Bouncy House. "I know you don't like to read but I think you'll like this book. I absolutely couldn't put it down." She took the gift wrap from my hands and crumbled it up. "Maybe this will be that one book to take your reading virginity." She forced a half smile. "Besides, I get half off." She wiped her cheeks and finished the smile.

I didn't tell her that during my journey of finding my inner self without her, I went to the library looking for the love of books in all the right places that she had once found it. I stumbled upon Kane and Abel sitting on a table with a sign that read "Summer reads by the pool." I checked it out and spent many nights alone in my room reading it. She was right. It was a great book. I couldn't put it down. I was becoming a bibliophile. The secret made me smile.

"Thanks," I said and then motioned to her outfit. "So what's up with the prom dress?"

She looked down and grabbed her dress and held it out. And just like that, Amanda Marrow was back to her normal, sexy, storytelling-self. "Well, it's a surprise but you have to come inside to see it."

I looked at my watch. There was nothing in the world I'd rather do then follow her into that house to whatever surprise was waiting for me, but I was also a Time Nazi and I had told Chuck that I would be at his place at seven. Amanda saw my situation.

"I know you're supposed to be at Chuck's at seven. But Ruth called him and told him you'd be running a little late."

"What!!!! Amanda, I just can't blow off my best friend like that, especially on graduation night."

"Ok," she said. "I understand." She reached over and gave me a departing hug. But, before she turned to walk away, she gave me the same Cheshire cat smile she gave when we first met. "But I think you'll really, really like this surprise."

And just like the disappearing cat in Alice's Wonderland, my concerns about blowing off my best friend on graduation night quickly dissipated into thin air.

In less than ten minutes, I went from writing the cold-hearted bitch out of my life and never wanting to see her again, to betraying my best friend at her request so I could be with her.

Amanda made her way back towards her house and I followed behind her and had I a tail, it would have been wagging hysterically.

CHAPTER FORTY-NINE

Amanda stopped at her front door, turned, and looked at me.

"Since prom was such a fucked-up night, I wanted to do it over," she said. "But this time we won't be dining at the Pipefitters Hall. We'll be eating at a table for two at the Marrow's Mansion." She opened the screen door and motioned for me to enter.

I walked into their tiny living room. It was ablaze with burning candles throughout. On the coffee table, the TV and bookcase, every step we took candles flickered and flared around us. We went through the bedroom, also adorned with an array of lit candles and stepped into the kitchen.

It was decorated like the Pipefitters Hall on prom night. There was a cover of Styx's album "Paradise Theater" hanging from the light above the table. Newspapers acted as a tablecloth. On the refrigerator was a poster that said, "Christian Hayes and Amanda Marrow are having The Best of Times." Sitting on the kitchen table, next to a small bouquet of flowers and another candle were two Steak 'n Shake glasses filled with Dr. Pepper. A large pepperoni pizza sat in the middle of the table.

"This my graduation gift to you." Amanda motioned to the entire room as she pulled a chair out and guided me to sit down. "My culinary skills aren't too proficient, but I was able to toss a pizza in the oven. Of course, it's probably cold now, since it's been sitting here while we were outside..." She paused to think of a choice word. "...conciliating."

Dr. Pepper. Pizza. Conciliating. I had no idea what the word conciliating meant but it sounded like kissing and making up.

"Wow Amanda, this is really awesome! I can't believe you did all this."

"Well, to be totally honest, Sara and Ruth helped. Sara did the newspaper tablecloth and hung the Styx album and Ruth made the poster on the fridge."

I looked over to the poster and recognized my sister's handwriting. The little secretive shit. No wonder she never came out of her bedroom when I was home this evening. Sara was already in there hiding.

"I'll warm the pizza back up." Amanda turned on the oven and placed the pizza back into it.

I pointed to the phone hanging on the wall. "Can I call Chuck? He's going to be really pissed if I don't let him know what's going on." I wanted to cover my social ass and not put all my pleasure eggs in the same basket. Amanda's apology, the present and the reenacted prom were awesome, but it was graduation night and the Time Nazi had made a commitment. "We should be done eating in say an hour." I looked at my watch. "I know you must have a party that you have to get to as well." I paused.

"You mean parties." She smiled. "It's still early. Chuck will understand. Besides I prefer to be a little late and make a grand entrance," Amanda said. Spoken like a queen.

We ate the pepperoni pizza and drank the Dr. Pepper and it was the best I had ever tasted. We talked about the rumors that went around school and what we each had been doing for the last month.

"I finished my freshman year with a 4.0 G.P.A.!" Amanda picked up her glass of Dr. Pepper and proposed a celebratory toast. I picked up my glass.

"To Lady Amanda, thy smartest and fairest maiden in all of Spanish Lake!" My English accent hadn't improved. Our glasses tinked and we sipped our soda. I made another toast. "And to Sir Hayes, the Vodka Watermelon White Knight, who was accepted into thy University of Kansas, in thy land of Lawrence." I raised my glass once more, but this time when I glanced over to look at Lady Amanda's sparkling smile, I was met instead by a sixteen-year-old girl who was doing her best not to show the sorrow she was feeling. She faked a smile of congratulations and held up her glass. "Here. Here. To Sir Hayes," she said. We sipped our soda once more.

"Is everything OK?" I asked.

She nodded her head yes but avoided my stare by looking down at her empty plate.

"You know, I've seen that look on your face before."

"I don't know what look you're talking about." She immediately began gathering the plates and dishes and put them in the sink.

"Do you remember the last words you said to me before falling asleep in my arms that night at Aloha?" I asked. She remained facing the sink with her back towards me, I watched as she took a deep breath and shook her head no.

We **both had parts of our memories with one another stolen away. Mine were of misery. Hers were of pleasure. Both caused by the same antagonist. And yet, had that antagonist not fought with either of us, there would have been no "that night" nor "this night."**
Thanks God. For the edits, the plot twists, and the antagonists of life.

"*My Tiny Treasure* was playing on the stereo." I reminded her. "You asked me if they wrote this song about us. Then you said, if I said they did, you were going to start crying." I got up from the table and walked towards her as she continued facing the sink. I put my hands on her shoulders and began gently caressing them. "And you hadn't cried since you were six years old, when you threw your Partridge Family lunch box at your fucking father." Amanda reached up and put her hand on my hand. "That's where I saw that sad and solemn look once before."

Once again, for the second time that evening, Amanda began to cry. She turned, and just as she did that night at Aloha, she buried her face into my chest and hugged me like I was the first man on the moon. And at that moment I was.

It was that evening. So many years ago. When this stupid, sex-starved, eighteen-year-old Vagina Hunter had my own epiphany.
I realized, it's the hugs, the caresses and the pats on the back that conveyed a person's true feelings more than anything. Sex can skew the senses and emotions. And words, no matter how loquacious and loving they may sound, can be deceiving. Lips will lie just to get you to fuck.

But when a person pulls you to them and hugs you like they want you inside their skin so that they can occupy the exact same space, time and feelings, when all the words, kissing, touching, sex and seduction is over, when you're lying naked (or not) in their arms, and they randomly begin to pat your back or caress your face for no reason.

That is the secret language of love. A wordless vocabulary where subconscious thoughts turn into physical actions that convey the deepest and purest feelings.

Squeezes. Pats. Caresses.

Those are the actions that are absent when love is fake or has faltered away. When sex is nothing more than sex.

Amanda, The Logosist, had a plethora of spoken words at her command. Amanda, The Freshman Fire, had a stable of young studs all begging and willing to satisfy her sexually. But Amanda, The Hoosier Girl, was starved of what she wanted and needed more than anything in life: The secret language of love.

Spoken, not by a Vagina Hunter, but a White Knight and done in a wordless way that translated the physical action of mere sex into the act of making love.

And to be totally honest, I wanted to be that translator.

That. White. Knight.

"It's time for dessert." Amanda leaned back and slowly wiped the tears from her eyes and tried to soldier on past her sadness. "I know how you like to eat healthy," she said as she escorted me back to my seat and walked to the refrigerator. "So, I started to get strawberries and angel food cake for dessert." She opened the refrigerator door. "But then I thought I'd go with something more exciting and rebellious."

She took a piece of devil's food cake and a bottle of chocolate syrup from the refrigerator and sat the cake in front of me. Then she popped the plastic cap open and began to pour chocolate syrup all over the devil's food cake until it was smothered in an orgy of chocolate syrup. We both laughed.

"Do you think it's a coincidence that devil's food cake is so much more sinfully delicious then angel food cake?" She proposed the idea.

"I surmise...no." I grinned.

And then my angel gave me a devilish smile as she licked the chocolate syrup off the cap of the bottle, so naughty and so seductive that it still makes my blood rush even to this day when I think about it.

This isn't THE END!

IT'S THE BEGINNING OF THE NEXT ADVENTURE OF THE HOOSIER GIRL AND THE VAGINA HUNTER

AUTHOR'S THANK YOU

I want to personally thank you for purchasing and reading my first book. It means a lot to me and I really appreciate it!! If you enjoyed what I have written (or even if you didn't:) please take a few minutes and give me a review on Amazon, GoodReads, Facebook or wherever you may have purchased "*The Hoosier Girl.*"

My goal is to retire from my job as a handyman and spend my days following my passion of writing full time. The more positive reviews I get, the more books I sell. The more books I sell, the faster I can retire and complete the second book in this series titled; "*The Vagina Hunter.*"

Also, please visit my website www.HarrySneed.me and get to know me better. Join my Readers Fan Club and get freebies and goodies from my store. And don't forget to follow me on my social networks.

I'm looking forward to meeting you at a book signing near you soon!

-harry
March 15, 2021

CPSIA information can be obtained
at www.ICGtesting.com
Printed in the USA
LVHW020017020521
686229LV00015B/487